THE BEST OF GLENCANNON

THE BEST OF
GLENCANNON

TWENTY-TWO STORIES

By Guy Gilpatric

DODD, MEAD & COMPANY

NEW YORK

FOREWORD

"I HAVE an idea for a story," Guy Gilpatric said to me one evening. "A man buys fifty parrots, and taking each one separately he teaches it a singing part. Pretty soon he's got them all trained and he thinks he's got the greatest act show business ever saw. The parrots singing together sound just like the Vienna Choir Boys. Except for one thing. One of the birds—the one with a voice like Pinza—always insists upon singing O'Reilly's Tavern right in the middle of Ave Maria. I haven't figured how it all turns out but it might be worth a whirl."

Guy never got around to working out the end to the story, and it's too bad, for in his hands it would have been a very funny thing. Now the story will never be written and thousands of people the world over will be denied the joy of that rare thing, the hearty, healthy, unfettered belly laugh. He never wrote the story, for on July 6, 1950, he and his beloved wife Louise died tragically in their home at Santa Barbara, California.

It doesn't seem right for tragedy to have had any part of Guy's life, for during it he brought so much laughter to the lives of others. Just a mention of Mister Glencannon and my elderly aunt starts to laugh. My young cousin's rowboat is the Inchcliff Castle, and he is an authority on an incredible variety of skull-duggery garnered from a certain walrus-mustached idol of his. I just spoke on the telephone to my wife's uncle and told him I was doing this foreword, whereupon he began to reminisce about his favorite Glencannons and soon he was giggling, spluttering and gagging so that he had to hang up.

This Glencannon disease does not seem to be confined to Americans. Once during the war I was sitting in the lobby of the Hotel Rock in Gibraltar when I saw a civilian in suspiciously deep conversation with two avidly listening British naval officers. I heard snatches of their conversation—"prisoner of the Japanese—disguise—sabotaged the water pumps"—and other bits that made me, as an eager young Vice Consul, think I had stumbled upon something BIG. For a brief moment, that is, until the phrase—"a couple of shots of the Dew"—floated over to me. I heard the laughter then and realized that here was just a pair of addicts catching up on the latest exploits of their hero.

Their *hero!?*

As a writer I have always been astounded by the phenomenon of the Glencannon stories. Every book on creative writing I've ever read has agreed that you "must like the main character and be in sympathy with his goal."

What the devil is there to like about Mister Glencannon! Here is an unmitigated, unvarnished, unredeemed scoundrel who in every story dedicates himself to a series of misdeeds which will merely hasten his unswerving path to the heated hereafter. The most charitable person could find absolutely nothing to recommend him. He is canny, aye, that he is, but canniness is not a virtue. He is also a liar, a cheat, a vindictive mercenary blackguard, and an incipient alcoholic. It's better not to go into what would happen if a poor feeble widow happened for some reason to be standing between him and a luscious dollop of Duggan's Dew when the thirst came upon him.

Think of the favorite rogues of fiction—they all have some saving grace, some lovable qualities, no matter how well hidden. Falstaff, Til Eulenspiegel, Robin Hood, Figaro, Candide, Tom Jones, Micawber, Huck Finn, Jimmy Valentine, the Cannery rogues, Hildy Johnson, Sheridan Whiteside, and the Kingfish . . . all of them have redeeming features which make you love them in spite of and because of their faults. Even Mr. Hyde had his good side.

But Glencannon! What can you say in defense of him? The Spanish have a word which suits him to a tee—*sinvergüenza*. It means "incorrigibly without shame." By all rights Colin Glencannon should be the most despised character of all fiction.

But he isn't. He's probably the most widely known and beloved rogue in modern-American fiction, and to heck with the books on creative writing!

It's incredible that such a character could emerge from the personality of Guy Gilpatric, for he was the antithesis of his brainchild. Gentle, warm, honest, generous, modest and painfully shy, perhaps he found refreshing outlets by making his character go to the opposite extreme of these qualities. Guy never liked to talk about Glencannon. He never liked to talk about his work at all, and whenever he did, it was always to laugh at it and dismiss it as being of no consequence to anyone.

He hated talking about himself. He was so modest that I knew him intimately for two years and only knew that he "didn't like airplane travel and always took the train." It was Louise who told me that he was one of the pioneers of American aviation or I never would have known that he'd even been up in a plane, much less held the world's altitude record for several years. He was also a fine fencer, a crack pistol shot, and probably the first exponent of the now popular undersea goggle fishing. He was a voracious reader, and the catholicity of his ideas and interests was highly stimulating to a young and very green writer. I would go up to Guy's two or three times a week, and over a mug or two of Duggan's Dew we would discuss everything under the sun, from spearing robalos in the Mediterranean, to stunting planes for the movies (which he once did also!). And of course, Monty. Monty, his adored dog, killed by a truck, always came into the conversation, and Guy and Louise would grow sad at the memory of their "only child."

Whenever I became stuck on a short story, which was constantly, I would run to Guy. With the greatest of willingness and with no apparent effort he would put his finger on exactly what was wrong with it. Once, by a simple yet ingenious suggestion, he turned a very commonplace story of mine into one which won several awards and is still appearing in anthologies.

Right now I am working on a short story, but I am stuck and I don't know what the trouble is. I wish Guy were here. He would know.

Guy would know for he was a consummate craftsman. He sold

his first story to Colliers when he was fifteen, and after that he never wrote a story that didn't sell. He wrote a lot of stories too, hundreds of them, and not all about Glencannon. Some—a very few—were serious, but most were calculated to make a person "express mirth by an explosive, inarticulate sound of the voice," (as the dictionary defines laughter). Even though Guy derided his work, constantly apologizing for it because it wasn't "serious stuff," he clearly believed with Rabelais that it is "better to write of laughter than of tears, because to laugh is proper to a man."

"Any darn fool can take a whack at tragedy," William Lyon Phelps once said, "but you have to be touched with genius to write comedy."

Josh Billings said: "Laffing iz the sensation ov pheeling good all over, and showing it principally in one spot."

Now it's time to board the old Inchcliffe Castle as she heads out to sea. I, for one, want to be along, because her infamous Chief Engineer gives me the sensation ov pheeling good all over. For Glencannon's gentle and warmhearted creator was touched with the genius that writes great comedy.

BARNABY CONRAD

San Francisco
California

CONTENTS

MARY, QUEEN OF SCOTS

THE *Inchcliffe Castle,* Para to Naples, stuck her rusty snout around the bend of Andalucia and ambled into sheltered waters across which sprawled the purple shadow of Gibraltar. Behind the Rock the sun had climbed an hour high; but Britannia's Lion, in its towering majesty, shut off all save a few ambitious rays which leaked around its edges, and framed it in a pinkly-glowing aureole.

The full moon, on the other hand—it would have been your left—swung over the white houses of Algeciras, in Spain, and sinking lower, paved a baleful pathway beyond Trafalgar for the wandering footsteps of Admiral Nelson's unquiet love-sick ghost.

In this strange and lovely moment of borning day and dying night, the *Inchcliffe Castle's* anchor let go with a shocking clatter of chains, a vulgar display of sparks, much profanity from the fo'c'sle head and even more from the bridge. The profanity was that of religious men, which is the kind that blisters paint.

The anchor caught in the mud, jerked loose once or twice, stirred up many bubbles and an evil smell, and finally hooked a fluke. Mr. Montgomery, hanging over the bow and seeing the chain stretch taut, waved his hands with the weary yet triumphant gesture of an orchestra leader bringing the Ninth Symphony to a glorious close.

Captain Ball, on the bridge, heaved a stertorous sigh. "Ring off the engines," he directed; and somewhere down below, the telegraph jingled. Suddenly, disturbingly, the decks ceased to throb and the stanchions to tremble. After eighteen pulsing days the ship seemed no longer to be alive. Silence, torrents of silence, poured in from all sides. And just then the sun, conquering the traditionally-unconquerable, scaled Gibraltar's heights and sent the night, its moon, and its lovely mystery scurrying away into Africa.

1

"Hell's bones!" remarked Captain Ball, unbuttoning his overcoat and taking a cigar from his night-shirt pocket, "What a trip
that was!" Resting his elbows on the bridge rail, his eye travelled
aft over the battered gear and salt-streaked superstructure which
told of a rough and troublous passage.

Mr. Glencannon, the Chief Engineer, appeared on the deck
below. At the heels of his oil-soaked carpet slippers toddled a jet
black female Scottish terrier with barrel chest, stump legs, and
whiskers such as one associates with natives of Aberdeen. Mr. Glencannon strolled to the rail, spat copiously over it, and considered
Gibraltar at length—meanwhile wiping his face with a handful
of greasy cottonwaste. Then he lifted the dog in his arms, and
placed her forepaws on the rail.

"Mary," he said, "this is Geebraltar, an heestoric port. I'll first
deerect your attention to the street which runs peerpindicular to
yon wharf. If ye'll note the fourth—no, the fufth building on
the left, ye'll be notin' a pub whuch sells the finest whusky South
of the Firth o' Clyde. And then, on the nuxt street, over toward
the naval coal docks, ye'll see a sma' house wi' a red roof. That's
a pub called '*The Royal Oak*,' after an old ancient freegate ship
whuch . . . oh, a vurra gude morning to you, Captain Ball!"

"Good morning, Mr. Glencannon," and the Captain nodded
over the canvas dodger. "How are you and Mary this morning—
fit?"

Mr. Glencannon shook his head dolefully. "As fur my ain puir
health, the less said the better. But Mary, the little lass, is ailin'
sore. I was aboot to crave yer kind permeesion, Sir, to tak' her
ashoor to a vetereenary, and get him to preescribe."

"Right-o," agreed the Captain cheerfully.

"Thanks kindly, Captain Ball," said Mr. Glencannon, setting
Mary on the deck and deftly brushing up her coat. "The lass and
I are grateful. We are indeed. Come on, Sweetheart—we'll ha' a
bit o' brukfust, we will, and then Papa'll put on his new unee-
furrm, and dress his ain little lass in her tartan collar, and hoot!
ashore for a romp we'll go!"

"Oh, now, my eye!" exploded Mr. Montgomery, the mate, who
had joined Captain Ball upon the bridge. "Did you ever 'ear such

blithering tosh in all your life, Sir?—Mr. Glencannon mykes a bit of an arss of 'imself over that dog when 'e sets 'is mind to it, 'e does!"

Captain Ball crinkled the corners of his eyes as do men who weren't born yesterday. "Well, I'll tell you, Mr. Montgomery, it's like this. I know as well as you do that he's going ashore to get drunk. Mr. Glencannon has his weaknesses, as who of us does not? Scripture says that 'To sin is human,' and though Mr. Glencannon drinks a full quart of whisky every day, and be damned if I haven't seen him drink five quarts, we must remember to let he without sin cast the first stone.—Particularly when he's the only Engineer on the high seas who can handle our rusty old tubercular junk pile of a blank-blanked engine."

"Well, all I can say is, God 'elp the Rock of Gibraltar!" grunted Mr. Montgomery, only half convinced. " 'Ere 'e comes now."

Mr. Glencannon, brave in his best white cap, the four gold stripes of his rank, and the medal awarded him for saving a German's life by mistake, stood at the foot of the gangway and invited bids from the yammering bumboatmen to take him ashore. He cut the lowest bid in half, kicked the chin of the nearest competitor, who had sought to seize his arm, and made the trip to the Commercial Wharf for thruppence. With Mary frisking at his heels, he passed through cobbled streets lined with whitewashed houses labelled, for example, "*Sgt. Major Alfred Hoskins, 67th Rgt. R.G.A.*," and "*Non-Com. Married Quarters—No Loitering.*" The latter sign he felt to be distinctly offensive in its insinuation. "Ha' no fear!" he muttered toward it. "I've better to do than loiter aboot with the she-beef o' the Royal Garrison Arteelery!" And forthwith he turned into an establishment the window of which displayed a spirited lithograph of the Relief of Lucknow, depicting several bottles of MacCrimmon's Very Old Liqueur Whisky being put to good use by the beleaguered defenders in the foreground.

He found MacCrimmon's Very Old to be distinctly creditable stuff—as good, in some respects, as The Laird's Selected Relics, Clammarty Royal Tartan Blend and Dunleven Particularly Choice. But none of them, of course, could compare with Dug-

gan's Dew of Kirkintilloch—most gorgeous of all liquids that
ever dripped golden from the nozzle of a still to mingle its perfume
with that of the heather in the cold Highland mists.

Now, like Duggan's Dew, Mr. Glencannon hailed from the
town of Kirkintilloch, in Dumbartonshire; and the picture on the
label made him first happy, then sentimental, and finally home-
sick. A great grief overcame him; tears coursed his cheeks as he
contemplated that label, and he was weeping copiously when he
finished the bottle. "Look," he sobbed, hoisting Mary to the table,
"Gaze, Lass, upon the dear fameeliar scenes o' your childhood!
'Tis there that our Mothers live. Ye played there as a bairn, and
so, alas, did I. . . ." And Mary, falling into the spirit of the occasion, tilted back her head and gave vent to piercing wails. Mr.
Glencannon purchased six cases of the whisky, ordered five to be
delivered aboard the ship and the sixth to be stowed in a cab. The
cab proved to be a spidery victoria driven by a Spaniard in straw
hat, short jacket and baggy trousers. Mr. Glencannon and Mary
scrambled aboard with the God-speed of the publican and some
assistance from the by-standers.

"Where to, Capitan?" inquired the Spaniard.

"How in the hell shud I know?" replied Mr. Glencannon. "Must
I act as guide to ye, on ye're ain native heath?"

"But I come from La Linea, Senor," protested the Spaniard.

"Vurra weel—let's go there, then," and with Mary perched on
the seat beside him, Mr. Glencannon dropped off to sleep.

They had clip-clopped out of the streets of the town and were
well in sight of the Neutral Strip—a barb-wired belt of land which
separates Spain from the Crown Colony of Gibraltar—when the
driver reined in his nag. Mr. Glencannon, opening his eyes, saw
that they were halted at a house before which paced a sentry in
the uniform of the Royal Garrison Artillery. A sign on the place
read *"H.Q. Frontier Guard. Passes for Spain."* Across the road,
under the flat face of the Rock, stretched a field filled with hurdles,
water-jumps, cricket greens, polo goal posts, and aeroplane hangars.
Upon this field, troops were playing football.

The driver dismounted, entered the house, and shortly emerged
with a little green slip which read "North front. Permit until first

evening gunfire. John Cochrane, Chief of Frontier Police."

Mr. Glencannon was considering this suspiciously, and was just about to ask Mary what country they were in, when a disturbing sound came from the distance. At first he thought he only imagined it, and instinctively he glanced at Mary for confirmation. But, yes—her ears were cocked, her tail was wagging, and she was craning her neck around the side of the carriage. It was the sound of bagpipes; and they were playing "Piobair o' Lochaber."

"Foosh!" exclaimed Mr. Glencannon, lurching to his feet. "Why, it's the Argyll and Dumbarton Highlanders!" Mary showed her front teeth in a broad smile and then her entire perfect set in a series of joyous barks. Her little hairy forepaws pattered on the cushions, and she wriggled with excitement. For there, down the long white road, was the head of the approaching column—kilts and sporans swinging to the time, white gaiters slogging up and down, tartan ribbons aflutter on the pipes, and the bass-drummer with his leopard-skin apron whirling his sticks cross-armed, overhead, and behind him in the wild inimitable Highland manner!— It was the Dumbartons, beyond a doot—and Mr. Glencannon's own Cousin Douglas was a Sergeant of the Regiment!

Nearer and nearer they came—the shrill chant and basso drone of the pipes leaping into the air and echoing against the great grey face of the Rock above the plain. Then came the muffled *clump* of sixteen hundred hobnailed boots, the rhythmic swish of eight hundred tartan kilts! The Dumbartons—the great and glorious Dumbartons!—were marching by! Wheeling smartly before his very carriage, they deployed into the field.

They were going to play football, and so they weren't carrying their rifles. Numerous sporting Majors, Captains and Subalterns had turned out with the team, and they swung along with their walking sticks beneath their arms and banter upon their lips. And over all, there was a friendly, comfortable smell of venerable Scotch whisky upon the soft Iberian air. . . .

Mr. Glencannon was sniffing deep when suddenly he and Mary beheld a sight which transfixed them. It was the regimental mascot —the handsomest, whiskeriest Scottish terrier in the whole wide world—a rakish, swashbuckling lad wearing a tiny Highland bon-

net cocked over one ear, the silver-and-cairngorm badge of the
Dumbartons pinned to the side of it. And he toddled along with a
man who stood full seven feet high—a giant with a chest the size
of the *Inchcliffe Castle's* main boiler, and great hairy knees like
the oak trees worshipped by the Druids of antiquity. This giant—
there could be no mistaking him!—was Mr. Glencannon's own
Cousin Douglas.

Mary cast virginal modesty to the winds, and shrilly yapped
her admiration. Cousin Douglas, spotting Mr. Glencannon, gave
vent to a joyous "Hoot!" and promptly fell out of the ranks. Mr.
Glencannon, not to be outdone, promptly fell out of the carriage.

"Heigh-nanny, lass!" said the terrier with the bonnet, swagger-
ing up to Mary and kissing her full upon her lucious black lips
without so much as a by-your-leave. "I'm Jock o' the Dumbartons,
senior dog o' the reegiment. Welcome to Geebraltar!" Mary stood
blushing, eyes downcast but heart throbbing wildly. . . . Mr.
Glencannon and Cousin Douglas were slapping each other on the
back, saying "Weel, weel, weel, I'll be domned!" and repeating it
over and over again.

"Foosh, Cousin Colin, and it's gude to see you!" roared the giant
at length. "Why, ye domned old ghoul, ye, when did we meet, the
last?"

"Let me think, let me think," said Mr. Glencannon, closing his
eyes and grasping the carriage lamp for support. "Why, o' course!
—it was thirteen years ago, when I was Second on the transpoort
takin' ye oot to G'llipoli."

"Thirteen years ago—eh, to think of it!" sighed Cousin Douglas,
and the sigh was as the sound of a locomotive plunging into a
tunnel. "Weel,"—and he wrinkled his nose, smacked his lips, and
cast his eye on the case of whisky partly concealed by the carriage
rug, "Weel, it's customarra in such happy ceercumstances . . ."

"—I was aboot to suggest it!" hastened Mr. Glencannon. "Coachman, I'll thank ye for the loan o' a corkscrew."

"Dinna trouble yersel'," said Cousin Douglas, seizing a bottle
and smiting it so lustily against his palm that the cork leapt out
as from the choicer vintages of Rheims. "Come, Cousin Colin, do
we mount yon carriage the twa o' us, an' go see the bullfight over

in Spanish Town. T'wull be better than the futball. But feerst, let us drink a drap to our happy meeting. Here—I'll open another bottle so we'll both have one." . . . He tilted his own quart beneath his bristly red moustache; and when he took it down again, lo, it was only a pint.

"Haw!" he snorted, closing his eyes ecstatically and holding the bottle at arm's length, "Tis the Dew o' Kirkintilloch! I dinna ha' to look at the label—I reecognize the way it treeckles doon an cozeys my sluggish liver! 'Tis a happy meetin', Cousin Colin— a happy meetin' indeed!"

He climbed aboard the carriage, which groaned in every joint and took an alarming list to starboard as he settled into the seat. Mr. Glencannon was about to join him, when he saw Mary and the mascot joyfully gambolling across the troop-filled field.

" 'Tis a-richt, peerfectly a-richt," Cousin Douglas assured him, "Let the little tykes frusk aboot while the lads are playin' futball. I'll tell MacPheerson and MacColquhoun to keep an eye on them, and leave them with Corporal MacClintoch at the Frontier guard house.—Ye see," he explained, "We're off juty today to play the 67th Arteelery—attendance optional. My time's my ain till evening gun. So, carra on, coachman!"

The driver beat several clouds of dust out of the hide of his nag, and headed for the border. At the British side they were halted by a Highlander who blanched perceptibly as he recognized Sergeant Douglas Glencannon.

"I'll thank ye for a look at your passes, gentlemen," he said, saluting.

"Tak' a gude look at this, Corporal MacClintoch!" replied Cousin Douglas, extending a fist the size of a hoof, and quivering it threateningly beneath the guardian's nose. "Tak' a verra gude look, while ye're still alive to see it!"

"Thank ye," said Corporal MacClintoch, backing up a trifle, and saluting again, "Yere passes are sateesfactorra."

They jogged across the Neutral Strip—a stretch of meadow in which the kine of Castile and Britain browsed in sisterly contentment—and paused again, for inspection at the Spanish Customs. The *aduanero* was a fat gentleman in a blue uniform and a sword

left over from the American War. "Have you tobacco or spirits?"
he asked in perfect English.

"I dinna ken your lingo," replied Cousin Douglas, smacking
a fresh bottle against his palm, and watching the cork sail into
a roadside cactus. "Drive on, gilly!"

The coachman was plainly troubled. "Tell heem you have no
the tobacco, no the alcohol," he whispered.

Without removing his feet from the opposite cushions, Cousin
Douglas leaned halfway across the road and seized the *aduanero*
by the throat. Dragging him to the side of the carriage he shook
him playfully.

"Pass!" gurgled the guard, retreating into his hut and swallowing diligently—"*Vaya con Dios!*" The driver clucked to his horse,
and five minutes later they turned into the main street of La Linea
de la Concepcion, headed for the bull ring. Evidently, from the
cheering, the *corrida* was already in progress.

Arrived at the Plaza, Mr. Glencannon dismounted first. "Do
ye please tak' charge o' the refreshments, Cousin Dooglas, while
I pay for the cab," he said, handing the driver a counterfeit Costa
Rican *colon* and three brass Chinese coins with holes in them.
The Spaniard raised his voice in protest, whereupon Cousin Douglas, standing in the carriage with the case of whisky under his arm,
jumped into the air thrice and so mightily that the vehicle broke
into two distinct halves. As he stood triumphant in the splintered
wreck of the rear section, the terrified horse, the driver and the
front wheels vanished in a dust-cloud down the street.

A crowd collected, and through it five cocked-hatted policemen
shouldered their way. They took one look at Cousin Douglas, and
shouldered their way out again.

Mr. Glencannon placed a shilling on the ledge of the ticket
booth. "Twa!" he ordered, holding up two fingers. The Spaniard
shook his head and pointed at the scale of prices. "*Dos duros,
Senores,*" he said.

"Twa duros!" snorted Cousin Douglas, "Why, 'tis rank extor-
tion! Dinna submeet to it, Cousin Colin, dinna submeet!" Seizing
the ticket booth by one of its upper corners, he rocked it back and
forth so violently that the Spaniard, the cash-till and two chairs

went rattling about the interior like peas in a withered pod. Then, reaching through the window, he seized a sheaf of tickets and led the way through the cool shadowy tunnel which gave access to the seats.

They entered the first vacant box and were about to sit down when the audience burst into a storm of frenzied *"vivas!"* Ortiz, the Seville Sticker, had manoeuvred his bull into a perfect *pase de la firma,* and dispatched him with a masterly thrust. *"Oreja! Oreja!"* screamed the crowd; and at a sign from the President of the *corrida,* a man sliced an ear off the bull and handed it—the highest of honors—to the *matador.*

Ortiz, in his heelless slippers, strutted bowing around the *sombra* side of the arena, amid a shower of hats, fans, and flowers.

"Oh!" exclaimed Mr. Glencannon, "Look, Cousin Dooglas— you can throw things! Foosh! what fun!" And falling wholeheartedly into the spirit of it all, he tossed a chair over the barrier and knocked the *matador* flat.

In that instant the cheers turned into the menacing roar of a mob whose idol has been desecrated. Wheeling about, Cousin Douglas saw a thousand Spaniards descending upon them with murder in their eyes. His bottle was almost empty; so hesitating only to empty it completely, he hurled it into the front rank with withering effect. Four chairs were handy, and he flung them with unerring aim. A policeman appeared with drawn sword. Cousin Douglas seized the sword, spanked him with it, and grasped him by the belt and threw him across seven tiers of seats. The seats were vacant—in fact by this time they had an entire section of the arena to themselves.

"Weel," he said, languidly settling himself beside Mr. Glencannon, who had been busy uncorking bottles, "We can better enjoy the speectacle the noo, without the fumes o' garlic from yon feelthy Spaniards."

"Ye're richt," agreed Mr. Glencannon, impatiently viewing the group which bore Ortiz from the arena on a stretcher, "But if they dinna proceed with their domned bull-sticking soon, I shall deemand our money back."

"A verra reasonable and tolerant deecision, Cousin Colin! We're

being imposed upon by these swundling foreigners, and it's time
we asseerted oursel's!"

Grasping the captured sword, he was about to go out and complain to the management when a fanfare of trumpets gave him
pause. A herald appeared upon the bloody sand below.

"Hoot!" applauded Mr. Glencannon, pounding his bottle on
the ledge of the box, "He's aboot to eloqute! Lusten closely, Cousin
Dooglas!"

Choosing his words according to the conventions of the *Corrida,*
the herald announced that El Vaquerito, the thrice-eminent *espada*
from Bilbao, would match wits with a bull *"con buenos adornos
en la pensadora"*—which meant a most intelligent bull indeed.
The bull, he went on to say, was none other than El *Maquinista. . . .*

"L. MacKinister!" exclaimed Mr. Glencannon, "Did ye hear
that name, Cousin Dooglas?"

"I canna believe my ears! Why, he must be a MacKinister o'
Kirkintilloch! A Scottish bull!"

Mr. Glencannon grasped him by the arm. "Cousin Dooglas,"
he hissed, "We canna permeet it!"

"Ye're domned richt we canna!" boomed Cousin Douglas, seizing his sword, shoving the two remaining bottles into his sporan,
and rising to his full seven feet, "Come, Cousin Colin—the Glencannons are gaein' to the wars!"

They vaulted the rail of the box and clambered over the barrier
into the arena. Three thousand Spaniards shouted, but only twenty
interfered. Cousin Douglas attended to fourteen, and Mr. Glencannon disposed of six. " 'Twas dry and theersty work," observed
Mr. Glencannon, surveying the scene of carnage,—"Thank ye,
Cousin Dooglas—I ha' a bottle o' my ain."

Occupied as they were, neither of them saw El Maquinista as
he rushed snorting into the sunlight. Spotting Cousin Douglas's
flaming scarlet kilt from afar, he thundered toward it. A mighty
shout came from the audience.

"Lusten to them, Cousin Dooglas—why, I do believe they're
giving us a cheer!" Mr. Glencannon raised his cap in a graceful
gesture of acknowledgment, and Cousin Douglas made a courtly

bow. As he did so, El Maquinista's horn very neatly removed his kilt, and left him with nothing below the waist save gaiters, shoes and stockings.

"Oh, shame, shame, Cousin Dooglas!" cried Mr. Glencannon, "Quick, lad—do ye stand in back o' me and pull down your sporan!"

" 'Twull be inadeequate," announced Cousin Douglas, "Look yonder, Colin—that domned bull has trompled my kilt all to nowt!"

A great rage came upon him. Despite Mr. Glencannon's scandalised protests, he strode across the arena and addressed the bewildered bull.

"Ye lout, ye!" he shouted, shaking his fist in the animal's face, "Ye ruddy garlic-eating impostor, ye! Ye're no Scot—ye're a feelthy, treecherous, back-knifing Spaniard, that's what ye are!"

El Maquinista bellowed, put down his head, and charged. Cousin Douglas stood his ground and met the charge with a right to the nose and a left jab to the eye. Stepping in, he landed blow after blow, every one of which jolted the bull from stem to stern.

"I'll knock ye oot, ye big booby, ye!" panted Cousin Douglas, "Another minute, and I'll uncoork the uppercut that made me Champion o' the Breetish Army."

Mr. Glencannon took out his watch, and stood solemnly by, ready to time the count. El Maquinista, both eyes closed and bleeding at the nose, was groggy on his feet when the bullfighters intervened. As they drove the bull out of the arena Cousin Douglas knocked out a couple of *toreros* for good measure. "Quick, Cousin Colin!" he shouted, "Help me borrow their troosers!" Together they had yanked most of the clothing off the limp Spaniards, when they saw five *picadores* galloping toward them, lances couched.

"Run for yere life, Cousin Dooglas—here comes the cavalry!" warned Mr. Glencannon; and dropping most of their spoils, they sprinted for the runway down which El Maquinista had vanished. He was standing just within the entrance, but he hastily stood aside when he recognized Cousin Douglas.

Climbing over the wall of the runway, they plunged into the labyrinthian foundations of the stadium. In the distance, they heard the hue and cry raised after them. Groping on their way, they came to a hole in the wall, and they crawled through it to find themselves in the back yard of a wine-shop.

"Foosh!" said Mr. Glencannon. "What a happy coeencidence! Let us gae in, Cousin Dooglas, and subdue the proprieter."

The *tabernero* was alone among his wine barrels, so Cousin Douglas imprisoned him within one, and sat upon it. "Oh, deary me, but I've a theerst on me!" he said, "Mak' haste, Cousin Colin, and let us quaff our fill."

"Verra weel," agreed Mr. Glencannon, inspecting the rows of bottles on the shelf, "I canna read any o' them, so we'll ha' to sample them all."

At this point things became curiously garbled. It seemed that a great deal was transpiring over a long period of time, but Mr. Glencannon's next really definite impression was of a splitting headache. He lay with eyes closed, his very soul cringing as white hot twinges of migraine surged through his brain.

Opening his eyes, he found that he was in his own room aboard the *Inchcliffe Castle,* and that he was wearing the green velvet jacket of a Spanish *matador.* Painfully hoisting himself to a sitting posture, he saw Mary Queen of Scots upon the floor, contentedly chewing a bull's ear.

"Bless me, I remember noo!" he chuckled, "Daddy brought it hame to his lass as a souvenir of Spain."

Mary wagged her tail and continued chewing.

"Weel," sighed Mr. Glencannon, lurching to his feet, "I wonder if we've coaled yet. Why! I do believe we're at sea!" He peered through the port at a blue expanse of Mediterranean across which trailed a long black smudge from the *Inchcliffe Castle's* funnel. He opened the port and gratefully gulped down the fresh, cool breeze. In the corner of his room were piled the five new cases of the Dew of Kirkintilloch, and uncorking a bottle, he poured himself a brimming tumblerful.

"Thur's no cure for dog-bite like the hair of the dog that bit ye!" he remarked to Mary, tossing it off and smacking his lips. Then, donning his working clothes, he made his way to the engine room—head clear, step brisk, and hand steady.

"Strike me ruddy, but the Chief's a wonder!" observed Mr. Swales, the Second Mate. "To look at 'im, this arfternoon, you'd think 'e was the H'Archbishop of Canterb'ry!"

" 'Is recuperating powers are remarkable," agreed Mr. Montgomery. "I 'ad 'Ell's own time gettin' 'im out of the tender larst night. There was 'im and another wild man—a non-com. 'Ighlander nine foot tall, with nothing on below the wyste but one of them 'airy Scotch tobacco-pouches, like. Singin' *'Scots wha hae wi' Wallace bled,'* they were, and drinking out of bottles. They 'ad another of them black tykes with 'em, syme as Mary—wearing a little Scotch bonnet, 'e was."

"Well, the Scotch are a mad race," said Mr. Swales.

"Mad as 'Ell," agreed Mr. Montgomery, "And Mr. Glencannon's the maddest of the lot. But despite 'is quart a day, not counting 'olidays, he's a great engineer, Mr. Swales, a great engineer."

Some weeks later, though (they had called at Naples, gone to Cattaro, thence to Odessa, and were westward bound in the Sea of Candia) Mr. Glencannon's madness took a disquieting form. He became preoccupied, morose. He spent long hours in his room with Mary. His appetite dwindled.

At first there was only a rumor. Then the rumor spread throughout the ship's company until it was discussed incredulously from fo'c'sle to engine room. *Mr. Glencannon had sworn off liquor!*

"The thing is serious," declared Captain Ball, shaking his head ominously. "A man who has drank all his life like Mr. Glencannon has drank, can't shut down on it all at once."

" 'E can't indeed!" said Mr. Montgomery, "But are you sure 'e 'as really sworn orff, Sir?"

"Yes. Last night I asked him if he'd lend me the loan of a little whisky to rub on my corns. He said 'Take all I've got and welcome, Captain—I'm quit o' the feelthy stuff!' "

"H'm," mused the Mate, "That looks bad, Sir.—Specially, offering you all 'e's got, 'im being of the Scottish persuasion, as you might say."

"Exactly! And he went moping off to his room saying he had to fix some medicine for Mary. She's sick or something, too."

"Sick my aunt, Sir! It's only the way 'e pampers the poor tyke!

Meanwhile, 'e's letting 'is engines go to 'Ell."

"H'm. I noticed we were quite a bit shy on yesterday's run."

In the engine room things went from bad to worse. The Assistant Engineers, though diligently they slaved, lacked the great genius of their Chief which could make the old coffee grinder behave like clock work.

South of Kapsali they ran into dirty weather, and the poor old *Castle* took a sorry buffeting. She went rails under every roll, and the forward well-deck was a surge of green water.

Captain Ball, a notorious coal saver, had laid his course close. They were less than a mile off the thundering white breakers, when the engines sighed, wheezed, and stopped. From the gratings and ventilators came clouds of steam, and the sound of hammers and scurrying feet. Mr. Montgomery leaped to the speaking tube, and addressed the engine room. " 'Urry up, you bleddy tinkers!" he screamed, "If you don't get way on 'er smartly you'll swim out through the condenser pipes!"

Captain Ball then stepped to the tube, and said a few words of his own. Those nearby could smell the rubber gums of his false teeth burning. When he had finished, he went alone into the starboard wing of the bridge and considered the situation. Things were bad—very bad. In an hour, at most, they would pile up on a lee shore. He started toward his room to gather the ship's log, his Bible, chronometers and hair tonic preparatory to ordering away the boats. Half down the ladder he was blinded by a stinging gust of spray, and as he groped on his way he encountered some one coming up.

"Hoot, Captain!" shouted Mr. Glencannon, grasping his superior officer in a joyous and drunken embrace. "I was just gaein' up to get you! Stup into my room a moment, Sir—stup into my room!"

"Hell's bones, not now!" gasped the Captain, as he dragged Mr. Glencannon into the lee of the house, "We're due to pile up any minute, man! Can't you feel that the enginees are stopped?"

"I was aboot to mak' appropreeate comment on the fact," said Mr. Glencannon, feigning a polite interest, "But if you'll just come wi' me a moment, Captain, and stup into my room, I'll go below in pairson and reepair them. It reminds me of a story I once heard aboot a . . ."

In desperation Captain Ball led the way across the rolling deck to Mr. Glencannon's room, and threw open the door.

"There, Captain," said the Engineer proudly, indicating the bunk with one hand and seizing a bottle with the other. "Look what the Angels ha' brought to Mary and her puir old Dad!"

On the center of the bed lay Mary Queen of Scots, feebly wagging her tail, and caressing six tiny squirming black shapes with a tender maternal muzzle.

"The reesponsibility!—Ah, the reesponsibility's been terrible, Captain! But noo I'm my ain old self again! Do ye mak' yersel' comfortable for half a moment, Sir, while I just stup below and start those engines."

Weak and trembling, Captain Ball settled in a chair. This, he thought, would be as good a place to die as any. For the first time in his life he felt his years, and the tragic grief of a master about to lose his ship. Smiling bitterly, he patted Mary's hot little head. She raised it from her puppies and gratefully licked his hand. And at this instant there commenced a rhythmic throbbing underfoot! The *Inchcliffe Castle* became alive again! Mr. Glencannon, the wizard of steam, had worked a miracle with the engines!

Captain Ball arose slowly to his feet. Yes, the *Inchcliffe Castle* was ploughing along on her course. "Thank God—and three rousing cheers for Scotland!" he said.

In less than an hour, the *Castle* was around the Cape and in calm waters. Mr. Glencannon, oily, happy and thirsty, came back to his room.

"Weel, Lass!" he said, picking up the bottle, "I see that the Captain has gone. And—why, the domned old teetotal hypocrite! Look, Mary—he drank up half a pint o' Papa's Dew o' Kirkintilloch!"

THE LOST LIMERICK

It was a fine sunny morning, and the *Inchcliffe Castle* was butting her nose into the turquoise swell which surges off North Africa—butting, then rearing back, and pouring cascades of white water from her rusty fo'c'sle head. Off to starboard, the saw-tooth Atlas Mountains loomed in the heat haze, with here and there an ancient crumbling Moorish watch tower repeating itself in the sky above their summits in obedience to the mad whims of Fata Morgana, or lying down sidewise upon a cloud some miles above its proper earthly foundation. Once, a three mile stretch of coast range wavered viscously, broke loose from its anchorage, and stood coyly on its head upon the horizon. . . .

Mr. Glencannon, viewing these phenomena from the *Inchcliffe Castle's* deck, paused on his way to breakfast to frown in sour disapproval.

"Asseenine, pairfickly asseenine!" he declared. "Fortunate it is that I'm no' a drinking mon, or those domned mirages wad gi' me St. Vittle's dance! Still"—and he settled an elbow on the rail the better to pursue his train of thought, "Still, yon's a hot an' theersty country, beyont a doot—and I'll be three days in Algiers wi' oot a saxpunce to bless myself.—It's a dry prospect, and a lesson never to send hame my savings unless present needs are provided for. But—Heaven will provide!" And with head bowed deep in thought he strolled down the deck and stepped through the doorway.

"Captain Ball and gentlemen, I bid ye a vurra gude morning," he said, touching his cap visor. "I hope your healths are better than my poor shattered ain." There was a scupping sound as he attacked his oat porridge—a heaping quart of which, lubricated with a lump of oleomargarine the size of a cricket ball, constituted his time-honored breakfast.

Captain Ball, who had heard the greeting and the scupping

16

every morning for nine long years, acknowledged the former with his usual polite concern.

"We're all quite fit, Mr. Glencannon, thank you; but we're sorry, m'sure, to hear that your own condition is still unsatisfactory.— Er, just what seems to be the trouble today, Mr. Glencannon?"

"It's my nairves," sighed the Engineer, pushing back his empty plate and producing an old plaid sock which served the dual function of tobacco-pouch and pipe-case. "Yes, it's my nairves. They've been all a-joomp and a-jangle since we cleared Melilla for Algiers. Yes, Captain, since we cleared for Algiers. . . . I fear that Algiers wull eventually be the death o' me." And as he filled his pipe, he glanced covertly from one to another of them, as if to appraise the effect of his lugubrious prophecy.

"Algiers?" repeated Mr. Montgomery, the First Officer, rising to the bait, "And wot, may I arsk, is so fatal about Algiers?"

"Weel," explained Mr. Glencannon, his canny Caledonian eye gleaming through the toxic mixture of smoke and steam which arose from his pipe, "It's a seetuation so strange as to be no less than eunuch. As some of you know, Captain Ball and gentlemen, I've always been a great one for lummericks—silly veerses o' poesy, like, for instance, the one aboot a cairtain young mon from Bombay who went oot a riding one day, and the Coolie who lived in Hong-Kong whose job was to hammer a gong . . . you know the sort o' thing? . . . O' course! Weel, there are leeterally hundreds o' them, a' more-or-less immoral, but a' o' them vurra comic—yes, vurra vurra comic indeed! It's been a hobby o' mine to collect and meemorize a lummerick for every port in the world—in fact, it's been a matter o' pride that no living mon, aship or ashore, could stump me when it comes to lummericks. Weel, when I heard aboot our nuxt port o' call being Algiers, I o' course thought o' the famous lummerick which goes—weel, the feerst line goes something aboot '*Algiers.*' Ye know it?" . . . And tensely he leaned forward.

"Oh, ha ha, why, my word, *certainly* I know it!" chuckled Captain Ball, patronizingly. "It goes . . . it goes . . . er, wait a moment, let's see, now . . ."

Mr. Montgomery spoke up. "Oh, I've 'eard *that* one, Sir! It's about the, er . . ."

"It's about Algiers, Sir!" volunteered the third mate, who was extremely young. "I've recited it a thousand times, I 'ave! Er—funny, though—it seems to eskype me."

Captain Ball shot him a withering glance. But the mate's eyes were closed and his fingers were beating time upon the table.

"Ah!" sighed Mr. Glencannon, "There, gentlemen, there is the deeficulty! *I* know that lummerick, *you* know that lummerick;—but I canna think o' it and neither can you! And because my health is frail at best, the domned thing has become an obseesion wi' me nicht and day, and my nairves are shattered in conseequence."

"Well, I'll think of it in a minute," said Captain Ball, doggedly, "That is, I will if you gentlemen will do me the favor to shut up and stop drumming on the table. I've got a pretty good memory for such things."

"So 'ave I," declared Mr. Montgomery.

"Well, mine's a bit above the average," said Mr. MacQuayle, the Second Engineer.

"Oh, and is it?" inquired Captain Ball. "Well, I'll have you know, Sir, that I'm in command of this vessel, and when it comes to memory . . ."

"'Old 'ard—I mean excuse me, Sir!" exclaimed Mr. Montgomery, springing to his feet. "The h'Algiers limerick goes like this . . . er . . . wyte a minnit now, 'arf a mo' . . . Oh, *'ell*, I do believe it's slipped me!"

The mess-boy paused in gathering the dishes, and cleared his throat respectfully. "Beggin' pardon, Sorrh, if Oi moight say a word to the Captain, Sorrh, O'ive 'eard that h'Algiers limerick monny's the toime, Sorrh! It's (ha ha!) it's something a, um, er . . . er, just a second, Sorrh, whoile Oi goes and arsks the cook."

There was silence at the table, broken only by tense mutterings and the ruminative drumming of fingers upon oilcloth.

The mess-boy returned, hand pressed to brow, and walking as if in a trance.

"Well?" snapped Captain Ball.

"Sorrh, the cook says 'e knows it loike a beggar in 'is cups—in fact 'e was on the very pint of tellin' me, Sorrh, when it slipped 'im, it did.—But 'e says as 'ow 'e'll 'ave it in a jiffick. . . ."

"Weel, I ha' me doots," declared Mr. Glencannon, wagging his head sagaciously. "Dinna meesunderstand me, Captain and gentlemen, when I say that if a meemory like mine—which has mastered Bobby Burns from cover to cover—fails in recalling a sumple lummerick, there's no' much chance on a ship like this!"

"Oh, we don't misunderstand you a dam bit!" bristled Mr. Montgomery. "What *you* mean is that the rest of us is so many 'arf-wits, so to say!"

Mr. Glencannon blew a stifling cloud and through it smiled a seraphic smile. "Oh, no!" he protested, "To you, Muster Mate, I wad no' say as much as that. . . ."

"Wait!" interrupted Captain Ball in a voice of frozen fury. "I said before, and I say again, that I've got the best memory on this ship, and what's more I've got money to prove it!—What's your answer to that, gentlemen?"

"You mean you'll bet, Sir?"

"Well," said the Captain, with such effort at repression that he almost bit off his palate, "That was the idea I intended to convey. But I doubt if there's anybody in the crowd who's sportsman enough to bet with me!"

"Let's myke it a pool—how about that, Sir?" suggested Mr. Montgomery. "All fork up a percentage of our pay, winner tyke all?"

"Right-o for me," agreed Captain Ball. "The more I win the merrier! What do *you* say, Mr. Glencannon?"

There was a pause while the Engineer thought it over. "A-weel," he said at length and doubtfully, "I'm no' a gambling mon, such being contrary to my streect Preesbyteerian principles. Also, I'm extremely conseervative in a' matters conceerning finance. But if you yoursel' wull admeenister the thing, Captain—taking it oot o' the hands o' the mates and thus assuring fair play—I'll cairtainly parteecipate."

And so it was arranged that the first man to hand Captain Ball a copy of the limerick, before the *Inchcliffe Castle* docked at Algiers the following day, would receive ten percent of the monthly pay of all of them.

This was, in itself, a tidy sum; but later in the morning the second mate was waited upon by Bo's'n Hughes.

"Sorrh," said the Bo's'n, "The fo'c's'le is in a h'uproar! Oi've 'ad to broike three 'eads, Oi 'ave, to muntain the discipline. And all h'about the ruddy limerick which the H'engineer arsked the Captain and the Captain arsked the mess-boy and the mess-boy arsked the cook.—All of us knows it, of course, but none of us can quoite *think* of it!"

"Ah," said the Mate absently, gazing toward a soaring sea-gull and moving his lips in futile quest of vague and fleeting words. "Ah? That is, I mean to say, yes?"

"Yes," said Bo's'n Hughes, "And wot Oi'd loike to s'y, Sorrh, is that the men would loike to come in on the pool, they would, syme as the h'orfficers, and settle once and for all 'oos got the best memory in this 'ere ship."

Thus the pool was swelled to mammoth proportions; and by mid-day the *Inchcliffe Castle* had taken on a strangely preoccupied air. On the bridge Mr. Montgomery was pacing back and forth, eating one cigar after another, and pausing at intervals to smite himself upon the forehead as does one who strives to summon an elusive memory. The man at the wheel was gnawing his moustache and peering off into space for minutes at a time, recalling himself to the binnacle and business only by the fear that Mr. Montgomery might glance astern, see the wavers in the wake, and kick him as Mr. Montgomery alone knew how. While the British Board of Trade, in its wisdom, has decreed that no officer shall strike a seaman, it has said nothing at all about kicking him; and the *Inchcliffe Castle's* mate, observing the letter of the law, had also mastered the technique of the boot.

Only, just now, Mr. Montgomery was too busy thinking of something else to bother about the extremely untidy wobbles in soapsuds. Suddenly his face brightened; he stepped to the engine room speaking-tube and whistled down it.

"Second Engineer," answered a voice.

"I'll speak to the Chief, if he's down there," barked Mr. Montgomery.

There was a long pause during which the mate beat time upon

the tube-nozzle. " 'Ell!" he growled impatiently, "If 'e don't 'urry up it'll slip me. '—*Da-de-de-de-de-de Algiers'* . . . I s'y, are you there, Mr. Glencannon?"

"No, Sir—it's MacQuayle again. The Chief says he canna speak to ye the noo, and says he's vurra annoyed at bein' deesturbed, Sir."

"Well, damn it all, tell 'im I almost 'ad it!"

"So did he, Sir, but he says ye bruck his train of thought. He's standing nuxt the crank-pit noo, Sir, seerching for it in the rhuthm o' the engines."

"Rhythm your eye!" shouted Mr. Montgomery, beating on the tube with his fist. "I *know* the rhythm—it's the *words!* The rhythm goes *'De-da-de-de-de-de Algiers'!"*

"I beg to deefer wi' ye, Sir!"—and the voice came through the tube a trifle tartly. "The proper rhuthm is *'Da-da-DE-da-de-Algiers,'* and ye'll obsairve it's wuth three *da's* an' twa *de's,* and no' wi' one *da* and five *de's,* as ye reheersed it, Sir."

"Wait, wait, *wait,* can't you!" screamed the mate. "There's first a *de,* then a *da,* then four—no *five* . . . oh, blarst your eyes, Mac-Quayle, you've got me all mixed up, you 'ave!"

Mr. Montgomery let the tube snap shut, glanced aft, saw the snakes in the wake, and advanced truculently toward the wheel-man—timing his stride like a hurdler who plans to elevate his right foot smartly and at the proper instant.

The wheelman didn't see him coming. Head back and eyes closed, he was murmuring, *"There once was a de-de Algiers . . ."*

"Right-*oh!"* exclaimed Mr. Montgomery, staying his foot in midair. "You've almost got it, you 'ave! Think 'ard, my man, think 'ard!"

The wheelman thought. He thought frantically, and in the process let the *Inchcliffe Castle* slide full seven points off her course. *"There once was a— There once was a—*er—oh—I'm afraid it's got me beat, Sir," he admitted feebly.

Mr. Montgomery tossed his head in disgust, remembered the wake, and launched his kick—all more or less in one motion. Then, becoming conscious of a monotonous and distracting sound, he scowled down at the well deck where three seamen were chipping paint. Their hammers rose and fell in unison in a vaguely familiar and yet unsatisfactory rhythm which they changed from time to time after prolonged and heated debate.

"Strike me pink," muttered the mate. "Why, I do believe the 'ole bloomink ship's gone barmy!"

And so, in truth, it seemed. At supper that evening scarcely a word was spoken or a mouthful eaten. So preoccupied were the officers with scraps of paper and stubs of pencils that none of them noticed that the meat was scorched or that the treacle was served on the potatoes instead of on the pudding.

"Weel," Mr. Glencannon broke the silence as he pushed back his chair, "I'll spend the evening in streect concentration. What time wull we be docking tomorrow, Captain Ball?"

"Eleven o'clock at latest. Please to notify everybody, Mr. Montgomery, to hand in their limericks by four bells sharp."

"Ye may rest assured that by four bells I'll hand ye the winning teecket, sir," declared Mr. Glencannon, retreating to the deck before a volley of vicious snorts.

Chuckling to himself, he went to his room, bolted the door, and hung a blanket over the porthole before he switched on the light. Then, pausing a moment to listen for footsteps outside, he took from a drawer a huge oilcloth-covered scrapbook and sat down upon the bunk.

He turned to the first page, which was a methodical and neatly hand-written index, and ran his finger down the columns. "No," he said at length, "No—it's even as I suspected. Under '*A*' there's nowt that wull sairve—absolutely nowt! But noo, let's conseeder the rest o' the alphabet. . . ."

For the better part of an hour he studied the index and thumbed the pages. At length an idea seemed to come to him, and eagerly he turned to the letter "*T*."

"There!" he exclaimed, triumphantly smiting the page, "I knew I cud find one! T'wull fit like a piston fits a cylinder! It's not only good, it's *pairfect!* And noo I'll write it doon, so's to have it a' in readiness for the morrow!"

Having written it down, tucked it into an envelope, and tucked the envelope into his pocket, he produced from beneath his bunk a bottle whose label bore the legend *"Duggan's Dew of Kirkintilloch."* He held the bottle to the light and sighed sepulchrally. "Less than a quart!" he said. "Losh, but I figured close—so close it was foolhardy! I should ha' laid in twa or three spare cases at Rabat before I sent my money hame. Why, just suppose we'd struck rough weather! . . ."

Shuddering at the thought, he poured himself a brimming tumblerful and drank it gratefully. "Saxty-foor poonds, nineteen sheelings, saxpunce," he mused. "That's what the pool comes to, by the most conseervative esteemate! 'Twull be a braw bricht festival in Algiers after a'!"

Replenishing the tumbler, he dragged an oil-skin case from beneath his bunk, and from it produced a bagpipe.

Then, filling his mouth with the *Dew of Kirkintilloch,* he removed the reed from the chanter of the bagpipe, and thrust it between his lips. Now, ordinary pipers, of course, suffer from the delusion that a chanter reed can be properly conditioned by saliva alone; but this is because such great *virtuosi* as The MacCrimmons of the Isle of Skye have jealously guarded as a secret of their art the fact that only Scotch whisky (and notably *Duggan's Dew of Kirkintilloch*) can so affect pipe and piper as to produce the so-desired soul-shivering result. Mr. Glencannon, religiously observing the ritual, let the chanter reed soak for full five minutes. Then he swallowed the mouthful, and drank what remained in the tumbler for his own benefit.

"Whoosh!" he said, tucking the bagpipe under his arm and stepping out into the moonlight, "God's in his heaven an' a's richt wi' the world! What cud be more feeting than an hour or two o' 'Cock O' The North?' "

"*Cock O' The North,*" as all good Caledonians know, is the greatest and grandest music ever composed by mortal man; but unfortunately none but the Caledonians are capable of appreciating it. The rest of mankind is unanimous in decrying the *opus,* and dismissing it along with all other bagpipe music as the merest mélange of savage groans, shrieks and catterwauls. And so, though Mr. Glencannon paced up and down the deck and played "*Cock O' The North*" as perhaps only four other living men could have played it, his efforts were not gratefully received by the rest of the ship's company.

The first manifestation of disapproval came from the Mate. Mr. Montgomery, tactfully awaiting a moment when Mr. Glencannon had laid down his pipes to take up his bottle, ascended the ladder to the upper deck.

"Orl finished?" he asked, hopefully.

"If ye're refeering to the whusky, yes," said Mr. Glencannon, hastily laying the bottle on its side behind the doorsill to conceal the fact that it was still a good quarter full. "But if, on the other hand, ye're refeering to the museec, ye've still a gude three hours to enjoy it. And noo," picking up the pipes and inflating the bag, "I'll beed ye' 'a vurra gude nicht, Muster Mate."

Mr. Montgomery was undaunted. "I s'y, now, see 'ere," he protested. "You've put the 'ole ship to a lot of trouble, you 'ave, with your ruddy limerick and orl, and it ayn't cricket for you to go disturbing the rest of us wot's trying to think of it. 'Ow can we think of this limerick—'ow can we think of *anything*, for that matter!—with you up 'ere pl'ying this bloody squealing yowler orl night? I arsks you, Mr. Glencannon, yes I arsks you,—is it cricket or ay'nt it?"

"No," said Mr. Glencannon, "It is no' creeket, which is at best a fool's game. It's *museec*, which is a gentleman's highest deevairsion! I'll reemind ye, Muster Montgomery, that ye wear but three stripes and I wear foor, and if ye dinna take ye're ugly face beyont my reach, I shall be forced to reesort to lusty meesures. . . ."

"Oh, so that's it, is it?" said Mr. Montgomery, backing down the ladder. "Well, just for that, my Scotch bucko, I'll go to me room, I will, and show you 'oos 'oo when it comes to remembering limericks on this 'ere ship!"

"*Scottish,* not 'Scotch,'" corrected Mr. Glencannon, patiently. "And for ye're further information, the true pronownciation is no' '*oo,* but *who,* wi' the 'H' audeeble, as in '*hoot.*'"

Mr. Montgomery's growl of rage was lost in the drone and shrill of the pipes, as for the two hundred and sixty-fourth time Mr. Glencannon launched into "*Cock O' The North.*"

Shortly, though, there was a hiss of steam, a rasping wheeze, a shower of warm water—and the *Inchcliffe Castle's* whistle gave vent to a bellow which shook the ship and shattered the night. The roar kept on—head-filling, terrible; and Mr. Glencannon, cocking his eye across the empty moonlit expanse of sea which lay ahead, realized that the whistle was being sounded solely in a malicious attempt to drown him out.

"On the bridge, there!" he hailed, "Muster Coyle, ye mannerless pup ye, if ye dinna stop wasting steam-pressure oot o' my boilers, I'll feerst come up and tromple ye, and then I'll go doon and tell the Captain why."

The whistling subsided and the piping resumed. Resumed, and continued for another ghastly hour at the end of which Mr. Glencannon, discovering that his bottle was almost empty, re-conditioned the chanter reed, laid away his pipes and prepared for bed.

He had switched off the light, said his prayers and composed himself for slumber with blissful thoughts of sixty-four pounds, ten shillings, sixpence, when he was stabbed into trembling wakefulness by a frightful fear.

"Foosh!" he exclaimed, his feet groping in the darkness for his slippers. "How cud I have forgotten him?" And with his nightshirt flapping around his shins in the warm African breeze, he tiptoed his way to the wireless room and peered furtively through the port.

There, sure enough, was Sparks—ear-phones in place, cigarette going, and his dark pimply young face illuminated by the eerie blaze of miniature thunderbolts which crackled and stuttered as his fingers set them free. Suddenly he abandoned the key, seized his pencil, and listened. Thin cold notes were coming from across the ocean spaces—coming in a broken whine which Mr. Glencannon visualized as flying fragments of pale blue thread. But Sparks knew their meaning, and eagerly wrote it down. When he had finished, and sat back reading the result, Mr. Glencannon threw wide the door and stood pointing an accusing finger.

"Swundler!" he shouted. "Gi' me yon paper befeer I do ye in!"

Sparks, who was a callow youth and typical of his calling, glanced him up and down, handed him the message, and shrugged.

" 'Ere you are, old walrus, and a fat lot of good it'll do you!"
he said. "I thought I'd cop the pool, as so would you if you 'ad
'arf my chance! I've been sending out a query *'Seek detailed information limerick about Algiers.'* Just now I gets this reply from
2 FMP, which is Funchal Madeira, the ruddy Portugee swine!
. . . 'Ere, read it for yourself!"

"H'm," said Mr. Glencannon, holding the pad beneath the
green-shaded light. "It says *'Limerick not about Algiers. Limerick
about 129 miles W.S.W. of Dublin Ireland.'*—Ha, ha, they completely meesunderstood ye, ye perishing young thief. Weel, noo,"
and he assumed a pious air, "Let this be a lesson to ye, young
Muster What's-Yer-Name, that honesty is the best policy!"

Very deliberately, Sparks switched off his receiving apparatus,
sat back, and lighted another Gold Flake. "My nyme," he said, "Is
not 'Whut's-Yer-Nyme'—it's Levy. There's quite a few of us is
trydesmen in Whitechapel. . . . But aside from that, 'ow would
you like to see the replies I've 'ad from nine other stytions and
twenty-two different ships—orl of which I got before you cyme
barging in 'ere where you 'aven't a mite of right to be, you being
a h'engineer h'orfficer, blarst your eyes, Sir! Do you know, I've arf
a mind to report you to the Captain?"

Mr. Glencannon paled, swallowed twice, and assumed his most
charming smile.

"Ah, noo!" he said, "Be paceefic, Muster Levy, be paceefic! I
did na' mean to inteerfere wi' your juties! It was only that . . ."

"It was only that you've got this swindle orl figured out, you
'ave, and you're afryde I'll crab it. Well, I *will* crab it! I'll go
stryght to the Captain now, and tell him that there simply ayn't
no such thing as a limerick h'about h'Algiers! Now wot do you s'y
to that?"

Mr. Glencannon's somewhat prominent Adam's apple travelled
up and down his throat like the conveyor-bucket of a Liverpool
coal barge.

"Er—why, noo, what ye say is rideeculous, young Muster Levy
—absolutely rideeculous! I don't mind telling ye that even noo,

a fair copy o' the Algiers lummerick is reeposing in my room, a'ready for the Captain in the morning."

"Then it's a fake—a ruddy fake!" declared Mr. Levy. "None o' them ships and stytions wot answered my query 'ave ever 'eard of a h'Algiers limerick! And besides that, the British Consulate in h'Algiers 'as an h'expert on limericks, and 'e says as 'ow there never was a h'Algiers limerick. So now I'll step below, I will, and tell the Captain that you're trying to swindle the ship. And I'll warn 'im not to settle the pool until after 'e's seen the Consul in the morning. . . ."

"Wait!" said Mr. Glencannon, restraining him.

Mr. Levy took several deliberate drags on his Gold Flake and lowered the lids of his extremely intelligent eyes. "I'll wyte while you mykes up yer mind—but remember, time is money!"

"Meaning what?" asked Mr. Glencannon, nervously.

"Meaning, what's my split?" explained Mr. Levy.

Mr. Glencannon licked his lips, and did some rapid calculating. "Ten percent—there, that's fair, isn't it?"

"Ha, ha!" replied Mr. Levy.

"Fufteen."

"Ha, ha, ha!"

"Twunty, then! *Twunty*—why, think o' it!"

"Twenty? Why, I s'y, listen 'ere, Mr. Glencohen, I thought you was a sensible business man, I did! Now I don't know just 'ow you're going to work your swindle, but I do know I'll go to the Captain this minnit unless you agree to split arf-and-arf. And that's that!"

Mr. Glencannon was on the verge of tears. "Fufty percent! Why, t'wull come to theerty-odd poonds!" he moaned.

"Well, maybe I'd better myke it sixty," mused Mr. Levy.

"Fufty percent! So be it, then," said Mr. Glencannon, hurriedly. But after a moment he chuckled and looked up. "Do ye know, Muster Levy, that ye're a most preecocious young mon? In monny ways, ye're a lad after my ain heart, and I preedict ye'll go far! What do ye say tomorrow we exploore Algiers together?"

"Orl right with me," agreed Mr. Levy. "Only, I wants my share right 'ere in my pocket before we starts ashore!"

II

Hot and humiliated, Captain Ball plodded up the arch-borne ramps which lead from the docks to the Boulevard de la République. His eyes, long accustomed to the grateful blues and greens and greys of the seven seas, winced at the dazzling whiteness which leaped out at them from all sides. . . . Well, he was getting old—that was the answer! Even his memory was deserting him. It had been a bitter pill to stand before the officers and crew, that morning, and bestow those sixty-odd pounds upon a blithering Scot with a memory no longer than the interval between drinks!

The dome of the mosque Jamaa-el-Kasbah seared his eyeballs, and he looked away. "Narsty town!" he muttered. "Damned if I don't write a letter to the Member from Dorking, demanding that the British Consulate be moved down to the water-front where a white man can get to it!"

At the Rue Bab Azoun he paused and glanced about him. On the corner, surrounded by spellbound Arabs, sat a snake charmer playing a bulbous brass instrument to the strident brayings of which sundry reptiles writhed and reared upon a rug. Beside him, a boy beat upon a tom-tom.

"Three damns to you, my man!" snarled Captain Ball, tossing his cigar butt into the snake-charmer's alms bowl. "Your profession is narsty, so are you, and your instrument sounds like a shuddering bagpipe anyway!" And crossing the street, he made for a building which bore the sun-blistered arms of Great Britain. That he had to climb two flights of stairs added nothing to his poise.

He entered a room on the third floor and introduced himself. His Majesty's Third Assistant Vice Consul, Major Cheynesyde, D.S.O., fiddled with hopeless courtesy at the lever of the electric fan.

"Shno use," he said, rather thickly. "Twelve fifty's all she'll rev., same's my old Sop Dolphin. Say, you weren't in jolly old Flying Corps during war, were you? Why no, f'course not—it was 'nother chap named Ball, but the Hun got him. Trust you'll pardon my undershirt, Captain. Bottle and splash are right there at your elbow, Captain. Clap your handsh twiche—*twice*—for ice, Captain. Realize it's breach of hoshtality to ask guest to clap own handsh for ice, but I'm not very good at clapping handsh. *Haw!*"

"Haw!" echoed Captain Ball, tartly. "Er, that is, I mean to say *haw* haw!"

"Thash spirit—haw *haw* haw!" roared His Majesty's Third Assistant Vice Consul. "I'd clap for you, Captain, only my right handsh made of jolly old aluminium. 'Riginal member got shot off during war by jolly old sphlosive bullet. . . . And now, Captain, I shpose you want me to sign ships papers and all that?"

"Yes, Sir, if you please," said Captain Ball in a businesslike tone. "Vessel, *Inchcliffe Castle;* thirty-six hundred tons; port of register . . ."

"*Inchcliffe Castle?*" repeated Major Cheynesyde. "Oh, of course, by all meansh! I hope you got my message?"

"Message?" repeated Captain Ball.

"Yesh—in reply to your wireless last night.—Always glad to be of shervice in such matters! You see, I'm an expert—yes, Captain, the world's greatest limming—er, *living* limerick expert alive in world today. Thash why I'm in position to say asholutely that there'sh never been a limerick about Algiers. I've spent years in research, burned gallonsh of midnight oil, in fruitless efforts to find . . ."

"Just a moment, Sir," interrupted Captain Ball, groping in his pocket. "I don't know what you mean about wireless messages from my ship. But I *do* know I've just awarded a pool of approximately seventy pounds to one of my officers for remembering a limerick which is most certainly about Algiers!"

"Indeed?" inquired Major Cheynesyde, his face lighting up like that of a book-collector who has discovered a Gutenberg Bible on a bargain counter. "Oh, read it, Captain, read it!"

Captain Ball cleared his throat, glanced at the servant, and blushed.

"It's a funny one—but, well, it's fair foul, Sir!" he warned. "Perhaps it would be better if you'd read it to yourself. It might demoralize the A-rab."

"H'm," said the Major, reaching for his monocle but finding his key-ring instead. "Er, haw! Er, really, I mean to say, haw haw!"

"Why, what's wrong?" inquired Captain Ball, hitching forward in his chair.

"Wrong? Why, my dear fellow, you've been had! Oh, my word, you've been imposed upon, yesh, frightfully! Why, *I* wrote this limerick myself in 1919! But I wrote it about *Ta*ngier, *not Al*giers! It ishn't about Algiers at all! There's no *s* on Tangier, so Algiers is a false rhyme. Can't you shee, Captain, that this line here— and this one (haw, it *is* rather neat . . . very neat, you musht admit it, Captain!) could apply only to *Ta*ngier? You see, I was in the Tangier Consulate before I came here, and . . ."

Captain Ball cleared his throat, gulped his drink, and cleared his throat again.

"Hell's bones!" he murmured. "I've been swindled, and no mistake!"

"You certainly have!" agreed the Major, "But it's not too late. Why not make him give the money back—face him with the swindle and jolly well make him cough up the cash!"

Captain Ball bowed his head upon his breast in thought. Dimly he heard the whine of the snake-charmer's pipe and the throb of the tom-tom. But suddenly there came an outburst of shouting and the sounds of strife. The music ceased, and then even the shouting died away.

"Well," Captain Ball broke the silence, "I guess in some ways you're right. It's plain we've been swindled, but I'm afraid it would be difficult to get the money back. You see . . ." and suddenly he paused, listened . . .

The snake-charmer's pipe had once more found voice—but now, it was playing *"Cock O' The North."*

Captain Ball sprang to his feet and strode to the window. "That's him now!" he announced. "Mister Glencannon himself —drunk as a fiddler, and wounded A-rabs heaped all around him!"

"Er—Glencannon? He sounds a bit Scottish," remarked the Major.

"He is! And why look there, Sir—there's Mr. Levy, my wireless man, selling the tom-tom to those American tourists!"

"Ah," mused His Majesty's Consul—"Glencannon, did you say? . . . And Levy? Well, Captain, er, I mean to say, perhaps, after all, you'll have to charge it to experience. Have a chair, won't you, and clap your handsh for ice."

HE MIGHT HAVE BEEN A ROOSHAN

THE great green mountain sloped down into the sea. Here and there among the trees above the city were farms, clustering hamlets, and wallgirdled villas of snowy white tenanted by asthmatic Britishers, opulent Portuguese, and jobless royal refugees from the lesser countries of Europe. On the beach beyond the breakers fishermen were painting their boats blue, lavender, pink. Across the water the breeze bore fugitive snatches of music from the bandstand in the square. It was Madeira. It was January. It was delightful.

Out in the open roadstead which the citizens of Funchal so optimistically term a harbor, several vessels swung at anchor. Among them were a Greek battleship which reminded one of a tin bathtub taking itself too seriously, and a tramp steamer with the woebegone air of an old gypsy crone fallen upon evil days. The latter craft was the *Inchcliffe Castle,* and she was streaked with the recent salt of Caribbean and Atlantic, and red with the rust of the sea-lanes of the world. Just now, her crew was engaged in desultory barter with a dozen jabbering bumboat merchants whose shallops bobbed and bumped alongside as she see-sawed in the swell.

In the wing of the bridge, elbows on rail, Mr. Montgomery and Mr. Swales were basking in comfortable silence broken only when one or the other languidly bestirred himself to expectorate down into a bumboat. During such an interlude, Mr. Swales, glancing aft, was aroused to sudden interest.

"Oh, my eye!" he whispered, nudging the Mate. "Do 'ave a look at the Chief!"

"Lawk!" exclaimed Mr. Montgomery, following his gaze to the deck below. "All swanked up like the ruddy First Sea Lord, ayn't 'e? 'E must be going ashore to throw 'is weight about a bit."

"—'Is weight, and m'ybe a bottle or so," suggested Mr. Swales.

"—Oh, good morning, Mister Glencannon!"

"Gude morning, Muster Swales, and to ye also, Muster Montgomery," said the *Inchcliffe Castle's* engineer, who was wearing his best uniform, an immaculate white cap, and his customary funereal air. "It's a braw lovely day the noo, but I fear twull be stormy later. There being nowt better to do, I was thinking I'd go ashore to yon toon and gi' it a bit o' a look-see."

"Oh, yes?" said Mr. Montgomery, raising his eyebrows and nodding prophetically. "Well, all I can s'y is, if them Portygees only knew wot's threatening 'em, they'd break out the 'urricane warnings and batten down the sidewalks!"

Mr. Glencannon paused on his way to the ladder to give the Mate a disdainful stare.

"Muster Mate," he said, "From what ye say, anybody wad think I was a drinking mon! Weel, I dinna choose to swallow the slur. Ye're insolent, untruthful, ugly, and no' overly clean."

"Oh, and am I?" bristled Mr. Montgomery, leaning on the dodger and shaking an irate finger. "Well, listen 'ere, you webfooted Scotch guzzler, I'll lay you five pounds 'ere and now that they 'ave you in jail by midnight. 'Ow about it?"

"Done!" agreed Mr. Glencannon airily, settling himself in a bumboat and pointing toward the wharf. *"Pronto, Portygee, row me ashore-io."* Then, selecting a pint bottle from the stock of wares displayed in the sternsheets, he negotiated its purchase and went about sampling its contents. By the time they reached the landing stage, he had decided that it was distinctly inferior stuff and quite unfit to exist upon this earth, so he swallowed the remainder at a gulp and tossed the empty bottle over the side. "Whah!" he shuddered. "If that is the best beeverage this sorry port affords, I'll drink no' another drap today!"

Strolling up the cobbled street he passed through the Entrada da Cidade and halted to look around him. "Ootlandish!" he announced sourly, dismissing the colorful scene with a scowl. "Ootlandish! And as for you—" he wheeled upon the group of beggars who had followed him, whining, from the wharf, "Foosh to ye! Do ye think I am Muster Rothschild, or what?"

"—It is really most annoying, is it not?"

Mr. Glencannon turned to see a large, flabby young man with yellow hair, pale blue eyes, and a mercantile marine officer's cap from which the house-jack badge had been removed. His speech had a faintly foreign flavor. Vaguely, and somehow unpleasantly, he suggested a second steward.

"It is vurra annoying indeed," agreed Mr. Glencannon looking him up and down. "—It is always vurra annoying to be accosted by strangers."

"Oh, no offense, no offense," smiled the flabby one, unabashed, "Smith's my name, and as for us being strangers, why, I fancy a spot of whisky would soon fix that. Will you join me?"

"A-weel," said Mr. Glencannon, smacking his lips despite himself, "when ye speak o' whusky, ye're putting a deeferent compleexion on the seetuation. Where can we get it, Muster Smeeth?"

"Across the street, at the Golden Gate," said the other, leading the way. "Come on, it's an English place."

Now it happened that the cellars of the Golden Gate afforded that choicest of all Highland nectars, Duggan's Dew of Kirkintilloch. Mr. Smith proved to be a slow and conservative drinker, so by the time the bottle was empty, Mr. Glencannon's mood was so expansive that he even said something about buying a drink in return. But he quickly retrieved the slip by looking at his watch and remarking that it was time for lunch.

"Oh, why so it is!" said Mr. Smith. "Hi, *arrieriro!*" he hailed a passing victoria. "Come on—let's drive over and take the switchback up to the Monte Palace.—You'll be my guest, of course?"

"Well, o' coorse, since ye insist . . ." agreed Mr. Glencannon, fumbling in his pocket while his host bought another bottle of Dew to sustain them on their journey.

Soon they were clicking up the rack-and-pinion railway between the lush green groves and flowery fields of the mountainside. Mr. Glencannon cocked his feet on the seat ahead of them, and considered the .view through the bottom of the bottle. "Sublime, sublime!" he said. "And to think o' that domned feerst mate, Muster Montgomery, betting me five poond I'd spend the nicht in jail!"

"Jail?" repeated Mr. Smith with sudden interest. "Why,"—he lowered his voice and glanced furtively over his shoulder, "—er, 'jail' is a most unpleasant word to me, too. I was just wondering if you'd do me a bit of a favor, Mr. Glencannon. . . ."

"Weel," said Mr. Glencannon, cautiously, "It a' deepends. If it's a question o' money, Muster Smeeth, I'm afraid I canna. . . ."

"Oh, no, it isn't money," the other reassured him. "But I do wish you could get me a job on your ship. You see I'm here in Madeira against my will. As a matter of fact, they—er—kicked me off my last ship. I haven't any papers or passport, so I can't get another berth. The authorities have been badgering me all week, but as I admit no nationality, they can't decide where to deport me. So they're threatening to put me in jail."

"No nationality?" inquired Mr. Glencannon, his brain a trifle muddled and his eye become glassy.

"No nationality whatsoever!" declared the flabby one, his voice suddenly vibrant with enthusiasm. "I, I am a citizen of the world! What are frontiers, boundaries, and all such capitalistic foolishness, compared with the vast unlimited freedom of internationalism? I might have been born a Russian, or a Serb, or a Polander —I might have . . ."

He was interrupted by Mr. Glencannon chanting at the top of his voice:—

> *"For he might have been a Rooshan,*
> *A Toork or French or Prooshan,*
> *Or peerhapsh an Eye-tal-i-AN;*
> *But in shpite o' a' tremtray-hay-shunsh*
> *To brelong to other nay-hay-shunsh,*
> *He remainsh an English-MON!*
> *He ree-may-hay-haynsh*
> *An ENG . . . lish MON!"*

"—Ah, that's exactly my point!" resumed Mr. Smith, with the ardor of one who expounds his most cherished religious belief. "It is the mistaken spirit of nationalism which . . ." But then he noticed that Mr. Glencannon was deep in slumber, so he subsided.

Arrived at the summit, the sleeper was aroused with some difficulty. "Dinna shak' me, dinna shak' me—I was no' asleep!" he mumbled. "I heerd every word ye' was saying, Muster Smeeth." The nap had done him good, and he was able to navigate the short distance from the station to the hotel without assistance. They were ushered to a table on the veranda, which commanded a breath-taking panorama of mountain, sea and sky.

"Whoosh!" sighed Mr. Glencannon, sinking into a chair which turned out to be a potted palm. "What a theerst these high altitudes do gi' a mon! What wad ye say, Muster Smeeth, to a little liquid refreeshment?"

As they were discussing the wine list with the waiter, three motor cars drew up beneath the porte-cochere and deposited a bevy of gorgeously-uniformed naval officers. "See, gentlemans!" said the waiter. "It ees the Greek admiral and his *attachés*. This afternoon, they will to visit the exile' Grand Duke."

"Giddy monkeys!" declared Mr. Smith, cynically.

"Ah, noo, noo, I canna' agree wi' ye there!" protested Mr. Glencannon. "It's unfoortunate, o' course, that they're only Greeks, but after a', an Admiral is an Admiral, and deesairving o' reespect." At this moment the dignitary and his aides were taking their places at a nearby table, so Mr. Glencannon beat lustily with his fork upon his plate and shouted, "Three rousing cheers for Admiral What's-his-name!"

The maitre d'hotel hastened over to restrain him. The Admiral, a paunchy gentleman with much gold lace, many medals and a black beard parted in the middle, arose and surveyed him belligerently through a monocle. Mr. Glencannon, not to be outdone, screwed a two-shilling piece into his eye and returned the stare.

"Ye're a mannerless lout, that's what ye are, and I'm deesappointed in ye!" he declared, shaking his fist. "You and yere gold lace and yere tupenny tin gunboat wad be at the bottom o' the sea in twa winks, if the Breetish navy ever got after ye!" Whereupon, having dropped the maitre d'hotel over the veranda railing into a flower bed, and spurred on by Mr. Smith, he climbed upon the table and sang *"Rule Britannia!"* with great gusto and impassioned gestures.

As it became apparent that the hotel staff was mobilizing for action, Mr. Smith suggested that they decamp.

"I agree wi' ye!" said Mr. Glencannon. "This is a second-class pub, the sairvice is atrocious, and the guests are so much riff-raff. Come, Muster Smeeth, do we be getting our caps and deeparting."

The vestiaire fled at their approach, so Mr. Glencannon helped himself to the admiral's hat—a notable fore-and-aft affair with gold braid, cockade and plume—and strode forth bravely into the sunshine.

At the edge of the hotel gardens they came out upon the Caminho da Monte, the famous stone-paved slide down which visitors to Madeira are wont to coast in runner-shod wicker chairs from the mountain summit to the town below. They hired a chair and a crew of two natives to guide it, and started on their way.

At first the slope was gentle, and their progress slow. Mr. Glencannon yawned in boredom, and took a deep and gurgling draught from his bottle. But soon the wooden runners commenced clicking over the smooth stones right merrily, and the crew, trotting along behind, held back on the guide-ropes to check the speed.

"Fuddlesticks!" complained Mr. Glencannon. " 'Tis a sorra spoort indeed! Do ye look doon there ahead o' us, Muster Smeeth, where it gets good and steep. Why do they no' cast us loose?"

"Because we'd jolly well go down like a bat out of hell if they did," said Mr. Smith.

"Hurroo! Here goes, then!" said Mr. Glencannon, reaching over the back of the seat and slashing the ropes with his clasp-knife.

The chair shot forward and Mr. Smith jumped for his life. Mr. Glencannon, waving his Admiral's hat in one hand and his bottle in the other, catapulted down the mountainside at breakneck speed. From time to time the chair hurtled high into the air, even as a chamois leaping from crag to Alpine crag. It caromed against the wall beside the road, reared perilously on one runner. It slewed around, proceeded backwards, and with speed no whit abated charged through a party of tourists who were sliding on their leisurely way. Their screams were answered only by a lusty "Hoot!" and the courtly flourish of a gold-trimmed *chapeau*.

At length, becoming a trifle dizzy from viewing the speed-blurred landscape, or perhaps because of the very considerable alcoholic cargo sloshing about in his hold, Mr. Glencannon closed his eyes trustingly and let gravity take its course. A cool wind blew against his fevered brow. He felt that he was sliding, spinning, flying through space. It was as though he were coursing the etheric regions of the outer cosmos. It was delightful. . . .

But suddenly there came a jolt, a splintering crash, a sickening thud. The flight was ended—Icarus had returned to earth. Dimly, Mr. Glencannon heard the murmur of voices, and felt sympathetic hands ministering to his bruised body. Feebly he motioned to his mouth, and swallowed the entire contents of the flask which was instantly proffered.

He opened his eyes. He was lying upon a lawn which was decorated as for a fete. Around him were grouped gentlemen in cutaways and others in uniform. At one side he saw a low stone wall upon which was draped the shapeless wreck of the chair-sled, and through which was a gate. Even as he looked, three cars halted at this gate, and disgorged the Admiral and his staff.

For a moment the new arrival caused much confusion among the guests. Some of them pointed to Mr. Glencannon, while others stared at the Admiral and shrugged. All of them were jabbering volubly. Plainly they had not been expecting two Admirals. . . .

The doughty Greek recognized his hat from afar, strode over, and snatched it from Mr. Glencannon's head. Then he snapped his fingers thrice beneath the Scotsman's somewhat-auburn nose, emitted a derisive "Bah!" and bade his henchmen summon the constabulary. When the *guardias* appeared, they found Mr. Glencannon snoring peacefully.

He was aroused by the bell in the spire of Sao Thiago as it boomed the twelve strokes of midnight. At first he thought he was in his room aboard the *Inchcliffe Castle,* but as he became fully awake, he realized that he was in a prison cell. Like a flash, he connected the time, the place, and his five pound bet with Mr. Montgomery.—He had lost! Ah, lackaday!

His gusty sigh brought response from the adjoining dungeon.

"Hello," came a vaguely familiar voice. "You're awake, are you?"

Mr. Glencannon, who was just discovering that he had a splitting headache and a thirst which had never been equalled within the history of man, was in no mood for conversation.

"Be quiet, my good mon," he said. "I dinna know ye, nor wad I care to."

"Don't know me, eh? Well, I'm Smith, the chap who footed the bills. They arrested me, too."

Slowly, Mr. Glencannon began to remember the events of the day.—Smith? Yes—a blond, pale-eyed flabby person with just the trace of an accent. . . .

"Weel," he confessed, "I can dimly recall ye, Muster Smeeth, but the reecollection is vurra unpleasant indeed. Ye ha' cost me five poonds, ye ha', so from now on, we're total strangers."

"But see here," came the voice, "How about that favor I asked you yesterday, getting me aboard your ship and all?"

"Dinna disturb me," growled Mr. Glencannon. "I ha' troubles o' my own." And mumbling "Five poonds, five poonds," he dropped off into fitful slumber.

In the morning he was routed out of bed by three policemen and brought before an official who scrutinized his papers, sputtered at him in broken English, warned him to beware the company he kept, and ordered him to go aboard his ship and stay there.

Mr. Smith was nowhere to be seen.

II

The *Inchcliffe Castle* was ploughing a furrow Eastward through the sea. Madeira lay a night and a day behind her. On the lower platform of the engine room—a gloomy cavern the air of which was hot and heavy with a mist of oil and filled with the clamor of machinery—Mr. Glencannon was deep in meditation. He was thinking of the five pounds which he would shortly pay over to Mr. Montgomery, and the thought was bitter indeed.

He was startled from his reverie by footsteps on the ladder, and turning, he beheld Mr. Montgomery himself—Mr. Montgomery, and yes, the pale-eyed Mr. Smith!

"Weel, I'll be domned!" exclaimed Mr. Glencannon, unable to conceal his surprise.

"Oh, then you do know 'im, do you?" inquired the mate in

credulously. " 'E's a bleddy stowaway, 'e is, but 'e said as 'ow 'e was a friend of yours, and that you invited 'im aboard."

"Ah, noo, there must be some mistake," stammered Mr. Glencannon, shaking his head. "I dinna know yon waster from Adam."

Mr. Smith laughed unpleasantly, and winked at him over the mate's shoulder. "Mistake?" he repeated. "Oh, why Mr. Glencannon! Don't you recall telling me about your five pound bet with this gentleman, and asking me to come and bear witness that you and I played cribbage all night in the Golden Gate Hotel?"

A great weight fell from Mr. Glencannon's spirits. "Ah, o' coorse, o' coorse!" he beamed. "I recognize ye noo! But why did ye hide yersel', and no' come to me before we left port?"

Mr. Smith simulated embarrassment. "Well, I suppose I have made an ass of myself. But you see," he laughed, "I'd been drinking a bit, and when the boatman put me aboard you in the darkness, I crawled under a lifeboat cover and didn't wake up till just a while ago."

"Well," said Mr. Montgomery, "It orl sounds fair fishy to me, it does. But if this cove's really a friend of yours, I'll leave it to you to fix it up with the Old Man."

"Vurra weel," said Mr. Glencannon. "Oh, and before ye go, Muster Montgomery, I'll just remind ye that ye're my debtor in the amoont o' five poonds."

"Oh, orl right, orl right!" grumbled the Mate, counting out five one pound notes. " 'Ere you are, and I 'ope it burns you."

"Ah!" sighed Mr. Smith, glancing after him as he departed up the ladder, "I certainly feel a whole lot easier. If I hadn't escaped from that damned jail, they'd have given me ten years in the Lisbon pen.—Yes," he smiled sourly, "Yes, and what's more, if I hadn't blackmailed you, just now, I'd have been sent back there from the next port.—I say, come to think of it, you're a pretty nasty specimen, aren't you?"

Mr. Glencannon winced. "Hold yere tongue, Muster Smeeth, hold yere tongue," he threatened. "Remember ye're in my engine room, where I have a pairfect right to clout ye!"

"Oh, go and take a good whistle for yourself!" replied Mr. Smith with irritating nonchalance. "I have half a mind to tell that Mate about your being in jail anyway."

Mr. Glencannon leaned back against the platform hand-rail and by dint of considerable effort arranged his face into a smile. "Ah, come, come, Muster Smeeth," he wheedled, "Canna ye no' tak' a jest?"

"Well, it all depends," said Mr. Smith. "And you know what it depends on. So just run along like a good fellow and fix things with the Captain.—I don't intend to work my passage, mind. I'm your guest, this trip, and I don't want you to forget it."

To Mr. Glencannon, the days that ensued were most unpleasant. Never for an instant did Mr. Smith permit him to forget the sordid pact between them. At meals, the passenger delivered tedious harangues on his pet subject of internationalism, and once Captain Ball was forced to call him to account for talking to members of the crew in a manner subversive to discipline. Mr. Montgomery was of the opinion that Smith was an escaped lunatic or a dangerous criminal, either status, according to his theory, fully explaining Mr. Glencannon's friendship for him. But young Mr. Levy, the wireless operator, had other ideas.

"I've seen that bloke before, I 'ave," he declared. "I can't ply'ce 'im to be sure, but I think 'e was standing on a soap box at 'Yde Park Corner myking speeches about the coal strike."

"That's reedeeculous, Muster Levy!" said Mr. Glencannon. "Muster Smeeth has been known to me for years." But just the same, he was bitterly disappointed when the mysterious passenger did not disembark at Gibraltar.

"I've got my own private reasons for steering clear of a British Crown Colony," said Mr. Smith. "Genoa's good enough for me, as long as you're buying my ticket."

"Stay with us till Geenoa, then," Mr. Glencannon acquiesced. "But I'd like to ask ye to explain what ye mean aboot my buying yere teecket?"

"I mean that you'll pay my passage out of those five pounds, you Scotch swindler!" snapped Mr. Smith. "If it comes to less, you can buy yourself some rat poison with the change."

Mr. Glencannon's eyes narrowed, and, quite automatically, his hands doubled themselves into fists. "Muster Smeeth," he said ominously, "I warn ye to be vurra, vurra careful."

"Same to you!" sneered Smith, glancing toward the bridge and
Mr. Montgomery.

III

Late one night the *Inchcliffe Castle* steamed slowly between the
granite walls of Genoa harbor and let go anchor in the sheltered
inner basin. The lights of the city danced in endless ranks upon
the water, and on the hill the Hotel Miramare glowed like a
giant liner passing at sea.

Mr. Glencannon, coming up from the engine room, stood viewing the scene and wiping his face with a handful of oily cotton
waste. Mr. Smith slid from the shadows of the deckhouse and
lounged familiarly beside him.

"Oh, so it's you," Mr. Glencannon greeted him coldly. "Weel,
I hope that as soon as we dock tomorrow, I'll be seeing the last
o' ye!"

"You will, if you give me a little friendly coöperation," promised
Mr. Smith. "Of course I can't set foot ashore without papers, unless
they think I'm an officer of the ship. But I fancy you won't mind
lending me a uniform jacket and cap, will you?"

"It's against my preenciples to lend things," said Mr. Glencannon. "And anyway, I've a mind to toss ye overboard."

Mr. Smith laughed a nasty laugh. "Better not do anything hasty,
comrade," he warned. "Now that our—er—charming association
is almost ended, it might interest you to know that I'm a rather
important person in certain circles, and not the half-baked article
you seem to imagine. Why see here, look!" He stepped into the
light of a porthole, and bared his breast.

"There!" he said, a strange, exultant note in his voice. "Do you
know what all this means?"

Mr. Glencannon looked, and gasped in amazement. "Weel,
weel, weel, I never!" he declared. "—That's certainly vurra interesting! Do ye pop into my room a minute, Muster Smeeth,
while I examine ye the closer." He opened the door and stood
politely aside. As Mr. Smith stepped confidently over the sill, a
horny fist caught him under the ear with a soul-satisfying smack,

and his knees seemed to melt from under him.

"There, my meesteerious friend!" chuckled Mr. Glencannon, dragging the limp form to the middle of the floor. "That was one I'd been saving for ye! Noo feerst, let us see what ye ha' in yere pockets . . . H'm—three and foor mak' seven and twa mak' nine —nine poonds and some odd sheelings.—Muster Montgomery must be reimbursed, though whoosh, how the idea rankles! And noo," he reached to the wash-stand for towels, "We'll just tie ye up, Muster Smeeth, and spend a pleasant hour improving ye. After that, if ye're conscious, ye'll go for a nice, refreshing swim in yon sewery water o' Geenoa!"

It was the following noon. The *Inchcliffe Castle's* officers were half through dinner when Captain Ball stormed into the saloon in his shore clothes and a towering rage.

"I say!" he demanded, scaling his bowler hat on to the locker cushions and taking his place at the head of the table. "Where in Gehenna is that blithering Scot?"

"Mr. Glencannon?" volunteered Mr. Montgomery. "Why, 'e nipped orf ashore as soon as we docked, the syme as 'e always does. 'E was acting a bit thirsty, Sir, if I might s'y so."

"Well, there's something damned queer been going on aboard this ship," snorted Captain Ball. "They've had me over in their Dago Scotland Yard all morning, trying to crime me for smuggling in that cove Smith."

"No, you don't s'y!" said the Mate. "Why, come to think of it, 'e 'asn't been around orl morning."

"Of course he hasn't—he's in jail," retorted the Captain. "His name isn't Smith, it's Petroslav or Slavovitch or something—anyway, he's a dangerous Bolshevik."

"Bolshywik? My word! Wot did you s'y to them, Captain?"

"Say? Why, I swore I'd never set eyes on him in my life. And then they stripped him to the waist and showed me the tattooing. Yes, tattooing! All over his chest, it was—pictures of red flags and Lenine and Trottersky and silly mottoes in furreign languages about the Revolution. He was literally covered with signs, like a ruddy London bus."

"Well, bly'me if I ever 'eard the like!" gasped Mr. Montgomery.

"Yes," Captain Ball continued. "But his chest wasn't the worst of it. It was his back. Across his shoulders, freshly tattooed in big black letters, it read *'God Save The King!'* And a little further down, it says, plain as day, *'Mr. C. Glencannon, Esq., is a better man than I am.'* "

"It did? W'y, blarst my eyes, Sir. And was there anything else?"

"Yes," said Captain Ball, lowering his voice and making sure that the steward was out of earshot. "Yes, Mister Montgomery, there was. Furthest South of all there was a picture—and to tell you the truth, Mister Mate, it was a crude but a very plain likeness of you."

THE SNYKE IN THE GRASS

OVER the way from the dockyard on West India Road, Poplar-on-Thames, there stands a house built of red bricks, the mortar between them painted white. Above the doorway swings a sign which bears the likeness of a four-bladed propeller and the legend "The Shipwright's Arms." In a region grown grimy through years of soft-coal soot belched from tall ships marching down to the sea, the place presents a grateful contrast of neatness. Curtains and potted geraniums are in the lower windows, and one of them, in addition, is graced with a beautiful picture. This is a lithograph in full color, suitable for framing, of Robert The Bruce, brandishing a mighty claymore with his left hand and a quart bottle of Duggan's Dew of Kirkintilloch with his right.

It was the lithograph, and not the sign, which caught Mr. Glencannon's eye that day, as relaxing in leisure, he strolled down the street from the yards. The S.S. *Inchcliffe Castle,* of which he was Chief Engineer, was resting on keel- and bilge-blocks in drydock, there to undergo a much needed refitting. For the nonce, Mr. Glencannon was free to rove as he listed.

"Foosh," he commented, pausing to admire the portrait of the Highland chieftain. "A braw bit o' art, indeed! 'Tis life-like, lusty and speerited—aye, and altogeether deesairving o' my patronage." Whereupon he pushed open the white-painted door and found himself in a bar parlor neat as a pin, the beer-pump scoured till its brass was as purest gold, and the ranks of glasses on the shelves polished to scintillant crystal. The barmaid was the very personification of scrubbed, starched and laundered spruceness, from her spotless linen cuffs to her soap-ruddied countenance.

"Gude morning, Muss," said Mr. Glencannon, touching his cap visor. "I'll thank ye for a dollop o' Duggan's.—Nice weather we're having." And then, as she reached for pitcher and water glass,

"Ah, dinna trouble yersel', Muss, dinna trouble yersel'—I'm no' sae extravagant as to dilute my whusky either before or after taking."

" 'Before or arfter tyking' . . . lawks!" she giggled. "Just farncy! Oh, ayn't you the comical joker, though?"

"Weel, Muss," said Mr. Glencannon, unfolding to her approbation like a morning glory to the dawn, "I'm widely known as a mon who combines deep weesdom wi' a keen sense o' humor. For instance, another droll way I sometimes put it is to say that if water'll sink a ship, what'll it do to a mon?"

"Oh . . . tee hee," said the barmaid, after an interval of profound pondering. "I tyke it you mean that water sinks ships and drowns men—is that it?"

"Yes, but wait!" chuckled Mr. Glencannon, wrinkling his eyes at the corners and preparing to launch a final and devastating shaft of wit, "Ye've often heard o' drunken men and sound ships, but did ye ever hear o' a sunken mon or a drowned ship?—Haw, Muss, haw!—D'ye get the point? Ye see, I mak' the joke simply by changing the d's and s's."

The humor and ingenuity of this sally appealed so strongly to the barmaid that she screamed with laughter. But at the very crescendo of her outburst, there came a voice from the distances beyond.

" 'Ortense!" it said admonishingly. "Remember you're a lydy and that this 'ere is a respectable 'ouse."

In the awkward silence which followed, Mr. Glencannon filled his glass again and glanced apprehensively toward the door.

"It's Aunty," whispered Miss Hortense, busying herself with the bar towel. "She'll not stand for no skylarking with the gempmen, Aunty won't!"

Mr. Glencannon, whose head at that moment happened to be tilted back, found his eyes focussed upon a framed document which hung on the wall behind the bar. It was an Excise License, by which permission to sell brewed, fermented and distilled liquors was granted to one Myrtle Bootle, spinster, at 27 West India Road, Poplar-on-Thames, London, E. Though his glass was empty, Mr. Glencannon still held it to his lips. He read the document again, and gave vent to a gusty sigh. His aesthetic soul was touched, for never, never had he encountered a name so lovely, so liquidly lilting, as Myrtle Bootle.

"Myrtle Bootle," he repeated aloud, as though reciting a sonnet. "Bootle . . . Myrtle . . . Myrtle Bootle. . . ."

"Yus," explained Miss Hortense, "My Aunt Myrtle—'er as owns this pub. 'Ere she comes now."

A purposeful step sounded in the hall. The door opened, and in swept a woman at once ample, majestic, and formidable. Mr. Glencannon, in his admiration, at first likened her to H.M.S. *Iron Duke;* but then, hastily estimating her tonnage, and taking in the full effect of her black satin dress and her necklace of red coral, he revised his decision in favor of the *Aquitania.*

"Good arfternoon, Sir," she said coldly. "Is everything as it should be, 'Ortense dear?" and she fixed the barmaid with a piercing gaze.

"Ah, noo, noo, o' course it is!" Mr. Glencannon interceded. "It was only that yere intelligent little niece was so gude as to laugh at some o' my jests and japeries. My name is Glencannon, Muddum. I'm Chief o' the *Inchcliffe Castle,* which is over the way in yon drydock."

"S'trewth, Aunty, it's syme's the gempman says," Hortense confirmed him. "Oh, but 'e's a comic one for fair, 'e is!"

"Is 'e indeed?" inquired Miss Bootle, melting a trifle. "Well, in that c'yse I'm very glad to 'ave you as a guest of the 'ouse, Mr. Glencannon. This 'ere's a new plyce, and we welcome tryde, but I do try so 'ard to m'ynt'yne respectability. Arfter orl, it's the decent pubs like this which is the cornerstone o' the British h'Empire, so to s'y, so let's keep 'em so, says I."

"Aye, a vurra comeendable seentiment," agreed Mr. Glencannon, who had been hanging on her words. "Will ye no' sit doon at yon table, Muss Bootle, and honor me by accepting a lemon sqush?"

Miss Bootle was about to decline, but so courtly was Mr. Glencannon's bow as he pulled back the chair that she changed her mind and seated herself.

"A lemming squash would be very refreshink," she said. "Mix it wif splarsh instead of water, 'Ortense dear, and fetch over Mister

Glencannon's bottle so's all will be 'andy and convenient." Then, lowering her voice that her niece might not hear, "Do you know," she said, "It's a pleasure, Mister Glencannon, to myke the acq'yn-tance of a cultured and cultiw'yted gempman like you, arfter orl the waterside riff-rarff that the 'ouse is forced to c'yter to?"

"Ah noo, Muss Bootle, ye're vurra kind," said Mr. Glencannon, blushing.

Myrtle Bootle was blushing, too.

Somewhere out beyond the docks, a passing tug-boat hooted a signal—two long blasts and a short one. The barmaid glanced quickly at her aunt, but Miss Bootle seemed not to have heard it. The tug-boat blew again, this time petulantly. Then, discouraged, it went snorting on its way down stream.

II

In the smoke-filled depths of the drydock, a gang of men were wielding scaling hammers against the *Inchcliffe Castle's* rusty plates, and a pneumatic rivet gun was singing its staccato song above the general din. It was Bedlam thrice multiplied, with Ypres and Jutland thrown in.

"What's this I hear about Mr. Glencannon?" asked Captain Ball, lighting a cigar and settling himself on the edge of his bunk. "Mister Swales tells me he's keeping company with a woman or something."

"Mr. Glencannon is? W'y, the ugly Scotch behemoth!" exclaimed Mr. Montgomery, the *Castle's* first officer. "I 'adn't 'eard about it, Sir. 'Oo is she, anyw'y?"

"I don't know, exactly, and that's the trouble," frowned Captain Ball. "They say she's in some pub on West India Road. From what I hear, we're likely to lose him, next trip or the trip after."

"Three cheers for that!" exclaimed Mr. Montgomery, with deep feeling.

"Oh, now, see here!" protested Captain Ball. "I know that you and him are antagonostic, so to say, but you'll have to admit that he's the best engineer twixt hell and the Hooghli River. The ship can't spare him, Mister Montgomery. It's your plain juty to break this up and keep him from getting married. That's what I got you in here about."

"Orl right, Sir, orl right, if you s'y so, Sir," said Mr. Montgomery with a grimace. "But I carn't see 'ow it's any of my business."

Captain Ball raised his eyebrows. "Mister Mate," he said icily, "I've already told you where your juty lays."

"Well," sulked Mr. Montgomery, reaching for his cap. "I'll see wot I can do, Sir, but I mykes no promises."

When the door had closed behind him, he paused for a moment upon the deck. Gradually a purposeful light kindled in his eye, and in his pockets his hands doubled into fists.

"I'll fix 'im!" he muttered. "I'll fix 'im so 'e's fixed for life, and juty be blowed!" Crossing the gangplank to the dry-dock's edge, he headed for West India Road.

The Shipwright's Arms was empty save for a barmaid who wore starched cuffs and a strangely preoccupied mien. As she drew Mr. Montgomery's beer and scraped off the foam with the lather-stick, she emitted a thin, whispery sigh.

"A-ha!" said the Mate to himself. "The young lady's love-sick, that's wot!" And then, aloud, "Nice little ply'ce you 'ave 'ere, 'aven't you, Miss—er—Miss . . . ?"

"Miss Bootle," said the barmaid absently, her eyes fixed upon the opposite wall.

"Please to myke your acq'yntance, Miss Bootle. I'm Mister Montgomery of the *Inchcliffe Castle*."

At the name, the barmaid almost dropped a glass. "*Inchcliffe Castle?*" she repeated. "Oh, why yus, Mister Montgomery, I've 'eard Mister Glencannon speak of you."

"Oh, Mister Glencannon!" said Mr. Montgomery enthusiastically. "A very charming gempman. 'E's a rare spirit, and the brightest man on our ship, Miss; indeed, 'e's probably the grytest engineer on the seven seas tod'y."

At this praise of Mr. Glencannon, Miss Hortense stopped polishing glasses and leaned eagerly on the bar. Mr. Montgomery, warming to his task, waxed eloquent. According to him, the engineer was a paragon of all the manly virtues, and even of those customarily reserved for saints. Miss Hortense drank it all in, though along toward the end, had Mr. Montgomery only observed it, she was swallowing hard. Also, what he mistook for the sparkle of love-light in her eyes might well have been a rising tide of tears. But he paid for his drink and departed, flattering himself upon a job well done.

"There," he said. "Now I know 'oo she is. And she knows that 'e's the grytest man 'oo ever lived—though of course 'e's told 'er so 'imself. O, I'll 'elp 'er 'ook 'im, I will!"

Meanwhile, Miss Hortense had crossed the room and cautiously pushed open a wicket in the wall through which, upon occasion, drinks could be passed to the private parlor in the rear.

Through the crack she beheld Mr. Glencannon, seated in a red plush morris chair. Miss Myrtle Bootle was massaging his head with Macassar oil, a considerable quantity of which flowed down to lubricate his celluloid collar.

"'E's in 'er clutches," sniffled Miss Hortense, dabbing at the corner of her eye with the bar towel. "It's just the syme as Samson and Delilah. Orl she's arfter is more business for the 'ouse."

". . . Ah, yes, my hair's a wee bit thin on the top, I ken it weel," Mr. Glencannon was saying. "It got blown awa', if ye'll believe me, Muss Bootle, in the course o' the hurricane which deevasted the unhappy island o' Porto Rico in the year Nineteen Hoonderd an' Twunty Seeven. Ah, whoosh, but yon was a feerocious wind! . . ." He groped in his pocket for his pipe, and when he had found it, Miss Bootle playfully captured it, filled it for him, and then held the match until it was gurglingly aglow.

"Oh, you seafaring men do 'ave such thrilling h'experiences!" she said. "I do wish you'd tell orl your friends about our little plyce 'ere, Mister Glencannon, because we're so anxious to attract a good clarss of ship's orfficer tryde."

"Ship's-orfficer tryde!" muttered Miss Hortense. "W'y, larst week I 'eard 'er telling that tug-boat captain that orl she c'ytered to was river and barge men. And 'im blowing 'is whistle to 'er every time he passes on the river, and 'er wy'ving 'er 'andkercheef to 'im from the upstairs window! . . ."

"I'll mak' a speecial point to tell a' my friends aboot yere vurra genteel establishment," said Mr. Glencannon. "Indeed, ye may deepend upon it. And noo, if ye'll permeet me, I'll endeevor to entertain ye with a little trick which has been accorded univairsal approbation wherever I've pairformed it.—Will ye ha' the goodness to hand me yon soup spoon from the table?—Ah, I'm obliged to ye, Muss Bootle."

With a preliminary flourish, he commenced whacking lustily upon the top of his head with the spoon bowl. He opened or closed his mouth at every beat, a hollow musical sound emerging with each percussion. Gradually the air of "Loch Lomond" took recognisable form, as though played upon a marimba sadly in need of tuning.

With the grand finale, which made up in volume what it lacked in verity, Miss Bootle burst into shrill paeans of praise, and produced from the cupboard a bottle and a glass.

" 'Ear, 'ear!" she cried. " 'Ave a spot o' this, Mister Musician! It's the Dew of Kirkintilloch, your special favorite. Lawks, lawks, lawks, wot talent! Is there anything that the man can't do!"

"Yus!" sobbed Miss Hortense, silently closing the wicket and burying her face in her apron. " 'E can't 'eal my broken 'eart, 'e can't: W'y, only the d'y before yestidd'y, when Aunt Myrtle was in there wif the tug-boat captain, 'e pl'yed Blue Bells O' Scotland· wif variytions, thumpin' it out on the top of 'is 'ead wif the 'andle of my h'ice pick. 'E said it was only fer me, 'e did! And 'e promised that next time 'e'd show me a trick wif a 'orse 'air and 'is h'Adams h'apple.—Oh, the g'y deceiver—the 'andsome snyke in the grass!"

III

Work on the *Inchcliffe Castle* was nearing completion. Her officers, instead of going their separate and devious ways ashore each day, were now engaged from dawn till dark in inspection, supervision and direction of the finishing touches of the refit. Mr. Glencannon, grease from head to foot, was lording it over a gang of mechanics who were replacing gaskets, pouring bearings and packing stuffing-boxes in the engine room. Mr. Montgomery was in charge on deck, while Mr. Swales, the second officer, his dungarees red with anti-corrosive paint, held forth on the floor of the drydock beneath the *Inchcliffe Castle's* keel.

The night that the dock gates were opened and the *Inchcliffe Castle* was towed downstream to load, Mr. Swales waited upon the Mate in his cabin.

"I s'y, 'ave a look at these," he whispered hoarsely. "But w'yte, we'd better be careful, Sir—'e might see us, 'e might."

" 'Oo might?" asked Mr. Montgomery.

"Mister Glencannon might," said Mr. Swales. "And if 'e did, 'e'd ryse 'ell for fair. Just w'yte till you read 'em!"

Behind closed door and shrouded portholes, Mr. Montgomery examined the sheets of yellow paper which the Second placed before him. "Oh, 'pon my word!" he muttered. "Why, dash it all, Mister Swales, this 'ere beats anything I ever 'eard. Did you read this one?"

> " *'I am Glencannon, a son of Neptune*
> *You are my lydy fair*
> *Though I roam the seas on juty*
> *My 'eart is always at 27 West India Road, Poplar,*
> *With my beautiful Bootle beauty.'* "

"Yus, 'orrible, ayn't it?" Mr. Swales shuddered. "And did you notice, Sir, 'e's got 'em orl marked in advance with the nymes of our ports of call for the trip—Lisbon, Gibraltar, Genoa, Nyples—ready to post at every stop? But 'e must 'ave 'ad a chynge of 'eart, or 'e wouldn't 'ave thrown 'em aw'y. M'ybe 'is love 'as grown cold."

"M'ybe," growled Mr. Montgomery. "But it's up to us to see that she gets them, orl the syme. With these 'ere pomes fer h'evidence, she can tyke 'im to court for breach of promise, and then 'e'll be 'ooked fer fair. And . . . oh, Lord lumme, Mister Swales, just listen to this:

> " *'Fair Lydy Bootle, I greet you from afar*
> *Glencannon's 'eart is lonely, this dark tempustrious night,*
> *I pray that you are well, and that the profits from the bar*
> *Continue satisfactory, also the bottle tryde*
> *And that the sun is shining bright.'*

"There!" he said, thumping the table with his fist. " 'Profits from the bar'! Profits is orl 'e's worrying about! 'E thinks she'll

inherit that pub some day, so 'e's trying to 'ook 'er for 'er money.
This one 'ere is a regular formal proposal . . .

" 'Soon will come the wedding d'y
And the organ it will tootle
If only "Yes" you'll s'y
And consent to chynge your nyme to Glencannon
Instead of Bootle.'

"—Oh, and underneath, it says, 'To be sung to the air of the
Piobaireached Cumha na Cloinne.' Well, I carn't s'y as I knows
the tune."

"No, and you wouldn't want to sing it if you did," said Mr.
Swales. I've 'eard Mr. Glencannon fair strangle 'is bagpipes on it."

"Well, this potery by itself is enough to strangle a h'octupus,"
said Mr. Montgomery. "The point is, now, that we've got to keep
the affair at w'ite 'eat, so's she'll be wy'ting 'im with open arms
when we get back. We'll 'ave to send 'er some more of them flowers
right aw'y. And meanwhile," he rose and locked the papers in his
dresser drawer, "Meanwhile, we'll s'yve these poems for our long-
rynge artillery."

IV

Ten weeks had rolled by since the *Inchcliffe Castle* put to sea,
and the bar-room of the Shipwright's Arms was filled with smoke
and bad language. A full score of alcoholized Scotsmen were
gathered at the tables, pounding upon them, scratching matches
on their white marble surfaces, and using them as footrests.

"Ye lie, MacFeergus!" one of the Scots was shouting. "Twas
no' the tail-shaft o' the *Ayleshire* that bruk, twas the crank-pin,
and ye know it!"

Mr. MacFergus, piqued, lurched to his feet and took his hand
out of his pocket. The hand was garnished with a set of brass-
knuckles. "MacCrummon," he said, "I fear ye're no gentlemon,
though I'll domned soon lairn ye how to be one!"

Mr. MacCrummon emitted the war cry of his clan, produced
a monkey-wrench from his overalls, and stood ready for the attack. But the rest of the company intervened, the belligerents shook

hands, and wept copiously upon each other's shoulders.

"Hoot!" shouted somebody. " 'Tis time for a drink! Please, Muss, I dinna mean to cavil at the sairvice, but will ye gi' us fresh glasses? These is reekin' feelthy wi' tobacco ashes."

Miss Myrtle Bootle swept into the room and viewed the assemblage with disdain. "Orful, oh, orful, ayn't they, dearie?" she whispered to Miss Hortense. "Are any of them buying anything tod'y?"

"No," said the barmaid. "Not a drop. They brings their own whisky, they does, buying it at 'oles'yle prices by the c'yse, and then they expects the 'ouse to furnish glarsses."

"Hmph," sniffed Miss Bootle. "A fine clarss of tryde that Glencannon ruffian brung us! Instead of being a 'igh-gr'yde waterman's pub, the ply'ce 'as turned into a boozing ken for cheap Scotch brawlers."

The loyal Miss Hortense was about to come to Mr. Glencannon's defense when the postman entered and placed two letters upon the bar—letters which bore Italian stamps and the post-mark of Naples.

The barmaid flushed and hastily picked them up.

" 'Ortense!" said Miss Bootle, ominously. " 'And those letters 'ere!"

"They're for me, Aunty," said Miss Hortense, her voice trembling. "They're from a girl friend of mine 'oo . . ."

" 'Ortense! They're addressed to me—'Miss Myrtle Bootle.' . . ."

"Well, that one is," Miss Hortense conceded. "But this one's for me. Yus, it's for me, and it's from Mister Glencannon, if you must know. From Mister Glencannon! 'E loves me, 'e loves me, 'e loves me—so there!" She stamped her foot and faced her aunt defiantly.

Miss Myrtle Bootle stared as though the girl had gone mad. "Oh, w'y, 'Ortense dearie, you're mistyken," she said pityingly. "It's me that Mister Glencannon pretends to be int'rested in, and 'e's been sending me pomes from every port, the impudent 'Ighland beast! W'y, 'ere 'Ortense—look 'ere, see wot 'e's written to me." And she handed across the slip of paper which she had taken from the envelope.

Through her tears, Miss Hortense read

"Bootle, Bootle, who loves a Bootle?
'I do,' said Certified Chief Engineer Glencannon
'If you will wed me, I will be your lifelong vassal,'
Said the Chief Engineer of S.S. Inchcliffe Castle."

"Oh, 'orrors!" wailed the barmaid. " 'E's been sending them to me, too. Let's see wot 'e 'as wrote me this time . . . Lawks, Aunty —w'y, the snyke in the grass! 'E's wrote us both the very syme thing!"

v

Before long it would be daylight; meanwhile the September sun was struggling its way up through the layers of fog and smoke which lay like a pall over sleeping London. Along the Thames the seagulls mewingly bestirred themselves for the day's duties of scavenging. Over in Limehouse Reach a liner's siren hooted, to be echoed by the throaty roar of an I. & C. freighter casting off from the company's wharf on the Isle of Dogs. Beyond the Millwall Docks a tug-boat churned upstream, her tow-line sagging back through the gloom to the bow of the *Inchcliffe Castle*, salt-crusted and freshly in from the sea.

Across the stern of the tug, in letters white and new, was painted her name. The name was *"Myrtle B."*

"Well, tod'y's the d'y 'e gets it in 'is ruddy Scotch neck," chuckled Mr. Montgomery as he was joined upon the bridge by Mr. Swales. "Before long we'll be s'ying good riddance to 'im."

"Yus," agreed the Second Mate. " 'E's planning to see 'er, right enough. 'E just now stopped me on my w'y up 'ere to show me a picture of the Juke of York wearing a pearl gr'y bowler.—Arsked me wot I thought of it, as one man of tyste to another."

"A pearl gr'y bowler, only farncy 'im in it!" said the Mate. "W'y, it would be more becoming on a walrus!"

Somewhat later in the morning, Mr. Glencannon retrieved his shore-trousers from beneath the mattress of his bunk, went over his fingernails with a bit of emery cloth, laundered his celluloid collar with a pencil eraser and a damp towel, and waxed the ends of his rather scraggly mustache into points like copper spikes.

"Oh, domn ye, Glencannon!" he exclaimed approvingly to the reflection in the washstand mirror. "Ye're a handsome beast when ye tak' the trouble to groom yoursel'! A-weel, I must be at my best today. Aye," and he nodded his head prophetically. "How dee-ferunt will be my condeetion and standing when I return to this vurra room tonicht!"

As a matter of fact, his condition upon his return was deplorable, and that he could stand at all was due solely to the friendly support of the *Inchcliffe Castle's* starboard rail. A full moon was bouncing up and down upon the rim of the *Castle's* funnel, and the masts were bowing politely to each other, like partners in the minuet. On Mr. Glencannon's left cheek were four scratches, deep, angry and parallel. Those upon his right cheek, while effective, were a trifle amateurish. But the egg-like bumps on the top of his head were palpably the handiwork of an expert—a tug-boat captain, for example.

"Meestery!" he said sepulchrally, gazing up at the bouncing moon. "Meestery, black meestery indeed! How them dommed pooms I wrote to Myrtle could ha' got to Hortense, too, is fair beyont me. Let's see, noo, let's rehairse the whole sorra business. . . .

"Feerst I composed the pooms in my room, whuch is here. Then I tuk the rough drafts and chucked them over the rail, whuch is still here. They fell into the water, which is there. But no!" he beat his brow in sudden inspiration. "The water's there the noo, but it was no' there the then! We was in drydock, so they fell into the bottom o' it."

He paused, chuckled, and politely acknowledged the bow of the main-mast. "Somebody picked them up and sent them to Hortense, that's what they did!" he declared.—"Who was it? Ah, Glencannon, there lies the meestery. Ye've either got a mortal eenemy aboard this ship, or else, conseederin' how trade has fallen off in yon pub, ye've got a fromned gude—er, domned frude— no, er, a *domned gude friend.*"

Whereupon he tossed the remains of his pearl grey bowler into the Thames, ripped off his celluloid collar, touched a match to it, and lurched happily to bed.

COCK O' THE NORTH

THE S.S. *Inchcliffe Castle,* Valparaiso to Cardiff and ports of call as ordered, lay in the harbor of Santiago de Cuba sweltering beneath the August sun. A lazy offshore breeze was stirring, and as it wafted across the vessel like breaths from a red-hot stove, it bore with it the smells of teeming tenements and of water-front warehouses where meat and fruit and vegetables lay steaming under corrugated-iron roofs. All around the *Castle,* great bubbles belched from the depths and gave forth fetidly upon the air. Occasionally a passing shark cut the surface with a steel-grey dorsal, but did not tarry on its passage toward the cooler, pleasanter waters of the open sea.

Mr. Glencannon, clad only in his cap and a pair of carpet slippers, sat in the shade of the awning slapping at gnats with a folded copy of *The Presbyterian Churchman.* On the deck beneath his chair stood a bottle of Duggan's Dew of Kirkintilloch, which beverage, despite its considerable calorific potency, he was consuming in frequent dollops and with purposeful mien.

"For ye see," he explained to the mate, who wore only a cigar and a palm-leaf fan, " 'tis a theory o' mine that when ye're thoroughly warm wi'in, ye dinna mind the warmest warmth wi'oot. In other words, the hotter ye are, the cooler, relatively, ye feel."

"Yus?" grunted Mr. Montgomery. "Well, it orl sounds like so much bilge to me."

"Aye, it wad," said Mr. Glencannon patiently. "It's complicated reasoning, weel do I ken, and ye yersel' are undootably no' capable o' comprehending it. But I'm gratified to obsairve that Professor Einstein agrees wi' me, onyway."

"Oh, blatherskite!" said Mr. Montgomery, dashing the drops from his chin. "You and Professor Einstein are welcome to your silly theeries and your bleddy whisky in this kind of weather. Me,

57

I'd tryde a shipload of such superstitions for a bit of a cool breeze."

"Supersteetions?" repeated Mr. Glencannon, his face clouding. "Supersteetions? Ah, noo, Muster Mate, I dinna lik' the word! I'll ask ye, sir, will ye be gude enough to explain yer thinly veiled in-seenuations aboot me being supersteetious?"

"Yus," said Mr. Montgomery promptly. "Orl wot you've been s'yin' about keeping cool with whisky is just ruddy rot. You Scotch 'as orlways been a superstitious, demon-ridden ryce, and wot's more, you orlways will be. Why, bless me. I wouldn't be surprised to 'ear you advocyte a h'eelskin wrapped around the wrist for curing rheumatism, I wouldn't!"

Mr. Glencannon studied him pityingly. "Weel, and why not?" he challenged. "An eelskin wropped aboot the wrust is a sovereign reemedy for rheumatism, aye, and for sciaticks too. O' course, for cheelblains a horsehair's better—a white one."

"Haw!" snorted Mr. Montgomery. " 'Orse'air for chillblynes, just farncy! Why, you'd ort to be ashymed of yerself, 'arboring such beliefs, you 'ad!"

Very deliberately, Mr. Glencannon tilted his bottle and took a long, gurgling draft. "Muster Mate," he said, "if ye wair no such a futile braying jockoss, I'd lose my temper wi' ye. But as a mon o' science, it befeets me to maintain my deegnity, e'en in the face o' yere gratuitous insoolts."

"Man of science? Witch doctor, you mean!" declared Mr. Mont-gomery, starting for the ladder to supervise the slacking off of the anchor chain, as necessitated by the rising of the tide. "You're worse than these 'ere voodoo niggers ashore and across in 'Aiti, you are!"

He had slid halfway down the handrails when he checked his descent and chuckled maliciously.

"Oh, and by the w'y!" he called over his shoulder. "Do you know wot day this is?"

"Weel," came Mr. Glencannon's voice, and in it were combined passion repressed and dignity injured, "Any fool cud tell fra' the steench o' keepered herrings arising from the galley that today is Friday. Friday—aye, Friday, the fufth day o' the week. But what aboot it?"

"It's Friday, yus, but it orlso 'appens to be Friday the thir-teenth!" And as Mr. Montgomery made his way along the blister-ing well deck toward the foc's'le head, he sensed, though he could not see, the consternation wrought by his words.

Mr. Glencannon was crossing his fingers, and fervently count-ing up to seven, which arithmetical exercise he repeated seven times. Then he rose, turned his cap visor backwards, and walked seven times around his chair. But not until he had spat seven times into the harbor of Santiago de Cuba did he even partially regain his poise.

"Gude losh!" he breathed. " 'Tis weel that I foond it oot! While customarily I dinna gi' heed to such things, 'tis always wiser to tak' the proper precautions."

Feeling that his temperature was in need of rectification, he groped beneath his chair for his bottle. His fingers had encircled its neck when a tickling sensation on his left leg gave him pause. He looked, and there—horrors!—he beheld a banana worm—giant green cousin of the inchworm—humping its way with great pre-cision up his calf in the purposeful manner of its kind when measuring a candidate for a coffin.

Mr. Glencannon sat fear-stricken. Then, with a cry, he sprang to his feet, immolated the worm with *The Presbyterian Church-man* and dropped the bottle. As the whisky trickled across the deck toward the scupper, he collapsed into his chair and sat breathing through distended nostrils, like a horse at the top of a hill.

" 'Tis the last straw!" he murmured weakly. "Black doom im-pends! Friday the theerteenth, a measuring worm and a brukken bottle! Aye, whoosh, Glencannon, ye've been thrice warned!"

He hurried to his room, knelt down and peered beneath the bunk. "There, noo!" he muttered. " 'Tis e'en as I feared! Yon was the last bottle o' whusky i' the whole domned ship!" He sat dis-consolate on the edge of the bunk and gnawed at the trembling fringes of his walrus mustache. At length, summoning his faculties, "A-weel," he sighed, "I've no doot I'll be safer ashore than aboord —at least, I will no' be sae theersty!"

Having clothed himself in spotless white and hailed a passing boatman, he was rowed to the foot of Cespédes Street. There he cast about him for a likely place wherein to attend to his temperature. Espying a mid-block *cantina*, he made towards it along a narrow sidewalk which naked brats were sharing with mangy dogs. As he was about to enter the friendly portal, a cat as black as night and twice as sinister went scurrying across his path. For an instant Mr. Glencannon stood frozen in his tracks, but only for an instant. Then he wheeled, and counting seven under his breath, he retraced his way in panic, being careful not to step on cracks.

For the ensuing hours of his quest, however, Mr. Glencannon seemed to have shaken off the ill fortune which had pursued him. True, none of the several *cantinas* which he visited could supply the Dew of Kirkintilloch, but they made good the deficiency with native liquors at once strange and strangling. Mr. Glencannon's temperature came gradually under control, and his confidence, too, was returning. In the course of his journeys to pastures new, he playfully tore signs from the fronts of stores, over-turned stands of fruits and vegetables, and shouldered jabbering Cubans from the sidewalk. And when at length he saw a sign which read: Bobo's Place English Speaken Foreign and Domestique Liquors, he felt that his luck had changed indeed.

Along one side of Bobo's Place stretched a zinc-covered bar behind which stood a fat mulatto in a pale green shirt. Upon the bar, American fashion, was a bowl of pretzels, and ranged on the shelves were row after row of bottles. Having helped himself to a notable mouthful of pretzels, Mr. Glencannon hooked his pipe-clayed heel upon the rail and ran his eye along the labels of this phalanx.

"Nice day-a, hey, Billy?" said the mulatto. "Have a dreenk-a, hey, Billy?"

"Dinna interrupt me, mon," said Mr. Glencannon sternly, as he reached for another handful of pretzels. "Can ye no' see I'm reading! When I've inspected yer mean wares at my ain gude leisure, I'll apprise ye o' the dictates o' my foncy."

"Oh, yaiss?" said the mulatto, with the trace of a sneer. "Okay-a, Billy, okay-a!"

"H'm," said Mr. Glencannon between crunches, considering

the stock with the half-closed eye of a connoisseur. "On the top shelf, I see nowt that's potable save Roderick Dhu's Blended Relics, and that's disteenctly infeerior. Over yon to the left, there's Dunleven Particularly Choice, the whuch is feelthy bilge water. Feerther doon I descry the sae-called Pride o' Argyll, and also Campbell's Tartan Vurra Speecial Liqueur, but both are the guttenest o'—er, no,—both are the rottenest o' rotgut. I say, my gude blackamoor, wad ye no' be dispensing Duggan's Dew o' Kirkintilloch?"

The mulatto smiled a disdainful smile. "Doogan's!" he repeated, shaking his head. "Doogan's, Billy? Ho, Doogan's eet ees no for the trade-a high class, no for *el bueno mundo*. Doogan's eet ees for the bums *Americano solamente.*"

"Ah, and say ye so?" inquired Mr. Glencannon, striving to smile a disarming smile and at the same time to masticate a fresh cargo of pretzels. "Weel, I ha' no asked ye yer opeenion aboot the merits o' Scottish whusky. What I asked ye, my fat and oogly friend, was sumply, do ye sell Duggan's Dew or do ye no'?"

"And I," said the mulatto, pausing in his work of wiping the bar, "And I, my boy, I have say I do not to sell such-a wash for the peegs."

Mr. Glencannon extended his horny right hand, seized the mulatto by the throat and dragged him half across the bar.

"Whurra!" he said. "So that's the way ye feel, is it? Weel, ye chooby mixture o' this and that, I see that I shall ha' to gi' ye a shoort ten minutes' lecture upon the subject o' ceevility! Noo, i' the feerst place— Oh, gude losh!"

The grip of his horny right relaxed and from his left the pretzels fell unheeded. For in the instant Mr. Glencannon had become aware that of all men in the Greater Antilles, the mulatto was the most shockingly, completely and ill omenedly cross-eyed! Bad luck was about to strike again!

It did strike—whop!—in the form of a lignumvitæ mallet such as is used to remove the bungs of beer kegs. Mr. Glencannon lapsed into a state of semiconsciousness—a shadowy realm of sawdust, cigar butts and cuspidors across which a green-shirted mulatto, bung starter in hand, approached with loud snorts to do him further mischief. He tried to struggle to his feet, but his knees wilted under him. He saw the bung starter raised on high. He saw the bloodshot misfit eyes gleaming balefully down into his own. This, then, was what the omens had foretold. This—this was doom.

But suddenly he heard heartening shouts, the scuffle of feet, the soul-stirring sound of a solid fist encountering a soggy jaw. There were oaths in Spanish and English, the crashing of furniture, the thin, cold tinkle of shattering glass. He felt his heels bumping over the floor tiles and he knew that he was being dragged across vast distances.

"C'mon, Scotty, snap out of it!" urged a voice. "This way, Scotty! C'mon, kid, lean on me!"

II

When Mr. Glencannon came more or less to himself, he found that he was lying on his back counting seven, and that the surroundings were dark, smelly and torrid. As his eyes became accustomed to the gloom, he saw that a hook-billed monster was glaring malevolently at him through a mist, so he assumed, quite naturally, that he was in hell. At first he was too terror-stricken to move, but gradually the mists cleared away and he realized that the monster was only a chicken perched upon his chest pecking the pretzel crumbs from his mustache, and that the cavernous inferno around him was actually a hen coop.

"Ah, noo, shoosh to ye!" he addressed the chicken indignantly. "Do you ken nowt better than to sully a mon's best white unifurrm?"

"Sh-h-h, pipe down, Glencannon!" came a whisper from the shadows beside him. "Do you want them spiggotty guys to come back here and start lammin' us with *cocomacacques?*"

"No," said Mr. Glencannon coldly. "Nowt cud be further from my wishes, but though yer voice, sir, is vaguely fameeliar, 'tis too dark to see ye; so micht I inquire how it is ye happen to ken my name?"

"Why, sure!" chuckled the voice, "I'm Delehanty. Jack Delehanty —remember me?"

"Delehanty!" exclaimed Mr. Glencannon. "Ah, surely, ye're no' Gob Delehanty fra' off the Yankee deestroyer 341, in Milford Haven during the War?"

"Sure, Chief Machinist's Mate John Delehanty—that's me nowadays. And how's old Scotty Glencannon, eh, the frolicking, rollicking—er—the worthy second engineer of the S.S. *Paxton Me;-chant?*"

"Fine as a fuddle!" said Mr. Glencannon, as they shook hands in the darkness. "Only the noo, Jock, bless ye, I'm chief o' the *Inchcliffe Castle*. Weel, weel, weel, 'tis a happy meeting! Why, if—"

"Sh-h-h, lie down and be quiet!" Delehanty warned him. "They're comin' out huntin' for us. I can see 'em through the crack. Here, take a look."

Half a dozen Negroes were creeping cautiously into the yard, poking with machetes and *cocomacacque* clubs behind piles of empty soda cases and beer barrels. The cross-eyed mulatto brought up in the rear, holding a chunk of ice against his swollen jaw. As they searched they chattered volubly.

"Some of 'em's Haitians," muttered Delehanty. "Do you hear that creole lingo? Tough *hombres*, by the look of 'em. Don't you dast make a sound, now, Scotty!"

"I will no'," replied Mr. Glencannon. "But look ye, Jock, I fear yon treecherous ongrate o' a cheecken is planning to inform on us."

The chicken, in truth, had run clucking from the coop into the open pen beyond, where it hopped, bowed and strutted before the Negroes. It was a white rooster—not one of the scrawny hard-bitten specimens of the tropical *fincas*, but such a bird as one sees bossing barnyards on the rich green acres of the North.

One of the Negroes, his machete held ready, was making for the door of the coop. Messrs. Glencannon and Delehanty prepared themselves for combat. But the cross-eyed mulatto pointed at the rooster, jabbered something, and waved his hand in a spacious gesture toward the fence.

"The rooster's saved us!" whispered Delehanty. "The big coon says the bird would raise hell if anybody was in the coop, and he's tellin' 'em we must of escaped. Look, he's going to feed the chicken."

As the bird gobbled the corn which was scattered through the wire, Mr. Glencannon heaved a sigh of gratitude. "Losh!" he said. " 'Tis e'en like when The Bruce was saved by the spider in the cave. Yon beerdie has my heertfelt vote o' thanks. If e'er I get oot o' this alive, I'll mak' it my juty to—"

"Sh-h-h!"

The American, his ear to the crack, was straining to hear the conversation of the departing Negroes. When they had disappeared within the house, "Well, by gosh!" he said tensely. "Did you get what they were talking about?"

"Nary a word," replied Mr. Glencannon. "I dinna ken the crude speech o' our Afreecan breethren. What was't?"

"Well, it was somethin' to make me want to get out of here *pronto!*" said Mr. Delehanty, with great feeling. "As near as I could get it, them men is voodoos—Haitian voodoos and Cuban *ñañigos,* which is the same thing! They're plannin' big doin's for tonight, and they've been fattenin' that rooster to kill for the sacrifice."

"Sacreefice!" gasped Mr. Glencannon. "Ye mean they're witch doctors? Foosh, lad, quick! Oot the back way, run for yer life!"

On hands and knees they crept out of the little door in the rear of the coop and scurried across the yard. Behind a pile of beer barrels they found a gap in the fence, through which they crawled into a dark, deserted alley.

"Seeven, Jock!" urged Mr. Glencannon as they lay there panting. "Count seeven, quick! And for the love o' heeven, mon, if ye've got a flask upon ye, hand it ower!"

Mr. Delehanty chuckled, unbuttoned his jacket, and after something of a struggle dragged a quart bottle from the waistband of his trousers.

As Mr. Glencannon drank, a look of surprise, of ecstasy, suffused his face. "The Dew o' Kirkintilloch!" he breathed. "Ah, Jock, where did ye e'er get hold o' it?"

"Oh, in a joint called Gallagher's, a coupla blocks from here. Same stuff you useter drink on the old *Paxton Merchant,* ain't it?"

"Aye," said Mr. Glencannon. "And this vurra morning a my bad luck started fra'—"

There was a menacing whir behind and above him. He grasped the bottle by the neck and sprang to his feet. The white rooster was perched on the top of the fence, peering at him with a reproachful eye.

"Ah, o' coorse, o' coorse!" exclaimed Mr. Glencannon, taking another drink. "Ye're here to remind me o' my vow to sheelter and proteect ye! Come, beerdie, come; do ye let me tuck ye under my arm, and I'll gi' ye a hame aboord the *Inchcliffe Castle,* such as it is. But feerst, Jock, I'll ask ye to conduct me to the pub where they sell Duggan's Dew. I'll be buying a case to tak' alang wi' me."

Having followed a devious course through blind streets and twisting alleys, they arrived at the Cantina Gallega coincidentally with the emptying of Mr. Delehanty's bottle. That Mr. Glencannon was carrying a rooster under his arm seemed not at all unusual to the Cubans who crowded the place; in fact, several of them were similarly laden.

"Ah, lovely!" beamed Mr. Glencannon, observing this. "A mon bringing his cheecken wi' him to enjoy the hospitality o' the neighborhood pub is indeed a commeendable custom! Do we reelax, Jock, and drink a nip or twa or three the while the publican is wropping up my case."

When they had drunk four or five or six, Mr. Glencannon had relaxed most expansively. Anxiety about his luck had completely left his mind. He noticed that the crowd, chicken-laden and otherwise, was filing out through a door in the rear.

"Come, Jock," he said. "Fetch alang the bottle and we'll see what's afoot."

They passed into a patio in the center of which was a fenced-in ring some twelve feet in diameter. Around this ring milled several hundred Cubans, shouting at one another and waving handfuls of banknotes on high. On the outskirts of the throng, each surrounded by a violently partisan group, men were grooming roosters, clipping their leg feathers and sandpapering their spurs.

"Hoot!" cried Mr. Glencannon delightedly. "Why, 'tis a cock-fight! Call the publican, Jock, and bid him annoonce to these speegottys that we'll motch our beerdie against the chompion o' Cuba!"

"You're dam' tootin' we will!" agreed Mr. Delehanty. "I'll make the announcement myself." He mounted a chair and in Spanish quaint but adequate, hurled a defy at the assembled flower of Santiago's cocking fancy.

At once they were snowed under with bets. Apparently, to the expert Cuban eye, this comfortable fat white bird would be as chaff before the formidable El Negrito, coal-black veteran of a hundred bloody battles.

"I'll lay every last sheeling i' my pooch on gude old Cock o' the North!" shouted Mr. Glencannon. "Tak' a' their bets, Jock, and let's you and me tak' a drink!"

The opening passage at arms was most discouraging. After a few vicious pecks from El Negrito, Cock o' the North, temperamentally unsuited to gladiatorial combat, cast aside all pretense of ferocity and fled. Unfortunately, the conformation of the ring prevented retreat in a straight line and to any place in particular, but Cock o' the North, making the best of it, ran around and around as fast as he could.

"Whurra!" grumbled Mr. Glencannon, thinking of the money at stake. "If 'twas only a foot race instead o' a fight, we'd be rich. But I fear 'tis a deebacle, Jock! If that black deemon e'er catches him up, our ain puir beerdie will be mossacred!"

Just then a bell rang and the owner of the black champion retrieved his charge and set about grooming it for the next round. He massaged its legs and the top of its head, and then, filling his mouth with water, blew it out upon El Negrito in a fine spray.

"Oh, ho!" said Mr. Glencannon, reaching over the side of the ring and seizing the jaded Cock o' the North. "If yon speegotty cheecken is trained on a diet o' water, we'll see what a quaff o' guid Scots whusky will do for a white mon's beerdie!"

He pried open the powerful beak and poured into it a sizable jolt of the Dew of Kirkintilloch. Then, at the clang of the bell, he tossed the bird to the center of the pit.

Cock o' the North, his eyes bulging, his neck craned forward and his beak wide open, stood choking and gagging. His black adversary was lunging savagely with bill and spurs. The air was rent with cries of the Cubans imploring the favorite to strike the fatal blow. Plainly, the fight was all but over. But suddenly Cock o' the North shuddered, ruffled his feathers and perked up his head. A dangerous glint had kindled in his eye. Emitting a most unchickenly note of rage and exaltation, he leaped high into the air and smote El Negrito with both spurs at once. The erstwhile pride of Cuba fell as dead as Sancho Panza.

"Hoot!" screamed Mr. Glencannon, springing into the pit and gathering the victor in his arms. "Gude lad! Stout fella! Aye, I knew ye cud do it! And noo, Jock, collect our winnings wi'oot delay, and let's be gac'ing before they expect us to stand drinks for the crowd."

III

Shortly before midnight Mr. Glencannon was making his unsteady way toward the water front. Under one arm, in a state of alcoholic somnolence, drooped Cock o' the North, and under the other was the case of Duggan's Dew. Some time before—just when, Mr. Glencannon's memory was not quite clear—sailors of the American shore patrol had gathered up Chief Machinist's Mate Delehanty, and Mr. Glencannon still sobbed as he thought of the parting. He was lonely—terribly lonely—and suddenly realizing how dark and empty was the street, he felt afraid.

"Hoo!" he breathed, glancing over his shoulder. "Ye're no' safe oot o' it yet, Glencannon! 'Tis still Friday the theerteenth, and ye're far, far fra' hame! If there was only a pub open, or some place where—"

From behind the shutters of a house across the street burst sounds of music and of laughter, and the heartening pop of a champagne cork. Mr. Glencannon hurried over and pushed open the door. In the brightly lighted room was a long table around which sat a group of Negroes wearing grotesque paper hats. At the head of the table stood a man, knife in hand. The man was the cross-eyed mulatto. He was preparing to cut a birthday cake. Mr. Glencannon turned and fled, with the Negroes in hot pursuit.

Though hampered by his burdens, he beat them to the dock by a matter of inches, fell into a rowboat and cast off the painter.

"Thief-a!" the mulatto's voice thundered after him. "You deed swipe my best cheecken for eat the birthday! Peeg, bum, rotten, dam'!"

Mr. Glencannon, bending to the oar, was too shaken to reply. On and ever on he rowed. At length he heard the water slapping against a vessel's plates and above him in the darkness he saw looming a familiar silhouette. He grasped the edge of the gangway platform and heaved a sigh of relief.

"There's no place lik' hame!" he declared. "Foosh, what a day it has been!" On his way up the ladder he stumbled once or twice. "Who the heel could ha' moved these steps?" he growled. "I'll wager 'twas that meddling lout, Montgomery."

Trying, but vainly, to walk on tiptoe, he lurched aft toward his quarters. From time to time strange objects barked his shins and shadows sprawled where no shadows should have been.

"Strange, strange," he muttered. "I'm no' clear o' the malign influences yet. Or maybe 'tis only the nairvous reaction."

Placing the case of whisky upon the deck, he opened the door of his room and laid Cock o' the North upon the settee. "Puir cheecky!" he said. "I've heerd the expression 'drunk as a rooster,' but ne'r did I see a rooster as drunk as yersel'. Why, I do believe ye're e'en drunker than I am!" He hung his cap upon the hook, but the hook was not there. "Oh, vurra weel!" he addressed the fallen headgear. "Ha' it yer ain way and stay where ye are!" And settling himself on the edge of the bunk, he went about unlacing his shoes.

From the darkness came a cry—shrill, bloodcurdling. A mighty force propelled him from behind. He catapulted across the room and crashed against the bulkhead. Coming toward him through the gloom he saw the figure of a woman in witch's robes—a woman who emitted a sinister hiss, seized him by the throat, and with the strength of a giant tossed him over her shoulder. Then she stooped, grasped him by the collar and dragged him out upon the deck.

Other figures appeared from the shadows—grotesque little black-robed witches who grouped around him chattering and gesticulating. Evidently, they were trying to decide his fate. Stark fear descended upon him and he made a break for the rail. Even the sharks would be better than this! He was seized by many hands and hurled into the air. His head struck the deck, but even as consciousness fled he heard a ship's bell sounding midnight. Friday the thirteenth had passed.

IV

When Mr. Glencannon opened his eyes and rubbed the lumps which throbbed on the top of his head, the sky above him was reddening with the sunrise. He saw that he was lying on the deck of the *Inchcliffe Castle,* and he wondered if it all had been a dream —nay, a nightmare, the most horrible ever visited upon mortal man. But there was the door of his room, still open as when the witch had cast him forth, and there, too, was the case of Duggan's Dew of Kirkintilloch. Cock o' the North was nowhere to be seen.

"Pairhops he, too, was a ghost!" thought Mr. Glencannon; but as he felt the wad of money in his pocket: "Ghost or mortal cheecken, he won me a muckle o' siller, onyway!" he chuckled. "Aye"—and he counted it delightedly—"if only 'twas a' as real and clear and pleasant as these twa hoondred and fufty-five dollars, I'd feel more at ease!"

Rising painfully to his feet, he leaned against the rail in baffled thought. Some distance astern rode a vessel which must have anchored there during the night. As idly he glanced at it, Mr. Glencannon became aware that its lines were familiar. Upon its bow he saw a row of beetlelike ideographs, and below them their equivalent in Roman letters.

"*Miyako Maru,*" he read. "—A Joponese tromp ship. No, I foncy I dinna ken her after a'. But still—"

Across the water came a clarion call—the crow of a rooster— the voice of Chantecleer summoning the day. Perched high on the bridge of the *Miyako Maru,* Cock o' the North was flapping his brave white wings. From several doors on the deck, squat figures in sleeping kimonos emerged and peered perplexedly aloft at the disturber.

"Weel, I'll be domned!" said Mr. Glencannon. "Sae that's where

I was! They must ha' brought me hame—yes, e'en my whusky!"
He spied a slip of paper thrust between two boards of the case
—a pencilled note which read:

You come wrong ship too drunk. We bring. Thank you very
welcome.

"Aye, sae far, sae gude!" He nodded. "But how did I find my
way aboot aboord her? And why does she look sae fameeliarly
fameeliar? But losh, let us see, let us see!"

Making his way up to the chart room, he hoisted out a ponderous volume entitled Lloyd's Register of Shipping.

"M," he said, leafing through it. *"M—Missourian, Mistley Hall,
Mitra, Mittelmeer*—ah, here we are! *Miyako Maru;* Owners,
Hoshino Kaisen Kaisha; Port of Registry, Hakodate, vessel, ex-
Magdalene, ex-*Odile,* ex-*Duke of York,* and ex—gude losh!—ex-
Paxton Merchant! And I had no' been aboord her for theerteen
years!"

"Thirteen!" At the thought of the accursed number, he glanced
at the calendar upon the table. Yesterday's sheet had not yet been
torn off; it read Friday—Friday, yes, but Friday the fourteenth!

"Weel, I never!" gasped Mr. Glencannon. "To think that 'twas a'
a false alarum! Yes, and 'twas a' the fault o' that lying scut o' a
mate. If—"

"Cheerio!" came the mocking voice of Mr. Montgomery himself. "I 'adn't expected to see you up this early! Oh, my word,
wot's 'appened to the top of yer 'ead?"

"I boomped it," said Mr. Glencannon shortly.

"Oh, no, you didn't, not arf! W'y, blyme, there's bumps on it
like h'orstrich h'eggs! W'y don't you wrap a blinkin' h'eelskin or
a 'orse'air around it, eh?"

"Because," said Mr. Glencannon, advancing very deliberately
around the edge of the table—"because, eelskins and horsehairs
canna cure bruises. But I'll ask ye, Muster Montgomery, did ye
ever try a slice o' raw beef for curing a black eye?"

"No," sneered the mate. "I never did."

"Weel, ye'd better!" advised Mr. Glencannon, putting heart and
soul into the blow.

THE FLAMING CHARIOT

IT WAS an afternoon of lowering skies and leaden seas on which
the white-caps gleamed with that unaccountable brightness which
presages a storm. A wind that had swept across four hundred miles
of Mediterranean since it took its leave of Africa was whisking
away these white-caps, turning them into spray, and then sullying
the spindrift with clouds of Tyne-coal soot which belched from
the funnel of a singularly ugly tramp steamer. This vessel was the
Inchcliffe Castle, and she was snouting her way Northward past
the Balearics towards Marseilles at a spanking clip of seven knots
an hour.

Now it happened that this rate of speed, although considerable
for her and being, in fact, about twice as fast as a man can walk,
was by no means satisfactory to Mr. Montgomery. Therefore, he
growled impatiently to himself, strode to the speaking tube, and
whistled the engine room. "The bridge'll speak to the Chief," he
said. "Oh, are you there, Mr. Glencannon?—Well, I s'y, ay'nt there
nothing you can do to choke another knot or so out of 'er? There's
a chap out 'ere 'oo's sculling past us in a punt!"

"Ah, noo!" replied a voice in which were combined the tin of
the tube and the timbre of Aberdeen. "What ye say, Muster Montgomery, is inaccurate on the vurra face o' it! In the feerst place,
the poont is a type o' craft unknown in these waters, and the waters
is too deep for it anyway. In the second place, I've got the old
teapot deleevering her maxeemum, and leaking steam at every
pore. And in the theerd place, I'll thank ye to leave the engines
to me and mind yere ain domned business." Whereupon, with
crushing finality, the tube snapped shut.

"There!" complained Mr. Montgomery to the quartermaster
at the wheel. "Bly'me if there ever was a man like 'im!" And returning to the starboard wing of the bridge, he trained his binocu-

lars astern at a three-masted barkentine which, close hauled and with all sails set, was scudding along in swift pursuit.

"Why, I never seen anything like it!" he muttered, in awed and reluctant admiration. "In another 'arf hour, that perishing old windjammer'll be showing us 'er 'eels! I'd better notify the Old Man. . . ."

Shortly, he was joined by Captain Ball, who borrowed his glasses and scanned the barkentine with an expert eye. "Well," he said after a thorough inspection. "He's certainly giving her all she'll take, but he'll jolly well yank her sticks out if he doesn't watch her!"

"Yes, and he'll jolly well pass us if we don't watch 'im!" said Mr. Montgomery. " 'Umiliyting, I calls it, Sir, being trimmed by a ruddy windjammer!"

"H'm," mused Captain Ball, "Sail beating steam . . . it is a narsty idea, at that! I'll just speak to Mr. Glencannon." And he, too, stepped to the tube and had a parlance with the choleric genius who presided below.

When he returned, his face was purple and his mustache was trembling. But soon the clank of furnace-doors and the scrape of coal shovels came up through the skylights—these, and a voice raised in profane exhortation. Then the pulse of the engines throbbed swifter to the stimulus of steam, and the deckplates set up a new vibration as the *Inchcliffe Castle* protestingly increased her gait through the water.

"Ah ha, now we're snorting!" said Captain Ball, glancing at his watch and peering through the glasses at the indicator of the patent log. "I bet Mr. Glencannon'll get a good ten and a quarter out of her."

Mr. Montgomery shook his head dubiously. "I suppose 'e could if anybody could, but just the syme, Captain, I'm afryde that blinking syle boat will shyme us yet!"

The crew, now, were watching the vessel astern. They stood in groups along the *Inchcliffe Castle's* well-deck, marvelling at the other's speed, waxing sarcastic about their own ship, and laying bets as to the time which would elapse before they took the windjammer's wake. For steadily, steadily, she was overhauling them.

Captain Ball beat his fist upon the bridge-rail in helpless exasperation. "Hell's bones!" he groaned. "She's an old-time racing clipper, or the ghost of one, that's what she is! I was fifteen years in sail myself, and I tell you no ordinary tub can travel like that.— No, nor no ordinary skipper, either!"

"I can't myke out 'er nyme—there's no 'eadboards on 'er," said Mr. Montgomery. "My word, Captain, look—'e's planning to shyve us close!"

"Yes—so's he can give us the horse-laugh when he goes by," growled Captain Ball.

High aloft above the barkentine's deck, tiny figures clambered out along the foreyards, while below, groups were hauling in on the main and mizzen sheets until the great sails stretched taut as drum heads. Heeled over until her lee rails hissed whitely through the water, she charged along like a massive pile of gale-driven thunderclouds. Her sails were dirty and frayed and patched; her black hull was streaked and lumpy as the outside of a leaky tar-barrel, and yet, despite it all, she was regal, majestic, beautiful. As she swept alongside the *Inchcliffe Castle,* the roar of water past her bows and the drone of wind through her towering pyramid of hemp and canvas made a hymn to honor the passing of a queen.

"By George, what a sight!" exclaimed Captain Ball. "I say, just ask Mr. Glencannon to step up here. He might as well share our shame."

By the time Mr. Glencannon, in overalls and carpet slippers, had arrived upon the bridge, the two ships were neck and neck. "Foosh!" he said disgustedly, wiping the perspiration from his chin. "So yon's the cause o' all the uproar! Weel, I've seen sail boats monny's the time before. . . ."

"—Yus, and I s'pose you've orften 'ad 'em syle rings around you, too," sneered Mr. Montgomery.

"No, I never ha'," replied Mr. Glencannon with unshaken calm. "And for the vurra gude reason that all the vessels I've sairved on in the past had speed enough to get oot o' their own way. But as lang as ye've seen fit to get pairsonal, Muster Montgomery, I'll just remind ye that . . ."

He was interrupted by a shout. Down on the *Inchcliffe Castle's* well-deck, the men were pointing excitedly toward the barkentine. "Look, look yon!" exclaimed Mr. Glencannon, following their gaze. "Why, domned if I ever beheld such a spectacle!"

The vessel's decks and rigging were peopled with characters who might have stepped from the pages of the Old Testament. Every man aboard her was clothed completely in black, and had hair that swept his shoulders and a beard that reached his waist! It was a strange and eerie sight. It made one think of the Flying Dutchman, and to expect the Klaboterman himself to clamber gibbering into the shrouds before the ghost-ship should vanish into mist.

"Lunateecks oot for a peekneek!" pronounced Mr. Glencannon, breaking the awed silence.

"Lunatics, and no mistake, but they're great sailors all the same!" grunted Captain Ball. "That's the skipper—the big brute there on the quarter-deck. I say, give the old shell-back a hail, Mister Mate."

"Barkentine a-hoy-y-y!" called Mr. Montgomery. "Wot's yer nyme?"

"What the hell is it to you?" bellowed a voice from between the cupped hands of the bearded skipper, and its accent was distinctly American.

"Haw!" chuckled Mr. Glencannon delightedly. "There's yere answer, Muster Mate! Yon is a master o' reepartee and a mon after my ain heart!" And reaching for the whistle-cord, he applauded the patriarch with three hoarse blasts of the *Inchcliffe Castle's* siren. Then, as the poop of the barkentine slid past the *Castle's* bridge, he removed his cap and waved it politely—a salute which the bearded one acknowledged by thumbing his nose.

Mr. Glencannon, outraged by this gratuitous discourtesy, leaned over the rail and shook his fist. "Why, ye whuskery Yankee goat!" he shouted. "Get 'oot o' our way or we'll run ye doon!"

"In a hawg's eye you will!" scoffed the bearded one, turning on his heel to glance into the binnacle. "Well, so-long, you limping

lime-juicers—I'll tell 'em you're coming in Marseels!" He paused
just long enough to thumb his nose once more—this time over
his left shoulder, and with something of a flourish.

The wind was freshening, and in response to a gust, the barkentine lay over and surged triumphantly ahead.

"Well," sighed Captain Ball mournfully, as her transom hove
into view. "That's that! What's her name, anyway?"

"*Flaming Chariot,*" read Mr. Glencannon, squinting his eyes.
"*Flaming Chariot, o*' Savannah, Georgia."

II

With much coughing and churning, two little French tugs
butted the *Inchcliffe Castle* between the granite walls of the Bassin
de la Joliette. She ran out her lines and made fast to the wharf.
Mr. Montgomery, his labors ended, waved to the bridge from the
fo'c'sle head and pointed to a stately three-master berthed in the
opposite side of the dock.

"Well, damme if it isn't the *Flaming Chariot!*" exclaimed Captain Ball. The Marseilles harbor pilot, hearing him, nodded, and
placing his forefinger against his temple, agitated it as though
scrambling eggs. "*Fou—ils sont fou*—all crez-zee," he declared,
indicating the barkentine. "*Crez-zee Americains!*"

"Yes, I fancy they are a bit cracked," agreed Captain Ball, observing that those members of the *Flaming Chariot's* crew who
were not engaged in labor were wearing long black robes and
smoking corn-cob pipes. "Who are those chaps, anyway?"

"*Crez-zee Americains,*" repeated the pilot, in full and final
explanation.

For the next few days the gentleman of the *Inchcliffe Castle*
were too busy to bother about their hirsute neighbors. But one
afternoon, when the cargo had been discharged and they were
awaiting orders from the agent, Captain Ball yawned, stretched,
and said something about paying the barkentine a visit.

"—Me wisit them impudent coves?—Well, orl right if you s'y
so, Sir," agreed Mr. Montgomery reluctantly. "But suppose we
tyke Mister Glencannon along. Arfter orl, it's 'im we 'ave to

thank for our disgryce."

"I'll deem mysel' honored to accompany ye, Captain," said Mr. Glencannon. "I'd like to mak' an inspection aboord yon Yankee zoo. The boorish behavior o' that whuskery skeeper still rankles beeterly."

They strolled down the dock and entered the gate at the opposite side. Over their heads soared the mighty jib-boom of the *Flaming Chariot*—a spar which jutted from her bow out over the traffic to the very center of the Rue Sainte Pauline.

"An old clipper hull—of course—I knew she was a clipper!" declared Captain Ball. "Look at the taper of her; why, she's built like a wedge!"

"Vurra curious," conceded Mr. Glencannon somewhat absently, as he abhorred all sailing ships and this one in particular. "But whoosh, Captain, do ye look at the rust and feelth o' her! 'Tis a wonder the old tub stays afloat!"

"You bet it's a wonder! Why, do you realize, gentlemen, that this craft must be at least sixty years old? Before they re-rigged her as a barkentine, I wouldn't doubt if she'd done seventeen knots or better."

"Only farncy!" remarked Mr. Montgomery, casting a sour glance at Mr. Glencannon. "Seventeen knots and not a h'engineer aboard 'er!—Bly'me, look!" he lowered his voice, "Look there, Captain—the silly blighters are wearing sandals!"

With their flowing black robes tucked up under them, a number of the crew were sitting in the shade of the deck-house, rolling dice. Two or three of them were smoking, and from the condition of the adjacent scupper, it was apparent that the remainder chewed tobacco. They looked, talked and behaved like a conclave of renegade saints.

Aft, beneath the awning, the skipper was engaged in darning a pair of red flannel drawers. Beside his deckchair stood a two-gallon jug and a tin cup, to which he referred frequently and with gusto. It was during such an interval that he spied the delegation from the *Inchcliffe Castle*.

"Well, damned if it ain't the limping limejuicers!" he roared. "Howdy, brethren, howdy! Come aboard and rest your hats!"

"A-weel," murmured Mr. Glencannon. "He seems a bit more ceevil, but I dinna trust him. There's the ladder to yere left, Captain Ball . . . after you, Sir."

They were welcomed on the deck by the bearded skipper, who towered at least six feet seven in his sandalled feet, and was broad and resonant in proportion. "I'm glad you-all dropped in, brothers!" he boomed. "We're clearing with a cargo for Barcelona tomorrer night. Jest unjoint yourselves under this-here awning while I go to my room and break out a fresh jug. Sho', it's the slickest home-made cawn you ever tasted! I can't abide these namby-pamby liquors, can you?"

Shortly, he reappeared with a jug and three tin cups. "Aft, the Mates!" he shouted, and then, uncorking the jug, "The Mates is my sons," he explained. "I'd like for you-all to shake hands with 'em."

They were joined by three hairy, bearded huskies who stood fumbling with their robes and digging shyly at the deck-caulking with their horny bare toes.

"Gents," said the skipper, "These here's my sons—Shadrach, Meshach, and Abednego. Tell the comp'ny howdy, boys.—You, Meshach, take your fingers out of your nose!"

"Do you look at yon Meshach," whispered Mr. Glencannon, plucking at Mr. Montgomery's sleeve. "I saw him this morning, wiping up the dock wi' five French stevedoors."

"Yes," the skipper was saying, as the trio shuffled away. "They're three good boys and three good mates. And now I'll interduce myself. I'm Ezekiel the Prophet." Quite oblivious to the startled expressions of his visitors he shook hands all around.

"I s'pose I ought to ax pardon for the way I acted, t'other day," mused the Prophet, as he tilted the jug over the crook of his mighty arm. "I'm always kind of short-tempered when I'm at sea. And then, besides, we'd lost the Prophetess only the night before."

"Oh, noo, let me understand ye, Sir," said Mr. Glencannon with ready sympathy. "Do ye mean to say that Mrs. Ezekiel is—er—dead?"

"Yop, you got the idea," nodded the skipper airily. "During the night, Ma heard the Call, so she clumb up to the cross-trees and jumped overboard. It was a mighty slick passing, I'm here to state!"

"Weel, weel, weel, I never!" breathed Mr. Glencannon in amazement.

"Why, sure you never!" beamed the Prophet. "I reckon it all sounds strange to you, brethren, because you don't understand our religion. Well, it's a danged good religion. I'm the boss of it, back in Savannah. I wrote it all myself." And helping himself to a sizeable snifter of corn whisky, he raised his cup, bowed politely, and tossed it off.

"Dawg-gone!" he exclaimed. "That there's the stuff for your bunions! How does it set with you, gents?"

"It's vurra deleecious," said Mr. Glencannon. "It tastes a wee bit like petroleum, only sweeter.—But aboot yere releegion, Sir, ye interest me. I'm a member o' the Kirk in gude standing and a bit o' a theologian mysel', so I wonder wad ye just briefly expoond yere doctrines for my benefeet?"

"Well, they're pretty complicated," said the Prophet, guardedly. "Besides, we don't want no Scotchmen in our religion anyway."

"Oh!" said Mr. Glencannon, gagging as the corn whisky reached his tonsils, and therefore failing to feel the kick which Mr. Montgomery landed in the bulge beneath his deck chair. By the time he had finished his drink and refilled his cup, the Prophet was telling Captain Ball about the ship.

"Why, sho', she's one of the oldest and fastest ships afloat!" he declared. "She was a clipper, built to run the blockade out of Charleston during the War, and . . ."

"The War? Well, that ayn't so long ago," chimed in Mr. Montgomery.

"Aye," agreed Mr. Glencannon, taking his nose out of his cup and feeling to see if his mustache was on fire. "I reecall the War as though it were yesterday!"

"—From 1863 to now ain't long? And you, Mister Scotty—you say you can remember it? Oh, why hell, boys, it's the Civil War I'm talking about—the American War of the Rebellion—not the German War!"

"Oh," said Mr. Montgomery. "A bit of a family brawl, so to s'y. Well, I 'adn't never 'eard of it."

"No, you wouldn't of, you being a limejuicer," said the Prophet, deep pity in his voice. "But I'll tell the world it must of been some war jest the same! Why, if you look sharp along them bulwarks and deckhouses, you can still find cannister shot and minnie balls under the paint and pry 'em out with your knife. Yes sir," and his eye twinkled strangely, "We've found some mighty funny things aboard this here old ship!"

Mr. Glencannon, engaged in further experimentation with the liquor, had heard comparatively little of this discourse. At about this time, as a matter of fact, he was surprised to find himself floating in a silvery fog through which voices filtered strangely. He peered curiously at the distance-dimmed faces to see if this sudden separation of his astral and physical selves was occasioning comment, but observing that the company was too busy having another drink to bother about such minor psychic phenomena, he banished his fears and joined them. It was really very pleasant, albeit a trifle confusing. . . .

Once, he was conscious of singing *"Scots Wha Hae Wi' Wallace Bled"* through all its several verses. Again, he realized that a whiskery giant was weeping upon his shoulder and that the whiskers tickled his ear.

There was a lapse of time, and then, magically, the scene shifted. He was seated at a table around which were Captain Ball, Mr. Montgomery, and four men with beards so long that the ends were hidden beneath the edge of the table. A Negro, similarly bearded but wearing a gingham apron over his black robe, was serving fried chicken smothered in a creamy white sauce, and pouring a colorless liquid out of a jug. The chicken was delicious. The liquid tasted something like petroleum, only sweeter. . . .

"Yea verily!" boomed a thundering challenge out of nowhere. "We Americans can outsail, outfight, outdrink and outspit any other nation on the face of this earth!"

"A-men!" came a basso response from three black figures seated in a row. "A-men and hallelujah!"

"A hoonderd poonds ye're wrong!" cried somebody, springing to his feet. "Though ye trimmed us at sea, ye domned Yankee, I'll bet ye five hoonderd o' yere ain dollars that ye canna do it again, and you to arrange the details!"

Mr. Glencannon was about to applaud these stalwart sentiments; but then, too late, he realized that the voice was his own,
and that, instead of springing to his feet, he had merely fallen into
the mashed turnips.

III

Mr. Glencannon was awakened by some one shaking him violently, and he opened his eyes to find himself in his room aboard
the *Inchcliffe Castle.* "Come, wyke up!" said a voice which he
recognized as that of the Mate. "Wyke up! You 'aven't any time
to wyste, you 'aven't."

With difficulty managing to disengage his tongue from the roof
of his mouth, "Any time to waste for what?" he inquired thickly.
"What is the necessity for a' the roosh and bustle?"

"Why, to get ready for the ryce—the life-boat ryce you challenged the Prophet to larst night!"

"Life-boat race? Why, mon, ye're daft! Whatever are ye talking aboot?" Mr. Glencannon sat bolt upright and then abruptly
lay down again.

"Well, it's you who's daft, if ye arsks me," shrugged Mr. Montgomery. "Nobody but a cryzy man would 'ave challenged them
gryte 'airy aypes to a rowing ryce and bet a 'undred pounds on it,
like you did!"

"A hoonderd poonds?" repeated Mr. Glencannon, weakly. "Ah,
noo, noo, Muster Montgomery, let's get this straight. I dinna reecall a word aboot it!"

It appeared, from the Mate's explanation, that the race would
be rowed over a course from the basin entrance to the Anse des
Catalans light-buoy and back; that Mr. Glencannon and the
Prophet Ezekiel would act as coxswains of their respective crews;
that the craft used would be two identical life-boats furnished
by the *Inchcliffe Castle,* and that the race would start promptly at
2 P. M.

"Yus, and you agreed to it yourself larst night," insisted Mr.
Montgomery. "Orl 'ands of both ships 'as been betting on it since
morning. It's 'arf arfter twelve now, so you'd jolly well better be

picking your crew and getting ready, you 'ad!"

"Whoosh!" said Mr. Glencannon, arising with a Spartan effort. "'Tis vurra plain that with a hoonderd poonds at stake I must summon a' my keenest faculties." And reaching under his bunk, he dragged forth a bottle of Duggan's Dew of Kirkintilloch, filled a tumbler to the brim, and drank it without a flicker of an eyelash.

"There!" he said, smacking his lips. "I shall noo pull on my troosies and set my intellect to work. Meanwhile," and he bowed his head and gnawed thoughtfully at his mustache, "Meanwhile, Muster Montgomery, I'll thank ye to order Number One life-boat lowered into the water richt away, and to have Number Three let doon so's it's exoctly opposite the loading door on the poort side. Stand by till I give ye the word to lower it the rest o' the way."

"Right-o!" said Mr. Montgomery, stepping briskly out on deck and blowing his whistle. Then, having given his orders, "Strike me if I don't believe 'e's sunk this time!" he chuckled. "Even that Scotch 'ighw'yman can't swindle his w'y past a boatload of ruddy seven-foot 'Erculeses!"

But later that afternoon as he stood with the cheering crowd upon the pier-head, he changed his mind—yes, and cursed himself for having bet his money on the *Flaming Chariot's* crew. Even though the racing craft were still beyond the Vieux-Port, it was evident that the *Castle's* was well in the lead. Through his glasses, Mr. Montgomery could see that the men were pulling along swiftly, easily, and that Mr. Glencannon, standing in the stern-sheets with the tiller between his knees, was fortifying his strength with copious drafts from a quart bottle. Several similar bottles, he observed, were in circulation among the oarsmen.

As the boats approached the finish line, the bearded giants were jaded, weary and sore beset. The Prophet Ezekiel, garbed in his flowing robes, raised voice and arms in futile effort to goad them on. "Row, row, ye shuddering sinners!" he stormed. "You, Shadrach, fer the love o' tunket put some beef into it! Hep! Stroke! Hep!—Wake up, Zeruiah, wake up, gol dang it, before I take this-here tiller and flail the livin' wamus off'n ye!"

But his eloquence was of no avail. Leisurely the *Inchcliffe Castle's* boat crossed the line a dozen lengths in the lead. As it did so, Mr. Glencannon turned, struck an attitude, and with a sweeping gesture thumbed his nose at his vanquished rivals. Then, reacting to the strain of it all, he took a final swig from his bottle and collapsed into the boat.

"Well, I never seen the like, Sir!" said the crestfallen Mr. Montgomery. " 'Ow in the world 'e ever myde that crew o' Liverpool riff-raff row like so many h'Oxford and C'ymbridge h'experts is a fair miracle to me!"

"Yes," chuckled Captain Ball, knowingly. "But you never want to forget, Mister Mate, that when it comes to miracles, Mr. Glencannon's a pretty handy chap to have about!"

"But 'ow did 'e do it, that's orl I arsk—'ow did 'e do it?"

"Huh!" Captain Ball snorted. "Why, when you was up there standing by for his word to lower Number Three into the water, what do you s'pose he was doing through that loading-door—fishing for bloaters?"

"I 'aven't the fyntest notion wot 'e was doing," sulked Mr. Montgomery.

"Well," whispered Captain Ball, glancing cautiously about him. "He was lashing a big steel ash-bucket to Number Three's keel, that's what he was doing! Why, it was a regular sea-anchor! It set up a drag in the water under that boat like towing a busted bass drum! . . ."

"Lawks!" gasped Mr. Montgomery! "An arsh-bucket! W'y, a team o' blooming lorry 'orses couldn't myke any speed dragging that!"

"No, nor neither could them whiskery psalm-singers," agreed Captain Ball. "Maybe it'll learn 'em some sea-manners!"

"It's learned me my lesson about Mr. Glencannon, anyw'y," said Mr. Montgomery ruefully. "And I 'opes them *Flaming Chariot* billy-goats sinks on their w'y to Barcelonia!"

Next morning bright and early, Mr. Glencannon strolled along the Quai du Port, and turned into the sunshine which flooded the broad Rue Cannebiere. There was a smile on his face and a song in his heart, for in the wallet directly over it reposed a portly packet of American bank notes.

"Weel," he chuckled. "It a' goes to prove ye dinna need whuskers to be sagacious! And it also proves that it's a costly pastime to gae aboot insulting decent people on the high seas. And noo I shall mak' arrangements for sending my winnings hame to Scotland. . . ."

Turning into the banking offices of the Crédit Marseillaise, he made known his wishes and presented his notes at the grilled window.

The cashier moistened his thumb on a sponge and prepared to count the neat stack of tens and twenties. Suddenly he paused, frowned, looked up.

"Monsieur," he announced coldly. "This money is not good!"

"Not good?" repeated Mr. Glencannon, grasping the marble ledge for support. "Ah noo, Mounseer, this is no occasion for humor! I'll thank ye to cease yere leevity and do as ye're bid."

"It is not an affair of the drollery," insisted the cashier. "Have the goodness to regard, Monsieur—why, one can easily see for one's self!" He pushed the bills back to Mr. Glencannon. "Read, Monsieur, read there carefully what is printed.

With trembling fingers, Mr. Glencannon picked up a bill and examined it. Across the top, in large letters, was engraved "*Citizens' Bank of Atlanta, Georgia*," and then, smaller, on the line below, "*Confederate States of America.*"

"Weel, I'll be domned," he murmured weakly. "That old Yankee swundler!" Then into his mind came a vague and tantalizing half-memory, obscured by a strange silvery fog. He tried to summon the rest of it, but it eluded him. He shook his head sadly.

"It's a' vurra peerplexing," he sighed. "Vurra peerplexing indeed. But, yes, I do seem to recall somebody, somewhere, saying something aboot an American Ceevil War. A-weel," and he stuffed the bank-notes into his pocket, and turned toward the door, "I foncy there's nowt to do but gae oot and find a pub where they haven't heard the war news!"

ODDS AND ENDS

IN THE broad expanse of mud-yellowed water which fans out from the Mafridgi delta to the surf-pounded bar, the S.S. *Inchcliffe Castle* lay nodding at anchor like an overfed dray horse asleep at the hitching post. She had wallowed down the East African coast from Zanzibar, loaded light, her propeller churning suds, and a good five feet of weed-grown boot-topping bared above the water line; but even with this shallow draft, she had negotiated the unbuoyed Mafridgi channel with scanty depth to spare. And now, when barge after barge had been towed out from the trading factory, and ton after ton of cargo had been lowered into her holds, she had settled down until even her upper Plimsoll mark— "Maximum loading for Indian Ocean, summer"—was buried beneath the swell. It would take a high spring tide to float her out safely, but as this phenomenon had occurred eleven days before, three days yet remained until the moon and the sun, crossing the meridian simultaneously, would again combine their mysterious forces and summon the waters in from the sea for the *Inchcliffe Castle's* special benefit.

"Yus, and a bleddy nuisance this w'yting is," grumbled Mr. Montgomery to Mr. Swales, as the pair of them finished checking their tide calculations with the almanac and Nautical Instructions. "I'm fed up with this plyce to the eyeteeth, I am."

"Orful, ayn't it?" agreed the second mate, gazing from the port at the monotonous line of mangroves which was broken only by the trees and thickets of the delta. " 'Ow an educyted, poetical cove like Bark can st'y 'ere year in year out beats me. I don't wonder 'e's fymous as the biggest bore in Kenya Colony."

"Well, 'e st'ys so drunk most of the time that he don't know whether 'e's in 'Onolulu or H'archangel," said Mr. Montgomery. "Did you 'ear 'im this morning when he cy'me aboard with them

84

invoices, and—"

The door opened to admit Captain Ball, perspiration on his brow and desperation in his eye.

"Hell's bones, Mr. Montgomery, you've simply got to help me," he puffed. "If I listen to that pest Bark another minute I'll have the wah-wahs complete. He's done in my second quart, and now he's pacing back and forth with the cuspidor in his hand, trying to recite 'Alas, poor Yorick! I knew him well.' Get him out of there, Mr. Montgomery; get him off the ship; get him some place—"

"Well, that's no easy contrack, sir," said the mate, scratching his head. "Lawks knows, sir, and in all respeck to you, I or Mr. Swales don't want to tyke charge of the blithering bore. But wyte —oh, my aunt, 'ere's an idea! Supposing I simply interjewce 'im to Mr. Glencannon, and may the best man win!"

"Well," said Captain Ball, mopping his florid brow, "don't you think—er, I mean to say, wouldn't that be just the least bit harsh on Mr. Glencannon?"

"No, sir," said Mr. Montgomery, "because if you was to arsk me to nyme the world's champion running, standing bore for any height or distance, I'd put my money on Mr. Glencannon." And chuckling sardonically to himself, he departed on his mission.

He found Mr. Bark in the captain's room, endeavoring to coax a drink from an empty bottle. "No use, Mr. Montgomery," he declared a trifle thickly –"no use at all. Love's labor lost. It's a dead soldier—er—haw—'immortal Cæsar dead and turned to clay.' 'Not a drum was heard, not a funeral note, as his corse to the rampart we hurried—' "

"Oh, wasn't there?" inquired Mr. Montgomery blankly. "Well, I s'y, Mr. Bark, 'ow about 'aving a little dollop of leopard spit with me in the saloon, wot?"

" 'Lead on, oh faithful watchman of the night!' " said Mr. Bark enthusiastically. " 'Take me somewheres east of Suez, where . . . a man can raise a thirst!' "

" 'East of Suez,' " muttered Mr. Montgomery, as he ushered the visitor aft from the lower bridge. "I wonder where 'e thinks 'e is now—Copen'agen?"

In the saloon they found a solitary figure, head in hands and lips moving, deep in a volume which lay between his elbows on the oilcloth table cover.

"Oh, 'ullo; 'ere's Mr. Glencannon!" the mate announced, feigning surprise. "Mr. Bark, I want you to myke the acquy'ntance of our chief engineer. . . . Mr. Glencannon, shyke 'ands with Mr. Bark, the tryder."

"Guid morning, Muster Bark," mumbled Mr. Glencannon, extending his hand but not otherwise bestirring himself. "Yere reputation has preceded ye, Muster Bark. Guid-by, Muster Bark."

There was an awkward silence, broken only by occasional lip sounds as the reader encountered difficult words on the page before him.

"Oh, now, see 'ere, Mr. Glencannon!" blurted the scandalized Mr. Montgomery. "That's wot I'd 'ardly call h'etiquette, I wouldn't. 'Ere I interjewce this gempman to yer, and—"

The steward entered with bottle and glasses. Mr. Glencannon glanced up from his book and blinked his eyes.

"Aye, aye, pairdon me, pairdon me!" he exclaimed, smiting himself on the brow and with apparent effort of will recalling himself to his surroundings and his social obligations. "I apologize to ye, Muster Bark, for my inteense preoccupation. But ye see, I am a student, Muster Bark—aye, a profoond student—and at times I get a' wropped up i' my studies and reesairches."

"Quite all right; perfectly all right; understand absolutely," said Mr. Bark. "I get the same way myself when I'm reading poetry. Er—haw—what's that book of yours, Mr. Glencannon—a bit of verse?"

"No," said Mr. Glencannon. " 'Tis prose, but ah, 'tis a delichtful thing! The name o' it is The Handy Man's Handbook, Or a Thousand Things to Mak' From Odds and Ends. Losh," he sighed wistfully, "if only I had some odds and ends, the things I could mak' to while away the time!"

"H'odds and h'ends of wot?" inquired Mr. Montgomery skeptically.

"Oh, odds and ends of anything," said Mr. Glencannon, with the spacious gesture of a sculptor over his clay. "For instance, here it tells how to build a cage wi' a self-repleenishing feed box, suitable for Beelgian hares or peacocks. A most ingenious and useful deevice it is."

"Useful?" snorted Mr. Montgomery. "Useful, yus, in Bucking'm-shire, m'ybe! But there ayn't no bleddy Belgium 'ares and pea-cocks aboard this ship, not so's you could notice 'em."

"No, o' course there isn't, Muster Mate—o' course there isn't," agreed Mr. Glencannon patiently. "That is why I preefaced my oreeginal remark by saying 'if I only had some odds and ends.' "

"Yus, but now wyte a minnit—wyte a minnit," persisted Mr. Montgomery. "Let's just get this stryght. Do you mean you want the h'odds and h'ends to myke something out of to keep some-thing in, or do you want to keep the h'odds and h'ends in the some-thing arfter you've myde it?"

"Made what?" inquired Mr. Glencannon, after a pause. "I'm afraid I dinna quite follow ye."

"Arfter you've myde a cyge," said Mr. Montgomery—"a cyge—a cyge to put Belgium 'ares and peacocks in."

Mr. Glencannon looked at him perplexedly. "Hares and pea-cocks?" he repeated. "Why, didn't ye just noo say that we had no hares—aye, ye e'en speecified Beelgian hares—didn't ye just noo say we had no Beelgian hares or peacocks on the ship? Foosh, Muster Montgomery, what wud we be wanting a cage for?"

Mr. Montgomery exhaled a long and exasperated breath. "Now look. See 'ere. Listen," he said, leaning across the table and shaking his finger. "In the first plyce, you started orff talking about h'odds and h'ends. Am I right?"

"Aye," nodded Mr. Glencannon judicially. "Aye, and so I did."

"Right! Orl right, then! And then you said something about huilding a some sort of a cyge with a gadget to feed Belgium 'ares and peacocks out of, didn't yer?"

"Aye," said Mr. Glencannon, "but—"

"No buts about it; now wyte! Then, when I said we didn't 'ave no Belgium 'ares and peacocks to put into no cyge, you said that was just the trouble, you didn't 'ave no h'odds and h'ends. Am I right or wrong, hey—am I right or wrong?"

"Ye're richt again," conceded Mr. Glencannon. "But whateever i' the name o' truth are ye driving at, Muster Montgomery?"

"Just this!" said the mate triumphantly, thumping his fist on the table. "Wot in the blyzes do you want anyway?"

"Why, odds and ends," said Mr. Glencannon, glancing at Mr. Bark for confirmation. "Odds and ends, lik' I said i' the vurra begeening. Guid losh, Muster Mate, how often must I explain it to ye?"

"Er—haw—I say," interrupted Mr. Bark, taking his nose out of his glass. "All this talk of hares and peacocks reminds me of those lines about the er—haw:

> "*Stately Spanish galleon, putting out from some place,*
> *With a cargo of something and—er—haw—something else*
> *And something and so forth and so forth,*
> *And——*

"Well, anyway, in the last line it turns out that they've got some peacocks aboard. Great poet, that chap Masefield! You remember the poem, of course?"

"Oh, vurra weel indeed," said Mr. Glencannon, rolling his eyes and reaching for the bottle. " 'Tis a lovely bit. Burns wrote it."

"It don't sound so bleddy lovely to me," said Mr. Montgomery.

"Well, it is, just the same," said Mr. Bark. "Yes, and it goes on to tell about a lot of different ships and their cargoes—for instance—er—haw:

> "*Dirty British coaster with a something—oh, yes, a salt-caked*
> *smokestack,*
> *Butting down the Channel in the mad March days,*
> *With a cargo of something and something and so forth,*
> *Pig iron, and something else, and cheap tin trays.*"

"Exoctly!" exclaimed Mr. Glencannon, landing a mighty slap upon the trader's shoulder. "Peeg iron! Trays! I get yer point, Muster Bark—I get yer point! Ye mean they had a shipload o' odds and ends. But aloss, there's nowt o' such aboard this whole dreary tub wi' whuch I can exeercise my creative faculties and dispel the frichtful boredom whuch peervades."

"Oh, gammon!" growled Mr. Montgomery, edging his way toward the door.

"Gammon?" repeated Mr. Bark, pricking up his ears. "Oh, I say, Mr. Glencannon, do you play backgammon?"

"Weel," said Mr. Glencannon, "provided the stakes were conservative, I ha' been known to indulge. I' fact, there was a time when I rather foncied mysel' as an expoonent o' the game."

"Oh, jolly!" said Mr. Bark. "Come on, then, nip ashore with me, and I'll give you an evening you won't soon forget. Yes, and you can pick up all the odds and ends you'll need from now till 'the oak that fell last winter shall upraise its shattered stem.' Er— haw—do you recognize that quotation, Mr. Glencannon?"

"Aye," said Mr. Glencannon, " 'Tis from the poom called Edinburgh After Flodden, whuch deescribes the one and only time in hustory when the Scots took a licking fra' the English." And he scowled at Mr. Montgomery, who, having made his escape into the alleyway, was thumbing his nose around the edge of the door.

II

On either side of the principal mouth of the Mafridgi River, the delta is seamed with dozens of lesser mouths—mere creeks which meander between steaming mud banks from which writhe the oyster-grown roots of mangroves. At certain seasons when the rains are heavy upcountry, the river joins forces with one or more of these creeks; and sometimes it cuts away the banks of a creek bed, scoops out the bottom and adopts it for its own. Thus what was the principal mouth of the Mafridgi last year may well be but a muddy trickle next, the restless parent stream having moved a mile along the coast.

So thick is the growth of rope vines which arches above the rivulets of the delta that even at noon a twilight gloom lies on the little waterways, and a silence as of night is with them always. Always, that is, save when Mr. Bark is journeying upcountry in his launch. Then the forest is awakened by the stutter of a petrol motor, and by the voice of the trader as he recites as much as he can remember of Marco Bozzaris, Lasca, or The Grave of the Hundred Head.

Mr. Glencannon, having listened to the motor and Mr. Bark

for something more than two hours with never a chance to get a word in edgewise, was becoming a prey to ennui. Also, due to the climate, his thirst was acute. Thus, in the midst of Mr. Bark's declamation to the effect that Mud-je-ke-wis was the beaver and that this was the forest primeval, he raised his voice and shouted, "Aye, 'tis a' vurra picturesque country, but guid losh, Muster Bark, what is the cause o' the drought?"

"Drought?" repeated Mr. Bark. "Oh, you really must pardon me. Gladstone—Gladstone, where's that other bottle?"

"Oh, thank ye, Muster Bark. After you," said Mr. Glencannon, when the Bahantou boatman had pulled the cork. "Er—yes, as I was aboot to reemark, the surroondings are vurra rural."

"Rural? Well, rather!" agreed Mr. Bark, wiping his chin. "Except for these chaps I'm taking you to see, there's not another white man nearer than Dares-Salaam. They're the monarchs of all they survey, the masters of their fate, the captains of their souls, and— er—haw—what was it I started out to say? Oh, yes, about these chaps we're going to visit! Well, they're quite mad, Mr. Glencannon—quite mad, I assure you. But very decently and quietly mad, if you know what I mean. Been alone too long, d'you see? I bring them visitors whenever I can, but the solitude's made them barmy."

"Aye," nodded Mr. Glencannon, "I once knew a lighthouse keeper who was daft the same way. He cut up an old rubber boot, boiled it for three days and ate it."

"What did it do to him?" asked Mr. Bark.

"It kilt him," said Mr. Glencannon.

"Er—haw—'boots, boots, boots, boots, slogging up and down again,'" Mr. Bark commented. "Well, we land just around the next bend. . . . Hold her in to the bank, Jim Bludsoe."

The Negro steersman grinned, wrapped his bare toes around the tiller and pulled it toward him like a monkey picking up a banana.

A tree branch brushed the gunwale, the craft slid gently up on the mud bank and stopped.

"Out we get," said Mr. Bark. "There's a trail of sorts right there ahead of you. But—haw—wait, look. Do you know what that is?"

Mr. Glencannon looked. "Weel," he said, "if ye mean that green glass bottle neck fastened wi' a spike to yon tree trunk, I'd say 'twas a green glass bottle neck fastened wi' a spike to yon tree trunk."

"Ah, that's exactly what it is," said Mr. Bark. "It's the neck of a Rhine-wine bottle. Er—haw—take me back to 'Bingen—fair Bingen on the Rhine'—what? But now, how do you suppose that bottle neck got there, eh? I'll give you three guesses!"

"I hae no' the slichtest notion," said Mr. Glencannon indifferently. "Nor hae I the slichtest eenterest i' Rhine wine, the whuch is nosty watered veenegar."

"Well, I'll tell you how it got there," said Mr. Bark, undismayed. "It was put there by the Hun in 1915, when this was still German territory. There's literally thousands of those bottle necks between here and Dar-es-Salaam. They were insulators for a telephone line from the *Essen*. Of course, you recall the *Essen?*"

"S and what?" asked Mr. Glencannon.

"No, *Essen*—the German cruiser *Essen*. Why, don't you remember how she came up here on a spring tide to hide, and our ships blockaded her for eight months until a couple of shallow-draft monitors came out from England and sunk her in the mud?"

"Oh, aye, I vaguely reemember noo," said Mr. Glencannon. "But what aboot it?"

"There's what about it!" said Mr. Bark triumphantly. "Just cast your eye ahead of you!"

Mr. Glencannon stepped into the forest clearing and beheld that which stunned him in his tracks. "Weel, weel!" he breathed. "Weel, weel, weel, and dom' my bunions!"

So astounding was the sight that for an instant he was persuaded that his breakfast oatmeal had made him the victim of hallucinations, and instinctively he reached for Mr. Bark's bottle. There, out of the dry land before him, loomed the mighty steel bulk of a battle cruiser. Four hundred feet long she was, with sides rearing full twenty feet above the surface of the smooth green lawn which encompassed her. No vestige of paint remained on hull or superstructure, and from her preposterous German ram bow to her shell-dented stern she was coppery red with rust. Her after funnel lay toppled crazily over the starboard side, and her ventilators were bent and blasted and pock-marked with the savage spatter of high-explosive shell. At what had been her water line yawned the three jagged punctures which had brought her to doom. Over in the far corner of the lawn—once, of course, the Mafridgi River's bed—Negroes were hoeing and planting in a thriving vegetable garden. From somewhere near at hand Mr. Glencannon heard the clucking of chickens.

Between the two eight-inch guns which projected from the forward turret there grew a luxuriant awning of vines.

Under this leafy shelter Mr. Glencannon saw two men seated at a table, deep in some kind of game. A Bahantou in the white uniform of a German mess steward stood handy to pour the drinks.

"They're playing backgammon," explained Mr. Bark. "They've got boards all over the ship. It's all they've been doing for fifteen years—that, and trading chunks of old battleship to the natives." Cupping his hands, "Essen ahoy-y-y!" he hailed. "I'm coming aboard with a visitor."

At the sound of his voice the two men left their game and hurried to the rail. They were clad in the German officers' uniforms, but it was instantly apparent that they were not Germans.

"Blyme, it's Bark," said one of them. "Look there, Charlie, it's Bark. But wot's that 'e's got with 'im?"

"Looks like a ruddy Scotch walrus to me, Jymes," said Charlie, considering Mr. Glencannon critically. "Come aboard, Bark, and bring the Caledonian carved coconut with you."

"Carved coconut!" repeated Mr. Glencannon indignantly. "Ah, noo, see here, Muster Bark, I'm weel o' a mind to tromple yon slack-tongued boor. Humor is one thing, but ronk impairtenance is another."

"Sh-h," said Mr. Bark. "Pay no attention to 'em. They're crazy, I tell you—mad as hatters, both of 'em." And he led the way along a conchshell-bordered path to the ship's accommodation ladder.

Within something less than fifteen minutes after he had settled himself in the shade of the gun-borne arbor and had consumed his second drink, Mr. Glencanon was wondering who was really the maddest man on the ship—Charlie, Jymes, Mr. Bark or himself.

The cruiser in the jungle, the Englishmen in German uniforms, the poetry-spouting bore of a trader were all too strange to be real.

"Astoonding! Astoonding!" he murmured as he gazed down across the leafy wastes which spread like the sea around them. "Ne'er did I think I'd view the joongles o' Ofrica fra' the deck o' a Gairmon bottleship!"

"I 'ope you'll h'excuse us," James interrupted his musings, "if I and Charlie nip up on the bridge for a 'arf a mo'. We'd orter just see 'ow she's 'eading and tyke a look at the weather, you know."

"Losh!" said Mr. Glencannon in amazement. "Why, my dear mon, I'll hazard the guess that ye'll find her heading the way she's been heading since 1915, when she soonk. And as for the weather, I can tell ye wi'oot leaving my chair that 'tis hotter than the high-preessure boilers o' heel."

" 'Ot?" scoffed Charlie. "Why, Mr. Glencannon, 'ow could it be 'ot? At the moment we're somewhere about 45° N, 40° W. Ayn't we, Jymes?"

"Yus, approximutely," James confirmed him. "We're right in the middle of the North Atlantic H'ocean, that's where we are. Br-r-r, I'm chilled to the marrow, if anybody should arsk yer. D'y'know, I shouldn't be surprised if there was h'icebergs about! Come, Charlie, let's go tyke a looksee."

"There, now, what did I tell you?" chuckled Mr. Bark when the pair had departed. "Could anything be madder than that? They think they're cruising around the world in fogs and monsoons and hurricanes, and what not, adventuring gloriously."

"Aye, but whurra!" said Mr. Glencannon, shaking his head in stupefaction. "How did they get here i' the feerst place, and noo why do they stay?"

"Well," Mr. Bark explained, "after the British monitors sunk this cruiser, they put these two lads aboard as a prize crew, as required by regulations and the usages of war, and all such silly rot. Of course, she'd only sunk about a foot and was resting on the bottom. The Huns had all barged off overland to Tanganyika, leaving everything behind, so James and Charlie lived high on the loot. They were only supposed to stay here for a month, but the navy got so busy fighting the war that everybody forgot about 'em. Finally, a whole year after the Armistice, a commission came out to inspect the *Essen,* found her on dry land and unsalvageable, and decided to let 'er sit. They discharged the prize crew with back pay and apologies, but that didn't make any difference to Charlie and James."

"No deeference!" exclaimed Mr. Glencannon. "Why, I should ha' thought that they'd ha' weelcomed their release wi' hymns o' grotitude!"

"Gratitude, nothing!" chuckled Mr. Bark. "Why, they were making money hand over fist. You see, they'd worked up a nice little trade with the natives, paying 'em with engine nuts, door knobs, and what not, so you couldn't have dragged 'em away. I clear their trade stuff for them through my factory. Er—haw, we're really business partners, in a manner of speaking."

"Astoonding!" said Mr. Glencannon, beckoning to the steward. "Why, 'tis lik' some strange tale oot o' the Arabbian Nichts!"

"Ah, but wait till they really get going!" said Mr. Bark. "Sh-h, here they are now."

"You can't be too careful in these 'ere waters at this time of the year," Charlie was saying. "We've told the natives to keep their eye peeled for bergs, but we've brought the thermometer down 'ere so's we can watch it fer ourselves. At the first sudden drop, we'll rejewce to 'arf speed."

Mr. Glencannon, examining the thermometer, was surprised to discover that its tube contained no mercury.

"It says 29 Fahren'eit," volunteered Charlie, looking over his shoulder. "You 'ave to h'understand that there thermometer to read it proper. But wot about the weather, Jymes?"

James took a barometer from under his chair and shook it violently. It emitted a hollow, rattling sound, and Mr. Glencannon concluded that its works had been removed. "Blyme!" said James, when the pointer had come to rest. "It's dropping farst, Charlie! Look 'ere."

"H'm, yus, we're in fer a bit o' dirty weather, I perdict," agreed Charlie ominously. "We'd better 'ave the mess boy put the racks on the supper tyble, in cyse she starts to roll. I s'y, let's go into the ward room; these mossqytoes is starting to snap like fox'ounds."

The ward room was spacious, cool and comfortably furnished. A jagged shell hole in the forward bulkhead had been patched up with boards, but otherwise the place was as the Germans had left it. Hanging between two of the ports, Mr. Glencannon saw a large, framed photograph, which he examined carefully. This was a flashlight of Kaiser Wilhelm, garbed as an admiral, standing with a group of officers at the table in this very room. All had champagne goblets in their hands, and a steward stood by with replacements on a tray. Evidently the occasion had been a notable one; probably, thought Mr. Glencannon, the ceremony of toasting the new ship when she had joined the fleet.

"Oh," said Charlie, "I see ye're looking at the pictcher of the 'Un picnic. That reminds me, we've still got eight or nine 'undred bottles of that fizz juice to drink up. Let's get started on it, eh— wot yer s'y?"

"Weel," said Mr. Glencannon, "I'm no' what ye'd call a drinking mon, and I preefair whusky anyway; but a wee spot o' yon champagan wud no' be sae greatly amuss."

"Righto," said Charlie. "We can drink it for chysers arfter the whisky. I s'y, Jymes, tell Wamba to fetch up fifty bottles of that Mummy or Momsie's or wotever its silly nyme is. And let's snag a couple of dozen of them tinned quail birds fer supper. Wot about it?"

"Tinned quail birds would be top'ole," agreed James. "I'm ruddy well sick of that caviar. Yus, it tystes like curdled buckshot to me. I don't see 'ow them 'Uns could stommick the filthy stuff."

"Er—haw—caviar? 'But he who hath never tasted the food, by Allah, he knoweth not bad from good!' " quoted Mr. Bark.

"Oh, shut up, do," James admonished him. "You wouldn't 'ave to tyste this caviar to know it was bad if you'd just got a whiff of the larst keg we opened."

III

The dinner was a gorgeous meal, consisting of turtle soup, asparagus and Uruguayan quail, all taken from the several tons of canned goods which still remained of the Essen's stores. The champagne flowed in torrents.

"Yus, and we've plenty more where this cyme from," said James. "Fill 'em up agyne, Wamba. Wot d'ye think yer 'ere for—to be embalmed or something?"

"I'm very sorry, gempmen, but the cockroaches et all the cigars," Charlie apologized. "But now, Mr. Glencannon, 'ow about a little gyme of backgammon?"

"Oh, vurra weel," said Mr. Glencannon with a languid shrug. "We can play or no', just as ye say." But through the smoke, steam and toxic gases which were billowing up from his pipe his eye gleamed dangerously.

The board was a homemade affair, the twenty-four points having been painted upon what was apparently a massive sheet of brass.

"It's an old 'Un tray with some kind of a whisky advertisement on it," said Charlie. "But it mykes a right nice board, just the syme."

"Yesh," said Mr. Bark, who had suddenly reached what is known in engineering parlance as the burble point. "Something else and something else and cheap tin trays!"

"Well, this 'ere's a brass one, so wot ye're s'ying don't myke sense," said Charlie. "Come on, now, Mr. Glencannon; wot'll yer play—red or white?"

Mr. Glencannon rolled high dice for first play, and then went carrying on to victory. Doublets literally poured from his dice cup, and his opponent's blots seemed always to be where they could most conveniently be hit. The second game, too, was an easy win.

"Backgammon!" he cried as he cleared his last man. "Ye've still three i' my hame table, Charlie! But guid losh, mon, why dinna we wager a few baubees and mak' it interesting? I've been bored a-muckle today!"

"Well, orl right, we'll pl'y fer money if yer s'y so," said Charlie reluctantly. "Of course, Jymes and I 'ave a little rule there's to be no gambling on the ship. But you won't mind fer just tonight, will yer, Jymes?"

"No," said James, "not fer just tonight. But it ayn't by no means usual."

"O' course not," said Mr. Glencannon, bringing out his pocketbook. "Gombling's against my preenciples, too, as a general thing.

But noo, Charlie, do we start in eernest for a sheeling a point."

"Whew! Blyme, that's pretty steep!" said Charlie. " 'Owever, we orlw'ys strives to please, don't we, Jymes? Bang! Double six! There, you can't beat that!"

As a matter of fact, from this point on Mr. Glencannon was unable to beat anything. Charlie's luck with the dice was uncanny —so uncanny that after losing his eighth straight game, Mr. Glencannon began to suspect that it was not luck at all, but skill. As though divining his suspicions and seeking to allay them, Charlie bade James take the dice and roll for him. But the slaughter was no whit abated. Later, when the pair of them commenced taking turns with the ivories, the slaughter became a veritable massacre. Several times Mr. Glencannon played lone men to points vital and remote, deliberately left them unsecured, and sat back to await the result. He did not wait long. Whatever the dice combination needed to hit them, that combination would show on either Charlie's or James' roll.

"So!" said Mr. Glencannon to himself. "There's something rotten i' Ofrica, and I dinna reefair to the caviar!"

So tensely were his adversaries occupied with the game that all signs of their earlier madness had left them. It was as though they had forgotten to play their parts.

"Weel," thought Mr. Glencannon, observing this, "if these swundlers are really crazy, then I am the Caledonian carved coconut whuch the blackhearted roofian said I was. Come, rise up, Glencannon; the time has come for drostic meesures!"

Peering ruefully into his wallet, "Foosh, gentlemen," he said, "there's only twa poonds remaining 'twixt me and complete insolvency. Aye, and there's monny a dreary week till pay day! If I only owned yon board, noo, I cud hope to recoup my foortunes by teaching the game to Muster Montgomery, but—"

He pushed his chair back from the table and spread his hands in a gesture of hopelessness.

"Now wyte a minute, Mr. Glencannon—wyte a minute," James restrained him. "Yer've still got yer two punds, ayn't yer? Well, why not be a sport and pl'y it? M'ybe yer luck will chynge!"

"No," said Mr. Glencannon sadly, "I dinna dare to tak' the rusk."

"Risk yer eye!" chided Charlie. "Why, look 'ere. Listen; I'll tell yer wot we'll do: You put up yer two punds and we'll put up four agynst it. Yus, we'll give yer two-to-one h'odds. That's fair enough, ayn't it? And wot's more, if yer lose, we'll myke yer a present of the blinking board with our compliments, won't we, Jymes?"

"Of course we will!" agreed James. "Come on, shyke up the dice and let's get going."

With seeming reluctance, Mr. Glencannon shook and rolled. "Ace-deuce," he sighed. "Aloss, 'tis as I feared. My luck is oot!"

All through the game he dribbled low numbers and made faulty plays, while his opponents swept around the circuit with doublets and the luckiest possible combinations. It was a rout.

"Well," said Charlie, smiling a sanctimonious smile and gathering up the money, "it's 'ard lines, Mr. Glencannon—it's 'ard lines. But then, we orl can't win, now can we?"

"No," said Mr. Glencannon, his voice vibrant with an emotion which the victors took for grief. "Ah, feeckle foortune! But onyway, noo that I own the board, I'll tak' it back to the Castle and do the vurra best I can wi' it."

"That's the spirit!" declared James. "Ye're a jolly fine sportsman, Mr. Glencannon, and I drinks to yer very good 'ealth!"

Shortly before noon the next day Mr. Montgomery discovered Mr. Glencannon seated in his chair outside his room, busily scraping the paint from a sheet of heavy metal.

"Ah, and so yer found some h'odds and h'ends, did yer?" said the mate. " 'Ow did yer enjoy the charming company of Mr. Bark and 'ow did yer myke out pl'ying backgammon, eh?"

"Weel," said Mr. Glencannon, "Muster Bark is the seecond worst bore I ever met, and one o' the three worst swundlers. And in as much as my opponents at backgammon had removed the mair-cury fra' a theermometer, loaded three sets o' dice wi' it, and spent a' their time since 1915 practicing how to switch them, I lost theerteen poonds."

"Lost thirteen pund? Yer did—haw-haw!—yer did?" exulted Mr. Montgomery. "Well, well, my word; you're 'ardly fit to go ashore alone, you ayn't! Why, you'd orter 'ave a guardian!"

"Aye, pairhops ye're richt," admitted Mr. Glencannon solemnly, scraping away at the paint. "Oh, by the way, Muster Mate, can ye read Gairman?"

"Not a word," said Mr. Montgomery. "Why?"

"Weel," said Mr. Glencannon, "then I'll just hae to read ye the inscreeption on this tray, whuch I hoppened to reecognize fra' a photograph I stoombled across. As near as I can puzzle it oot through the paint, it says:

"THIS TOKEN OF PUREST GOLD, TO A SHIP
OF PRUSSIAN IRON
PRESENTED TO THE OFFICERS OF THE
CRUISER ESSEN
BY
HIS IMPERIAL MAJESTY, WILHELM II
KIEL
DEC. 31, 1909."

SCONES UPON THE WATERS

Toward midnight clouds blew over the moon. The storm which had been brewing off the coast of Murcia came creeping up the gulf and pounced upon Marseilles like an angry black tomcat. The breeze turned into a gale which sent straw hats and café tablecloths sailing through the dust clouds, and brought a shower of roof tiles clattering to the pavement. Rain came lashing through the Rue Cannebière, filling the gutters with torrents which raced down to the Quai and cascaded whitely into the Vieux Port. The street lights blinked twice and went out for the night. Five minutes, and the avenue was empty of all save stranded tram cars which sparked and sputtered futilely on their wires.

Within the Brasserie Maritime, Mr. Glencannon listened to the rain, looked at his watch, then at his glass, which was almost empty, and then at the bottle, which was entirely so. Then he looked at the backgammon board, at Messrs. MacCrummon and Campbell, and at his own considerable winnings. The winnings decided him. Surreptitiously he clicked up his watch stem and spun the hands two hours forward.

"Weel, guid friends and scholars," he yawned, gathering the flimsy French bank notes to him and rising just a bit unsteadily to his feet, "it's after two and the tromways is stopped, and I hae a lang, lang tromp through the highways and byways to get back to the ship. Therefore, I'll regretfully bid ye a vurra guid evening. But"—he smiled jovially and hastened to change the subject— "noo that I've mentioned highways and byways, I'm reminded o' Loch Lomond, that grond old Scottish bollod in whuch I feel we shud meengle our voices."

Stuffing the bank notes into his pocket, he tilted back his head and sang:

100

> *"Oh, I'll tak' the hi-i-gh-rud*
> *And you'll tak' the lo-o-ow-rud*
> *And I'll be i' Scotland afor-r-re ye.*
> *For me and my true love*
> *Wull neever-r-r meet again*
> *On the bonnie, bo-o ——"*

"Ach, domme, hold hard!" Mr. MacCrummon interrupted him. "To heel wi' yere bonnie bonnies, Glencannon! Ye've mulcted us o' heavy winnings in the game, ye have, and if ye think ye can quit this airly i' the evening by braying a bollod i' yere disgusting whusky barytune, ye're vurra sodly i' error!"

Mr. Glencannon's song ended on a soul-piercing note. Three Frenchmen, realizing that it was not, after all, the Marseillaise, replaced their hats and sat down again.

"Ah, swith!" protested Mr. Glencannon, putting tears into his voice, but at the same time putting on his waterproof. "I feel that ye're onkind and onjust, Muster MacCrummon. There's nowt I'd rather do than sit here and game wi' ye till dumsday, no' caring a feeg whether I won or lost. Money? Foosh to money! But alos, 'tis two-fufteen, as ye can see by my watch, and juty calls. As brother engineers, ye weel ken its exactions!"

"Aye," said Mr. Campbell hotly. "Being brother engineers is precisely why we ken dom weel that ye've nowt to do aboard yere ship tonicht, and that ye're merely scuttling off i' the rain to fleece us o' our money, ye nosty sonctimonious Dumbartonshire yellow-belly!"

Mr. Glencannon winced, thrust his hands into his pockets and hung his head in sorrow. "Onjust!" he murmured. "Onkind! Oh, but I'm cairtain ye'll repent, gentlemen, and sae I bear ye no ill will. That I dinna offer ye my hand at parting is only because I hoppen to be wearing a rather cumbersome knuckle-duster wi' half-inch steel spikes on it, just i' case either o' ye shud behave uncouth."

"So!" said Mr. MacCrummon, lighting his pipe, but going about it very slowly, lest Mr. Glencannon mistake his intentions and unlimber the knuckle-duster. " 'Tis no surprise to lairn that ye're a thug as weel as a sharper, and if my ain slungshot was no' oot o'

reach i' my rain coat yonder, I'd vurra quickly teach ye the tricks
o' yere trade!"

"Weel, I've no doot ye cud teach me more aboot thuggery than
ye did aboot backgammon," conceded Mr. Glencannon. "I've
lairned nowt tonicht except that ye're a pair o' poor losers." And
snorting to himself, he fared forth into the storm.

Something less than a minute after his departure an individual
who had been observing the proceedings from a near-by table arose
and strolled languidly toward the door. This person was slight,
pasty faced and inconsiderable. He wore a gray cloth cap, scarlet
shoes with fancy brass eyelets, and sickle-shaped side burns which
curved up in points almost to his cheekbones.

Pausing in the vestibule only long enough to hearten himself
with a good fat sniff of cocaine, he turned up his collar and set out
after Mr. Glencannon. After the bank notes, rather. What might
befall their custodian was wholly incidental to Le Requin. For
Le Requin, at least to himself, was no longer slight, pasty faced
and inconsiderable. He was eighteen feet high, had killed a hundred and seven policemen in single combat, and had just sniffed
up a bucketful of Turkish snow. He paused in the shadows and
took one up the other nostril, for luck; whereupon, magically, his
height increased to thirty-six feet. He walked along beside himself
and gazed up admiringly, like a newsboy who has recognized the
heavyweight champion on the boulevard. "*Eh, bravo!*" he applauded.

In the gloom ahead, the bank notes were singing a crazy English
song about *Ah! ni l'oreille*. They were hurrying along the Quai du
Port—and staggering slightly. The bank notes were drunk—all
three thousand francs of them.

Well, it was about time for Hermine. Le Requin slid her out
of his pocket, clicked her open, and spat upon her blade. Hence,
he told himself, the cloudburst in Marseilles.

II

As Mr. Glencannon hurried down the dark, rainmisted street,
he was oppressed with a feeling that someone was following him.

What with the storm sounds and the shadows, he was unable to verify this; but, nevertheless, he walked all the faster. Far ahead a solitary arc light blazed through the night like a beacon, and by it he shaped his slightly devious course. Once, to hearten himself, he sang a few bars of Annie Laurie, but finding that the rain blew into his mouth, he quickly subsided. "Brrh, guid losh, guard yere health, mon!" he shuddered. "Tonicht's no nicht to be taking raw water into yere system!"

A stealthy footfall pattered in the gloom behind him. Fearfully he peered over his shoulder, and in so doing collided full tilt with a gentleman hurrying in the opposite direction.

"Bondit!" gasped Mr. Glencannon, unleashing a mighty swipe with his knuckle-duster. Due to the ragged state of his nerves, the blow went wide. Before he could aim another, the target backed away and stood cowering, his hands thrown up in abject surrender.

"Don't 'it me, guv'nor!" he pleaded. "I didn't mean to jostle yer, so 'elp me. I wouldn't 'arm a fly, I wouldn't. Orl I want is to get out of Marseel as quick as 'eaven will let me. Look 'ere, guv'-nor, as one Britisher to another, could yer spare a 'undred francs to syve a man's life?"

"No," said Mr. Glencannon, regaining his poise. "Positeevely no. Why, deary me, my guid mon, the sum ye meention is appruximately sixteen sheelings, and sixteen sheelings are a muckle o' money! Wi' the world i' its preesent sod state, it behooves us a' to proctise the most reegid economy. Come, walk alang wi' me, my mon, and tell me yere troobles." It was good to have company, and Mr. Glencannon was disposed to make the most of it.

"Well, orl right," said the other reluctantly. "But see 'ere, guv'nor, let's just cross the street and get aw'y from that light."

Mr. Glencannon looked ahead at the light, then back into the shadows.

"As ye prefair," he shrugged. "But what's wrong wi' yon light?"

"Plenty!" said the other. "Why, if them coves in the guardroom once saw 'oo I was they'd nab me in a jiffick. That's Fort St. Jean, that is, and don't you ferget it!"

Mr. Glencannon observed that the light hung above the gate

of a drawbridge which spanned a moat, beyond which a prisonlike structure of granite bulked black in the rain. Beside the gate was a corrugated-iron sentry box occupied by a khaki-clad colonial. A sign on the gatepost read:

> Dépôt de Passage
> ire et 2me Rgtes.
> Légion Etrangère.

"Foosh!" exclaimed Mr. Glencannon. "The Furreign Legion! Why, they're a disgraceful oggregation o' roofians whose behavior has brung blushes to my cheek i' monny a cinema."

"Yus," said his companion. "And it's the Furreign Legion I'm deserting from right now. I enlisted yesterd'y when I was drunk, I did, and when I cyme to my senses a while ago I found that they'd 'ave me in uniform and shipped orff to H'afrikker fer five years' service in the desert first thing tomorrow. I bided my time and I nipped orff, but they rysed the hue and cry arfter me. If the patrols tyke me h'up now, they'll shoot me out of 'and."

"Weel," Mr. Glencannon commented unsympathetically, "ye've been vurra ondiscreet, and I hope 'twull be a lesson ne'er again to look upon the wine when it is red."

"It wusn't red," said the deserter. "It wasn't even wine. It was coggernac, which is something like whisky."

"Oh, and say ye so?" inquired Mr. Glencannon, evincing interest. "Come alang and watch me drink a drap o' it, then, the while ye're telling me the rest o' yere story."

"No," declined the fugitive, "I don't dare show myself. I've got to get going, I tell yer! To Spain! I've got to 'ave the price of a ticket. Come on, now, guv'nor, you can't let me down! A 'undred francs is orl I arsks, and—"

Mr. Glencannon made as if to move off, but paused as a sudden wave of good will surged warmly over him. His eye became moist with tenderness and pity for a distressed fellow being. Impulsively he slipped off his knuckle-duster, plunged his hand into his pocket, and extended a five-centime copper piece.

"There, my poor mon!" he said, choking a little. "Tak' it, tak'

it, but dinna emborrass me wi' proteestations o' yere grotitude!
After a', 'tis only Christian chority, and—"

A woolen sock descended upon him. The sock was filled with
sand, and Mr. Glencannon subsided into a puddle in what appeared to be sweet and dreamless slumber.

"There now!" the deserter addressed him. "That's fer you and
yer five-centime Christian charity! Well, it serves me right to 'ave
wysted my time on a ruddy Scotchman anyw'y. I'll just see 'ow
much yer've got in yer pockets, and—oh, my aunt! Two thousand
—three—no, four blinking thousand francs!"

"And four t'ousand t'anks to you for counting it," said a cold
voice behind him. "I thought it was but three. Stand up, my leetle
friend Charley, and hand them over to me."

It was Le Requin. Hermine was gleaming dully in his hand.
Charley winced, and stood up, trembling.

Le Requin snatched the money, and chuckled. "Leetle friend
Charley," he said, "I have warn you before and I warn you again,
you must to leave these affairs of importance to me. I have work
on theece in the Brasserie Maritime all evening. I saw theece man
ween *trois mille* from his two friends, and make his queeck depart.
En futur play your beggar's game of the *Légion* deserter all you
weesh, but do not interfere weet me!"

Once more he spat upon Hermine. Then, sneering contemptu-
ously after the scurrying Charley, he swaggered toward a café.

III

In the Brasserie Maritime, Messrs. MacCrummon and Campbell, halfway into a fresh bottle, were calling down anathemas
upon the name of Glencannon. They were calling them down so
loudly that the proprietor strolled over to ask them to desist.
Observing, however, that one of them was whanging upon the
backgammon board with a canvas-covered slungshot while the
other was knocking chips out of the marble table with a ten-inch
spanner, he changed his mind and strolled back again.

"A mean, mean, mean, pairsimonious mon!" Mr. MacCrummon was complaining. "Why, guid losh, to think that it's only

one o'clock the noo! We shud ha' followed him oot and tuk the money awa' fra' him, that's what we shud ha'!"

"Aye, I shall ne'er forgi' myself for being hoodwunked by the grosping ghoul!" agreed Mr. Campbell fervently. "Fufteen hoonderd froncs apiece— think o' it, think o' it! Weel, let's drink black confusion to him, and may a tree grow oot o' his back!"

"Two trees," corrected Mr. MacCrummon, lifting his glass. "And may he be hung on the pair o' 'em."

A stranger stood before them—a shifty, cringing specimen. As he twisted his cap deferentially, water dripped from it to the table.

"I arsks yer pardon, gempmen," he began. "I met a cove 'oo said as 'ow yer was 'ere, and sure enough, 'ere yer are."

"Aye, sure enough, here we are," agreed Mr. Campbell coldly. "But who are you, and who cares onyway?"

"My nyme is Charley," said the newcomer, unabashed. "Some calls me the Liverpool Wasp. I just cyme to tell yer that yer drunken Scotch pal was slugged a few minutes ago, and orl his money stole orff o' him. 'E wasn't 'urt bad, and 'e's probably back on 'is ship by now with nothing worse than a 'eadache. But I thought if you'd myke it worth my while, I'd point out to yer the chap wot done it. 'E's still got your friend's four thousand francs on 'im, and m'ybe you'd like to get it back."

"Four thousand francs—four thousand, ye say? Why, ye're dom richt we wud!" exclaimed Mr. Campbell, springing to his feet and reaching for his coat. "And we'll pay ye a hoonderd francs for the tip, won't we, Muster Mac?"

"Glodly," said Mr. MacCrummon. "Oh, we'll gi' yon lout Glencannon a proper lesson i' sportsmanship, as lang as he's paying for it wi' his ain money! Lead on, Muster Leeverpool Cockroach— ye're aboot to wutness wonders!"

"Righto!" said Charley. "Let's get going."

Glowering and silent, they followed him through the rain. At the bend in the Quai du Port he halted. "We're about there," he announced. "But if it's orl the syme to you, I'll just st'y outside till the barshing is over. I'll point out yer man from the door, and I warn yer 'e's a very 'ard customer!"

"He'll be a vurra soft custard when we get through wi' him!" predicted Mr. MacCrummon, toying with his slungshot.

"I 'ope so," said Charley, curling up his lip like an angry rat. "Oh, I've many an old score to settle with that slimy bucko, I 'ave! But now gempmen, 'ere's the plyce 'ere. And, yus, there's yer man, sitting there f'ycing us h'opposite that other chap in the larst little booth on the left. Well, good luck, gempmen. Toodly-oo! I'll be wyting across the street!" With shoulders hunched, he oozed away into the darkness.

Messrs. MacCrummon and Campbell paused in the vestibule and peered into the dim interior. Save for their quarry, his companion and the barman, the place was deserted.

"Weel," said Mr. Campbell, "sae far, sae guid. Our mon himsel' doesna appear difficult, but as ye've dootless obsairved, his friend has a cairtain oogly expression aboot his posterior. We'd better tak' a drink at the bar the while we plan the battle."

They had scarcely wet their whistles when they heard from the booth a voice as from the tomb—the voice of Mr. Glencannon addressing Le Requin across a table which they shared in alcoholic amity.

"Aye, the futpads!" he was saying. "Fra' the way ye describe them, sir, I hae no' slichtest doot that they were MacCrummon and the rogue Will Campbell. 'Twas vurra lik' them, too, to creep behind a mon engaged i' admeenistering sweet chority, and smite him doon the while he was heelpless and onsuspecting!"

"But yes!" agreed Le Requin, quite evidently enjoying the situation. "I stand in the door. I look across the street. I see you to speak with the beggar, and put your hand in the pocket. I see then that the two do creep behind, with *trique* upraised. I shout '*Eh, la!*' but too late! I think you are dead, and so I come inside and sit down. For *zut,* in theece Marseilles, monsieur, one learns that it is wise to mind one's business!"

"Aye, *zoot!* Naturally," said Mr. Glencannon, who fancied himself as a linguist. "But I'm grateful for your guid intentions, and still more grateful"—he reached for the bottle—"for yere kind hospitality since I blundered i' here, battered, dazed and sore beset."

Mr. Campbell nudged Mr. MacCrummon. "Weel, did ye ever!" he whispered. "The swundling French frog is blaming it on us!"

"Aye," answered the scandalized Mr. MacCrummon. "And the droonken jockoss is confairming him! Come, come, Muster Campbell, 'tis time we settled it, and to heel wi' discreetion!"

Shoulder to shoulder, they strode down the room and stood squarely in the entrance of the booth.

"Glencannon," said Mr. MacCrummon, ominously and without prelude, "ye've been robbed, e'en as ye robbed us, and we mean to have it back!"

"Aye!" chimed in Mr. Campbell. "And here ye sit and lollygog wi' the scoondrel that robbed ye!"

It was a tense moment. Le Requin sat forward in his chair and sniffed a carefully gauged shot of cocaine. The emergency, he estimated, would require the services of a man fifty-three feet high, and he intended to be prepared.

Mr. Glencannon set down his glass without spilling too much of the contents, and surveyed the intruders coldly.

"For shame to ye!" he said. "For shame, ye thieving hypocrites! Was it no' enough that ye assaulted and pillaged 'me i' the public streets? Must ye noo come slondering my vurra dear friend—an eestimable gentlemon who—"

"*Espèces de salauds!*" screamed Le Requin, springing to action. The heavy marble table upended, caught the two Scots violently amidships, knocked the wind out of them, and crashed down upon their legs.

In a split second, Le Requin was astraddle of Mr. MacCrummon, going through his pockets like the wind going through trees.

The barman, although less expert, was doing a competent job on the inert Mr. Campbell. Like all good craftsmen, the pair were concentrating on their work.

There was a sudden sound, *thwuck!* and Le Requin measured his length upon the floor. His length had decreased from fifty-three feet to a mere five feet seven. There was another *thwuck!* and the bartender folded up with a whistling sigh.

"Noo then," said Mr. Glencannon, setting down the cognac bottle which had served him so nobly as a war club, "I'll proceed wi' the business i' hond before ony o' these foor blacklegs become restless."

Kneeling beside Le Requin, he took from his pockets seven thousand two hundred and eighty-five francs.

"Losh!" he chuckled, tucking the money into his wallet. "This is what I micht truthfully call a braw clever evening's work! But no"—the smile left his face and he scratched his chin pensively—"but no! On second thought, 'tis vain o' ye, Glencannon, to tak' the creedit unto yersel'. Though ye may be several thoosand froncs the reecher, 'tis only because i' lavishing alms upon that Furreign Legion futpad, ye caught his sondbag on the shoulder i'stead o' the head. It was yere chority, yere Christian chority, that saved ye, Glencannon! Aye, ye cast yere bread upon the waters, and ye got back buttered scones!"

THE FOUNTAIN OF YOUTH

AFTER weeks in fog and gray waters, the S.S. *Inchcliffe Castle* was snouting through the blue just south of Cancer, where skittering squadrons of flying fish coasted down the valleys of the rollers, and dolphins flashed like flames beneath the surface upon which, here and there, broad patches of Sargasso weed lay yellow as wheat fields ripening for the harvest. On the morrow she would call at San Juan, Porto Rico, to coal, proceeding thence to Campechuela, on the eastern end of the island, for a half cargo of sugar, coffee and cigars for Philadelphia.

On the lower bridge of the vessel, Mr. Glencannon was gratefully gulping the bland West Indian breezes and also, from time to time, the contents of a bottle which he kept within easy reach. Meanwhile, without cessation, he gently pounded a small canvas bag upon the arm of his chair. This bag contained a dozen gold sovereigns, two tablespoonfuls of powdered emery, and half a pound of birdshot. After a week or so of pounding, Mr. Glencannon planned to remove the birdshot, the emery and the coins— the latter by that time slightly shopworn, but acceptable for deposit by any bank—and burn the bag. From the ashes, then, he hoped to extract sufficient gold dust to compensate for the reduction in interest upon savings accounts which the Glasgow bankers, in their sniveling parsimony, had recently seen fit to declare. Like knitting and solitaire, it was a happy device with which to while away the hours, and as Mr. Glencannon thumped his bag, he sang a little song about a clergyman named MacDermott, who strangled his wife, chopped her into nine pieces with a cleaver, and threw them into Cromarty Firth.

Captain Ball emerged from his room with a bundle of back numbers of The London Saturday Guardian which had come aboard at Halifax, and settled himself to catch up with the news.

Presently, too, Mr. Montgomery appeared, equipped with razor and strop, and went about paring his corns. Save for the recurrent chink, chink of Mr. Glencannon's bag, the occasional scream of a long-tailed tropic bird, and the familiar creaks, rattles and swishes of the ship, a peaceful silence reigned. Here, you would have said, were three cronies so close in spiritual harmony that mere words among them were superfluous.

At length, however, Captain Ball fell to rattling his paper and champing his false teeth. "Why, hell's bones!" he growled. "D'you chaps remember about the *City of Leyden*, that Miller & Sarthey motorship that went ashore off Portugal last December? Well, the courts have cleared the owners of criminal negligence for having George Flaherty in command, but the Board of Trade has suspended poor George's ticket for six months. Fat chance he'll ever have of getting another berth, if he lives to be a hundred!"

"Yus, or even ninety," observed Mr. Montgomery, a crafty glint kindling in his eye. "Wasn't it Captain Flaherty's h'advanced years that was just h'exackly the mooty point of the 'ole h'inquiry?"

"It was," said Captain Ball, sorry that he had brought up the subject of age, but hastily girding his loins to debate it. "The underwriters claimed that the owners had no business leaving a chap of sixty-eight in command. Well, the truth of the whole thing was, George took chances in a fog by the owners' orders, trying to beat one of the Ruthven ships around to Huelva for a cargo. They floated the *Leyden* and refitted her like new, and Miller & Sarthey got out of it all right. But they made a scrapegoat out of poor George."

Mr. Montgomery, logical successor to the elderly Captain Ball as commander of the *Inchcliffe Castle*, shrugged his shoulders. "Well, there's two sides to every story," he declared. "I 'eard a different side of it from 'Ennery Puddle, 'oo was Captain Flaherty's chief h'orfficer when the h'accident 'appened. 'Ennery is in command of the *Leyden* now, of course; but 'e'd been trying for years to convince the owners that Flaherty was too old and h'antiq'yted fer the job."

"Ontiquated, foosh!" scoffed Mr. Glencannon, coming to Captain Ball's support. "Why, sixty-eight is mere puling puberty, and e'en seeventy-five is nowt but advonced youth. My ain ree-spected reelative, Jock Glencannon, Esquire, o' Milngavie, is spry as ever at the age o' a hoonderd and five."

"Ah, quite so!" said Captain Ball gratefully. "And what, may I ask, is his occupation?"

"Drinking," said Mr. Glencannon.

"Well, be that as it may," persisted Mr. Montgomery, ignoring the interruption. "But h'according to modern scientific h'opinion, the crumbling stone should be replyced and the dying branch should jolly well be pruned. Yus, pruned, just like these 'ere corns 'ere!"

Captain Ball, feeling that he was cornered, launched out on an impetuous offensive. "Well now, that just goes to show how much you know!" he roared. "You and your bally corn pruning! Haven't you got sense enough to realize that to a man in your position, a good set of corns is a priceless asset, and it's a howling shame to sacrifice 'em to mere vanity?"

Mr. Montgomery, toe in hand and razor poised, looked up de-fiantly. "It ayn't vanity, it's necessity," he declared. "They 'urt like 'ell, and I intend to prune 'em, let the chips fall where they may. But 'ow—yus, 'ow—can corns be reckoned as a h'asset to a mercantile-marine h'orfficer?"

"How, hunh!" snorted Captain Ball. "Well, mister, I fancy you've still got a lot to learn about your job if you've never trained your corns to tell the weather!"

"Oh, that!" said Mr. Montgomery, with a patronizing sneer. "Why, good lawks, there ayn't the slightest sensible basis fer no such superstition. It ayn't scientific—now is it, Mr. Glencannon?"

"Ah, i'deed it is!" declared the engineer solemnly, sliding his right foot out of his carpet slipper and considering the gnarled small toe with admiration and respect. "Aye, there's a muckle o' science to support Captain Ball's conteention. Noo, tak' my ain corn here"—he extended it for their inspection. "Ye can see for yersel's 'tis no' a large one; i'deed I'm weel aware that it deesairves to be ronked as a corn o' no more than the second mognitude. But ne'ertheless, that corn is sae deelicately adjoosted that I've used it for years to locate dry bearings i' the engines. At the vurra feerst treemor o' untoward vibration, it infoorms me infollibly."

"Oh, and does it?" inquired Mr. Montgomery sarcastically. "Well, m'ybe it will h'interest yer to 'ear that there knob on yer toe ayn't a corn at orl. It's only a callus, so there!"

"Aye and what then?" countered Mr. Glencannon. "Even assuming that ye're richt, which I doot, does it no' merely indicate that calluses are adapted to engineering, while corns are best for meteorology?"

"Oh, twash!" snorted Mr. Montgomery. "Give me a good old h'aneroid barometer any time! But 'ere, 'old on—'old on a minute"—he peered through the port at the shiny brass instrument hanging on the bulkhead above the captain's bunk. "Now, then, I've myde a barometer reading, I 'ave, and I respeckfully challenges Captain Ball or h'anybody h'else to see 'ow close they can come to it with corns, calluses, bunions or fallen h'arches! Yus, gor blyme, or h'ingrowing toe nyles even!"

"Wait, captain," intervened Mr. Glencannon, reaching for his bottle. "Had ye no' better seensitize them feerst wi' a brusk whusky rub? Come, tak' off yer shoes, sir!"

"No," declined Captain Ball, with hauteur. " 'Taint necess'ry, not with these corns of mine. I've consulted 'em regular twice a day for forty years, and the less I tinker with 'em the better, that's been my experience. They function in all climates and through all kinds of footwear, though I must admit they've given their most extraordin'ry results with galoshes. Now—ker-hem—just hold hard, everybody, and I'll put 'em to work."

He closed his eyes, tilted back his head, and wiggled his toes within his shoes. It was apparent that he was deep in concentration. At length he stirred uneasily, like a trance medium communing with the spirits. "H'm," he said, as if to himself. "They twingle to beat hell, 'f you know what I mean. Just half a mo' now, I want to check 'em back again; yes—yes, by Jupiter, there's no doubt about it! Gentlemen"—he sat bolt upright and shook his finger impressively—"gentlemen, we're in for a spell of dirty weather!"

"Haw!" laughed Mr. Montgomery triumphantly, "Dirty weather indeed! Dirty weather my eye! The barometer's at 30.20—the 'ighest it's been fer a week!"

"Oh," said Captain Ball, wilting visibly, but still defiant. "Well—er—I mean to say, we'll see what it says tomorrow."

Next morning, though, as the *Inchcliffe Castle* wallowed in the swell that sweeps through Mona Passage, the glass and the weather were even more favorable than before.

"As of course they was naturally bound to be," Mr. Montgomery exulted. "Well, we'll be in port between noon and a quarter arfter, and Mr. Glencannon and I'll nip stryght ashore and attend to about the coaling and what not. We'd ought to myke Campechuela on h'easy schedule, we 'ad."

"Oh, there really ain't any rush," said Captain Ball vaguely. "I mean to say—well, you see what I mean—"

"Wot?" Mr. Montgomery pressed him. "Wot d'yer mean, sir?"

Instead of answering, Captain Ball rose, walked out on deck, and stood studying the eastern horizon. Then, very carefully, he commenced tapping his foot against a ventilator, pausing between each tap to sense and measure the effect upon his nerves. At the tenth tap he nodded his head in the satisfied manner of one who has brought conclusive proof to sustain a disputed theory. Emitting a single derisive sniff in Mr. Montgomery's direction, he went into his room, slammed the door, and took from the shelf a volume entitled The Laws of Storm.

Back in the saloon, the mate turned to Mr. Glencannon. "It's 'is ayge," he said pityingly—" 'is ayge. The Old Man's crazy, you mark my words. Why, 'is brains is so ruddy ayncient that they're addled!"

II

Señor Camparez, manager of the Barboza depot of the Antilles Marine Fuel Supply Company, escorted Messrs. Glencannon and Montgomery to their dinghy, being careful, as he walked, not to scuff coal dust upon his immaculate white shoes.

"Guarantee!" he said. "Theece affaternoon we geev you the coal. Ho, coal you queeck, zip! Have cigar, meesta? Have cigar, meesta?"

"Thanks," said Mr. Montgomery, tucking the long slim corona into his pocket. "I'll smoke it lyter, if you don't mind."

"Weel, I'll smoke mine the noo," announced Mr. Glencannon,

examining the beautiful specimen of handcraftsmanship with the eye of a connoisseur. "Cigars, ye see, are my seengle vice, and this one looks sae vurra tempting that I've no' the streength o' choracter to reseest it." He broke off approximately a third of the cigar, crumbled it between his palms and stuffed the fragments into a pipe the cracked bowl of which was bound with copper wire.

"Losh!" he exclaimed delightedly, blowing a cloud that smelled not unlike the climax of a martyrdom by fire, "I didna ken that Porto Rico produced cigars sae ripe and juicy! When we get aroond to where's-this-we're-gaeing I really must lay in a supply."

"Campechuela—that's where we're going," volunteered Mr. Montgomery.

"Ah, Campechuela!" said Señor Camparez, fanning the smoke away from his nostrils with his hat. "See"—he indicated a vessel, pale gray and funnelless, which lay farther down the water front taking on fuel oil—"see, we are joosta now furnish oil to other sheep Inglés, she ees also for Campechuela. A motorsheep, yes, no?"

"Yes," said Mr. Glencannon. "Yes, that's the word ye're groping for, senior. Ye see, the English longuage is really vurra simple, once ye get the hong o' it; but ye shud ne'er say 'yes' and 'no' togeether, because they dinna agree i' gender and particeeple. If ye want to say 'yes' i' English, 'yes' is the word to say. But if, on the other hond, ye wish to say 'no,' why then, ye simply say 'no.' To spell it, ye feerst write the letter *n*, and then ye follow wi' an *o*. But why dinna ye just jot doon these rules the noo, Muster Coalmonger, and commit them to meemory at yere leisure?"

"Oh, my word, shut up!" Mr. Montgomery admonished. "Wot we'd better do is 'urry back aboard and tell Captain Ball about this 'ere motorship. They load cargo from lighters at Campechuela, and they can only work one ship at a time. Unless we beats 'er around there, we'll cool our 'eels in the bleddy h'offing till they've done with 'er. I s'y, wot's 'er nyme, Mr. Comparison?"

"Her name," said the Porto Rican, "ees *Ceety of Leyden*."

"Well, well, yer don't s'y!" exclaimed Mr. Montgomery. "Why, as soon as we've reported to Captain Ball, I'll just 'op aboard of 'er and s'y a friendly 'ullo to my old chum 'Ennery Puddle."

III

Mr. Montgomery and Captain Puddle were seated in the latter's spacious cabin behind the bridge of the M. V. *City of Leyden.*

"Why, I never heard the like!" Captain Puddle was sympathizing "Go on, Chauncey; what happened then?"

"Why then," said Mr. Montgomery, his face red with rage, "Then, I goes h'up to 'is room to tell 'im we're promised a barge that will deliver a 'undred and fifty tons an hour, to start coaling us direckly arfter lunch. And 'e says—now mark this, 'Ennery—'e says, 'Oh, there ayn't no 'urry, Mr. Myte; 'ave it wyte till tomorrow or the next day!' "

"Wait till tomorrow or the next day?" repeated Captain Puddle. "Why, my word, Chauncey, whatever ails the ruddy old ram?"

"That's wot I'm arsking," said Mr. Montgomery, spreading his hands. "There 'e was, with the Virgin Passage and Vieques Sound charts on the tyble, studying h'up on Campechuela, like. And 'e says to me, 'e says, 'Tyke yer time, Mr. Myte—tyke yer time! Yer still too young and h'impulsive, that's yer trouble,' 'e says. 'We won't go beggaring around down there on a lee shore in Vieques with a bleddy storm brewing, not if I knows it!' 'e says."

"Storm!" scoffed Captain Puddle. "Why, hell's hornets, don't he never look at the glass?"

"No," said Mr. Montgomery, making lavish use of the handsome brass cuspidor which stood beside the table. " 'E navigates the ship with 'is corns, 'e does."

"Ah, yes," nodded Captain Puddle, "just like Old Fool Flaherty —only he had an idea he could tell when there was going to be fog by the hairs in his ears wilting. Confidentially"—here Captain Puddle shifted slightly in his chair—"confidentially, the silly old pot did say something about fog that night, just before we run ashore, but nobody paid no attention to him. Of course, he had sense enough to leave that part out of his testimony, when they had him on the carpet, because he jolly well knew they'd say he was crazy."

"Well, I should 'ope so," agreed Mr. Montgomery. "But then,

orl these old shellbacks is alike. 'Ere I've strove fer years to do my duty by ship and owners, and orl I gets in return is h'abuse from a blithering h'imbecile. Oh, I've just about 'ad a bellyful of it, 'Ennery, and that's why I 'urried right over 'ere to see you."

"You mean you'd like to sign on with me?" suggested Captain Puddle.

"No," said Mr. Montgomery, leaning across the table. "I 'aven't come to arsk no fyvors, 'Ennery. I've come to 'elp you myke a nyme for yerself with yer owners, and because I mean to get command of the bleddy *Inchcliffe Castle!*"

He paused impressively and fixed the other with his eye.

"H'm, well, that sounds fair enough," declared Captain Puddle. "I'm an ambitious bloke, I don't mind admitting it. If your helping me will help you help yourself, well, I'm for it, I am. Just what's your scheme, Chauncey?"

"It's simple," said Mr. Montgomery. "Now look. You'll be at Campechuela tomorrow, won't yer? Right! Yer supposed to load 'arf a cargo fer New York, ayn't yer? Right! Well, s'posin' you picked up another 'arf fer Philadelphia—that wouldn't myke yer owners mad, would it?"

"No," admitted Captain Puddle. "They'd be tickled no end, especially in these rotten times. We was supposed to fill up the other holds with Haitian lumber, but there's damn scant profit carting that."

"H'exackly!" said Mr. Montgomery, "h'exackly! Now then, 'Ennery, get this: The only reason them people at Campechuela are splitting this cargo between two ships is because they 'opes to st'y on friendly terms with your owners and orlso with Clifford & Castle. H'aside from that, they don't give a cobbler's Monday cuss who gets the freight, as long as the stuff is delivered in the United Stytes on schedule. Well, thanks to Captain Ball's ayge, 'is corns, and 'is general inefficiency, Clifford & Castle are going to fall down on their contrack!"

Captain Puddle stroked his chin and smiled thoughtfully. "By dod, Chauncey, I get your drift," he said. "But if I talk these Campechuela Spiggottys into giving me both consignments, how's it going to help you?"

" 'Ere's 'ow!" said Mr. Montgomery, his voice tense. " 'Ere's 'ow! When Clifford & Castle learn that we've lorst this freight because of lyte arrival, they'll ruddy well want to know why. Well, gor blyme, I'll myke it my business to tell 'em why—yus, corns, old ayge, Captain Ball and orl!"

IV

That night there was not a breath of breeze to rustle the palm trees or to waver the single wisp of smoke which lazed straight upward from the *Inchcliffe Castle's* funnel. Across the glassy waters of the harbor came the distance-dimmed sounds of San Juan—the shrill of traffic whistles, the purr of motor cars, the shouts of newsboys and *refresco* sellers. In Barboza, nearer at hand, a man was playing an accordion, a woman was spanking her brat, and dogs were holding a community choral in praise of the yellow moon which floated above the sawtoothed mountains in the background.

In the shadows of the coal sheds and clustered oil tanks along the waterside, a great gray ghost came sliding along toward Palo Seco Point. The ghost was muttering snicker-chuck, snicker-chuck, snicker-chuck. From a spindly pipe which jutted from its topside came little flurries of incandescent carbon which winked like swarms of fireflies as they swirled down to drown in the wake. The M. V. *City of Leyden* was putting out to sea.

Captain Ball heaved himself ponderously from the chair in which he had been dozing, and stood scowling at the *Leyden's* running lights until they rounded El Morro and were blotted out.

"Well, there she goes!" he said, in the wistful tone of one who sees opportunity slipping from him. "Now, just supposing I'm wrong, what then? Or just supposing I'm right? Well, I can't be wrong, although—although—" He paused in troubled thought— thought which he strove to stimulate by polishing his bald head with the palm of his hand.

"If I was only younger!" he sighed. "Then, by George, I'd take the chance. Yes, I'd take it because I wouldn't know enough not to! But I ain't old—at least not too old. Yes, and I'll tell 'em so any time—Montgomery or Hazlitt or Sir John Castle even! Tell 'em! Why, no, by cripes, I'll show 'em!" He pounded his fist upon the rail. "I'll order steam right away, and I'll beat that toy tugboat around to Campechuela if we have to make the trip on bunker sweepings!"

Resolutely he strode aft and delivered a thunderous kick upon Mr. Glencannon's door.

A twinge of agony shot through his corns. His resolution left him. Into his mind flashed visions of storms, shipwrecks, courts of inquiry, suspended certificates, and foreclosed mortgages on a certain cottage in Surrey. The sequence of tragic pictures was interrupted only by the realization that Mr. Glencannon was standing in the open doorway addressing him.

"Er—beg pardon?" asked Captain Ball, partially recovering himself. "What was it you were saying?"

"Weel," said Mr. Glencannon, "my reemark—haw-haw!—uttered spontaneously, was more than a wee bit jocose. I said that when ye're standing on one foot, as ye are the noo, ye closely reseemble the provairbial pelican, except that yere beak canna hold more than yere belly can. A vurra comical whimsy, captain—haw—ye must admeet it!"

"Ah, indeed, quite so!" said Captain Ball, hastily putting down his foot. "Er—pelicans, you say? Come to think of it, I didn't see a single pelican all day, did you?"

"Not a seengle one, nor e'en one that was married," chuckled Mr. Glencannon. "Guid losh, captain, did ye hear that last quip? But come in, sit ye doon and listen closely, sir, while I regale ye wi' some more japes equally droll!"

"Oh, please don't bother," said Captain Ball. "Er—you see, I only came back here to ask you how about a—hem—a little drink?"

"Swith, I'd be delichted!" answered Mr. Glencannon, smacking his lips. "What hae ye got, sir?"

"Me? Why, I haven't got a thing," the captain confessed. "What I meant was that maybe you could spare a drop of something. To tell you the truth, I'm—I'm—well, I'm not quite myself tonight, Mr. Glencannon."

"Ah, neither am I, and for the vurra same reason," sighed the engineer. "As a matter o' fact, I was just thinking aboot gaeing ower to San Juan to see what heaven micht provide."

"Well, I'll go ashore with you," said Captain Ball. "Only, I won't go to San Juan. San Juan's too far, and tonight I—well, frankly, Mr. Glencannon, I want to be near the ship."

"Vurra weel, let's gae to Barboza then," Mr. Glencannon suggested. "After a', the whole island is Yonkee prohibition territory, sae getting a drink one place will be as easy as the other."

Barboza was a hamlet behind the coal docks. Its single street, garnished with telegraph wires made thick and fuzzy by air plants, extended for a quarter of a mile until it reached the Plaza de Ponce de Leon.

Although the hour was well after midnight, it had not occurred to any of the inhabitants to go to bed. Throughout the boat trip ashore and the walk up the Avenida del Gobernador Teniente Coronel Theodore Roosevelt, Captain Ball had been clicking his teeth, shrugging his shoulders, and muttering to himself. But not until they were making their way around the monument in the center of the square did Mr. Glencannon become definitely alarmed by his companion's behavior.

There, the captain halted beneath an electric light and stood staring intently upward. After a pause:

"No bats!" he announced sepulchrally. "No bats! You've noticed it, of course?"

Without waiting for an answer, he got down on hands and knees and studied a crack in the sidewalk. "No ants, by gad!" he rasped in a stage whisper. "No ants! No bats! No pelicans!"

"Aye, and no whusky, either," said Mr. Glencannon, hastening to divert the captain's thoughts into rational channels. "Come, come, sir, we'll hae to look aboot us sharply i' this sorra toon, if we hope to find a drink."

"A dreenk, *señores?*"

They turned and saw a little mud-colored *rustico* with straw hat, white cotton pants and leather sandals, grinning at them across the back of a pack horse which was tethered to the railing of the monument. The panniers of the saddle were laden with coconuts.

"Have dreenk, hey, *señores?*" he urged. "Ees good stuff, some keek, *muy forte,* ho, damn!"

Mr. Glencannon considered him sourly. "Foosh to ye, my mon," he said. "D'ye think we've nowt better to do than lave our insides wi' the inseepid bilgewater o' the coconut?"

"Ho!" said the Spiggotty, delivering a grimace intended to be a wink. "You wait; one taste, you see!"

He selected a coconut from the left hand pannier and deftly chopped a hole in the thick green husk with his machete. "Now," he invited, presenting the cuplike result to Mr. Glencannon, "joosta try one taste, *señor!*"

Mr. Glencannon, who prided himself upon maintaining an attitude of dignified tolerance toward the benighted foreign races, decided to humor the fellow. He took the nut, bowed to Captain Ball, and tossed down a truly notable swig.

His first thought was that he had been struck by lightning, but then he concluded that he had merely been knifed through the liver. He opened his mouth to scream "Ossossins!" but was able to utter no sound save a series of wheezy chirps, like the bickering of fledgling meadow larks.

"Well, how is it?" inquired Captain Ball, skeptically. "Wishy-washy, sweet and swillish, I'll perdict!"

Mr. Glencannon, mouth open and eyes protruding, passed him the nut. The captain quaffed. The nut clattered to the pavement. He grasped his chin with one hand, and with the other pointed frantically down his throat.

"Quick!" he gasped. "Quick! I've shwallowed m' falsh twee-tee-teeth!"

Mr. Glencannon, still fighting for breath, hastened valiantly to his aid. "Why, yere dentistry is a' shipshape, sir," he reported after a conscientious inspection. "What ye felt was only the doonward progress o' yon Porto Rican nectar. But whoosh, captain, 'tis a warm and cozy tipple, once ye get the upper hand o' it!"

"Gig-guh-huh, yes," said Captain Ball, wiping his eyes with the end of his necktie. "I must confess it's got a certain distinctive— er, bouquet, sort of. Brrh—I mean to say, what in the hell is it?"

"Ees *cañita*," volunteered the spig, with evident pride. "Rum, most fine rum of the sugar cane. Have more another?"

"Oh, vurra weel," said Mr. Glencannon. "As lang as ye put it

that way, I'm forced to yield to yere blondishments. After a', I
suppose that lairning to drink it is only a motter o' proctice, lik'
sword swallowing. Hae one yersel', captain!"

In the course of the succeeding hours their investigations dis-
closed that small holes had been bored in the bottoms of the nuts,
the milk withdrawn, and *cañita* substituted. All the nuts in the
left-hand pannier had been thus treated, while those in the right
were intact.

"Vurra ingenious!" declared Mr. Glencannon. "Our genial host
can cheer the theersty pilgrim and mak' a profeet oot o' him, be
he teetotal, teemperate, drunk, or merely a government spy. But
speaking o' cheer, captain, may I osk if yere no' feeling a bit more
cheerful yersel'?"

"Well," said Captain Ball, "I fancy I would be if it wasn't for
the ugly mug of that statue reminding me of Mr. Montgomery.
Fons Juventutum—that's who that statue is—at least that's all I
can read of it on the pedestal. Well, I don't like his face, and I
don't like his name, and I don't like his face either. I say, Mr.
Spiggotty, just drag your nag around to the back of this here
statue, so's I'll not be bothered by looking at it. Mr. Glencannon
and I'll just have another little drink and forget about that swine
Montgomery for another little drink with Mr. Glencannon. It
takes more than a bleddy brass barometer to make a sailor, that's
what I told him! Not a single maiden ant or a married pelican—
haw-haw—now wasn't it? Oh, yes, and bats. And so that's why I
said if Puddle wants to take his ruddy motorship around to What's-
Its-Name tonight, well, let him take his ruddy motorship around
to What's-Its-Name tonight, if he wants to take his ruddy motorship around to What's-Its-Name tonight."

"Aye, by all means!" said Mr. Glencannon politely, though feeling a trifle embarrassed that the point of the captain's remarks had
somehow escaped him. "Yere logic, sir, is onassailable."

"Yes, but what's age got to do with it?" Captain Ball demanded.
"What's age got to do with our having another drittle link? What's
age got to do with our having a drother nittle nink, heh. Mr. Glencannon, you damn old pelican you?"

"Nowt," said Mr. Glencannon, falling into the spirit of the

thing. "Nowt at a' sir, save that the more o' it we drink, the younger we'll feel!"

"Younger!" exclaimed Captain Ball, thumping himself on the chest. "By crickey, I'd noticed that! Maybe Mr. Montgomery was right about my being too old this morning. Too old for what? Who said that? Why, I did. Oh, you did, did you? All right, blast you, here's your answer right back in your impudent teeth! Now, in the first place—in the first place—yes, and in the second place, there ain't any bats. Moreover, I can read that blackleg Montgomery like a book. Read every thought he has! He hasn't any! When he was right here in my room talking to me, I could read in his face he was going to tell Puddle to beat us around there and snaffle up that freight. So he went aboard the *Leyden* and he told Henry Puddle that Captain Ball's just an old fool. I know what Montgomery told Puddle. I know what Puddle told George Flaherty, and I know they'll run ashore in Portugal, so who'll pay the mortgage? Who'll pay the mortgage? There's Mrs. Ball to think of, just think of that! If I lose my ship, who'll think of her? If I lose my job, who'll think of her? If I lose my ship, I'll lose my job. If I lose a cargo and don't lose my ship, I'll lose my job any-way. But thank heavens I haven't lost my health, Mr. Glencannon! Faculties alert! Hand steady! Eyesight keen! Oh, can't I? I don't like your tone, sir! I'll bet you the drinks I can read every word on that monument. Listen:

> JUAN PONCE DE LEON
> GOVERNOR OF PORTO RICO
> 1509
> HE SOUGHT THE FOUNTAIN OF YOUTH
> BUT HE FOUND IMMORTALITY

"Bravvio!" applauded Mr. Glencannon, knocking two coconuts together. "Bravvio!"

"Thank you, madam," said Captain Ball, removing his cap and bowing to the horse. "But that ain't the significant phase of it. Remember awhile ago I couldn't read but a couple of words on that statue, and them in a furreign tongue? Well now, by gosh, I can reel the whole thing off like boxing the compass! Eyesight's as keen as a hic—beg pardon—hawk, that's what it means! Getting younger every minute that's what it means! What else could it means, Mr. Glencannon?"

"Weel," said Mr. Glencannon deferentially, "it micht mean that the words on the other side o' the statue are i' Latin, but on this side they're English."

"English!" shouted Captain Ball, lurching against the pack horse. "English—haw—now you're talking! If this country was English, sir, a man wouldn't have to worry about ants and bats and pelicans and Mr. Montgomery and ants. You and I would be in a decent pub somewheres, drinking drinks like Englishmen should. Why, this place"—he curled his lip and glanced disdainfully about the plaza—"this place, faugh! Mere boozing ken! Place is filthy! Look at the bar, sir—look at the bar! Yes, looka bar, Mr. Glencannon! Bar's so filthy there's hair growing out of it! Why, just let the London County Council see a bar with hair growing out of it, and they'd close up the place like—ouch!"

His right foot clasped between his hands, Captain Ball went hopping briskly across the plaza and headed down the street toward the harbor. For a man of his bulk, his years, his condition, and his manner of locomotion, his speed was phenomenal. He covered fully a block before Mr. Glencannon could overtake him.

"Come on!" he urged breathlessly. "Hell's due to pop any minute! Not a second to lose, Mr. Glencannon! Got to get back to ship, Mr. Glencannon!"

Shortly, though, the effort of highspeed hopping became too much for him, and at length even walking overtaxed his strength. It was only by dint of the greatest exertion that Mr. Glencannon supported him through the faint gray of the dawn, eased him into the dinghy, and rowed him out to the *Inchcliffe Castle*.

Their progress up the ship's ladder was not without difficulty and a certain amount of thumping. Mr. Montgomery, awakened by the noise, appeared upon deck in his cap and underwear. It was daylight now, and flat calm, though the air was filled with a fine, white rain. Hundreds of gulls were mewing above the harbor and endless strings of them were flapping in from the sea.

"Ah, good morning, gempmen!" mocked the mate, sizing up the

situation. "Well, it's a gryte relief to 'ave yer h'aboard agyne, now that this 'orrible storm is ryging. A regular teapot tempest, ayn't it? Come, 'elp the captain in out of the drizzle, Mr. Glencannon, before 'e catches cold in 'is corns!"

Mr. Glencannon was so busy fighting back an attack of vertigo that the sarcasm passed unnoticed, and together they assisted the captain toward his room. They were about to pilot him through the narrow portal when he opened his eyes and saw that he was aboard his ship. A tremor passed through him. He grunted, waved them away, and stood majestically erect.

"Mr. Mate," he bellowed, suddenly sober as a judge, "order up all hands, tighten stays, and batten everything down. Slack her off another twenty fathoms of chain and stand by to let go the other anchor. Well, what are you waiting for—an Act of Parliament? Hep, jump to it, you lily-livered son of a mangy Limehouse rat-catcher!"

Mr. Montgomery winced and went pale. He advanced a step, lips quivering and fists clenched.

"See 'ere!" he blurted. "I've stood fer enough, I 'ave! I refuse to tyke the orders of a senile 'arfwit! I refuse, d'ye 'ear me? Why should we batten down in a bit of a summer sun shower? Why should we let go h'extra h'anchors in a dead calm? Why—"

"Now just a minute," Captain Ball interrupted him, his manner suddenly become paternal and kindly. "What you're saying, m' dear young lad, is out-and-out mutiny, and of course you know it. I could have your ticket if I wanted it, but I don't. The only thing I want is for you to look over there at that signal station and tell me what you see."

Sullenly, Mr. Montgomery turned and peered across the harbor toward the Morro. There, climbing up the halyards in the misty rain, were two red flags with black centers.

"The 'urricane warning!" he gasped, his knuckles whitening as he gripped the rail, "The 'urricane warning!"

"Ah, quite so!" beamed Captain Ball, delivering a soul-satisfying kick in a region which caused not the slightest discomfort to his corns.

* * *

Three days later—it was so bright and peaceful and calm that you could tell it was Sunday—the *Inchcliffe Castle* steamed out of the shelter of San Juan harbor and headed along a coast which bore melancholy testimony to the might of the unleashed wind. For mile after mile the palms stood naked as telegraph poles, and entire plantations of green banana trees sprawled prostrate, like praying pilgrims at Mecca. Here and there shapeless smears of wreckage marked what had once been villages. At the eastern tip of the island, the storm had struck with a fury stored up throughout its howling rampage from the hurricane nest off Africa.

"Queer," said Mr. Swales, steadying his binoculars on the rail of the bridge. "That ought to be Campechuela over there, but my word, just look at it!"

Captain Ball looked. Mr. Montgomery looked. Mr. Glencannon looked, and momentarily left off pounding his little canvas bag. As the word went round, the whole ship's company looked—and wondered. For there on the beach, white geysers of surf spouting over it, lay the wreck of the *City of Leyden*. Directly in its lee, protected by the battered steel carcass, the warehouses of the Campechuela Company stood unscathed.

"Well, gor blyme!" said O'Rourke, the cook, to Jessup, the captain's steward, as the pair of them gazed shoreward from the well deck. "The Old Man's a ruddy old bucko, syme's we've orlw'ys h'agreed, but 'e's a s'ylor, Jessup, and don't you never forget it!"

"'E is!" agreed Jessup, resuming his labors with sponge and pipe-clay. "'e is! But look, O'Rourke! Wot I wants to know is 'ow the 'ell 'e got this 'ere 'orse's 'oofprint on one of 'is new white shoes, which is three sizes too narrer fer 'im anyw'y?"

X

JUST BETWEEN SHIPMATES

THE Italian Peninsula, as everyone knows, is shaped in the profile of one of those gilded wooden boots which identify shops of the Caesars' cobbling sons throughout the cities of the world. The heel of this boot is Cape Santa Maria di Leuca, its sole is the southern coast of Calabria, and its arch is the Gulf of Taranto, a body of water customarily churned to a lather by the Italian Royal Navy in its manoeuvres against fictitious hostile fleets, of which, with boundless verve and valor, it immolates as many as six at a time.

One sunny blue morning in November, a cargo steamer was wheezing along southwestward beneath the boot's great arch, serene as a bug which has just escaped being crushed on a pavement. This vessel was the *Inchcliffe Castle,* of London, but so altered was her appearance that you would scarcely have recognized her. Ever since leaving Pola, which is up near the tip of Istria, the *Inchcliffe's* crew had been scaling her with hammers, scrubbing her with soojie, and coating her with paint, until now she looked neat, clean, and to a tolerant eye, respectable. The finishing touches had just been applied, and the Bo's'un was escorting the Chief Officer over the ship with the flustered air of an academician towing a duchess around a *vernissage.*

"Well, it ayn't 'arf bad," declared Mr. Montgomery as he ran an approving eye along the immaculate white superstructure. "I'll tell yer wot, Hughes, if them stingy swine in the h'office wouldn't orlw'ys go cutting our paint requisitions in two, we could keep the old 'ooker looking like a yacht."

"Ah, indeed we could!" sighed Hughes wistfully. "Oi'm only hoping now, Sorr, thot t' paint'll droy before we stroikes bod weather, or before them ash cats below go stoking her so's she'll get all sooted up, loike."

"Yus, soot would certainly ryse the deuce with 'er," agreed the

Mate. "I'll 'ave to speak to Mister Glencannon about it."

"Aye, but I'll speak to ye feerst, and that richt the noo!" came an irate voice from around the corner of the deckhouse. "Foosh, Muster Mate, and what hae ye got to say to this?"

The Engineer appeared in his shirtsleeves, waving on high like a banner a jacket profusely smeared with white.

"Wet paint!" he fumed. "Wet pairt here, wet paint there, wet paint all over the whole dom ship! Can ye ne'er lairn to let weel enough alone, Muster Montgomery, or must ye foreever hae a' hands fuddling aboot wi' paint pots, mucking things up? Look at the sorra state to whuch ye've brocht my brond new jocket!"

Mr. Montgomery surveyed the garment, and, having audibly collected his liquid resources, expectorated over the rail. "Well," he said, "wot about it? 'Aven't yer got wit enough to st'y clear of fresh paint? Yus, and while we're on the subjick, just wot the 'ell do yer mean by rubbing yerself agynst the 'ole ruddy ship and messing up my brand new paintwork?"

Mr. Glencannon dashed his jacket to the deck and shook his fist across it. "Oh, horns o' the deevil!" he stormed. "Sae ye're oot to add insoolt to injury, are ye, ye tin-chinned Cheapside cockney?"

"'Oo're yer calling cockney?" demanded Mr. Montgomery, struggling out of his coat and hurling it down upon that of Mr. Glencannon. "Why, see 'ere, gor blyme, I'll barsh the narsty fyce of any Scotch tinker 'oo dares to call me cockney!"

"Ah, so?" said Mr. Glencannon, thrusting out his jaw. "Weel, here's one Scottish face ye'll atteempt to bosh at yer deadly peril, Sir! Tak' a guid look at it whilst ye may, for 'tis the last thing ye'll see upon this airth!"

As the pair squared off, the delighted Hughes mentally offered himself seven-to-five on Mr. Montgomery; but chancing to observe the handle of a monkey wrench protruding from Mr. Glencannon's hip pocket, he hastily shifted the odds to ten-to-one the other way. Well, any second now, and the carnage would begin. . . .

Suddenly, above the soft scuffle of feet, the swish of the breeze through the funnel stays, and beat of the engines below, there came a new sound—a head-filling drone which throbbed upon the eardrums like the surging pulse of apoplexy. On the bridge, somebody shouted. A great shadow sped over the three hundred and fifty feet of the *Inchcliffe Castle's* length, and down to the water beside her swept a seaplane almost as large as the vessel herself. It landed in a series of bounces which threw white clouds of spray high into the air, and finally came to rest a quarter of a mile off the *Inchcliffe's* starboard bow. From one of the twenty motors arranged in pairs along the top of the huge wing, flames and black smoke were pouring; but even before way was off her, a dozen mechanics had scurried up from the wing hatches and were stripping the motor nacelle, squirting extinguishers upon the blaze, and beating it out with their kapok life-jackets.

Messrs. Glencannon and Montgomery, secretly much relieved by this interruption, exchanged a final salvo of horrid snorts; the mate went hurrying up the bridge ladder after Captain Ball, while Mr. Glencannon joined the excited group at the rail.

"Great swith!" he exclaimed. "Yonder floats the most munstrous bird o' its species I've e'er beheld!—An Eyetalian naval plane, judging fra' the red-white-and-green on the rudder o' it."

By this time the *Inchcliffe Castle* had swung off her course and was headed for the seaplane. Mr. Glencannon bethought him of his camera, and was turning away to fetch it when the two abandoned jackets caught his eye. The sight gave him pause. He picked up the Mate's spruce garment, bundled it into a wad, and with it scrubbed approximately two square yards of wet paint from the cowl of a ventilator. Then he spread it upon the deck and very carefully stamped upon its eight brass buttons until they were flat as so many pennies, albeit a trifle lopsided.

"There, noo!" he chuckled. "Pairhops that will teach him the ruddiments o' eetiquette, and wean him away fra' his spit-and-polish mania for destroying peace aboard ship!" And tossing his own jacket over his arm, he continued aft.

In his room, he went about loading his camera. He heard the *Inchcliffe Castle's* engines rung off, and the squeaking of the blocks as the starboard lifeboat was lowered. By the time he emerged upon deck, this boat, with Mr. Montgomery at the steering oar, had crossed the narrow strip of water that separated ship and seaplane.

With all its motors stopped, the flying giant was rolling majestically in the swell, and the Mate and his oarsmen were gazing in wonder at the massive wing, so new and shiny, which hung above their heads like the roadway of Tower Bridge. The fire was extinguished now, but the reek of leaking motor-fuel was heavy upon the air.

"H'airyoplyne ahoy!" Mr. Montgomery hailed. "Do yer need a 'and? Do yer want any 'elp?"

"No," snapped a voice from the streamlined conning tower which jutted from the turtleback abaft the great stubby bow. "Go away at once."

Mr. Montgomery looked up and saw a swarthy gentleman in a pale blue uniform, the left breast of which was graced with gold pilot's wings and four rows of ribbons. There were gold oakleaves on the visor of his cap. "Go away," this officer repeated angrily. "Do not to interfere. Go away, I tell you!"

Mr. Montgomery's jaw dropped in pained surprise, but he instantly recovered himself. "Oh, so that's yer gratitude is it? Why blarst yer eyes, look 'ere!" he retorted. "Yer on the 'igh-seas now, you ill-mannered squid-eating bum, and Britannia rules the wyves, don't yer never fergit it! Fer bleddy tuppence,"—he thumped the resounding cork breast of his lifebelt—"Fer bleddy tuppence I'd come aboard yer ugly flying swill-barge and . . ."

He was interrupted by shouts and the pounding of feet upon the wing overhead. The mechanics were pointing toward the *Inchcliffe Castle,* and raising indignant outcry. The cause of their excitement was Mr. Glencannon, who, still in cap and shirtsleeves, was levelling his camera over the rail.

The Italian commander leaned far out of his porthole and waved his arms. "No photo, no photo!" he screamed. "Photo prohibit! You officer weeth white shirt! Stop, stop, I say you!"

Mr. Glencannon snapped the shutter and looked up with an austere frown. "Oh, do be quiet, ye impairtenent garlicky barber!" he admonished.

With an oath, the commander ducked back into his conning tower. The lifeboat crew could hear him shouting orders. Another officer appeared and trained binoculars upon Mr. Glencannon.

An excited voice within the cabin was repeating the same words over and over again, like a formula.

"Why, 'e's calling fer 'elp by wireless telephone!" announced Mr. Montgomery. "Listen there—'e's got through to 'em now, and is telling 'em 'is tyle of woe. Haw, strike me if I ever 'eard such chatter! It sounds like a zoo full of them gaudy purple-sterned kangerangoutangs!"

There came a throaty blast from the *Inchcliffe Castle's* whistle. On the bridge, Captain Ball was beckoning the lifeboat back to the ship. The oarsmen gave way, and Mr. Montgomery brought her alongside smartly. The painter was thrown, and the falls hooked on. "Set taut!" called Mr. Montgomery to Mr. Swales, who was in charge on deck. "Right-o, 'oist aw'y!"

The boat had scarcely been swung inboard on her davits when one of the deckhands swore and pointed astern. There, a few hundred yards to windward, six destroyers were charging in line-ahead formation. They were doing 35 knots, and as they sliced through the swell, sheets of white water came curling out from their concave bows like pine-shavings from a chisel.

"Ah, lovely!" murmured Mr. Glencannon, winding in another film. "If yon laddies will only trot oot their soobmarines and bottleships, noo, I'll hae snopshots o' their whole dom navy!"

But suddenly, as the leading destroyer overhauled the *Inchcliffe Castle,* dense torrents of black smoke came crawling and tumbling out of her funnels, looking, in the instant, for all the world like bloated greasy worms. Abruptly the five other craft followed suit. As the wind caught their smoke, mingled it, spread it, and dragged it like a quilt across the *Inchcliffe Castle,* the sky vanished, the sun was blotted out, and lo, at high noon there was darkest night.

Mr. Glencannon stood his ground for a moment, and then, coughing and strangling, he groped his way to his room and slammed the door. Mr. Montgomery, still in his lifebelt, went storming up and down the decks, tripping over obstacles and screaming futile curses into the Stygian gloom.

"Our paint!" he raged. "Good lawks, yer've ruined the 'ole job, yer treacherous soot-slinging beggars, yer!"

His feet became entangled in something soft, and he went sprawling. Dragging the object close to his eyes, he saw that it was a paint-smeared uniform jacket.

"There!" he snarled, "It's orl 'is fault, 'im and 'is blarsted camera!—Get us caught in a smoke-screen, would he? Well, by cripes, I'll learn him!" and whirling the garment thrice above his head, he cast it far out into the smoke-smothered sea.

II

The *Inchcliffe Castle,* currently and by long odds the filthiest vessel afloat, was tied up alongside the Quai Papacino, in the Port Lympia of Nice. Her winches were grinding, and a gang of French and Algerian stevedores were working below as the derricks lowered great casks of wine into the holds. Endless ranks of these casks were arranged upon the wharf, and as the noon sun beat down upon them, they gave off a smell that was at once sour, stuffy and sickening, like the air in a Leningrad tramcar.

Mr. Montgomery, a picture of melancholy, was standing on the quai gazing up at the vessel. "Oh, wot a rotten shyme!" he groaned. "Not a clean spot on 'er the size of a chilblain. Yus, and the blarsted soot 'as 'ardened right into the paint!"

"—A charming little harbor isn't it?"

Mr. Montgomery turned and saw a venerable English gentleman, red of face and kindly of eye, standing beside him surveying the scene. "The hills, the colors—" the stranger waved a gold-headed malacca stick, "The gem of all France, I'd call it."

"Oh, and would yer?" grunted Mr. Montgomery, his thoughts still on soot.

"I would indeed!" said the old gentleman, limping nearer and extending a morocco cigar case with a crest done in platinum. "Yes, and this ship, this—er—*Inchcliffe Castle,* so perfectly rounds out the picture. A typical toiler of the sea!"

"Well," said Mr. Montgomery, melting a trifle and accepting a cigar, "She looks like a toiler in a 'Indu burning-ghat just now, if you should arsk me. I'm orlmost ashymed to h'admit that I serve on 'er."

"You serve on her!" exclaimed the other. "Ah, fancy! Well, well, how interesting! You're her, ah, captain, perhaps?"

"No," said Mr. Montgomery, "I'm the Chief H'Orfficer."

The old gentleman removed a gray silk glove and offered a cordial hand. "Mister Montgomery," he beamed, "My name is Forsythe-Connor, and I'm very happy to make your acquaintance."

"Yus, er, that is, so'm I," stammered Mr. Montgomery. "But see 'ere, Sir, 'ow does it 'appen that you know my nyme?"

Mr. Forsythe-Connor playfully tapped him on the shoulder with the ferrule of his stick.

"Well," he laughed, "it must seem most mysterious, Mister Montgomery, most mysterious—but before I explain, here's a bit more mystery for you. If you will drive back to the Ruhl and have luncheon with me, I'll take great pleasure in restoring to you your uniform jacket which you lost four days ago. Now, what've you to say to that?"

Mr. Montgomery gasped, swallowed, and pushed his cap to the back of his head. "Why, good lawks . . ." he began.

"Enough!" beamed Mr. Forsythe-Connor. "Follow me!" And with Mr. Montgomery at his heels, he limped shoreward between the rows of winebarrels.

III

It was the middle of the afternoon, and in the depths of the *Inchcliffe Castle's* fireroom, Mr. Glencannon was drying several strips of newly printed photographs before a furnace door. As his countenance was illuminated by the glow of the smouldering coals, it looked like that of an alchemist engaged in the distillation of some unholy brew, or even—as Mr. Montgomery decided as he approached through the gloom—like one of those grotesque conceits which the Germans delight to carve upon the bowls of meerschaum pipes and the far ends of fiddles.

At the sound of footfalls, Mr. Glencannon looked up, but recognizing the Mate, he grunted and looked down again.

"See 'ere," said Mr. Montgomery, his voice tense with excitement, "I'd like to talk to you."

"Weel," said Mr. Glencannon, rustling his prints, "I regret that I canna return the compliment. In view o' the recent onpleasantness betwixt us, I . . ."

"Now wyte!" interrupted Mr. Montgomery. "Let bygones be bygones, can't yer? If yer'll only ferget yer silly grudge, 'ere's a chance fer you and I to myke a tidy bit of money."

"How tidy?" inquired Mr. Glencannon, evincing interest.

Mr. Montgomery advanced a step and leaned toward Mr. Glencannon's ear. "Fifty pund h'apiece, that's 'ow tidy!" he answered in a stage whisper.

"Fufty poonds apiece!" exclaimed Mr. Glencannon. "Fufty . . . why guid losh, my dear friend, ye can count upon my fullest cooperation! Ye surely didna think that I'd hold a groodge against an auld shipmate, did ye? Come, lad, dismuss yere fears and teel me all aboot it!"

"Right!" said Mr. Montgomery, with evident relief. "Now listen! I 'ad lunch tod'y with an old gimp-legged cove nymed Forsythe-Connor 'oo's st'ying at the 'Otel Ruhl. 'E's a retired King's Counsel from London, but 'e 'appens to 'ave stood as godfather to a local kid 'oo is now grown h'up to be a 'igh-ranker in the h'Eyetalian navy. It was 'im 'oo was in command of that h'airyoplyne the other d'y. D'yer begin to get the connection?"

"Aye, vaguely," said Mr. Glencannon. "But gae on, gae on, dinna tontalize me!"

"Well," Mr. Montgomery continued, "That there h'airyoplyne was something new and secret, and the h'apple of this 'ere navy's h'eye. If any news was to leak h'out h'about it, old Forsythe-Connor's godson would be cashiered, or m'bye h'even get carst into the brig. That's why 'e rysed such a stink when you was tyking them snapshots, and why 'e 'ad that smokescreen laid down and orl."

"Aye, exoctly," nodded Mr. Glencannon. "And I suppose it's also why he's sae onxious the noo to buy yon snopshots at ony price."

"'E'll buy 'em for a 'undred quid, like I told yer," declared Mr. Montgomery, licking his lips. "Fifty fer you and fifty fer me."

"H'm," mused Mr. Glencannon, "How vurra romontic! But teel me, Muster Montgomery, how did yere spy friend get i' touch wi' ye, and why did he no' come direct to me?"

"Spy?" scoffed Mr. Montgomery. "Haw, he ayn't no spy! 'E's just a soft-'earted old dotard trying to get a lad out of a jam, and it's really orl very simple. Yer'll recall that when yer was tyking them photos, yer didn't 'ave no coat on. Neither did I, but I was wearing a lifebelt, so they didn't notice it. Orl they saw through the glarsses was a chap with an H'orfficer's cap and a white shirt tyking h'eighteen pitchers of 'em. They kept count. Lyter on, when they picked h'up my jacket with some of my letters in the pocket, they naturally thought it was me."

"Aye, noturally," nodded Mr. Glencannon. "And did ye tell old Muster What's-his-name that it wasn't?"

"Of course I didn't!" said Mr. Montgomery. "I let 'im go on thinking that I 'ad the pitchers, and I myde an h'appointment to give 'em to 'im in 'is rooms at h'eight o'clock tonight. 'E's to pay me the 'undred when I deliver 'em."

Mr. Glencannon rose and laid his hand upon the Mate's shoulder. "Muster Montgomery," he said, with a catch in his voice, "I'll mak' no secret o' the fact that there hae been times when ye've tried my patience sorely. But noo, but noo—weel, I must confess ye've won my deepest odmiration."

"Er, haw, well, I 'aven't done so badly at that," admitted Mr. Montgomery. "After all, fifty quid apiece is a nice bit of oof!"

"It is i'deed!" agreed Mr. Glencannon. "But noo, if ye'll excuse me, I must hurry ashore to the bronze foondry, aboot those new bushings. I'll see ye at tea-time."

A shrewd glint flickered in Mr. Montgomery's eye. "Yus, but wyte a minute," he said. " 'Adn't yer just better give me them prints and negatives before yer go?"

Mr. Glencannon sighed gustily, and his face was shadowed with sorrow. "Why cairtainly ye can hae them!" he said. "Ah, but it grieves me sorely, my guid friend, to see ye suspect that I micht sell them elsewhere. Here, tak' them, tak' them wi' my blessing!" And pondering the universal mistrust which pervades mankind, he disappeared up the ladder.

IV

At 7:45 that evening, Mr. Glencannon presented himself in the foyer of the Hotel Ruhl, told the clerk that Mr. Montgomery was calling upon Mr. Forsythe-Connor, and was at once requested to go up to the latter's rooms.

As he walked through the scarlet-carpeted corridors of the fourth floor, he patted his hip to make sure that his monkey-wrench was readily accessible, and thrust his left hand into his coat pocket to conceal the fact that it was adorned with a spiked knuckle-duster of rather clever design. "Aye," he muttered, as he rapped upon the door of room 431, " 'Tis a'ways weel to be on the safe side, e'en wi' that jockoss Montgomery's fairy godfathers!"

He heard limping footsteps within. The door was opened by the beaming Mr. Forsythe-Connor, who stood leaning on his stick. "Come in," he invited, "Come in, Mister Mont—er, oh, who are you, Sir?"

Mr. Glencannon slid into the room and closed the door behind him. "Ne'er mind who I am," he whispered hoarsely. "It's aboot those peectures. . . ."

With a fluid gesture, Mr. Forsythe-Connor's hand came up from the top of his stick and brought with it a twenty-inch stiletto, the needle point of which he pressed against Mr. Glencannon's ample Adam's apple.

"Put up your hands—higher, higher," he ordered, the paternal smile never leaving his face. "Now, who are you anyway? What pictures are you talking about?"

Mr. Glencannon gulped once or twice, but the blade scratched so uncomfortably that he decided to give it up.

"Muster Forsythe-Connor," he said boldly, "if ye dinna tak' that sword away fra' my tonsils this vurra minute, ye'll be i' the domdest fix o' yere nosty spying life!"

"My good man, my good man!" the other protested incredulously. "Pray what in the world are you driving at?"

"Just this," said Mr. Glencannon. "That black hoond o' a Montgomery has robbed me and betrayed you. He didna' mak' those snopshots—I did. He was oot i' the lifeboat at the time, as the ship's log will prove. But he told me this afternoon aboot the bid ye made for them, and I told him to accept it. Then he tuk to wondering if he cudna get more money fra' somebody else. . . ."

"Who?" snapped Mr. Forsythe-Connor, momentarily forgetting to smile.

"Just who, I dinna ken," said Mr. Glencannon. "As a motter o' fact, I didna osk him, because I cudna accede to such a swundle. But just before I discovered that he'd stolen my peectures, he did mention something aboot meeting somebody at eight o'clock tonicht."

"Where?" The voice was strident with alarm. "Where?"

"Weel," drawled Mr. Glencannon, tilting back his head and smiling blandly at the crystal chandelier, "I'm a mon o' few wurrds, so I'll mak' ye a proposeetion. Noo feerst, o' course, there'll be the amount ye agreed to pay Montgomery. . . ."

"Yes, two hundred pounds," barked Mr. Forsythe-Connor. "Be quick, man!"

"Aye, twa hoonderd poonds, I thocht so!" chuckled Mr. Glencannon. "He only mentioned one hoonderd to me, but pairhops he'll be more accurate next time.—Twa hoonderd for the peectures, and three hoonderd for taking you to Muster Montgomery. I'll gae alang wi' ye, but ye can pay me the five hoonderd i' advonce."

"Yes, yes—here!" said Mr. Forsythe-Connor, unlocking a little steel drawer in his wardrobe trunk and feverishly counting the banknotes into Mr. Glencannon's hand. "Now where is he?"

Mr. Glencannon hauled out a massive silver watch and consulted it sagely. "Just noo," he said, "We'll find our vurra guid friend stonding under the theerd tree on the richt as we turn into the Rue d'Alger fra' the Boulevard Solferino."

"Rue d'Alger!" gasped Mr. Forsythe-Connor, snatching up his hat and hobbling toward the door. "Good lord, there're half a dozen consulates on that street! Come on, my car's downstairs!"

There were chauffeur and footman in the car, and even as it pulled away from the curb, Mr. Forsythe-Connor was snapping instructions to them through the speaking tube. When he had finished, they were purring along the Boulevard Solferino.

"You and I," he said to Mr. Glencannon, "will remain quietly in the car until this little affair is, ah, settled.—You, especially." There was a faint click as the safety-lever of an automatic pistol was released within a pocket.

They turned into the Rue d'Alger. In the shadow of the third tree on the right, Mr. Montgomery was pacing back and forth. As the car slowed down beside him, the footman leaned out from the running board and beckoned. Mr. Montgomery stepped eagerly to the curb, and directly into the swishing downward course of a flexible rubber blackjack.

"Ah, losh, what technique!" breathed Mr. Glencannon.

In an instant the car was under way again. The footman passed back a wallet and a crumpled envelope. Mr. Forsythe-Connor, switching on the light, hastily examined its contents. ". . . Sixteen, seventeen, eighteen, yes, eighteen prints and eighteen negatives. Correct!" he announced with evident relief.

Again there came the click of the automatic's safety, but this time it was being moved the other way. "Everything, ah, seems to be quite in order," he smiled. "Shall I drop you at your ship? Right-o! By the way, Sir, these are extraordinarily good photographs."

The car halted at the corner of the Rue Gauthier, and Mr. Glencannon descended.

"Well, au revoir and many thanks," said Mr. Forsythe-Connor. "If you ever happen to have any more pictures of, ah, technical subjects—ships, drydocks, aircraft or what-not—I'd be awfully glad if you'd let me know."

"Aye, no doot ye wud!" chuckled Mr. Glencannon, as he watched the car disappear toward Ventimiglia and Italy— "Especially, the eighteen duplicate prints whuch are noo i' my room, but whuch will be somewhere i' the Rue d'Alger tomorrow!"

It was midnight when Mr. Montgomery returned to the ship, but Mr. Glencannon was waiting up for him.

"Weel," the Engineer greeted, "hae ye got the money? But whurra mon, what's hoppened to yer head?"

"Oh, I've 'ad a 'orrible time!" wailed Mr. Montgomery, sinking into a chair. "I was slugged, I was, and everything stole orff me.

Lawks, but I've got a 'eadache!"

"But the money, mon—the snopshots! Ye dinna mean to say . . ."

"Yus," confessed Mr. Montgomery. "They—they swiped the pitchers, too. Yer see, this afternoon, a 'all boy from the Ruhl brought me a note from Mr. Forsythe-Connor telling me to meet 'im in the Rue d'Alger, instead of coming to the 'otel. So tonight, I . . ."

"Let me see the note!" thundered Mr. Glencannon, and his wrath was terrible to behold. "Great swith, ye gowk, d'ye think ye can mulct me o' my richtful due wi' ony such cork-and-bull story as this? Ye've sold the peectures, that's what ye've done, and noo ye're holding oot on me!"

"I ayn't, I ayn't!" protested Mr. Montgomery, his lip trembling. "Strike me green and 'ope to die, it orl 'appened h'exackly like I've told yer. They stole the note. Why, they even stole my wallet with three quid h'eighteen shillings in it!"

Mr. Glencannon sat back and contemplated him sternly. Then, gradually he seemed to relent. "Weel," he said at length, "I'm a mon wi' a trusting nature, and I've no alternative but to tak' yere wurrd fer it onyway. I bear ye no ill-will, Muster Montgomery—i' fact, if ye're finoncially emborrassed alang toward the end o' the month, I micht even conseeder loaning ye a few sheelings, just between shipmates. The rate o' interest, o' course, will be steepulated i' advonce."

THE ROLLING STONE

To STUDENTS of Scotland's history and to collectors of those stirring ballads, poems, and pibrochs which laud the prowess of her sons, the name "Glencannon" is one with which to conjure. Though the precise origin of the clan remains shrouded in the Scotch mists of antiquity, we may reasonably assume that its founder patriarch was a shaggy barbarian who painted himself blue and who used his whiskers to filter out the tadpoles, wigglers and lesser animalculæ whenever he sucked up a mud puddle, as was customary in the benighted eons before mankind bestowed upon itself the priceless boon of whisky. The earliest traceable mentions of the Clan Glencannon occur in the lays of the Gairloch minstrels, and though the patronymic is there variously rendered, the student cannot fail to be impressed by the frequency of its repetition in drinking songs. The first individual member of whom we have record is Skene Dhu Glencannon, who, in A. D. 1211, fell into a fit of pique, brained five Englishmen with a bottle, skinned the cadavers with his dirk in the High Street of Ecclefechan and nailed the pelts to the door of the church—a devotional gesture for which, so the chronicle tells us, his fellow pew holders "were toe hym most deeplye beholden." In the year 1507, three Glencannons of Ballachulish were drawn and quartered for "stealing a tunn of spirits, the whych they dyd then and there most greedilye drinke, quaffe, imbybe, swill, swigg and swallow," and on Saint Andrew's Day, 1740, one Malcome of the ilk was pilloried and given sixty lashes "for that he did mayke a horryd noise when the Duke passed bye." Even as recently as June twelfth of last year, a certain Colin Glencannon, variously describing himself as a temperance worker, a three-toed sloth, and the Dowager Queen of Rumania, but actually chief engineer of the S.S. *Inchcliffe Castle,* was detained at Dundas Street Police Station, Glasgow, for disorderly conduct, as the charge sheet duly attests.

Now, from this last circumstance it is apparent that the Glencannon family is still actively engaged in upholding traditions established through the centuries; and so, to bring its history up to date, it is our purpose here to review the series of incidents leading to Mr. Colin Glencannon's incarceration.

Let us begin with the bright, warm Mediterranean morning when the *Inchcliffe Castle,* London to Dar-es-Salaam and ports of call as ordered, headed down past L'Ahrash Point on the western tip of Malta, skirted the pile of rocky hills growing out of the sea, and swung between St. Elmo and Ricasoli into Calcara Creek in the frowningly fortified Grand Harbor of Valetta.

The anchor down and the engines rung off, a great and peaceful silence descended upon the ship. The accustomed rushing tumult of angry waters, the throbbing pulse beat of mighty mechanism, the squeaks and rattles and groans of rusty riveted iron, all, all were stilled, and in their stead reigned a calm which was almost palpable, like that of Sabbath in a city.

Mr. Glencannon, perspiration dripping from his chin, emerged from the torrid depths which were his special realm, slouched to the rail and spat disconsolately over it. Before his eyes the turreted walls and rock-hewn bastions of the town reared like imperishable monuments to the Knights of the Maltese Order who had for centuries sallied forth to knock seven bells out of the Saracens. But Mr. Glencannon, if he saw Valetta at all, was less concerned with the glories and architecture of the past than with the finances of the present and future.

"Forty-seeven!" he muttered plaintively. "Aye, forty-seeven years auld today! More than half o' life's appointed span is spun, and I'm still nowt but a rolling stone! Twenty-eight weary years slaving in the bowels o' tromp ships, and what, oh, what do I amoont to?"

"Do you really want to know, ye crankous auld sweer?" inquired a truculent voice behind him. "If ye do, weel, we're both off juty, so it wud give me great pleasure to tell ye straight to yere walrus face!"

Wheeling, Mr. Glencannon saw his nephew Duncan, the *Inch-*

cliffe Castle's third engineer—a red-headed, keg-necked youth with pale-blue eyes and hands like the scoops of a dredger. He observed with concern that the red head and keg neck were thrust forward, that the scooplike hands were slowly contracting into fists and that the pale-blue eyes were fixed intently upon the point of his chin.

"Ah, Duncan, dear lad, what a start ye gave me!" he exclaimed, at the same time prudently edging out of range. "I was just the noo refleecting to mysel' that today's the forty-seeventh anniversurra o' my birth. Congrotulate me, Duncan, congrotulate me!"

"Congrotulate ye what for?" snorted the nephew, emitting from between his teeth a high-pressure jet that sizzled past the clump of hairs which sprouted luxuriantly from Mr. Glencannon's left ear. "If there's any reason to congrotulate ye, it's that ye're still alive, and that's nowt to shout aboot. But noo, as I started to say, you and I are off juty, so I'll just mak' bold to osk what the heel ye meant by writing on the slate that it was my fault she primed three times during my watch the other nicht, and why ye reported yesterday to Captain Ball that—"

"Haw, tush, come, come!" interrupted Mr. Glencannon, retreating still another pace. "As ye say, we're off juty the noo, so dismuss yere professional worries! Dinna be so conscientious, lad! It's my birthday—my birthday, and—"

"And what?" Duncan took a quick step forward.

"W-w-weel," stammered Mr. Glencannon, cornered, but desperately groping for a figurative, distracting glove to cast to the wolves and thus stay their onslaught—"weel—Haw! Haw!—it's my birthday, don't ye see, so I—I was aboot to invite ye ashore to drink my health in honor o' it!" He spread his hands and smiled a smile that was fairly convincing in the middle, but which petered out in palsy at the edges.

For an instant, Duncan Glencannon stood as one stunned. "Eh?" he gasped incredulously. "Ye mean ye're actually inviting me for a drink? You, Uncle Colin? Inviting me, meaning that ye'll pay? Why, o' coorse I'll drink yere health, for yere mind's completely gone!"

Relieved at the success of his stratagem in so far as it had saved his person, but smitten with dismay as he estimated the havoc it would play with his pocketbook, Mr. Glencannon relaxed dismally against the rail.

"Aye, lad, we'll mak' high holiday!" he promised. "Put on yere shore clothes whilst I do the same, and then we'll hire one o' yon bumboats to ferry us ower to town."

"Vurra weel," agreed Duncan, turning somewhat doubtfully toward his room. "I'll be ready in three shakes o' a whustle, so dinna ye dare attempt to scootle off without me, ye sliddery auld strunt luggie!"

A short time later, still shaken by his narrow escape and more than ever melancholy over the stormy course of life in general, Mr. Glencannon followed his nephew up a steep, cobbled defile, half stairway and half street, which had echoed the shouts of warriors long dead and which smelled as though they were still in the neighborhood. At length, warm and thirsty, they emerged upon the Strada Reale.

Malta being a link in the mighty chain of fortresses and dockyards which stretches from England to India, the Strada was bright with the uniforms of His Majesty's army and navy. At sight of them, Mr. Glencannon's spirits improved.

"For after all," he explained, "Valetta is a white mon's town, and thus, instead o' the usual dom dog wash, it affords a wide choice o' really potable liquors—by whuch, o' coorse, I refer to whusky. So come, Duncan, do we turn into yon estoblishment so amiably labeled 'Amabile's' and dompen our puir parched gullets wi' a dollop o' genuine imported Scots bagpipe juice."

What with the soldiers, sailors, marines and aircraftsmen assembled therein, Amabile's was doing a rushing business. "Duggan's Dew o' Kirkintilloch," ordered Mr. Glencannon, when he and Duncan had shouldered their way to the bar. "Aye, Duggan's Dew, my mon, and leave the bottle here before us. 'Tis my birthday, do ye see—a braw wet festival at my expense for all proud bearers o' the name Glencannon!"

"Oh, aye?" boomed a great voice behind them. "Then mak' way, gentlemen, for a Glencannon to slake his raging theerst!" Through the crowd, and towering above it, they saw approaching them a man—a colossus—full seven feet high and built to scale all over. He was clad in the forest-green tunic and scarlet-and-heather kilt of the Argyll and Dumbarton Highlanders, and on his sleeves were the chevrons of a sergeant. Through some oversight, he was wearing his Glengarry bonnet hindside foremost; its two black ribbons dangled down over his face, and he was forced to blow them out of his way with frequent gusty blasts which sounded like the *Inchcliffe Castle's* main exhaust.

"Cousin Dooglas!" gasped Mr. Glencannon, clutching the bar for support as recollections of this giant's liquid capacity bore in upon him. "Weel, weel, how are ye, Cousin Dooglas? Four years since I've seen ye! Why, I thocht ye were still in garrison at Gib!"

·"I dinna doot it!" chuckled the giant, reaching for the bottle and playfully whacking Mr. Glencannon across the trousers with a swagger cane made from the butt of a billiard cue. "Ye'd no hae been so free wi' yere invitations if ye'd thocht I was in the neighborhood! But how are ye yersel', Cousin Colin?"

With black ruin staring him in the face, Mr. Glencannon could do nothing but make the best of it. "I—I'm as ye see me," he said, filling his glass again. "Ye understand, Dooglas, that I—"

He winced as a violent kick caught him in the shin. "Exockly who in the heel is this great loomp, Uncle Colin?" demanded Duncan loudly, considering Sergeant Glencannon with a hostile eye. "Losh, when I consented to be yere guest at this debauch, I didna onticipate ye'd osk me to consort with freaks and munstrussities!"

Cousin Douglas, scowling cross-eyed through his ribbons, leaned over to obtain a better view of the speaker. Mr. Glencannon hastily intruded himself between.

"Ah, pairdon, pairdon!" he apologized. "It ne'er occurred to me that ye didna know each other. Nephew Duncan, this is Cousin Dooglas, and *visa versus*. Ye're both Glencannons, and so—"

"Weel," Duncan broke in, "if there's one thing that clogs my liver more than one Glencannon, it's another Glencannon, and yon brute"—he jerked his head toward the Highlander—"yon brute amoonts to at least three Glencannons any way ye look at him."

"Shoosh, Duncan!" Mr. Glencannon admonished him. "Cousin

Dooglas is no beauty, 'tis true, and he's no' even vurra inteeligent, but that's no reason ye shud forget yere manners, lad!"

Cousin Douglas shifted his feet, and the sound was like that of moving furniture. "Noo, hae a care, the two o' ye!" he warned. "I'm a patient mon, and I'll stand for just so much, but when I've stud for just so much, I've stud for just so much!"

"Let's all hae a drink!" Mr. Glencannon strove to stem the rising tide of war. "Come, we'll move the bottle ower to yon table and mak' it a guid auld family reunion!"

"Oh, vurra weel," Cousin Douglas agreed. "I can drink just as weel sitting doon as I can stonding up, e'en though I canna stond up as weel when I've been drinking sitting doon as I can sit doon when I've been drinking stonding up."

"Blosh!" commented Duncan, disgustedly. "What ye say doesna mak' sense, ye hulking mullet, and what's more, I dinna lik' yere looks!"

Sergeant Glencannon was arranging his elaborately accordion-pleated kilt preparatory to settling himself into a chair, but Duncan's words gave him pause.

"Cousin Colin," he said, "just so's I'll know whose gore it is I'm spilling, will ye please explain to me exockly what relation yon snirtling, pig-eyed boor is to the two o' us?"

"Aye, mak' it plain to him, Uncle Colin," Duncan urged. "As plain as yere ain mean faculties will pairmit. And dinna be such a miser with that whusky!"

Mr. Glencannon's hand trembled as he filled the three glasses. "Weel," he said, "the geneology o' our clan is reediculously sumple. Cousin Dooglas, here, springs from that bronch o' our ilk whuch inhobits Inverfarigaig on Loch Ness and the nearby foothills o' the Monadhliadths. Salmon poachers they are mostly, although one of them got bruk on the wheel for piracy in Kingston, Jamaica, in the Year o' Our Lord Seventeen hoonderd and something, or thereaboots, A. D. His grondson was one o' the MacFeergus Glencannons, some o' whom still live aroond Craigellachie-on-Spey, as weel as in Tillieludlem, doon Larknark way. Their cousin by her second marriage—no, it was his third—was Tamish Glencannon, o' the Ichnadamph Glencannons, though his mother, as we hae just seen, was born in Drumlanrig. The sole fruit o' this union, the Reverend Strathallan Glencannon, got transported to Tasmania for sheep stealing in 1853, but shortly after sairving his time, he came into a tidy bit o' money by dynamiting a safe in Hobart. He died wealthy and in the cairtitude o' a glorious resurrection, amen. The Drumochie Glencannons, on the other hond, a collateral bronch originally o' Balquhidder and sodly addicted to alcohol, later migrated to the Island o' Muck, one o' the small isles north o' Ardnamurchan, and to Llanndydnowyddykilthragowrfydd, a picturesque little hamlet lost in the northeast corner o' the map o' Wales. Does that mak' everything clear?"

Cousin Douglas and Duncan nodded, and took a drink in silence.

Mr. Glencannon, feeling the tension relaxed, took one himself. "Aye," he said, settling back, "that's how it comes aboot that the three o' us here, but especially you two, are the logical heirs to the estate o' auld Uncle Jock Glencannon, o' Milngavie, and so he arranged it in his will. Strange," he mused, "but this is the feerst time—the vurra feerst time—that the three o' us hae been together. Hae ye had any news o' Uncle Jock lately, Dooglas?"

"Nowt that's encouraging," said the Highlander, gloomily chewing the ends of his cap ribbons. "The last letter I got fra' a friend o' mine in Milngavie said that the domned auld rip is getting tougher every day. E'er since he bruk his collar bone falling oot o' the tree, that time on his hoonderd-and-eighth birthday when he foncied that he was an eagle, he'd been taking vurra guid care o' himsel'. He's turned streect vegetarian, consuming nowt whatsoe'er except a quart o' whusky, a quart o' oatmeal and a packet o' snuff per day."

"Aye," nodded Duncan, "I heard, too, that he's guarding his health and spending all his money doing it. He's e'en bocht an owercoat—an owercoat, think o' what that cost! Ho, domn it all, gentlemen, unless the auld reeprobate dies pretty soon, there'll be nowt left but the property for the three o' us to inherit!"

Mr. Glencannon pursed up his lips and frowned judicially. "Aye, Duncan's richt—he's absolutely richt," he declared. "When I was hame last year, I made it my business to check up on the cash estate, and I found that it amoonted to proctically nothing. Whoosh!" he sighed with relief. "Ye can weel believe me, dear reelatives, I didna sleep a wunk o' nichts until I'd contrived to get mysel' weel clear o' the rotten business!"

"Clear o' it?" repeated Cousin Douglas, hitching his bulk forward in his chair. "Why, what do ye mean, ye got clear o' it, Cousin Colin?"

"I mean I got clear o' the whole domn inheritance, and especially the taxes that will go with it, that's what I mean!" said Mr. Glencannon, chuckling happily. "Ye see, I hired a Glesga lawyer to figure it all oot, and he deemonstrated conclusively that the estate tax on my share wud run to approximately a hoonderd and seventy-three poonds, three shillings and saxpunce more than my third o' the property is worth. That's because the tax assessment stonds at the original purchase price; since it was made, o' coorse, the whole tract has depreciated way doon in value, due to their running the new Glesga highroad richt oot in front o' it and putting in sewers and all. Ah, losh, ye wudna reecognize the puir auld place noo!"

"But great swith, Cousin Colin!" exclaimed the Highlander. "Do ye mean to tell us that when Uncle Jock dies, Duncan and I will be called upon to foork oot a hoonderd and seventy-three poonds, three shillings and saxpunce more than we'll get?"

"Aye, do ye mean it?" gasped Duncan.

"I mean worse than that!" said Mr. Glencannon placidly. "Noo that I've succeeded in getting oot o' my share o' the inheritance, leaving it divided in two instead o' in three, each o' you will hae to pay a tax o' two hoonderd and fufty-nine poonds fufteen shillings and thruppence. Aye, and there'll be no dodging it, either! On matters o' that sort, ye canna diddle the King!"

Cousin Douglas and Duncan wilted back in blank dismay. "But —but how did ye monnage it?"

"Weel," said Mr. Glencannon, "it was a vurra deelicate job. Uncle Jock had made up his mind to leave it to the three o' us, and it tuk me many a weary hour to pairsuade the stooburn auld ram that you two were more desairving than I, and shud therefore hae the whole thing between ye. But finally he acceeded to my blondishments, changed his will and left me oot."

"Ho!" snorted Duncan, half rising from his chair. "So ye fixed it so Dooglas and I wud get stuck and soddled with the whole thing, did ye? Weel, ye putrid miscreant, I've a guid mind to—"

"Wait!" Cousin Douglas restrained him, brushing his ribbons out of his face and then petulantly yanking them off. "Hold on for just a minute, lad, and then I'll help ye tear him up by the roots as he domn weel desairves! But feerst I want to osk him what's to prevent us fra getting oot o' the mess the same way he did?"

Mr. Glencannon licked his lips and rolled his somewhat fishy eyes. "Weel," he said, "Article III o' the Act Pertaining to The Bequeathment o' Lands Entailed by Freehold, Fief and Fee leaves auld Jock no alternative but to leave it to his nearest kin, whuch, as ye've seen by the geneology I just noo explained to ye, clearly indicates you."

"Ah, fush!" groaned the Highlander. "Is there no way, no way at all, that Duncan and I can dodge this frichtful colomity?"

"And if there isn't"—said Duncan ominously—"and if there isn't—weel—" Very slowly he removed his cap, hung it on the back of his chair, and went about unbuttoning his jacket. Mr. Glencannon, glancing furtively at Cousin Douglas, saw that the Highlander was unhooking his belt and sporran. The moment, he realized, was critical, and filled with dire potentialities.

"Noo, wait!" he protested, at the same time signaling the bar boy to bring a fresh bottle of Duggan's. "Dinna wax violent, dear reelatives—dinna wax violent, for aloss, 'twull avail ye nowt! E'en though ye batter and buffet me aboot fra noo till Dumsday, ye'll still each hae to pay yon two hoonderd and fufty-nine poonds fufteen shillings and thruppence tax! The only way in the world ye cud possibly get oot o' it wud be to sign ower yere shares to somebody else, and there's a fat chonce o' anybody in his richt mind letting ye do that! Oh! Haw! Haw! Haw! M'lads! Pairdon my laughter, but I fear ye're vurra badly stuck!"

"Oh, aye?" One of Duncan's dredger-scoop hands shot out and clamped itself around Mr. Glencannon's forearm. "So we're vurra badly stuck, are we? There's a fat chonce o' anybody in their richt mind accepting our shares, is there? Weel, Uncle Colin—Haw!

Haw! Haw! to ye, and pairdon my laughter—you yersel' are going to accept our shares richt here and noo, as we mak' them ower to ye in black on white! In return, ye're going to give each o' us a written receipt, assuming full responsibility for all taxes and everything else, and releasing us completely. Aye, that's exockly what he's going to do, isn't it, Dooglas?"

"Losh, why, o' coorse it is!" thundered the Highlander joyfully. "Bless me, Duncan, ye're a braw clever lad, e'en though yere looks belie ye! . . . Ho, barman!" He clapped his hands with the sound of a salvo of field artillery. "Fetch us pen and ink and paper! . . . And noo, Cousin Colin, ye swundling sneak in the grass, we'll just compose some documents in triple dublicate that'll cost ye twice two hoonderd and fufty-nine poonds fufteen shillings and thruppence, or five hoonderd and nineteen quid ten bob sax, by yere ain canny colculation!"

Mr. Glencannon turned gray. He tried to speak, but his voice failed him. He sat as one crushed by weight of woe. Once, but only once, he glanced toward the door, like a caged beast planning a desperate break for freedom.

"Oh, dinna attempt it!" his nephew warned him. "If ye do— weel, Dooglas will clout ye feerst, and then I'll tromple on what I can find o' ye!"

A dry sob escaped from Mr. Glencannon as he watched Cousin Douglas preparing the papers, but tears were in his eyes as he read and finally signed them. Without a word, he stuffed his copies into his pocket and staggered from the room, an aged and broken man. So deep was his despondency that he even neglected to pay for the whisky.

Once out upon the Strada Reale, however, a surprising change came over him. He squared his shoulders. Smiles wreathed his face. He stepped along like a man who walks on the very top of the world.

"Swith!" he gloated, patting his pocket. "Two shares added to the one I've got mak's three, and three mak's the whole domn estate! Hoot, lad, ye're noo sole heir to the entire Glencannon fortune! Losh, what a forty-seeventh aniversurra! Many hoppy returns o' the day!"

From Malta the *Inchcliffe Castle* went down to Dar-es-Salaam and to the Cape of Good Hope. From there she proceeded across the South Atlantic to the Plate, traipsed around through Magellan up to Valparaiso, and then clear over to China. Fourteen months had rolled by when, early one evening, just as the smell of fried kippers was rising from the galley, she swung out of the North Channel and stuck her snout into the dark gray waters of the Firth of Clyde.

The light on the tip of Arran, winked cheerily through the gathering dusk, and Mr. Glencannon winked cheerily back at it. "Glesga in the morning!" he chuckled. "And oot to Milngavie to see Uncle Jock in the afternoon! Ah, little did I think when I set forth on this voyage that I'd return fra it with my prospects o' foortune increased two-thirds! He's a hoonderd and ten years, eight months and fufteen days o' age, and it won't be long noo!"

Shortly after noon the next day, he donned the somber garb which he affected when going ashore, took a drink of whisky for his stomach's sake, another to ward off pyorrhea, a third against dandruff and a fourth because he felt like it, and shaped his course along the Dumbarton Road toward the Glasgow-Milngavie motor-bus terminal. He had not proceeded far, however, when a thought occurred to him.

"O' coorse it's no' customarra for the Prodickal Nephew to fetch alang his ain fatted calf," he mused, "but pairhops, in the caircumstonces, a gift o' some kind wud be no more than diplomatic. Some little token––an offering from the heart—a quart o' Duggan's Dew o' Kirkintilloch, for exomple." And crossing the street to an establishment labeled The Riveter's Rest, he made known his wants to the bar-maid.

"Wrop it up, if ye please, muss," he requested. "And while ye're doing so, I'll just wrop mysel' aroond a dollop o' the same." As a matter of fact, he wrapped himself around several and had partially enveloped still another when he realized that someone was wringing his unoccupied hand and emitting loud protestations of friendship. Turning, he recognized a certain John MacColquhoun, boon companion of his youth and now generally conceded to rank among the three outstanding liquor consumers of Glasgow.

"John!" he cried. "Ah, guid auld John, how are ye, how are ye?" In the instant, the dear scenes of his boyhood flashed cinematographically through his mind; he saw himself and John throwing red-hot counterfeit pennies over the wall to the little children of the orphanage, and—grandest of pranks!—sawing the rail of the church pulpit in such a manner that it broke when the minister leaned against it, pitching him into the transept and fracturing his jaw. Nostalgia surged over him, and as he signaled the barmaid to do her duty, the scalding tears welled in his eyes and coursed down his checks. Mr. MacColquhoun, who bore signs of having done considerable wrapping on his own account, wept loud and unashamed. It was a touching reunion, but at length:

"Come, come, John," Mr. Glencannon urged. "Pull yersel' together and tell me the news o' Milngavie at first hond. I'm on my way oot there to pay my respects to dear auld Uncle Jock."

"Aloss, puir Colin, o' coorse ye are!" sobbed Mr. MacColquhoun. "Ah, it came as a bitter shock to all o' us, Colin, but when I think o' how you must feel, my heart aches in sumpathy!"

"Eh?" gasped Mr. Glencannon. "A shock, did ye say? Swith, John, d'ye mean to—"

"Aye, exockly—it was sudden as a boat from the blue! Apparently Auld Jock was his ain reegular sel', in full possession o' his health and faculties, except sometimes Soturday nichts when his faculties got scrambled, and then his health wud be a wee bit low on the Sobbath in consequence, as who in the heel's is often sometimes not, I osk ye? But none o' us drumpt that the end—"

Mr. Glencannon's glass slipped from his fingers and crashed upon the floor. Before his eyes myriad yellow specks went dancing —specks which turned into bright golden sovereigns.

Uncle Jock was dead! The patriarch had passed! The Glencannon fortune was his! He was rich, rich, rich!

". . . and so the Reeverend Muster Lamb will officiate," Mr. MacColquhoun was saying. " 'Tis for three o'clock this afternoon, in the little ivy-grown kirk at the foot o' the hill, exockly according to Auld Jock's wish. All o' his few friends will be there, but whurra,

Colin, how I admire yere ain fortitude in soobmitting yersel' to the ordeal!"

With great dignity and no little effort, Mr. Glencannon drew himself erect against the bar. "John," he said, "no mon o' our name was e'er known to shirk a fomily juty, howe'er sod the occasion and heavy his heart! I shall attend yon rites, e'en though my tears blind me!"

Shoving the bottle into his coat pocket, he squared his shoulders and strode bravely through the door. Fortunately, the plate-glass panel shattered outwards, so he escaped with minor lacerations. For a moment he believed that this little misadventure had passed unnoticed, but then, hearing the voices of the publican and his staff shrill in wrath behind him, he scurried across the street through the flood of traffic and into the gateway of a shipyard. A high board fence was between him and his pursuers, and in its concealment he proceeded on his journey, undisturbed by the hue and cry raised upon the thoroughfare.

From time to time he sang, and once, moved to dance, he launched into an airy *pas seul*. He had trod but the first few steps of the measure, however, when he was overcome by an irresistible tendency to spiral. Also, his feet felt heavy—so heavy that he was scarcely able to lift them. Suspecting a trap of some kind—fly paper, perhaps—he waxed righteously indignant.

"Ho, send for the headwaiter!" he cried. "If ye think I'm a mon to soobmit to such horseplay, ye're dom weel mistaken! I'm Muster Colin Glencannon, Esquire, one o' the most influential men in Scotland, and—"

At this point, abruptly, his right foot came up with a viscous "sluck!" and carefully reviewing the situation, he found that he was standing ankle deep in ooze at the river's edge. The ship yard's boundary fence terminated just above the tide mark.

"Dearie me!" he muttered, stepping back to dry ground like a cat on a tarred roof. "I fear this barrier must hae turned a corner unbeknownst to me!" Leaning against the end of it, he proceeded to unwrap the bottle. "Weel, here's to yere meemory, Uncle Jock!" he toasted. "I bocht it as a gift, but noo it's yere monument!"

The word "monument" gave him pause. He wrinkled his brows

in thought. "Monument!" he repeated. "Monument! Aloss, the monument's an item I had completely owerlooked! Naturally, as his sole heir, 'twull devolve upon me to erect a suitable meemorial, but I hae no doot that all such mortuary knickknocks run into a muckle o' money. Oh, dom it, Glencannon; 'tis plain to be seen that yere new-gained status is no' all milk and honey!"

Still gloomily pondering the matter, he waded around the end of the fence and headed across a mud flat. "Marble is the usual thing, o' coorse, but a shoft o' marble is a costly confection! Bronze? Bronze is entirely oot o' the question, judging from the price we had to pay for those three-inch tapered phosphor bushings for the ship. No, it must be something sumple—sumple, deegnified and inexpensive, in accordance wi' the consairvatif tendencies o' the times! What, oh, what cud— Och!"

A sudden shocking agony stabbed his left shin and traveled up and down it in white-hot twinges. He clasped his hands around the injured region and endeavored to hop upon one foot. At the second hop the foot became so deeply embedded in the mud that he sprawled headlong.

"Ah, strange, strange!" he muttered, shading his eyes and scrutinizing the landscape. "Whate'er it was that smote me, it's no here noo. But what cud it hae been and where cud it hae gone? . . . Swith, I've guessed it! It must hae been a boomerang! Ho, be on yere guard, Glencannon; the bushmen are on the rompage again!"

Rising cautiously, he had just leaped forward in a frantic sprint for cover when his right shin was seared with the same sickening anguish.

As before, he went down; as before, the piercing twinges coursed through him like high-tension electric currents. But this time— ah, horror!—he knew their cause. For there, scarcely a yard from his face, reared a giant cobra, hood expanded, ready to strike again!

This, then—this was the end! Mr. Glencannon's eyes closed and his hands clutched convulsively. One of them fastened upon something solid. A bit of driftwood! Lashing out blindly, he felt the club strike an immovable object and shatter in his grasp. Opening his eyes, he saw that the rearing cobra, the immovable object, was in reality the flat, triangular fluke of a kedge anchor. The other fluke was hooked in the mud, this securing a motorboat which lay tethered by a rope some twenty yards out in the stream.

"Hah, so 'twas you, was it?" he rasped, shaking his fist at the offending hardware. "Weel, ye dom treecherous shin breaker, if 'twas no' fer my wealth and social poseetion, I'd leave my mark on ye, I wud! The idea o'—er—er—"

Suddenly his annoyance gave way to gratification. "Why, 'tis the vurra thing!" he cried. "The anchor, emblem o' security, symbol o' rest and repose in the last quiet harbor o' life's journey! Ho, Glencannon, here's Uncle Jock's monument all ready for the taking, wi'oot the expense o' a single soliturra farthing!" He cut the line several fathoms above the rusty mud hook and rigged it into a sling by which to support the burden on his back. With staggering footsteps he set off toward Dumbarton Road. The motorboat, freed from its tether, went spinning merrily downstream toward the Firth of Clyde.

"A coat o' gilt will mak' it the brawest monument in the kirk yard!" gloated Mr. Glencannon. "Though aluminium paint wud be less extrovagant, as I can snoffle a tin o' it when I go aboord the *Inchcliffe Castle* to say my farewells tomorrow. Also, I must remember to filch a bit o' bross upon whuch I can engrave a suitable inscription. H'm—r—for instance—let's see:

> *"Here rot the bones o' J. Glencannon,*
> *Whom grim Death from amongst us took.*
> *His stormy voyage through Life is finished*
> *And noo he'll never drag his hook."*

"Losh, there's a pairfect epitoft! Ah, ye've talent, m'lad—rare talent—I've told ye so a mullion times!"

Having plodded through the marsh and regained the highway, he found the going easier. To be sure, the rope cut into his shoulders and the anchor chafed large areas of his back, but so cheerful were his spirits that he was oblivious of physical discomfort. When he turned into crowded Greenock Avenue, however, he com-

menced encountering difficulties. Several times the wide, projecting anchor flukes hooked and maimed innocent bystanders, and
once, in the course of a sudden lurch, the starboard stock smashed
an apothecary's window. The din was considerable. Perceiving
a policeman approaching on the gallop, Mr. Glencannon dodged
around the corner and strolled unconcernedly down a side street.

Arrived at the terminal, he set about hoisting the anchor into a
Milngavie bus.

"Hold hard, muster!" the conductor objected. "Ye canna bring
yon giant's pick ox or whate'er it is in here! What d'ye think we're
running—an iron-monger's lorry?"

Mr. Glencannon considered him severely. "Yoong mon," he
said, "were it no' for my belief in the wisdom o' that wise old
provairb, 'A soft dancer turneth away wrath,' I'd smosh yere dom
ugly snout for ye. This object is no' a pick ox; it's no' a tool o' any
sort. It's a monument, a meemorial, a work o' art, and I insist
upon yere transporting it."

After much bickering, it was agreed that the anchor be carried
on the roof. Assisted by the conductor, he boosted it aloft and
made fast the end of its rope to the railing of the baggage rack.
Unfortunately, in the course of the boosting a window was broken.

"Faw!" he snorted. "Whate'er has come ower the glass in this
town, anyway? It's as brittle as glass!"

The beginning of the journey was uneventful. In the outskirts
of Glasgow, Mr. Glencannon leaned forward and observed to an
elderly gentleman that the country thereabouts looked rather like
the outskirts of Glasgow. The elderly gentleman changed his seat.
Mr. Glencannon moved along and sat beside him, but finding the
other to be discourteous even to the point of refusing a snifter
from the bottle, he fell to romping up and down the aisle and
knocking off hats. Tiring of this he recited Gunga Din, complete
with practical illustrations of the drinking scenes, and then
launched into a highly technical discourse on the Pirie-Lossington
acid-vapor method of removing scale from boilers.

Approaching the long, steep hill beyond which lies Milngavie,
the chauffeur hit up a lively clip. At the foot of the grade, where
the tram rails cross the highway, there was a sudden jerk, a violent
rending, and lo! the bus roof was whisked away like a topsail by a

typhoon.

There was a crash in the road behind them, shouts, and the shrill of brakes. The crew and most of the passengers piled out in consternation.

"Ah, noo, see here, conductor!" complained Mr. Glencannon, standing on his seat and leaning over into the great outdoors. "Fresh air is one thing, but too much o' it will suffice. And another thing, ye scut—what hae ye done with my anchor?"

"Here's yere anchor back here!" the conductor retorted. "Aye, dom, ye've ruint the bus, ye hae, and twull cost ye a pretty penny before ye've heard the end o' it! If ye want yere nosty anchor, get doon and lug it yersel', for ye'll ride no langer with us!"

"Haw, hae no fear!" Mr. Glencannon assured him, vaulting over the side. "I'd no' ride another step in yere rickety auld dump cart, so just put that in yere smipe and poke it!" Walking back, he found the remains of the roof lying in the ditch. The rope was stretched taut from the baggage rack to the anchor, which was securely hooked under the tram rail. "Ah, a bit o' luck, I call it!" he exulted. "Why, if it hadna caught the track and yanked the roof off, I'd ne'er hae known it had boonced owerboard. Weel, 'tis only a stroll from here to Milngavie, so I micht as weel get gaeing."

Though the distance was short, the hill was steep and the cargo heavy. After a hundred yards, he found himself so sorely tuckered that he sank down in the grass at the wayside to regain his strength. He lay studying the anchor and wondering how best to mount it upon the sepulcher. "Naturally, a peedestal wud set it off to the neatest advontage," he decided. "But there again the ugly question o' finonce intrudes itsel'." Just then his glance fell upon a bowlder in the high grass beside him. It was perhaps three feet in diameter, rounded and smoothed by the weather of the centuries. He balanced the anchor upon the stone and stood off to view it like a connoisseur before a Rodin. "The vurra thing!" he declared. "Why, ye'd swear 'twas made to order! . . . Er—m'm. . . .

> "*Rest ye tranquil, Uncle Jock;*
> *Though ye strive from noo till Dumsday,*
> *Ye will never budge this rock!*"

This epitaph was more truth than poetry, as Mr. Glencannon discovered when he tried to roll the bowlder out into the road. Once there, moreover, it exhibited a perverse and almost irresistible tendency to coast back down the hill. He dug his toes into the macadam; he sweated, groaned and strained; the veins of neck and forehead stood out like bunches of grapes. "Push, Glencannon, push!" he panted. "If it eludes ye the noo, ye'll be squashed beneath it lik' a caterpillow!" Fortunately, he was able to block it with the anchor; then, jamming a fluke beneath it, crowbar fashion, he found that he could make some forward way. Inch by inch, he levered the great stone up the slope. His muscles ached. He had a scorching thirst. But the summit was attained at last.

Mopping his brow, he gazed down into the valley where lay the town of Milngavie. Through the still, warm air of the June day he heard the solemn tolling of a bell. He shaded his eyes and watched a line of carriages slowly approaching the graveyard of the ivy-grown church at the foot of the hill.

"Come, come, ye must hurry!" he urged himself, falling to work again.

On the down grade his problem, though reversed, was even more difficult than before. Now the bowlder seemed determined to roll merrily on its way. He tied the rope around it; then, straddling the anchor and bracing backward with his full weight, he managed to keep the procession under a fair degree of control.

Half down the hill, the slant of the road increased. Despite his efforts, he felt himself walking faster and faster; felt the walk turn to a trot, the trot to a gallop and the gallop to a wild nightmare stampede. Faster he went, and ever faster. He was covering five yards with every stride. The stone was bouncing high into the air. He saw an ornamental iron gate, the entrance to a private driveway, standing ajar some fifty yards farther down the hill.

"Praises be!" he panted. "Pairhops I can check it there!" With a final desperate burst of speed, he managed to hook the anchor into the iron grille. The rope snapped taut and tore the portal from its hinges, whereupon gate, rope, rock and anchor went careering down the road until halted by a tree.

"Ah, whurra, more trouble!" gasped Mr. Glencannon. "How I

yearn for the guid auld days lik' this morning when I was penniless but carefree! Aloss, we rich! Our obligations! Our reesponsibilities! For instance, for example, what am I to do aboot this gate? It's not a bad bit o' ironmongery but—but—why, losh! I can mak' it part o' the meemorial! Aye, Gates Ajar, no less. Wait—ahem. . . .

> *"Oh, he has gone to his heavenly home,*
> *Has canny Uncle Jock.*
> *For once he's left his gate ajar,*
> *So ye need no' pick the lock!"*

"Oh, needn't we?" said a gruff voice behind him, "Well, here's a lock that even you can't pick! . . . Put the handcuffs on him, Campbell!"

Wheeling, Mr. Glencannon saw four husky gentlemen descending from an automobile upon the door of which was stenciled GLASGOW METROPOLITAN POLICE. "You're wanted, mister!" said one of the newcomers. "You've done enough mischief for today. We've had nineteen telephone complaints about ye in the last two hours, and if ye don't go quiet—"

"Ho, tak' care, officer; I give ye fair warning!" cried Mr. Glencannon, propping up the gate and thumbing his nose over it. "Ye see me here safe in the sonctity o' my ain private domain, and ye dare no' illegally violate the threshold wi'oot a search warrant! A Briton's home is his castle, so come in and arrest me at yere peril! Phut to ye, I say! Phut, phut, and phut again!"

He attempted disdainfully to slam the gate in the intruder's face, but just then a great lassitude overcame him, and he sagged to the ground in slumber with the gate on top of him. The anchor, jolted loose, joined company with the bowlder in its mad career downhill toward the unsuspecting village of Milngavie.

III

Disturbed by the sound of voices, Mr. Glencannon opened his eyes and found himself in semidarkness. He was reclining upon a hard, narrow and unfamiliar cot beneath a blanket which reeked unpleasantly of disinfectant.

"Aye," a thin voice was cackling, "it's him, richt enough, the shameless, roistering gowk!"

Mr. Glencannon sat bolt upright and beheld a gnarled and gnomelike figure peering at him malevolently through an iron-barred door. His blood froze with horror. "Uncle Jock!" he screamed. "No, no, no, go away! Dinna come haunting me, ye ghost! Help! Help! Police!"

"Police, eh?" sneered the ghost. "Weel, if it's police ye want, dear Nephew Colin, ye've come to the richt shop to find 'em! . . . Aye, hasn't he, Sairjunt MacNab?"

"Indeed he has!" agreed a voice from the corridor. "But noo, sir, do ye plan to press the charges o' attempted murder or not? In view o' the fact that he was one o' yere principal heirs and therefore had everything to gain by preventing the wedding and killing you and the bride, I think he'd get twenty years at hard labor at the vurra least."

"Um," mused the ghost. "So he wud, and so he shud, but in that case I mysel' wud hae to pay for rebuilding the wall o' the kirk where the boulder smoshed it in. No, sairjunt, I willna press the charges. I'll temper justice wi' economy, and I know that my housekeeper, Muss MacDuck—er—I mean to say, my wife, Mussis Glencannon—will agree with me. And so, Colin, I'll leave ye alone with yere conscience, ye treecherous, tarrybreeked thigger, ye!"

The footsteps grew faint in the corridor, and suddenly the light was switched off. Mr. Glencannon settled back in the darkness. His head ached, his back was sore, and his mouth as parched as that of the worn hart which panteth for the water brook. But, strangely enough, his spirits were gay.

"Foosh!" he chuckled, "Muss MacDuck, his housekeeper! Weel, she's ninety-four years auld at least, and noo that he's married her, her monthly wages will be just that much saved for the estate. Be patient, Glencannon, be patient, and think o' the compoond interest!"

STAR DUST AND CORN

EARLY one evening in October of the past year the inhabitants of Catalonia, in Spain, and of the neighboring maritime provinces of France, were witnesses of a strange and awful spectacle. It was at precisely 7:46 that the good citizens of Port Vendres, in the French department of the Pyrenees-Orientales, glanced up from their afterdinner *marcs* and saw that which caused them to look twice. For the clear autumnal heavens were laced and lashed with light as stars streaked madly across in hundreds, in thousands, in myriads, until the regular old stellar standbys were lost in the crazily-rushing barrage. Some of the meteors flashed fast and wild as lightning. Some sped with sinister purposefulness, like tracer bullets. Others drifted slowly as half-becalmed balloons. But all left behind them long red trails of sparks which hung suspended for awhile, dripped bloodily earthward and in falling reluctantly faded.

That night the mistral wind was stirring in the valley of the Rhone and the chill transmontana came hurrying down after it from the cork-oak forests on the Pyrenees. The air of Port Vendres harbor was brisk with the first threat of winter; one could see one's breath in it, and Mr. Glencannon, seeing his own, wondered if it were not, indeed, the explanation of the whole extraordinary phenomenon.

"Swith!" he muttered, resting on the oars of the dinghy which he was rowing uncertainly shorewards from the tramp ship *Inchcliffe Castle*, of which he was Chief Engineer. "I do believe I've stoombled upon a discovery that will reevolutionize the whole science o' astrom-astromon—the stars! Why, sumply by breathing into the air, I increase the visibility the same as with a teelescope! —In other wurrds, the alcohol fumes act as a reflex, convex and dooble-refroctory prismotic lens o' appruximately theerty-two

160

thoosand diometers o' mognification.—That is, o' coorse, if Einstein's colculations are to be accepted, whuch I doot. Noo wait, noo wait, let's vurrify the new Glencannon theory—*Whoosh!*" He puffed out a gust that was redolent of Duggan's Dew of Kirkintilloch and eagerly peered skyward through the vapor. The results were stupendous. "Aye, losh, just look at them! Mullions o' meteors —mullions upon mullions o' them! And noo when I hold my breath I'll wager I canna see a thing!" He closed his lips—and sure enough the flashes, as well as his hiccups, abruptly ceased. More astounding still, even the usual stars vanished and the entire vault of heaven became an inky black void. Still holding his breath he was gloating over this gratifying confirmation of his theory when the dinghy's gunwhale bumped against something solid, and he found that he had drifted under the stern counter of a sailing ship which was completely obstructing his celestial view. The ship was tied up alongside a wharf. Petulantly fending off into the clear with an oar he resumed his respiration and his researches and was chagrined to note that the meteors were streaking overhead even more brilliantly than before.

"Weel, never mind!" he consoled himself, thumbing his nose at the looming black bulk of the windjammer, "it took a vurritable giant's intellect to conceive o' it, all the same!"

Again the dinghy encountered something solid, and as the beam of his flashlight probed the gloom Mr. Glencannon saw the stern of a sardine boat protruding from between the piles of the wharf. It was loaded to the gunwales with round, red objects like small Edam cheeses. Beyond it, deep-hidden in the damp black forest of piles, were two more craft similarly laden.

"Oh, ho!" he muttered. "Oh, ho! There's some kind o' skuldoogery afoot! No doot it's a plot to smoogle Dutch cheeses into . . ."

His suspicious musings were interrupted by a voice from the windjammer's deck. "And lo, ye sinners!" it boomed, "Behold the heavens flash with fire and brimstone in awful warnin' of war! I've let the meteors loose tonight, Brethren, so Hell's all ready to pop! Let us join in singin' that grand old prophetic hymn-tune— 'I Saw the Heavens Drip With Blood'—Ready? One . . . two . . . three!"

A deep chant swelled up into the star-streaked night:

> *"I know the woe the meteor brings*
> *When it on high doth flaming range;*
> *Storm, famine, plague and death to Kings*
> *War, earthquake, flood and direful change."*

"Ho!" gasped Mr. Glencannon. "It is—it must be, the Yonkee shipful o' lunatics and corn whusky we met in Marseels five years ago!" With a stroke of the oars he sent his dinghy clear of the vessel's counter and trained his flashlight on the name on her transom. " '*Flaming Chariot. Savannah.*'—Losh, I knew there cudna be two lik' her! Weel, I've got a little finoncial score to settle with her whuskery skipper; 'twull be lik' squeezing blood oot o' a scone, but the sooner I settle it, the better. On deck, there!" he hailed. "Is the Prophet Ezekiel aboard?"

"He sho' is, Suh, in all his glory, directin' the heavenly fireworks!" replied a voice. "Jes' you-all come for'ard hyah to the ladder and I'll fetch a lantern." As Mr. Glencannon skulled along the barkentine's side, he saw strange Old Testament figures, black-robed and bearded, peering down at him over the rail. The condition of his boat soon attested that a number of these saintly anachronisms chewed tobacco, but suddenly there appeared one who towered head and shoulders above the rest and who, as the lantern beams fell upon the dinghy's occupant, boomed "Well, praises be, if it ain't Bre'r Glencannon, the drunken Scot! How are you, brother, how are you?"

"A-weel, Muster Ezekiel," said Mr. Glencannon with hauteur, negotiating the ladder up the *Flaming Chariot's* side, "as lang as ye've seen fit thus boorishly to libel my condition, why do ye tak' the trooble to osk?"

"Oh, now, shucks!" the Prophet grinned apologetically. "I been so busy steerin' the meteors around the heavens this evenin' that mebbe I didn't choose my words. Sho', sho', I don't really mean that the jag you're totin' now is the same one I seen you with five years ago!"

"O' coorse it's not," said Mr. Glencannon, stepping on deck into the midst of the black-robed whiskery group. "It's no' even appruximately similar. The one yere refairing to was the result o' my being internally lacerated with some o' yere ain fulthy corn whusky, o' whuch I'll have none o' the same this evening, thonk ye! But how are ye yersel,' Sir?"

"Oh, toilin' hard, but I reckon I can't complain! Sho', I done put on two earthquakes in Japan and one in San Salvador since last I seen you and a couple of tidal waves here and there besides. Also I been widdered three times again, but man is born to trouble as the sparks fly upward,—you know what contrary critters the fair sex be! But how do you like the little taste of Hell I've turned loose on high tonight, Brother?—Nifty, hey? Come on aft, and we'll see if we can't scare up a snort of cawn a little less athaletic than that which you was speakin' of. Oh, you needn't be afraid of this batch, Brother—it's smoother'n the milk of Georgia's hummin' birds buzzin' in the summer sunshine! Shadrach! Meshach! Abednego!" he bellowed. "Rustle up a fresh jug, one of you! Can't you-all see we got company aboard?"

As Mr. Glencannon followed the Prophet aft along the splintered deck from the seams of which the caulking protruded in lines of fuzz, he glanced aloft at the rotting rigging, the rusty chains and the sloppily-furled sails from which streamers of frayed canvas hung like ghosts of drowned mariners and he felt as though he were aboard some spectral ship of the dead.

"Yop!" said the Prophet, reading his thoughts. "She's old, old, old! Clipper-rigged, she was, Baltimore built, and durin' the War Between The States she run the blockade out of Charleston till the Yankees captured her in '63. Sho', I shouldn't wonder but what these very planks might of heard the voice of Dave Farragut damning the batteries of Mobile!"

"Aye, vurra probably," agreed Mr. Glencannon, his knowledge of American history vague and his mind half occupied with plans for collecting his money and half with the strangeness of his surroundings. "In the early days the motor car was a target for much bod longuage." He descended the cabin companionway without bumping his head too badly on the edge of the sliding hatch and settled himself at the table opposite the Prophet. Upon the bulkheads of the lamplit saloon Biblical texts had been painted, and he was dismayed to note that all of them were of a solemn, even a threatening nature. " 'Prepare to meet thy doom,' " he read; " 'The wages of sin is death.' Braw!" he shuddered, turning toward his host, who was just then tilting a gallon jug over his elbow. "Everything aboot this evening, including yere ain prophecies, is o' a distinctly chill and dismal nature. As ye've already said, colomity seems imminent! But teel me, Muster Ezekiel, how is yere private home-made religion getting alang?"

"Oh, I reckon I can't kick about the religion," said the Prophet, raising his tin cup politely. "I invented it, I wrote it and I run it, so it's O.K. in spite of hell.—Incidentally, runnin' a private sea-goin' religion is a dang good way to git a crew to work for nothin', I don't mind tellin' you! Of course once and awhile I have to sorter pep 'em up and impress 'em with a waterspout or a hurricane or sump'n, like them meteors I done turned loose tonight. The only thing is, though, I ain't the Prophet Ezekiel any more. I'm the Prophet Elijah. I changed just after I killed that last jug yesterday evenin', for a divine revelation was vouchsafed unto me, and, zippo!, I seen the light!"

"Ach, to be sure!" nodded Mr. Glencannon, gagging as the corn whisky buffeted his esophagus and squinting his eyes to prevent them from exploding in their sockets. "I thocht I'd (ga-haff! gr-h-h! P-p-pairdon me—this whusky is, as ye say, lik' the milk o' Georgia's buzzards in sunimertime) I thocht I'd noticed a soobtile difference in ye, but I cudna quite put my finger on it. How do ye find it agrees with ye thus far?"

"Sho', I thrive on it!" boomed the Prophet. "The change has done me a world of good! After all, Mr. Glencannon, I really didn't have no business bein' the Prophet Ezekiel in the first place. It was Elijah, not Ezekiel, which rode up to heaven in the flaming chariot, as you'll find set forth in Chapter Two of the second Book of Kings. Well," he spat a sepia gob into a parrot cage which hung conveniently in the corner, "it seemed meet and fitting unto me that as long as this here ship was named 'Flaming Chariot,' I'd orter be named Elijah to go with it.—Especially," he turned and cocked his eye at the disc of star-streaked firmament that was visible through the porthole "—Especially as any minute, now, the whole danged world is libel to go blooey, so it behooves us one and all to have our affairs in order. Savvy?"

"Aye," Mr. Glencannon squirmed uncomfortably at the prospect and hastened to fortify himself with another jolt of corn, "I canna but odmire yere logic. But as lang as the scales had fallen from yere eyes, why did ye no' sumply paint a new name on the ship?"

"Oh, I dunno!" shrugged the Prophet, removing from his beard a minute organism which he cracked beneath his thumbnail and then contemplated intently in the light of the lamp. "There'd of been a lot of legal duck-plucking, I reckon. And besides," he spread his hands resignedly, "we ain't got a drop of paint or a penny to buy it with.—Hell, brother, ain't you heard about the depression?"

"Aloss, indeed I have!" sighed Mr. Glencannon, preparing to drive a wedge into the long-awaited opening. "That was the vurra reason I was so cheered to reecognize yere voice tonicht, despite yere dire prophecies. For ye'll no' be forgetting, Muster Elijah, that ye still owe me the five hoonderd dollars I won from ye that time in Marseels harbor, betting on the rowing race between the crews o' our reespective ships, and noo, with everything doon in the sloomp, I'd be vurra grateful to ye if ye'll kindly hond it ower."

The Prophet Elijah's face melted in a sad and seraphic smile. "Ah, Brother!" his voice throbbed piously, "Ah, my dearly beloved Brother, how I pity thee in thy greed! Knowest ye not that gold is dross? And aside from that, good gosh, didn't I just get through tellin' you I ain't got a lousy cent?—Five hundred bucks, says you?—Haw, haw, haw!"

"Ah, but noo, see here!" protested Mr. Glencannon, beginning to feel his corn. "If the deprussion mak's it impossible for ye to pay, that's one thing, but haw-haw-haw is another! With due respect for yere cloth, I've a vurra guid mind to bosh yere oogly prophetical snout for ye. Do ye octually mean to say ye canna e'en give me summat on account, ye sneeveling scoondrel?"

"Yea verily, I sho' do!" answered the Prophet softly and in the manner which turneth away wrath. "Why, even when we do git a cargo, like you take these here thingumajigs we was lucky enough

to pick up in Barcelona, with the revolution going on and all—
well now, the dang French Custom House says we can't land 'em
here, and the consignor's agent says we've got to take 'em back. He
won't pay us and Jehovah alone knows who will!"

"What thingumajigs are ye refairing to?" asked Mr. Glencannon, obviously downcast but inwardly alert.

The Prophet reached over to a pile of spherical objects wrapped
in red tissue paper which stood on the cupboard, selected one and
rolled it across the table. It was identical with the red, cheese-like
globes which Mr. Glencannon had seen in the hidden sardine boats,
but he gave no sign of recognition. Instead he thumbed a charge
of Black Wool Mixture into his pipe, lit it, and murmured "Aye?
What is it?"

"It's a fruit," the Prophet explained, "though be dam if it looks
it. Pump-granite's the name, or sump'n' such. Well, jest you try to
bite it once and you'll understand the 'granite' part!"

Mr. Glencannon picked up the pomegranate, stripped off the
paper and examined it with seeming casualness. It was the size of
a large apple but several times as heavy. It was covered with what
appeared to be hard, dry calfskin, and from its top protruded the
stump of a thick fuse-like stem. He essayed a vicious snap at it but
his teeth glanced futilely off the leathery surface.

"There, whad I tell you?" chuckled the Prophet. "—Reckon the
French and Spaniards must eat 'em with a can-opener and a hack-
saw. But, well, the whole dam cargo, three thousand crates of 'em,
is layin' out there in the wharf shed, every crate with a French
Custom House seal on it so's we can't open 'em. Tomorrer we've
got to load 'em aboard and take 'em clear back to Spain again."

"But what's amuss with them?" demanded Mr. Glencannon.
"Why canna ye land them here, and why has the French Custom
House gone to the trooble o' sealing them up?"

"Oh, they found some kind of a pest in 'em—sump'n like the
corn borer or the boll weevil.—Afraid it'll spread to the French
orchards, I reckon. Here—"

He tossed across the table a bulletin issued by the Ministry of
Agriculture, printed in English, which read:

From July 22, 1928 until further notice, all oranges, lemons, peaches, pomegranates, pears and other fruit emanating from Spain shall be subject to examination by the Phyto-Sanitary Service of this department to determine the presence or otherwise of the *Aspidiotus perniciosus* ("St. Joseph's Louse") and similar crop-destroying insects. Until such examination is made all fruit (if bulk cargo) must be held aboard the delivering vessel or in lighters; if crated, crates may be landed at wharf side, sealed by the Customs Guards and there held pending report on samples at the shipper's expense and responsibility. Fruit showing evidence of contamination must be removed from French territory within twenty-four hours of receipt of report to that effect. Violation of these regulations will be punished by a fine.

"Weel, dearie me!" said the Engineer, frowning at the paper suspiciously. "As lang as these rules have been in force since Nineteen Twunty-Eight, I shud think yere Sponish consignors wud have had sense enough to mak' sure there was no bugs in their fruit before they shipped it."

The Prophet shrugged. "So should I! But then, of course, hell is popping in Barcelona and them parts, and, well, I reckon they was all so busy shootin' and reverlutin' that they just didn't bother. Oh, these be strange and awful times we're livin' in, Brother Glencannon, and all them there meteors a-zippin' around in the firmament don't bode us a bit of good!

> *"The meteor is Satan's eye*
> *All red with lust it flames on high*
> *While here below the earth drips gore*
> *Of peoples slain in civil war."*

While the other sang, Mr. Glencannon was busy piecing together this and that strange circumstance in this strangest of evenings. Although as a rule which he had learned to his sorrow he could not handle the Prophet's blistering brand of Georgia corn, tonight he felt that it had sharpened his wits to a point almost occult in its ability to penetrate the obscure. There was, he was certain, something fishy afoot. He thought of the boatloads of pomegranates hidden beneath the wharf—but no, his instinct told him that there was bigger game! The Prophet, of course, was not as mad as he seemed—if at all. As for the Spanish shippers blindly dispatching a contaminated cargo clear up from Barcelona, even with the excuse of the revolution, it was incredible! "Revolution!" The word flashed back into his brain like a skyful of meteors, and only with the greatest difficulty was he able to suppress a start. Very deliberately he drained his cup and as he did so the entire plot became clear to him.

The Prophet continued his song:—

> *"Protect us from the meteor*
> *The star of war, the star of gore!*
> *When once it flashes, ruin and*
> *Stark famine follow through the land."*

At the last note Mr. Glencannon banged his tin cup down on the table. "Weel, ye whuskery auld goat, that confirms it!" he shouted with crushing finality. "I've heard enough o' yere pacifistic blether aboot ruin and famine and civil war! Ye're getting rich on war yersel', ye smoogling hypocrite, so noo I'll thonk ye to pay me my five hoonderd dollars withoot delay. And if ye refuse," he leaned forward and shook his fist in the Prophet's beard, "if ye refuse, I'll just stup ashore to the Custom House and teel them aboot the three boatloads o' contraband hidden under yon wharf!"

"Eh!" the Prophet seemed stunned. "Which three boatloads of what did you say? Why, what in the world is eatin' you of a sudden, Brother?"

"Ho, ye dom weel ken whuch three boatloads!" snarled Mr. Glencannon. "The three boatloads o' grenades, that's whuch three boatloads—grenades, bombs for the Sponish reevolutionists, all wropped up in red paper and disguised exockly lik' these pomegranates! Ye've come up here from Barcelona with a buggy cargo ye knew in advonce wud have to be shipped back—and I'll bet that richt noo yere hairy crew is oot there in the wharf-shed prying the bottoms off the crates and packing a dozen-or-so bombs in each withoot disturbing the customs seals on the top! Noturally, when ye get back to Spain, the Sponish customs won't bother to examine them. It'll be domestic cargo returned unopened, and the French seals will be there to prove it!"

The Prophet wilted in his chair and that portion of his countenance not covered with hair turned from red to purple and back to red again. "Well, g-good gosh-a'-mighty!" he stammered at length, and in his tone was awe and reluctant admiration. "I—I guess I got to take my hat off to you, Brother! Why, we've worked this game twice at Sete and once at Agde without a single solitary soul seein' through it—and—and here you-all happen along and tumble to it in less'n an hour!"

Mr. Glencannon acknowledged these tributes to his perspicacity with a bow. "Weel, all that ye say is merely fact," he admitted modestly. "Ye shud have realized at the ootset the utter futility o' trying to diddle a mon who comes from one o' the oldest and most parsimonious families in Scotland. But fronkly, if ye'd no blabbed so much aboot colomity and war and deesolation, I'd ne'er have guessed yere secret. Ye layed it on a bit too thick—aye, ye owerplayed yere part, that was yere trooble! Ye took me for a fool, Sir, the whuch I'm dom weel not! And noo, how oboot paying me my money?"

The Prophet spread his hands helplessly. "Natcherally, I'll pay you!" he said. "I ain't got no alternative. Sho', you don't reckon I want to have my ship confiscated and do a ten year stretch in no French bullpen for arms-smugglin', do you?"

"That," said Mr. Glencannon, "is entirely up to yersel'. I'll waive the accrued interest on the debt in reecognition o' yere hospitolity and because ye'll pay me cash doon in the hond richt here and noo."

Again the Prophet launched a gob at the parrot cage. It was greeted by a flutter of wings and an angry, "Nuts to you, Brother!". "Well," he said, "I ain't got the money here on board, but if you-all'll jest set here and make yourself to home with the jug, I'll mozey across to the agent's office and git it."

Mr. Glencannon wagged his head cannily. "Ah, no ye don't, no ye don't!" he demurred. "I'm too wise an owl to sit here and twiddle my thumbs and let ye calmly sneak oot on me!"

The Prophet scratched his beard. "Okay," he assented. "If you won't trust me, you can go over and git it yourself, then there won't be no arguments. Old Man Douane speaks English, so I'll give you a note to him."

He rooted around in the cupboard and returned with a pencil and paper. "Look," he invited as he wrote, "how's this? 'Please pay to the bearer, Mr. Glencannon, $500 U.S. money or 7500 francs and charge same to my account. Elijah.' "

"That," said Mr. Glencannon, scanning it, "is eeminently sotisfactory. Where can I find the gentlemon?"

"In the office across from the wharf—there's a big sign 'Douane' on the front. Ask for Mr. Sheff D. Douane, the senior partner. And —well, shucks, Mr. Glencannon, I s'pose I'll be back at sea tomorrer, but I hope you'll just join me in one last drink now to show there's no hard feelin'!"

"Glodly!" said the Engineer, filling his cup and raising it on high. "Here's to me, my money and—yere meteors!" He drained it at a draught, gasped for a moment, threw out his chest and stumbled up the stairs.

II

Mr. Glencannon found the agent's building, entered the hall and presented himself at the desk of the attending functionary.

"My guid mon," he said, "I'd thonk ye to present my compliments to Muster Sheff D. Douane and osk him for a moment's interview."

"*Parfaitement, Monsieur,*" said the other. "*Par ici.*"

He led the way across the corridor to an office in the center of which was a small flat desk. Behind the desk was a large round Frenchman.

"A vurra guid evening to ye, my dear Muster Douane," said Mr. Glencannon, with a charming smile. "I won't detain ye but a minute. I understond ye speak English?"

"I do," bowed the Frenchman.

"Then," said Mr. Glencannon, presenting his note, "ye've only to hond me the cash and I'll give ye a receipt. Pleasant weather we're having."

"Er, very," agreed the Frenchman, frowning at the note and reaching for his spectacles. "Er—just what does this mean, Mister

—ah—Glencannon?"

"Weel," replied the Engineer airily, picking up a letter opener from the desk and excavating his nails with it, "it means appruximately what it says. In other wurrds, ye're to hond me ower five hoonderd dollars and charge it to the Prophet Elijah."

"The Prophet Elijah! But my dear Sir!" the Frenchman looked slightly alarmed, "there must be some mistake! Do—do you know who I am?"

"Noo, noo, none o' yere shilly-dallying!" retorted Mr. Glencannon, his ire mounting. "I know who ye are and I know enough aboot ye to have ye thrown into jail. Ye're Muster Sheff D. Douane, the head *serang* o' this nest o' smooglers, and ye'd better no attempt to flim-flom me!"

The Frenchman stiffened. "I am, as you say, *Chef de Douane*— the Chief of the Custom House, as you call it in English. But," he pressed a button; two guards entered, and at his nod seized Mr. Glencannon by the elbows, "—But I also exercise police powers. Therefore I'll just hold you over until the morning, my man, to see whether you are a dangerous lunatic or merely drunk. Perhaps," he tapped his forehead and nodded toward the ceiling, "perhaps it is the meteors!"

"Ho, so that's yere ottitude, is it?" Mr. Glencannon bawled, at the same time kicking in the side panel of the desk. "Weel, ye bondit, there noo remains no doot that ye're involved in the whole cruminal tronsoction! Ye know as weel as I do that there are three boats loaded with Spanish grenades hidden beneath yon wharf, and I know as weel as ye do that ye know it as weel as I do!"

"Naturally I know it," said the *Chef de Douane*. "Those grenades *d'Espagne*—'Spanish Pomegranates,' to translate it into English—came off a ship from Valencia this afternoon and will be landed tomorrow as soon as three thousand crates from *The Flaming Chariot,* which have been approved by the Phyto-Sanitary Service, are removed from the wharf. But—but what about them?"

Mr. Glencannon's mouth opened, but no sound emerged. There was a wild look in his eye.

"*Voilà!*" the *Chef de Douane* nodded to his henchmen, "*Au violon!*"

Some hours later Mr. Glencannon awoke, and in the darkness of his cell lay wondering whether the throbbing in his head was actually due, as it felt, to multiple hammer-dents in his brain pan. Painfully he arose, groped to the narrow barred window and gazed up at the heavens. He even blew his breath towards them; but the meteoric shower had definitely subsided, now, and the old familiar stars were doing business at their old familiar stands.

"Aye," he murmured, picking out the various constellations, "there's puir auld Orion, with his sword belt, though it looks more lik' a truss. And there's the Pleiades, the six ancient plotinum blondes who donce in the heavenly nicht-club o' the univairse. And there's the Dipper—the Big Dipper—the constellation whuch all Glencannons are born under. And speaking o' dippers, guid losh, what a frichtful theerst corn whusky leaves a mon!—'Corn'? Brr!—They oucht to call it 'bunion'!"

Just then, from out of the still cold night, came the chant of many voices. Mr. Glencannon strained to catch the words, but though he could not distinguish them clearly, they seemed to run:—

> *"There's madness in the unleashed star,*
> *Its flaming path misleads afar.*
> *So do not trail the meteor*
> *And if you do—*
> *Haw!*
> *Haw!*
> *Haw!*
> *Haw!"*

THREE LOVESICK SWAINS OF GIBRALTAR

LATE one summer afternoon the S.S. *Inchcliffe Castle* rounded Europa Point into Gibraltar harbor and let go her mud hook just off the coal wharves at the base of the Rock. A fly swarm of bumboats headed for her, their owners bending sweatily to the oar, screaming invective at one another and beseeching the crew of the *Inchcliffe,* gathered along the rails, to "looka-looka-looka, gentlemans; vair fine goods, vair chip price." The merchandise in question consisted of rotten fruit, pink soap, tin razor blades and nickel-plated junk at exorbitant prices, as well as the usual bottled corrosives bearing forged labels of the world's great vineyards and distilleries for which Jack Tar—whose name, signed on the ship's articles, is likely to be Olaf Olafson, Gus Schmidt or merely X—will cheerfully trade his eyeteeth.

Mr. Colin Glencannon, the *Inchcliffe's* chief engineer, emerged upon deck and peered over the side at the cargo of the shallop bumping the plates immediately below him. "Duggan's Dew o' Kirkintilloch," he murmured wistfully. "Yon is the dear familiar label, but I fear 'tis nearly counterfeit, pasted on a bottle o'some hell broth distilled from the dondruff o' the octopus and sweetened with the venom o' the cobra. Weel, I'll have to nurse my thirst till I go ashore to congrotulate Cousin Douglas on his engagement. But then—but then—"

His anticipatory musings were interrupted by a renewed burst of shouting from the bumboats as into their bobbing midst there plowed a new arrival. This craft, propelled by a terrified Spaniard, was so heavily laden aft that its bow rose clear of the water. The reason for this was a passenger of colossal proportions, clad in the brave bright uniform of the Argyll and Dumbarton Highlanders, who sat sprawled in the stern sheets in a basket of Malaga grapes. This giant was sobbing garbled fragments of a song about a heart bowed down by weight of woe, and beating time with a bottle. Suddenly spying Mr. Glencannon, he lurched half erect, bellowed "Cousin Colin!" in a tragic basso, and then collapsed back into the grapes with a mighty squashing sound.

"Cousin Dooglas!" Mr. Glencannon winced as he returned the greeting. "I got yere post card aboot yere great hoppiness just before we left Naples! But come aboord, dear lad, and teel me what in the world's the motter with ye!"

After some slight unpleasantness with the boatman, who demanded payment for a quart of whisky and a stick of shaving soap which he claimed his passenger had eaten under the impression that it was nougat, Mr. Glencannon succeeded in assisting his kinsman over the side. The boatman headed back, whining plaintively through a broken nose.

"Swith, Cousin Colin," sighed the Highlander, leaning against a stanchion and wringing grapejuice from the tail of his kilt, "I come to ye sore beset and in a muck o' trouble. But flood is blicker than thud is flicker fl—" A great sob shook him and he wilted upon Mr. Glencannon's shoulder.

"Noo, noo, control yersel', Dooglas; ye've imbibed too much o' yon bumboat bilge," the engineer admonished. "As ye say, the ties o' blood are strong, and if ye're in trouble o' any sort—except o' coarse, finoncial—I'll do my best to help ye oot. If ye'll just kindly stond off my foot wi' yere domn great hobnailed boots, ye can unburden yere soul to sumpathetic ears."

Cousin Douglas took three steps backwards, two sideways, and brought up abruptly against the rail. He expelled a long breath and several soap bubbles. "Cousin Colin," he blurted, "the mact o' the fatter of fact is, her domn father has slondered me to her. Though I'm sure she still loves me, she's—she's thrun me doon!"

Mr. Glencannon pursed his lips beneath his walrus mustache and nodded judicially. "Weel, I'd already deduced that something had slipped, but do ye pull yersel' together and give me all the details. Who is she, for exomple?"

"Her name," said Cousin Douglas, "is Clematis Mahoney, and she's the daughter o' Sergeant Major Marty Mahoney, o' the Sixty-Seventh Royal Garrison Artillerillerill—er—wait, wait, I

can hondle it!—illery. Here"—he groped in his breast pocket—
"here ris ser snopshot."

Mr. Glencannon considered the photograph critically. "Vurra
attroctive, vurra attroctive," he murmured. "What are these things
in the foreground?"

"Teeth," said Cousin Douglas, peering over his shoulder. "Pairhops I shud hae explained it to ye. That other part, there, is the
drain pipe o' the veronda."

"Ah, precisely!" nodded Mr. Glencannon. "The camera doesn't
lie. And as lang as it doesn't, there remains no doot that the owner
o' this uniformed and chevroned arm whuch she's holding—the
rest o' whom ye've so carefully scissored off the picture—is a corporal in the Royal Garrison Artillery. A corporal and"—he nudged
the other slyly—"yere rival! Am I richt, Cousin Dooglas—am I
richt?"

The Highlander scowled, and the effect was that of a thunder-
cloud's shadow falling upon a shoulder of raw prime beef.

"Aye!" he said. "Richt ye are! A corporal, a newly promoted
corporal—a domn conceited young smarty by the name o' Alf
Chatterton. And here am me—my—I, twunty years in the King's
sairvice, with the Mons Star, throrty-five furreign-sairvice ribbons,
a hoonderd 'n' foorty-three battle clasps and eighty-two wound
stripes. Er—weel, at least I've been recommended for them—that
is, I shud have been!"

"Exockly!" Mr. Glencannon nodded. "Ye've everything in yere
favor, so I fail to see why ye've let this other lad cut ye oot. And
besides, as ye say, he's only a vurra junior corporal, while you,
Dooglas, are a vurra senior sergeant."

A sob escaped Cousin Douglas. Hesitantly he extended his arm
and nodded toward the sleeve. There, where sergeant's stripes
should have been, Mr. Glencannon saw only a few ends of snipped-
off threads.

"Dooglas!" he gasped. "Dooglas! D'ye mean to say—"

"I mean to say I'm nowt but a private, as ye see!" bellowed the
giant. "I've—I've been rejewced to the ronks! Yon squirt o' a
Chatterton is noo my superior officer, and when I meet him in The
French Poodle tonight, I'll smosh his nosty smirking mug for him!"

"Oh, deary me," said Mr. Glencannon. "But why did they re-jewce ye, Dooglas?"

"For being drunk," explained the Highlander. "Aye, I got drunk because I was hoppy, I lost my stripes because I was drunk, I lost my girl because I lost my stripes, and noo I'm drunk again because I lost my girl. Cousin Colin, I want ye to go to see her parents—to intercede for me—to help me win her back!"

Mr. Glencannon glanced again at the photograph of Miss Clematis Mahoney and shuddered. "Weel, fronkly, Dooglas, I canna help but feel that in some ways ye're luckier than ye realize. How lang had ye been keeping company with her?"

"For months and months! Aye, I loved her e'en before she'd got the letter."

"Got whuch letter, Dooglas?"

"The letter from the solicitors in Liverpool, aboot her aunt eating the tinned salmon. The tin was rusty, the salmon was musty, and noo her number's up. Sairves her richt, the auld skinflint! Why, if I had a foortune o' ower two thoosand poonds, I'd no' eat tinned salmon or e'en tinned angels. I'd—"

"Two thoosand poonds!" gasped Mr. Glencannon. "Two thoosand poonds! Ye mean she's aboot to inherit her aunt's money? Great swith, ye lummox, why did ye no' say so before? Come, Dooglas, come; we must get ashore at once! . . . Bumboat ahoy-y!"

II

Arrived at the Commercial Wharf, Cousin Douglas commenced mumbling that he needed sleep, so Mr. Glencannon led him into The French Poodle, an establishment on the Ramps much frequented by noncoms of the Garrison Artillery, and assisted him to arrange himself on a settee in the corner of the bar parlor. The Highlander lapsed into slumber at once. Mr. Glencannon was about to take his departure when he saw a bottle protruding from the other's sporran. Capturing it, he drew the cork and sniffed the contents. "Braugh!" he shuddered. "More o' that bumboat bilge wi' the Duggan's label! He must have stolen it on the trip in." Prudently shoving the bottle under the bench, he went on his way.

Hurrying across the town and through the Gardens, he came at length to a little street called Balaklava Row. On the lamppost at the corner was a sign:

MARRIED QUARTERS
67TH REGT. R.G.A.
NO LOITERING

Mr. Glencannon had observed this sign in the course of previous visits to Gibraltar; its insinuations had always rankled him, but today he nodded at it cheerily.

"Richt ye are!" he chuckled. "There'll be 'no loitering,' because there's no time for it. After all, I'll be sailing day after tomorrow, and I must mak' hay while the sun shines. Noo let me see, let me see; No. 3 is the address, and ower the way it is."

No. 3 Balaklava Row was one of a double rank of red-brick cottages so exactly alike in their ugliness that they could only have been built by military engineers, and in Victoria's reign at that. Each was surrounded by a border of grass and a whitewashed fence which seemed to choke it like the Sunday collar of a steve-dore. In the garden of No. 3 a young lady was beating a strip of carpet. The carpet was sending great clouds of dust up into the summer twilight, but through them Mr. Glencannon recognized the damsel of the snapshot. He was dismayed to note that, as usual, the camera had not lied.

Bolstering his courage with thoughts of the two thousand pounds, he leaned over the fence and doffed his cap politely. "Guid afternoon," he said. "I believe I have the pleasure o' addressing Muss Clematis Mahoney?"

The young lady paused in her labors and surveyed him with evident distaste. "The pleasure is orl yours," she replied.

"Haw, copital, copital!" the engineer applauded, stepping through the gateway. "Wit and beauty seldom go hond in hond, but when they do—weel, 'tis a pity for the hond to wield a rug beater! Pairmit me, Muss Mahoney!" He was about to seize the rattan when, with a might full-arm saber swing, she whacked it stingingly across his coattails.

"Stand yer ground!" she snapped. "Keep yer 'ands orff! I'll teach yer that no narsty civilian can myke free with a 'igh-ranking non-commissioned horfficer's daughter!"

"Aye, pairdon, pairdon!" Mr. Glencannon apologized, hastily retreating with his hands pressed behind him. "There, see? I dinna mean ye harm! Oh, quite the contrary! My name is Glencannon, muss, and I—"

At the name, Miss Mahoney emitted a piercing scream and launched into a fit of hysterics.

From the house came a rumble and clatter like that of a battery of field guns unlimbering for action, and down the veranda steps hurtled a lady who might well have posed as model for the Rock of Gibraltar itself. In one hand she clutched an unsheathed bayonet and in the other a raw mutton chop.

"Yus, Clematis, wot is it, dearie?" she demanded, thrusting her bulk between her daughter and Mr. Glencannon, and scowling down upon him. " 'Oo is this 'ere walrus and wot's 'e been up to, hey?" She brandished the chop threateningly, realized what it was, and dropped it into her apron pocket. "Well?" she demanded, presenting the bayonet to his throat. " 'Oo are ye, mister? Speak hup!"

Mr. Glencannon swallowed his Adam's apple out of the range of the bayonet point and assumed his most charming and magnetic smile.

"Oh, why, Mussis Mahoney," he said, "I'm surprised ye're no expecting me! As soon as I heard the news, in Naples, I sent ye a cablegrom. Oh, guid heavens!" He trembled with sudden apprehension. "Ye dinna mean to teel me ye didna get it? Ye dinna mean to say I'm—I'm too late?"

Mrs. Mahoney lowered her bayonet. "Cablegram?" she repeated. "Why, I never got no cablegram in orl my life! 'Oo are yer, that's wot I want to know?"

"My name is Glencannon, moddum," he answered, bowing his head in shame. " 'Tis an auld name, an honest name and I shud be prood to bear it despite him! But"—he dashed the tears from his eyes—"he—he has drogged it in the dust! Ah, he's the black sheep o' the family, Cousin Dooglas Glencannon is! When he wrote

me in Naples that Muss Clematis had succoombed to his blondishments and consented to be his bride, I saw where my juty lay.
At frichtful expense I sent ye a cablegrom o' warning. At e'en
more frichtful expense I've come here the noo in pairson to con-
fairm it."

Slowly a look of understanding dawned upon Mrs. Sergeant
Major Mahoney's large face. "Oh!" she said apologetically. "Oh,
why, you poor man! Now I hunderstand yer, Mr. Glencannon!"
The bayonet slipped from her fingers, and though the engineer
leaped sideways as the point of it grazed his foot, she caught his
arm and dragged him toward the house. "Come in, come in!" she
urged cordially. "Oh, 'ow can I ever apolergize fer the way Clematis
'as treated yer? . . . No, you stay houtside, Clematis! Stop yer
crying and beat them carpits! Yer've done enough 'arm fer today!"

Once in the parlor, Mrs. Mahoney tossed the mutton chop into
a polished-brass howitzer-cartridge case which had the scene of
the Nativity painted on the side of it, and waved Mr. Glencannon
to a violet plush armchair. "Yus, yus, I see it orl now," she said.
"Yer wanted to bryke up the match between Douglas Glencannon
and my daughter! Well, I can't never tell yer 'ow gryteful I am
to yer fer yer kindness, Mr. Glencannon; even though we orleady
broke the 'ole thing orff as soon as 'e lost 'is sergeant's stripes fer
drunkenness. Yus, we told 'im never to dock on our door agyne!"

"Ah, thonk heavens!" breathed Mr. Glencannon. "Ye've saved
yer daughter from the clutches o' a wastrel, a rakehell and a
foortune hunter o' the deepest sty!"

"Well, well, well, is 'e really as bad as that?" she gasped. "I was
saying only yesterday that if 'e could get 'is stripes back, I wouldn't
mind 'im calling on 'er agyne. But in view of what yer say—ugh,
no! The only throuble is, I'm afryde 'e's broke 'er 'eart."

Mr. Glencannon dismissed her fear with a wave of the hand.
"A brukken heart will heal," he said, "but a ravished foortune,
never!"

"True!" agreed Mrs. Mahoney. "But she 'asn't really got Aunt
Jezebel's money yet, because it tykes tinned salmon a long time
to work. In fack, I arsked the medical sergeant about it only
yesterday, and 'e says 'as 'ow in Egypt' and Iraq 'e's seen it tyke as

long as two months. But then, of course, 'e's talking about ordinary gov'ment rations."

"Two months!" said Mr. Glencannon. "Ah, my dear Mussis Mahoney, ye've snotched yere daughter from the clutches o' a foortune hunter in the vurra nick o' time. I mysel' am heir presumptive to a conseederable foortune and have lang been a prey to adventuresses and vompires seeking to snoffle it. I know how they operate. For ye see"—he coughed diffidently—"in addition to my present comfortable means, I expect ere lang to inherit the vast wealth o' my uncle, Muster Jock Glencannon, Esquire, o' Milngavie, one o' the most eminent misers in Scotland."

"Indeed?" and Mrs. Mahoney pricked up her ears. "Well, I seen as soon as I set eyes on yer that yer were a man o' substance, Mr. Glencannon. Er"—she leaned forward slightly—"do yer 'appen to be married, if I might myke so bold as to arsk?"

"No, moddum, I'm a lonely botchelor," he sighed, but it was obvious that the news pleased her. "I'm a wanderer, a globe trotter, forever traveling from one great copital to another in my yacht, the *Inchcliffe Castle,* seeking by means o' study and culture to fill the void in my heart whuch ought to be occupied by a wife, a home, a loudspeaker and a litter o' streectly legitimate offsprings. And—oh, yes, Mussis Mahoney, I almost forgot to mention to ye that I'm a hoonderd per cent teetotaler, shunning alcohol in all its forms."

"Well, good lawks, yer a regular paragon of orl the virtues, I must say!"

"Aye, and I'm generous to a fault," said Mr. Glencannon modestly.

Mrs. Mahoney sat back and beamed upon him with appraisal and approval.

"Mr. Glencannon," she said at length, "yer've showed yerself to be a true friend of the family. I can see 'ow a gent of yer experience and character can be a gryte 'elp to Sergeant Major Mahoney and I regarding about planning Clematis's future. She's a charming slip of a girl, like yer've olready seen, and we wants 'er to marry well. Just now—er"—she hesitated—"there's a young man my 'usband brought around 'ere 'oo's just been permoted corporal—Alf Chatteron, 'is nyme is—wot's paying 'er court. But just between us, Mr. Glencannon, 'e's only a calf fer orl 'is conceit, and 'e' asn't myde much progress as far as Clematis 'erself is concerned."

"Aweel, fronkly," said Mr. Glencannon, "I'm vurra glod to hear it. In the feerst place, moddum, I feel that yere daughter shud mak' a more advontageous motch than is possible in the army. In the seecond place"—he blushed and shuffled his feet in callow embarrassment—"in the seecond place, I—I— Ah, foosh, Mussis Mahoney, I canna say what I want to say!"

"Oh, go on, do!" she urged him.

"No," he said firmly, "No! I really must leave ye the noo and look up my runagate cousin. And besides, 'twud no' be genteel o' me to speak what's on my mind after such short acquaintance. Pairhops tomorrow—"

"Yus, tomorrow, by orl means!" gushed Mrs. Mahoney. "Come and tyke a dish o' tea with us, do! I'll 'ave Clematis byke a kyke. Oh, she's fair wonderful at cooking, that girl is. The sergeant major's orff juty tomorrow arfternoon and I want you to give 'im yer views about Clematis not marrying a soldier. Yer see"—a troubled look crossed her face—"well, frankly, my 'usband is very strong fer a military marriage, and now yer cousin is out of the running, 'e's very strong fer Corporal Chatterton."

"I'll be delichted to discuss it with him, and have no doot I can mak' him see the licht o' reason." Mr. Glencannon rose to take his leave. "Haw, wud ye believe it, Mussis Mahoney, ye really mak' me feel lik' a member o' the family?"

III

As Mr. Glencannon cut back through the town toward The French Poodle, he was more than a little pleased with himself. "Progress!" he chuckled. "Progress! Cousin Dooglas is clearly eliminated and noo nobody remains but this scut o' a Corporal Alf Chatterton. By hook or by crook, I must fix him so he'll lose his corporal's stripes. 'By crook,' preferably—aye, the crook o' his elbow!"

He found Cousin Douglas still wrapped in slumber, tossing fitfully and muttering to himself. "I dinna care if ye're the Archbishop o' Dundee," he was saying, "ye've stolen my umbrella!"

Mr. Glencannon peered apprehensively beneath the bench, but the bumboat whisky was still there. He settled himself at the table, ordered a drink and looked around the smoke-filled room. It was now nearly ten o'clock and the place was doing a rushing business; a double rank of artillerymen and Highlanders were standing at the bar, an electric piano was hurling forth large quantities of galloping melody, and in the center of the floor, numerous gentlemen in the uniforms of His Majesty's forces were treading a hobnailed measure with dark-eyed daughters of La Linea de la Concepcion. The engineer was just about to call the waitress and inquire if Alf Chatterton was present when the street door opened to admit a group of new arrivals. One of them, a raw and ruddy young artillery corporal, spied Cousin Douglas, sneered superciliously, and strode across the room.

"Well, strike me if yer ain't blotto agyne!" he addressed the sleeping Highlander. "Yus, ye're blind to the wide!" Then, turning, he winked at Mr. Glencannon. "Pal of yours?"

"Hardly," replied Mr. Glencannon with an indifferent shrug. "He hoppens to be my cousin, but ye must odmit it's through no fault o' mine."

Cousin Douglas stirred uneasily. "Ye can stop dog fights with an umbrella too," he mumbled. "Stick it betwixt 'em and snop it open."

"Lawks, 'ear 'im!" chuckled the corporal. "Would yer believe it, it's the third time 'e's been tiddely this week! If it wasn't fer 'is twenty years' service, they wouldn't 'ave stopped with tyking 'is stripes. No, sir, they'd 'ave chucked 'im into the clink."

Mr. Glencannon nodded sadly. "Aye," he agreed. "There's no doot he desairves it. I beg yere pairdon, young mon, but do ye hoppen to be Corporal Alf Chatterton, by any chance?"

"I do, but there's no chance about it," replied the other grandly. "They permoted me to be corporal because I'd ought to be corporal, and that's just why I am a corporal. Yus, sir, Corporal Alpheus Chatterton, at yer service!" He clicked his heels and saluted smartly.

". . . Eight steel ribs and a bit o' a black rag are all ye need to mak' an umbrella," came the sepulchral voice from the bench.

"Ah, foosh, corporal, pay no attention to him!" Mr. Glencannon dismissed the interruption, at the same time wringing the other's hand. "Sit doon, sit doon, lad! After all the guid things I've heard aboot ye today, it's a pleasure indeed to mak' yere pairsonal acquaintance!"

Corporal Chatterton's bulging chest bulged still farther as he settled into the proffered chair. "Well, I'm orlways glad to 'ear good things about myself," he admitted blandly. "Just 'oo did yer 'ear the latest reports from—my horfficers or only from my pals?"

"From neither," replied Mr. Glencannon. "From neither—and from better than either! This afternoon, ye see, I had the difficult tosk o' calling upon Mussis Sergeant Major Mahoney, to apologize to her for the way yon droonken oaf has behaved toward her charming and talented little daughter. While I was there, the guid Mussis Mahoney confided to me the great hoppiness whuch is shortly to be yours and—and—weel, I hope ye'll honor me the noo by drinking a drop o' whusky to the bride, Corporal Chatterton."

". . . The Joponese, however, mak' them oot o' split bomboo and paper," said Cousin Douglas.

"Whisky?" repeated Corporal Chatterton. "Well, rather! A man on private's pay don't often get a bite at anything better than beer, and of course I won't draw my first noncom's screw till next Friday a fortnight. Yus, indeed, sir, I'd relish a spot of whisky no end!"

"Pairfict!" said Mr. Glencannon, reaching under the bench and dragging forth the bottle of bumboat bilge. "Ye're aboot to mak' the acquaintance o' whusky in its most deleectable form. Noo, this bottle o' Duggan's Dew o' Kirkintilloch"—he placed it reverently at the center of the table—"is one o' the last remaining o' a cherished private stock whuch has been in the Glencannon family for ceenturies. We keep the priceless auld stuff under lock and key until one o' the clan is aboot to wed. Then—then— Weel, corporal"—there was a catch in his voice—"ye can imogine my feelings, after having brocht this ceremonial bottle half way aroond the world, to lairn aboot our family's shame."

"When the wind blaws it inside oot, sumply turn aroond and let it blaw it back again," soliloquized the sleeper on the bench.

"There, ye see?" Mr. Glencannon appealed, at the same time flagging the waitress. "Losh, Corporal Chatterton, may none o' yere babies be dipsomoniacs! . . . F-s-s! . . . Here, muss! Please fetch a corkscrew, two glosses and a bottle o' arrack. . . . I'll leave ye to drink the whusky by yersel', corporal. For sentimental reasons, whuch I know ye'll appreciate, I—ugh—no, I cudna touch a drap o' it!"

"Well, yer sentiments does yer proud," said Corporal Chatterton, eyeing the brimming glass which the waitress had poured for him. " 'Ere's to the blushing bride and the 'andsome bridegroom! Hupf! Hapf!" He unfastened his collar hooks and wiped his eyes. "Why, d'yer know, this stuff is a bit of orl right! It tystes something like hornets boiled in boot polish in a slop pail."

Mr. Glencannon smiled as he gulped his arrack. "Aye, that's because it's ower four ceenturies auld," he explained unctuously. "Four hoonderd years—think o' it! When that whusky was laid doon, the Rock o' Gibraltar was only a pebble, the giant thesaurus was roaming the earth, and men and women were riding aboot on velocipedes." He poured himself another jolt of arrack.

"Well, it certainly 'as one 'ell of a muzzle velocity," agreed Corporal Chatterton. "In fack, I wish I 'ad time to myke this bottle larst. But at midnight"—he glanced at his bright new chromium wrist watch—"at midnight sharp, I've got to tyke my men up on the Rock, so I 'aven't any time to wyste. We've target practice at sunrise in the morning."

"Her Mojesty the Queen invariably carries one," said Cousin Douglas, saluting in his sleep.

"Target proctice? Ho, I envy ye!" said Mr. Glencannon. "I mysel' am a famous shot with firearms o' all descriptions, including bross knuckles. When I was a boy, I used to think nothing o' shooting the eye oot o' a tomcat at five hoonderd yards with a .22 pustol."

"Twenty-two pistol!" scoffed Corporal Chatterton, replenishing his glass. "Oh, 'oo the 'ell wants to bother with a .22 pistol? We—er—I—why, tomorrow morning, I'm going to fire a fourteen-inch rifle!"

Mr. Glencannon's shoulders shook with patronizing mirth. "A foorteen-inch rifle!" he scoffed, measuring the distance between his hands. "Haw, guid losh, corporal; d'ye mean to teel me that His Mojesty's troops are rejewced to playing with miniature pop-guns whuch e'en the Boy Scoots would scorn with derision? A foorteen-inch rifle, to be sure! Oh, haw, haw, haw! Noo I under-stond why ye're so cautious aboot drinking that whusky. Whusky is a mon's drink!"

"Oh, yus?" retorted Corporal Chatterton truculently. "Well, just to show yer that I'm a man [gluck] there goes a whole ruddy tumblerful, see? And just to show yer agync, I'll drink a [gluck] another! And as fer that fourteen-inch rifle yer giggling about, let me tell yer that fourteen inches ain't the length of it, it's the bore! Yus, a fourteen-inch bore—now wot do yer think of that?"

"Swith, the Royal Garrison Artillery can boast the biggest bore in the world!" replied Mr. Glencannon heartily. "Come, have an-other drink, corporal, and tell me more aboot this mommoth popgun o' yours."

"Don't call it a popgun!" cried Corporal Chatterton, pounding his fist on the table. "It's a cannon, a cannon—a Mark XI Vickers fuitreos rifle, the very larst word in 'eavy hartillery! It's a thirteen-point-six, to be hexact, or three 'undred and fifty millimeters. It's sixty feet, three inches long from muzzle to breech, and it'll throw a four 'undred 'n' fifty pound Mark XIV shell thirty-one thou-sand yards, or happroximately eighteen miles. Up there on the Rock, we—"

". . . His Royal Highness, the Juke of York, carries a silk one whuch has an electric floshlicht cunningly concealed in the hondle," announced Cousin Douglas oracularly.

"Oh, shut up, do!" snapped Corporal Chatterton. . . . "Up there on the Rock we've got twenty of them guns in emplacements between O'Hara's Tower, which is thirteen hundred and sixty-three feet above sea level, and Rockgun Battery, which is thirteen hundred and fifty-six. I'd like to see the ruddy Red navy try to get through the Strait when I'm on the job!"

"Haw, so shud I!" said Mr. Glencannon. "Come, let's drink to yere vurra guid aim!"

Corporal Chatterton needed no urging; in fact, he followed the drink with another. But though he was now outside the greater part of the quart, it seemed to have little effect on him.

Mr. Glencannon, who had done nobly with the arrack, observed the corporal's apparent sobriety with amusement. "Losh!" he chuckled to himself. "He's got the vurra worst kind o' a jag— the kind with revairse English on it, when ye're so drunk ye're sober! But just wait till he gets ootside and the fresh air hits him! Aye, and wait till he reports for juty at the barracks!"

"It's quarter to twelve," the corporal announced briskly. "I'll just swill the rest of this 'ere whisky, and then I must shove orff. Well, cheeri-ho, Mr. Glencannon! Many thanks fer yer 'orspitality, and if yer'll tyke my tip, yer'll walk yer ruddy cousin around a bit before 'e tries to get back to quarters. If yer don't, 'e'll get fourteen days in the clink."

"Thonk ye, I will," said Mr. Glencannon, suddenly realizing that his own faculties were becoming somewhat arrackized and that a walk might prove beneficial to himself. "Weel, Corporal Chatterton, in love and in target proctice, may ye have all the success ye desairve! Guid nicht, my brave lad."

"In Siam, the golden umbrella is the inswignia o' royalty," declared Cousin Douglas.

"Weel, shove it doon yere throat and open it, then!" retorted Mr. Glencannon, shaking him violently. "Come, it's time to wak' up, ye great drunken booby, ye!"

Cousin Douglas opened his eyes and then sat bolt upright. "Colin!" he cried. "Did ye see her? Did ye see her mother?"

"No, they were both oot; I'll see them in the morning. Come on, Dooglas, get up; we're gaeing for a bit o' a stroll."

"Stroll?" repeated the Highlander. "Foosh, Cousin Colin, what are ye leaning against the wall for? Why, I do believe ye're in yere cups! Weel, dinna worrit, lad. I'll see ye safely back aboard yere ship." He snatched up the arrack bottle, gulped what little remained in it, grasped the table by a leg and tossed it over the heads of the surrounding drinkers.

"Ah, Dooglas, Dooglas!" Mr. Glencannon chided him. "Are ye no' yet sober enough to realize that a donce floor is no place for furniture?" Lurching between the startled couples, he picked up the table and hurled it back into the corner.

Not without difficulty, then, they assisted each other into the night and headed for the water front. "Funny," muttered Cousin Douglas, gazing up at the stars, "I thocht it was raining. Then I thocht I was Kitchener. Then I knew I was sober. Weel, I must have been dreaming. On the other hond, I may have been drunk. But domn if I can find the other hond. . . . Whoa, steady. Canna ye stond up straight?"

"'Tis ye that's teetering, no' me," Mr. Glencannon protested thickly.

"Weel, somebody's teetering," said Cousin Douglas, "but at this time o' nicht I dinna suppose there's any way o' finding oot who wrote it."

"Is there no British Consulate in this sorra town?" demanded Mr. Glencannon, scratching his pipestem against a lamppost and throwing away the match. "It seems to me that in 1926, when I was here, I was there. They guorontee it to give ye thirty-five shaves per blade."

"Exockly!" agreed Cousin Douglas, helping himself to a six-pence from the cup of a blind Moorish beggar. "The following nicht they sairched his bag and found eleven packs o' marked cards."

"Weel, it's Foscism, Communism, Socialism—call it what ye will!" Mr. Glencannon's countenance opened in a cavernous yawn: "Whoo-a-ah! Guid losh, Dooglas, control yersel'! Dinna ye ken that yawning is contagious?"

"Yo-a-whoo! Um! M'm!" The Highlander stretched and nodded sleepily. "But why did ye sign it withoot reading it?"

"A vurra guid suggestion," said Mr. Glencannon. "Let us lie doon in the shade o' this signboard by the water's edge and enjoy the customarra noontime siesta."

Cousin Douglas unstrapped his wrist watch, wound it, and tossed

it over the signboard into the inky water. "Wak' me airly, airly,
mother, for I'm to be queen o' the May," he mumbled, settling
down beside Mr. Glencannon.

IV

Mr. Glencannon was awakened by the roar of express trains
rushing by behind the sign board. Ordinarily he would not have
minded them, but this morning he had a splitting, or arrack, headache and he found their clatter definitely annoying. For a while
he lay without opening his eyes, trying to piece together the events
of the preceding day. At length, through the mental association
of express trains and honeymoons, he remembered Clematis Mahoney, and her inheritance of two thousand pounds.

He sprang up. "Be still, my heart, be still!" he murmured
ecstatically.

The sun, he noted, was half an hour high and the water of the
Strait, deserted save for a government tug steaming slowly along
a mile or two away, was a brilliant pink. Cousin Douglas, his
Glengarry cap pulled over his face as though it were a feed bag,
was emitting snores like the soughing of the wind in a graveyard
cypress.

"Puir lad!" mused Mr. Glencannon, contemplating him. "I mis-
doot he'll be in a muckle o' trouble again for absence withoot
leave. Weel—haw!—yon prig o' a Corporal Chatterton will keep
him company in the clink for showing up drunk at target proctice.
. . . Corporal Chatterton! Private Chatterton, I shud say, because
no doot they'll rejewce the drunken swine to the ronks and—"

He paused to listen while another express train sped past.
"Strange, strange!" he muttered, strolling along the heavy timber
at the wharf edge. "There wasn't any railroad in Gibraltar yesterday, so they must have built it owernicht. Weel, we live in a
progressive commercial age! Odvertising, there's the secret! I dinna
doot, for exomple, that the front o' this hoarding bears a poster
o' Duggan's Dew o' Kirkintilloch, identical with those that they've
plostered all ower the British Isles. Ah, the Dew o' Kirkintilloch!"
He smacked his lips. "How snoogly a dollop o' Duggan's Dew
wud do me the noo! Weel, I—" Suddenly his voice became a cross

between a croak and a shriek. "Dooglas!" he ordered. "Quick! Come aroond here!"

Cousin Douglas rose, blinking, and stumbled around the end of the signboard. He found his relative staring stupidly toward the town. Toward it, yes, but the town wasn't there! Instead was a vast expanse of water, with the sunbathed peaks of Andalusia and the summit of the Rock just showing above the distant horizon.

"Oh, losh!" he gasped. "Why, domn it, Colin, we're oot in mid-ocean on a roft! There must have been an earthquake during the nicht; the wharf bruk loose and—"

He was interrupted by the roar of another approaching train— a fast train, a heavy train, which sounded as though it were crossing a trestle.

"Duck!" he screamed. "Lie doon!"

The invisible express thundered overhead. Instantly, out of the sea beyond the raft, leaped a towering white geyser which climbed up and up. For aching minutes it hung suspended; then it collapsed upon itself in a patch of steaming spume. Faintly from across the waters rolled a muffled "Boom!"

"Colin! The fourteen-inch rifles!" Douglas gasped. "It's target proctice—and we're—we're on the target!"

Mr. Glencannon's blood turned to cold jellied consommé. He rolled up his eyes toward heaven, observing, as he did so, that the fencelike structure which he had mistaken for a signboard was in reality a white-painted oblong of wooden slats. Large sections of it had been crudely and recently repaired.

"S-s-shr-r-o-o-o-oof!" another projectile came ripping through the air. "Pl-l-osh-h-h!" it hurtled into the water a scant fifty yards from the raft. The solid wooden hull dithered in the swell, and as countless gallons of chill sea water crashed down upon him, Mr. Glencannon emitted a piercing scream.

Then there was a rush, a deafening roar, a shattering crash. A thirty-foot section of the target soared into the air and vanished in a seething maelstrom which swept over the raft and stood it on its beam ends. Gasping for breath, Mr. Glencannon felt that a pile driver had hit him in the diaphragm.

"Ah, Dooglas, ye lout!" he was finally able to snarl. "If I only had my bross knuckles, I'd mak' ye think that shell had struck ye square! Ye call yersel' a soldier? Foosh, why did ye no' have sense enough to see it was a target last nicht?"

"Oh, aye?" countered Douglas hotly. "Ye call yersel' a sailor? Blosh! Ye cudna e'en distinguish this roft from the wharf it was tied up to."

"Ho, so it's my fault, is it?" Mr. Glencannon seized a splintered timber and started for his cousin. "Weel, ye stuppid sot, ye, I'll soon show ye whose fault it is!"

When the speedboat from the target tender arrived to ascertain the damage done by the direct hit, its crew was horrified to find two limp forms sprawled side by side upon the narrow raft.

v

Col. Sir Basil Burton-Melville, O.C. 67th Regiment, R.G.A., acting provost marshal of the Crown Colony of Gibraltar, scowled across his desk at the two battered prisoners.

"Well, my man!" he snapped at Mr. Glencannon. "What did you think you were doing out there on that target? Have you any idea of the fate you escaped?"

Mr. Glencannon drew himself up with vast dignity. "Sairtainly I have, as ye'll lairn to yere cost!" he retorted. "I escaped being murdered by yere domn Vickers Mark XI fortress rifles, throwing a four-hoonderd and fufty poond Mark XIV shell appruximately thirty-one thoosand yards. I know that ye've got twenty such guns up there on the Rock betwixt O'Hara's Tower and the Rockgun Battery, and I know, furthermore, that I intend to drog ye into the law courts and sue ye for domages for yere cruminal neegligence in shooting them at me. Foosh, 'tis an ootrageous state o' affairs when—"

"Wait!" barked Colonel Burton-Melville. He sat back, frowned and placed his finger tips together. "H'm! It seems to me you know a good bit more about our artillery than you've any business to know, my fine fellow!"

"Aye, sir, he's a spy!" blurted Cousin Douglas. "He's a distant reelative o' mine—a sort o' cousin—and I've lang been suspicious o' him. Last nicht I shadowed him doon to the water front and saw him sneak aboord the roft. I snuck aboord too and hid on the other side o' the target. I thocht I'd denoonce him when they started towing us oot to sea before daylicht. Then I thocht it wud be better to wait and catch him red-honded, actually obsairving the fire. No doot he plonned to jump owerboord and get picked up by a boat. I—"

"Well, by gad, that was plucky of you, I must say!" the colonel nodded approvingly. "As an infantryman, you, of course, didn't know that they try to straddle the target, not to hit it—although they often do hit it accidentally, as they did this morning. Oh, I'll see that you get your stripes back for this. Yes, by gad, you can consider it all settled! I'll recommend you for the D.C.M. for bravery too! But as for you"—he turned accusingly upon the engineer—"where did you get all your information about the Rock armament? Speak up!"

"From yerc ain lout o' a Corporal Chatterton," said Mr. Glencannon. "I didna give a hoot aboot yere guns, but he inseested on teeling me."

"Corporal Chatterton, eh!" fumed Colonel Burton-Melville. "Well, he'll be rear-rank Private Chatterton and cooling his heels in clink, when I get through with him! Blab military information to civilians, will he? . . . Send for him at once, Mahoney!"

"I just 'ad a phone call from the Rockgun Battery that they've put Corporal Chatterton under arrest, sir," reported the sergeant major. " 'E was acting orlright when 'e went into the emplacement, but then it happears 'e was suddenly tyken drunk, sir—in fact, it was 'is fault that they laid that gun wrong and smarshed up the target. The charge is intoxication, insubordination and removing 'is breeches on 'Is Majesty's fortified property to the prejudice of military discipline, sir."

"So! I'll attend to his case later. Now you!" The colonel leaned across his desk and shook his fist in Mr. Glencannon's face. "You get out of Gibraltar in two hours' time, or I'll put you under arrest! Spy? Spy? You're not a spy; you're just a damned nuisance! . . . Sergeant Glencannon, show your precious cousin to the door and boot him through it! . . . Boot him, I said! Boot him, sergeant! . . . Harder! Harder! . . . Ha, that's the way!"

THE LADIES OF CATSMEAT YARD

ALONG the left bank of the Thames where it winds through Limehouse Reach is a dismal cluster of slums like an old dead growth of barnacles. It is a neighborhood of mean streets upon which the sun seldom shines, for even when the fog clears off, as it sometimes does, there still remains a sable pall from factory chimneys and the funnels of great ships sliding down to the sea. It is a cheerless region any way you look at it, though it were well not to look too hard lest one of its denizens mistake you for a copper's nark and bryke yer hinquisitive nose fer yer.

At the center of this teeming faubourg is Catsmeat Yard, a narrow cobbled rectangle walled in by a dozen two-story brick dwellings. It is a community within itself, a Pomander Walk strewn with fish spines and potato peels, a placid backwater in the torrent of traffic which city folk call life. For nothing much ever happens in Catsmeat Yard; there hasn't been a murder since the days of Jack the Ripper, wives are seldom beaten and then only on Saturday nights, and the three counterfeiters—decent blokes, they were —who occupied the basement of No. 5, went off that peaceful that a body'd have said they were bound for evensong if it hadn't been for the handcuffs. Once, long, long ago, Queen Victoria was pleased to honor the Yard with her presence, coming to bestow a bronze medal upon a certain Thomas Tugg, a good bit of whom, including several arms and legs, had been lopped off by a chainshot at the Siege of Sebastopol. Her Majesty graciously sustained Mr. Tugg with the thought that as he still had one eye remaining, he could look at the medal whenever he felt like it, and the fact of the royal visit was duly recorded for posterity upon a brass plate on the wall of No. 3. In 1899, however, when scrap brass was fetching tuppence the pound, posterity stole the plate and so the event is now all but forgotten.

A couple of the houses in Catsmeat Yard are occupied by

families who live at leisure on the Dole and who therefore hold themselves grandly aloof from such members of the working class as Mrs. O'Halloran of No. 11, the Jessups and the Gonigles of No. 6, the Flynns of No. 8, and the Smiths of No. 1, together with their numerous lodgers. But these humble toilers are joined by a dual bond of interest, for not only do they all work, they all serve the same masters. Bert Jessup is Steward of the S.S. *Inchcliffe Castle;* the mountainous Veronica O'Halloran, relict of the late Tom O'Halloran, A.B., is charwoman in the offices of Messrs. Clifford, Castle & Company, Limited, owners of that ship; the brothers Flynn are Bosuns of the *Swalecliff Castle* and the *Hardcliffe Castle* respectively, while the worthy Joseph Gonigle is donkeyman in the *Ormcliffe Castle.* The paying guests in these households include the wives, mothers and children of deckhands and firemen aboard various other vessels of the Clifford & Castle cargo fleet, in such numbers that a summer evening in Catsmeat Yard is like unto a Board Meeting in the company's offices, except that a great deal more is decided.

It was on such an evening that Mrs. Alf Flynn, sitting on her door-step to catch a breath of air, glanced over the rim of her pot of 'arf and 'arf and spied Mrs. O'Halloran ponderously settling herself in her portal across the way.

"Lawks, Missus O'Halloran!" she screamed. "Fair wilted, I am! Phew, dearie, did yer ever feel such 'orrible 'ot 'eat? Oh, the menfolk is lucky to be orff at sea on a night like this, though at that I hexpecks some of 'em's in 'otter plyces than Lime-'ouse, poor chaps, and I means no disrepeck to yer lyte 'usband, 'im being dead and rotting in 'is gryve and orl. Why, no longer than tea time ago I was saying to Myrtle, I says, ' 'Ot? Yus, it's perishing 'ot, but 'ow'd yer like to be in poor Veronica O'Halloran's corsets, slaving aw'y up there in the owners' orffices fer fussy old Mister 'Azlitt, and 'er not even able to so much as slip into a kermoner, the poor dear?' —Them was hexackly my words, wasn't they, Myrtle?"

"Yus," screamed Myrtle from the window above. "That's hexackly wot she says to me, Missus O'Halloran, and then I says the very syme thing to 'er."

"Well, I must say it did get cruel sultry this arfternoon," screamed Mrs. O'Halloran in turn, helping herself to a swig from the pint of bitter which she had placed beside her on the step. "We 'ad a very busy day at the orffice, a very busy day indeed."— Then, impressively, "—There's—there's something going on in the wind, Missus Flynn, something 'ighly himportant, you mark my words!"

"Oh, yus?" Mrs. Flynn pricked up her ears and Myrtle hitched forward on the window sill. "Well, I 'opes they ain't planning another cut in the wages, that's orl I 'opes! In these 'ere 'ard times, with orl the lines laying hup ships and laying orff men, a body can't call its soul her own from one day's end to the next.—But just wot 'appened, Missus O'Halloran dear, if I might myke so bold as to arsk?"

There was a soft rustling sound as dim, kimonoed figures appeared in the windows and doorways on all four sides of Catsmeat Yard and prepared to tune in on the broadcast. Mrs. O'Halloran took another dollop of the bitter and then, to give her audience time to settle, very deliberately lighted a Woodbine.

"Well," she explained, "Sir John Castle and Mister 'Azlitt and the other gempmen 'ad their Hannual Meeting this arfternoon, and a shocking narsty brawl they turned it into.—'Ammering on the tyble with their fists, they was, and 'ollering at each other that scandalous you'd 'ave thought it was Satiddy closing time at the Pot and Puddink."

"Indeed, Missus O'Halloran!" Mrs. Tousey chimed in from the steps of No. 3. "It must 'ave been most hundignified, I must say! But just wot was the question at tissue?"

Mrs. O'Halloran took a thoughtful puff, and nodded good evening to Mrs. McCoy and Mrs. Regan, who were bulging from the parlor window of No. 9. "Well," she said, lowering her voice so that it carried a scant eighth-mile, "I couldn't get it orl in detyle, so to say, because they shut the door and it 'asn't got no key'ole. But as far as I was able to 'ear—as far as I was able to 'ear—there's been something very serious 'appen to the dividends!"

For a moment there was a stunned silence. Then Mrs. McCoy cleared her throat diffidently. "Something very serious 'as 'appened to . . . to the wot did yer say, Missus O'Halloran?"

"To the dividends, Missus McCoy, and I 'eard 'em say it with my own ears. Why, it happeared from wot they said that Clifford

& Castle ain't declared a single solitary dividend fer three years, and them was the very words they used!"

"You don't mean it!"

"Oh good lawks!"

"Fer pity's sakes!"

Again there was a pause. "But—but 'ow do you hexplain it, Missus O'Halloran, dear; 'ow do you hexplain it?" inquired the perplexed Mrs. Jessup, hoping like the rest of them to glean from the answer at least some faint clue to the meaning of it all.

Mrs. O'Halloran shrugged. "Well, I suppose that furreign countries 'ave just simply stopped shipping 'em, or else the dirty Rooshan Commonists is dumping 'em in 'ere fer next to nothing or something. Any'ow, old Lord Tilligrew flew into such a flyming styte of ryge about it that they 'ad to lead 'im outside, loosen 'is waistcoat and feed 'im a good stiff peg of whisky to keep 'im from catching the hapoplexy."

"Well bless me, I don't wonder!" gasped Mrs. Tousey, the gravity of the situation, whatever it was, finally dawning upon her. "Fancy trying to run a line of freighters without no dividends!"

"Ah, you may well say it, Missus Tousey! I gathered from the 'orrible 'ullaballoo that the cargoes on dividends the ships used to carry must of been the company's very bread and butter, so to speak."

"Dearie me, 'ow 'orrible! Was they imported dividends, Missus O'Halloran, or them as is manufactured at 'ome?"

"Imported ones—no doubt the very finest," said Mrs. O'Halloran. " 'Declared' dividends means the kind that 'as to go through the Customs 'Ouse, don't yer see? Oh, I'll tell yer wot, lydies, the business is in a cricketal styge!"

"Hunh, it means a lay orff, if you should arsk me!" opined the pessimistic Mrs. Dill.

There was a thin chorus of sighs. All around the yard the heads shook sadly in the gloom.

Mrs. O'Halloran, gratified by the effect of her baneful intelligence, rewarded herself with a gulp from the growler. "But of course," she continued, wiping her mouth on the back of her hand and working up to the high spot of her news, "of course, Mister

'Azlitt is too smart a fiddler to be caught without two strings to 'is bow. If Clifford & Castle can't book dividend freights with the rotten old ships they've got—and 'e said 'imself as 'ow 'e was fair sick and tired of trying to get the Captains to operate 'em more hefficiently—why then, 'e says, there's nothing fer it but to go in fer a new type of ship altogether."

"—Motorships!" gasped several ladies in unison.

"Ah, motorships, blyme, I knew it!" wailed Mrs. Bossert, whose husband was a coal trimmer. "Clifford & Castle are going in fer motorships to throw a lot of honest men out of work! Why, orl it tykes to run a ruddy motorship is an happrentice to turn a spiggot and a Dutchman to tend the stove!"

"Now wyte a minute, 'old 'ard!" and Mrs. O'Halloran's voice was vibrant as she prepared to cast a figurative lifebuoy to the drowning. " 'E didn't say motorship at orl, and I didn't say 'e did. 'E spoke of a ship that's something entirely new—I couldn't catch the nyme of it, but 'e perdicted that in six months' time the 'ole shipping world will be talking about it. 'Gempmen,' 'e says, 'Gempmen, when this thing is hannounced, it will shyke the British Mercantile Marine to its very foundations!' Yus, girls, them was Mister 'Azlitt's own words, and you know 'e's not one to boast!"

"Oh, and indeed 'e ain't, not 'im!" agreed Mrs. Tousey eagerly. "Why, my good grycious, if sly old 'Azlitt mykes a stytement like that, it means the 'ole difficulty's as good as settled!"

There were cries of " 'Ear! 'Ear!" followed by a relieved and assenting babble. Mrs. O'Halloran sat back, sloshed up a head of foam on the bitter which remained in the can and drank it, a moth and several gnats with audible satisfaction.

"Ah!" she mused with a knowing chuckle, " 'E's a clever one for fair, old squint-eyed 'Azlitt is!"

"—Oh, 'e'll get them dividends some'ow!"

"Trust 'im!"

"Lawks, wot a hintellect!"

"Well, 'ere's to 'im!"

Somewhere out in the Reach a steamer's siren bellowed, and in the distance, very faintly, Big Ben chimed nine strokes. Still clicking their tongues and nodding their heads at Mr. Hazlitt's astounding shrewdness, the good ladies of Catsmeat Yard gathered their kimonos around them and went their optimistic ways to bed.

II

. . . TEN . . . ELEVEN . . . TWELVE; Big Ben boomed the midnight. Mechanically, at the final solemn note, Mr. Hazlitt snapped open his watch and squinted at the dial. Then he sat bolt upright in his chair.

"Ha!" he ejaculated. "Well, by gad!"

At every hour of every one of the cruelly-long working days which he had imposed upon himself throughout his forty years with Clifford & Castle, Mr. Hazlitt had been trying to catch Big Ben in error, and now, at last, he'd succeeded! He'd begun it as a Junior Clerk; he'd continued it as General Manager. It was his hobby, his sole diversion; and it was characteristic of him.

"Eleven Fifty-Eight and a Half!" he gloated, waving his watch on high. "Ah, I knew it, I knew it! —Big Ben, the master timepiece of the greatest city in the world, one minute and thirty seconds fast! Well—" he leaned forward and harangued the empty gloom which hemmed in the pool of light from his green-shaded desk lamp "—Well, it just goes to show the sorry state to which the whole world's fallen! We preach Efficiency, but how do we practice it? We rant about the value of Time, the raw material of which all things are made, and yet we can't even measure it! We're heedless, we're careless, we're sloppy, we're inefficient—er, well, most of us are. I've sounded the warning for years, a still small voice crying in the wilderness, and now—" he brought down his fist upon the pages of figures, mostly red, which lay before him on the desk "—and now, perhaps too late, they believe me!"

He twisted the flexible neck of the lamp so that it lighted a large-scale map of the world which hung upon the wall. Thrust into this map were twenty-three pins upon each of which was a little paper flag bearing the name of one of the company's ships. These flags dotted the seaports, rivers and watery wastes of four hemispheres; they jutted from the harbors of Wai-hai-wei and Vadso, Saigon and Samarang, Barcelona and Boston; there was one in the Plate below Buenos Aires, another in the Suez at Timseh; two were in the Mexican Gulf off Galveston, and in the desk lamp's beam, the remainder cast their little oblong shadows upon three printed oceans and half a dozen seas.

Here, to a layman's eye, was romance, but not to Mr. Hazlitt's. For he was seeing red—the danger signal red of those ominous figures on his desk. He shook his fist at the map, and though the gesture was intended for the twenty-three ships, the whole inefficient world was included.

"Oh, the slackers!" he rasped. "The sluggards, the wasters, the dolts! Well, by gad, I'll try once more to make them listen to reason!"

Switching on the current in his electric stenophone, he seized the mouthpiece, cleared his throat and dictated:—

"Form letter to Captains of all C. & C. ships. Address individually, in care our agents. My dear Captain: (a-hem) The showing of your vessel continues to be deplorable in all departments. Despite my frequent letters urging upon you the vital necessity for offsetting decreased tonnage and starvation freight rates with increased efficiency, the S. S. (fill in the name of the ship, Miss Melcher, and mind that you do a neat job of it) is a burden upon the company, a disgrace to the fleet, and a constant proof of your utter inability to command. As you are aware, Clifford, Castle and Company, Limited, are among the few owners who have not yet laid up a single ship, it being our theory that a vessel at sea with half a cargo is better than one laid up to rust, just as you yourself are better off afloat, even with your present reduced wages, than you would be ashore and out of a berth. To turn this theory into practice, however, we must accomplish what so many other lines have failed to do—in other words, we must increase our efficiency (type that all in capitals, Miss Melcher) er, we must increase our efficiency in every branch of our operations. But instead of that, what are you doing, question mark. You are burning more coal than any other two ships under the house flag. Your engine room repair costs are shocking. Your Steward's catering average would be high even for a Transatlantic liner. You waste time through missing tides, through clumsy docking, and due to bungled working of cargo. Your record is atrocious, a-hem, er, period. H'm, let's see, oh yes, paragraph. This is a time when all of us have got to put our shoulders to the wheel. We've got to work, work, work, exclamation point. Here in the office we do not spare ourselves, we do not watch the clock—, er . . ."

Abstractedly, Mr. Hazlitt dragged out his watch and consulted it. Behind his *pince nez,* his nearsighted eyes protruded like those of a frog. "No!" he gasped, and the mouthpiece of the stenophone slipped from his fingers. "No! Why damme, it's impossible!" But there was no dodging the fact that the hands of the watch still stood at Eleven-Fifty-Eight and a Half—stood there, because Mr. Hazlitt had forgotten to wind it.

"Good heavens!" he muttered dully. "Hazlitt, Hazlitt, what in the world has come over you?" He slumped down in his swivel chair and realized for the first time in his life that he, like the rest of mankind, was fallible. Big Ben had been right and Virgil Hazlitt wrong.—Wrong!—Careless!—Inefficient!

It was a bitter pill to take. As he sat there, his head in his hands, he seemed to grow smaller. Smaller, and older, and grayer.

Big Ben spoke once.

Mr. Hazlitt stirred, shook himself, wound his watch and set it. Then, very slowly, he removed the record from the stenophone and smashed it in the wastebasket. "The pot," he murmured, "was about to call the kettle black."

Taking up his hat and stick, he moved toward the door. But halfway across the room he seemed to remember something. He turned and bowed to the little paper flags which jutted from the map. "—My most humble apologies to all of you!" he said. "Good-night, gentlemen, good-night!"

III

It was noon, and the sun blazed like a magnesium flare in the blue above the Darsena del Comercio in Barcelona harbor. The S.S.*Inchcliffe Castle,* John Ball, Master, lay alongside the Muelle de Pescadores, heat waves dancing giddily on her rusty steel decks and the once-white paint of her super-structure pouting up in great gummy blisters. Wafting out of her in all directions came that peculiarly-discouraging effluvium combined of steam, grease, garbage, members of the crew and the dusts and juices of many ancient cargoes, by which even a blind man with one nostril may recognize a tramp ship stewing in the sun.

"Well, gentlemen," beamed Captain Ball, taking his place at the head of the dinner table and mopping his brow with his napkin, "here we are enjoying a pleasant little holiday, as you might say, and from the look of things out there—" he nodded toward the doorway, which framed a shimmering vista of idle cranes and laden freight cars on the mole beside the ship "—from the look of things out there, we're likely to enjoy it for another week at least."

"Yus," agreed Mr. Montgomery, the Mate, with an effort managing to reassemble the two halves of his face at the finish of a capacious yawn. "If it wasn't fer them there soldiers lying hasleep, yer'd say the bleddy plyce was a deserter's village, yer would upon my word!"

"Is Mister Glencannon back from huptown yet?" inquired young Mr. Levy, the Wireless Operator. "—I mean to say, I wonder if they're still shooting in the streets?"

"No, 'e ain't back, so per'aps, please God, they are!" said Mr. Montgomery, with fervor. "Ho, wouldn't it be a jolly bit of luck if, er—oh—" his face fell and so did his voice "—ere 'e comes now."

"Aye, here I come, lik' Wallace trioomphant fra the wars!" proclaimed the Chief Engineer, a stocky walrus-mustached personage whose visible, audible and smellable characteristics were all unmistakably Scotch. "But whurra, Captain and colleagues, such is the parlous state o' politeecs in Spain that I can thonk my lucky stars and a vurra neat knuckle-duster o' my ain design that I got here at all! If yon is the Catalonian idea o' a 'paceefic deemonstration,' gi' me the guid old days in the Dardanelles ony time!"

"Ah yes, Mister Glencannon, but a general strike is a general strike, and you can't get away from it," Captain Ball reminded him. "What I mean is, you can't have a general strike without undergoing all the goings-on which generally goes on in all general strikes, if you follow me. Well," he sat back and stretched luxuriously, "let 'em take their own good time to settle it, says I! We can't get loaded till they do, and a few days more rest won't do us a bit of harm."

" 'Ow's things going in the city?" asked Mr. Swales.

"Ah, they're going something frichtful," replied Mr. Glencannon. "Fra what I was able to obsairve, the Repooblicans, or Purple Shirts, are going for the Syndicalists, or Gray Shirts; the Syndicalists are going for the Separatists, or Green Shirts, and the Separatists are going for the Foshists, who wear the conventional black. The Black Shirts are going fer the Communists, or Red Shirts, and they're all going for the Royalists, who hae no shirts at all. Except for them, a mon wud think it was a war among the haberdashers!"

Captain Ball puffed out his fat cheeks jovially. "Heh, well, a fine chance there is of settling a rat-fight like that! But what are they all quibbling about, Mister Glencannon;—what's the *casus belli*, heh?"

"I dinna ken the cause's belly," said the Engineer. "In foct I dinna ken its head fra its tail. All I can tell ye, at feerst hond, is that in the street whuch they've christened the Paseo de Colon in honor'o' the lower intestine, a dense mob made up o' all factions were joyfully setting fire to a tram car. Hae'ing lighted my pipe on it, thus saving mysel' a motch, I continued on my way to the agent's office and picked up the mail. Among it was this letter for you, Captain."

"Ah, mph!" sniffed Captain Ball, considering the envelope. "It's from Hazlitt, dam his gimlet eyes! I'd been wondering all these weeks what'd happened to the ruddy old ram;—I haven't had one of his bellyaching letters since the one at Rabat about how we was using too much red lead or vanilla extract or something. Well, I fancy he's heard about the strike and now he's writing to blame all this delay on me." Cleansing his knife of mutton gravy with a skill which would have aroused the envy of even the most talented sword swallower, he slit open the envelope and scowlingly perused its contents.

Presently, though, the scowl gave way to a look of bewilderment. He spread the letter flat upon the oilcloth and studied it with the fascinated wariness of a guinea pig confronted by a cobra. His lips moved as he spelled out each word, and strange noises issued from his throat.

"Well, wot is it this time; some more of the usual?" inquired Mr.

Montgomery, unable longer to restrain his curiosity.

"No!" bellowed Captain Ball, violently recalling himself, "it's not the usual, not by a dam sight! Why gentlemen—gentlemen, the sneaking little sniveller has actually got the insolence to try to get chummy with me!—Yes, chummy, after twenty-four years. of the vilest abuse, the meanest blackguarding, the most niggling er—er, but here, listen:—

" 'My dear John,' he says (yes, 'John,' there it is in black on white, but who in hell ever give him leave to call me John, that's what I want to know, heh?) 'My dear John: Just a line to let you know that I'm thinking about you and hoping that you are well. I am glad to note that your ship is upholding its usual standard of efficiency; indeed, its record is the envy, the inspiration and the goal of the entire fleet. The Board of Directors held its Annual Meeting yesterday; business continues bad, but I do not want you to worry about it. If you or your officers hear any rumors, please dismiss them from your minds. I hope you'll drop me a note whenever you're not too busy, and give me the news of yourself and your ship. Please convey my warmest personal regards to Mr. Glencannon, Mr. Montgomery and all the others. As ever, Cordially yours, Virgil.' "

"—'V . . . Virgil'?" gasped Mr. Montgomery. "Do yer mean 'e hactually signs 'imself Virgil?"

"Aye, Veergil, there it is, ye can see it plain!" said Mr. Glencannon, who had been reading the letter with his head cocked sideways. " '—As ever, Cordially yours, Veergil!'—Weel, weel, weel!" He sat back and gnawed his mustache thoughtfully.

"But what's it all mean?" demanded Captain Ball. "Why, there's not a single word of complaint in it! —I mean, aside from its nasty, sticky drooling familiarity, what in blazes do you make of it?"

"Well, I'll tell yer wot I myke of it," blurted Mr. Montgomery. "I myke of it that 'Azlitt's gone stark, ryving cryzy! Arfter all these years, 'is own natural narstiness 'as finally poisoned 'im and drove 'im as mad as a March 'atter!"

"Why of course!" agreed Mr. Levy. "The bleddy old curmudgeon's completely orff his chump."

"H'm," mused Captain Ball, "I fancy you're right.—I mean to say, insanity's the only sane explanation.—Come, come, don't you think so, Mister Glencannon?"

"No!" declared the Engineer. "Absolutely no! Yon Hazlitt is a vurra shrewd auld glaggy, and going daft is the last thing he'd do as a favor to his fellow men. I give ye solemn warning, Captain and gentlemen, that this thing is a snare, a pitfall, a trop—aye, it's a plot whuch Hazlitt has hatched for our undoing!"

"A plot?—A plot what about?"

"A plot to get rid o' us—to sack us oot o' our jobs—to beach us! Why, ye ken as weel as I do that he hates every mon in the *Inchcliffe Castle,* and his ain past letters prove it! But having lairned through experience that he canna pin a single thing against us in line o' duty, he hopes the noo to lull us into a false sense o' security, catch us off our guard, and lop off our heads—squirp!—lik' that! When he says 'If ye hear ony rumors, please dismuss them fra yere mind,' it's plain he's afraid we've already got wind o' his neefarious mochinations and is striving further to hoodwunk us."

Captain Ball heaved ponderously. "Well, ker-huff, now wait a minute! What I want to know is, why should he think we've heard any rumors, heh? What kind of rumors from where, for instance? —Have any of you gentlemen heard any rumors?"

Around the table there was a searching of memories and a shaking of heads.

"Well, there you are!" said Captain Ball. "—I mean, there you are, aren't we?"

From the doorway of the pantry passage came the sound of a discreet cough. "I begs yer pardon, Captain. . . ."

"Yes, what is it, Jessup?"

From the pocket of his white jacket, the Steward produced a letter. "Per'aps this 'ere may carst some light on the subjick, Captain," he said. "It's just come from my wife in London, Sir, 'oo's very friendly with Veronica O'Halloran, 'er as is the widder of Tom O'Halloran wot broke 'is neck when 'e fell down the 'old drunk that time, as no doubt yer'll remember, Sir. Well, it 'appens that Veronica is char in the owners' orffices, and she hinforms my wife very confidential that Mister 'Azlitt says as 'ow the comp'ny is going to buy a new ship."

"A new ship?" repeated Mr. Swales. "Wot kind of a ship?—A

motorship?"

"No, Sir," said Jessup, "and that's the strynge part of it. Haccording to wot Missus O'Halloran told my old woman, it's a very special ship—a new kind of ship entirely; in fact—" he consulted the letter "—in fact, Mister 'Azlitt was over'eard to perdict that it would shyke the British Mercantile Marine to its very foundations."

"Oh, ho!" exclaimed Mr. Glencannon. "Noo we're getting doon to bross tocks! Clifford & Castles buying a new ship o' some kind, Hazlitt is afraid we've heard rumors o' it, and doesna want us to believe them.—Why?—why?"

Captain Ball's clenched fist descended like Thor's hammer upon the table. "—Why? Well, here's why, and we might have guessed it at the start! I'm maybe one of the most senior Captains in the whole C. & C. fleet, ain't I?—Same way with Mister Montgomery among the Mates, and with you, Mister Glencannon, among the Engineers, ain't you? Well, then, by every rule of precedence, this here new ship, whatever it is, should go to us, and Hazlitt knows it. But he's scheming to rob us of our rights; he wants us to turn slack and inefficient and ruin our records, so's he can hand the new ship over to McCartney or Dwight or Swithy or one of his other particular pets! He wants to trap me into writing him chummy letters like one pal to another so's he can show 'em to Sir John Castle and get me fired for insubordination! Yes, it's a plot, a plot, exactly like Mister Glencannon says!"

"O' coorse it is," declared Mr. Glencannon. "It's plain as the nose on Muster Levy's face!"

"Yus, Sir," said Jessup, "such is my own 'umble hopinion. But Mister 'Azlitt's 'atred of the *Inchcliffe Castle* hincludes not only the horfficers, but even me and the Bosun, the Cook and the crew, Sir. Why, gorblyme!" his face clouded and he snapped his dish towel savagely, "them letters 'e wrote about me at the time of that plum jam hincident is sumping I ain't ever likely to ferget, Sir!"

"Aye!" growled Mr. Glencannon, his brows knitted in thought. "He's got it in for all o' us, o' that there is no doot!"

"No doubt at all," admitted Captain Ball, who was by this time somewhat pale around the gills. "And now, rot the luck, here we are stuck here in Barcelonia by this rotten strike, with not a chance to load, and the wharfage charges and everything mounting up on us and making our record blacker every minute, and, and I mean to say, oh hell!" Into his mind flooded thoughts of dismissal, of his wife, and of a snug little cottage in Surrey completely thatched with mortgages.

"But noo, look ye here," and Mr. Glencannon shook his finger impressively, "if there was one way at all to save our skins, it wud be to save coal and food and time and charges—to mak' things hum sae briskly that e'en auld scrooge Hazlitt wud be forced to reecognize our merit. Ye ken as weel as I do that we could do it. That we haven't been doing it in the past is sumply because o' our notural and justified spite o' him."

"Yes, of course, I mean to say, there's something in that," Captain Ball's false teeth were clicking like castanets to the wild measures of a *flamenco*. "I know very well that we could tighten up on things and run 'em smarter, now that we're faced with a—a dread alternative, sort of. But how's that going to get us loaded and out of Barcelonia, heh?"

"Here's how!" barked the Engineer. "We'll put the crew to work loading richt noo! The Ship's Articles, whuch they've all signed, require them to work cargo in emeergencies. When Jessup has explained to them that Hazlitt's ondootedly scheming to beach them alang wi' the rest o' us, they'll load wi'oot a murmur or a brukken head, won't they, Jessup?"

"Yus, Sir!" declared the Steward stoutly. "Oh, they'll get arfter it 'ammer and tongs, if it's a question of spiting 'Azlitt!"

"Richt ye are! And noo, Captain," Mr. Glencannon rose to his feet, "wi' yere pairmission, let's get started. Muster MacQuayle, I'll thonk ye to hae steam on deck immediately. Mysel', I'll gae wake up the soldiers, bestow a bottle o' whusky upon them and osk them to protect our operations fra the strikers. If Muster Montgomery will be guid enough to loan me six men wi' crowbars, we can jockoss yon cars alang the track and smosh their doors open in a jiffick. I, pairsonally, will tak' charge o' the wharf cranes. Hoot, gentlemen, we'll fox the auld fox yet!"

Somewhere off the Nash in the raw dusk of a December day, Captain McCartney and Mr. Rollands stood shivering in their oil-skins on the bridge of the S.S. *Northcliffe Castle,* cursing the slowness of the Cardiff pilot whose boat was even then struggling toward them across the expanse of nasty lead-gray chop.

"Hell!" complained Captain McCartney, passing the binoculars to the Mate. "If he keeps on at that rate we'll miss the bleddy tide, and . . ."

"Hell!" complained Mr. Rollands in turn, but rather louder. "Why look, look there, Captain! That there other ship's cutting in on us, it is!—Yessir, he's going to pick up that pilot right out from under our noses, arfter us wysting arf the arfternoon 'anging around out 'ere wyting fer . . ."

"Haw!" snorted Captain McCartney. "Yes, blow me if he isn't! Well, by George, I'm not the man to submit to no such insolence as that, by George, and when I get ashore I'll tell him so to his face, I will, and I don't care who he is! But—who is he?"

Snatching back the glasses, he trained them upon the other ship which, pilot now on board, was driving ahead into the murk to landward. "Why, she's another C. & C.!" he announced, studying the funnel markings. "Yes, another C. & C.!—Tell you what, Mister Rollands, I'll bet you it's Ball! I-n-c-h—of course, *Inchcliffe Castle!* Well, the dam double-dam old pirate!"

"—Still up to 'is tricks, just like we 'eard!" grunted Mr. Rollands. "Good grycious, wot could've come over 'im, these past six months? 'E used to be just a big fat blob of suet, and with just about that much biff to 'im; but now they say 'e's a regular driving 'ellion!"

"Here's the glasses, take a lok at him," said Captain McCartney. "That's him on the bridge."

With a following wind and sea, the *Inchcliffe Castle* came plunging along like a scout cruiser, racing the black wisp of smoke which swept in a long low streak ahead of her. She was her own battered self, as always, but now, strangely, there was about her something bold and brisk and businesslike. She lacked paint, but she wasn't rusty. She was vomiting soot like a crematory, but she was clean as her own whistle—which, along with all her other brightwork, was burnished golden as the handle of a beer pump. Upon her decks, men were moving with that efficient unhurried swiftness which marks a well-disciplined, intelligently-officered crew. And calmly lording it over everything, the monarch of all he surveyed, was Captain John Ball.

"Yus, it's Ball sure enough!" sneered Mr. Rollands. "Strutting about like Hadmiral Jellicoe, no less, or Nelson in Trafalgar Square! And look there, Captain! 'Ere 'e is, still out 'ere at sea, and blyme if 'e ain't getting the tarpaulins orff the 'atches, and steam on deck orl ready to unload!"

Captain McCartney smote the wind-tautened canvas of the dodger with an exasperated fist. "Oh, and is he? Well, that's the way he does things, blast him! That's why he's Hazlitt's precious pet! And that's why I and you and everybody else on this ship has got to shake a leg, Mister Mate, or that rat Hazlitt'll put us on the beach just like he's scheming to do!" He seized Mr. Rollands by the shoulder and shoved him toward the ladder. "Rout out the men and lay onto them hatch covers, you!" he bellowed. "Get steam on deck, and clear the derricks! Smartly, now, Mister —jump to it, d'ye hear! I'm going to drive this swill barge in without a pilot, and fight it out with the Port Authority or anybody else who says I can't!"

Thus it came about at a late hour of the evening that Mr. Mac-Lean, the *Northcliffe's* Chief Engineer, ashore in Cardiff to stretch his legs and wet his whistle, espied a familiar figure approaching. This person walked briskly and in the purposeful manner of one without time to waste, but despite the quickness of his step and the military swing of his arms, his gait was markedly peculiar. This was because, through some oversight, he walked with his right foot upon the curb and his left in the gutter.

Mr. MacLean, whose own course was none too steady, contrived to time a violent sheer to starboard so that they collided.

"Weel, weel, Glencannon!" he roared as they clung together teetering. "I thocht it was yersel the moment I got a breath o' ye! Come, lad, hoist yere foot oot o' the gutter and let's gae somewhere and imbibe!"

"Imbibe?" repeated Mr. Glencannon. "Imbibe?" Then, squinting his eyes and managing to bring Mr. MacLean into focus, "Ah, guid losh!" he exclaimed. "If it isna auld Davey MacLean in pairson! How are ye, Davey, how are ye? I crave yere forgiveness for no haeing reecognized ye at the ootset, but my mind was entirely occupied wi' the monnifold affairs o' business. I must get back to the ship, Davey, I must get richt back to the ship!"

"Ah, swith, what's yere hurry, Colin? Canna we e'en hae a little drink together? I've a-muckle I'd lik' to talk to ye aboot."

Before replying, Mr. Glencannon took a monkey wrench from his pocket, shook it, held it to his ear, and consulted it gravely. "A-weel," he said with a thoughtful frown, "inasmuch as ye hae broached the subject o' a drink, pairhops I can arrange to spare ye fufteen minutes." And linking arms, they assisted each other across Bute Street and into the bar of the Royal Edward.

"Noo then," said Mr. MacLean, when they were seated to a round of Duggan's Dew of Kirkintilloch, "We both o' us ken that there's a-muckle o' rivalry and back-biting betwixt the ships o' the Clifford & Castle Line, but you and I are auld friends, Colin, so we can talk as mon to mon. Therefore, let's lay our cards on the table."

Mr. Glencannon examined the table minutely, but being unable to discover any cards upon it, he returned his attention to the whisky.

"Ah!" he murmured, "by all means!"

"It's aboot this new ship which Hazlitt's haeing built," continued Mr. MacLean, lowering his voice confidentially. "Ah, dinna deny that ye've heard aboot it, Colin! Full five months ago one o' our firemen got the news fra his wife, who got it straight fra that fat Missus O'Hell-'n'-what's-her-name who works in the office, and I ken dom weel that by noo it's all ower the fleet. The point is, what sort o' a ship is it, and who's slated to get command o' her?"

Mr. Glencannon extended his hand in a searching gesture. It chanced to encounter his glass. "Ah, Davey!" he said, "What kind o' a ship it is still remains a dark, onfathomable and most mysterious mystery. But I dinna mind telling ye betwixt friends that though for the past six months Captain Ball and the rest o' us hae been breaking our backs and sweating blood to force auld Hazlitt to appoint us in charge o' it, as is our richtful due, he's still plotting to knife us, blost his nosty pale-green soul!"

"Meaning exoctly whuch, Colin?"

"Meaning he's still trying to throw us off our guard by writing us the most soft-soapy, goody-goody letters I e'er set eyes upon! He's hoping we'll slock doon and get lazy, and . . ."

"Letters?" exclaimed Mr. MacLean. "Colin, mon!—D'ye mean to say he's trying to work that letter game on Captain Ball too?"

Mr. Glencannon's jaw dropped in amazement, just in time to make way for the rim of his glass. "Foosh, o' coorse he is! But— But I'm stunned to gather fra what ye say that Captain McCartney's in for it as weel!"

"Aye, but he is! And so's Dwight o' the *Hardcliffe* and Swithy o' the *Marlecliffe* and Howard o' the *Bournecliffe,* and guidness knows how monny more. Each o' them conseeders himsel' entitled to the berth, and each believes that Hazlitt's trying to bilk him, as no doot he is. But what hae ye o' the *Inchcliffe* been doing about it, Colin?"

Mr. Glencannon's face darkened in a scowl. "Weel, we've been fighting!" he rasped. "Fighting, and we'll keep on fighting to the vurra last ditch, deespite McCartney and Dwight and Swithy and the rest o' them! E'er since we feerst got wind o' it, in Barcelona, we've been slaving lik' horses, and running the auld tub lik' a bottleship! We loaded her oursel's that day;—aye, and we've done it monny's the weary time since, to save time and expense. We're still living on three or four carloads o' tinned quails and calves' tongues and goose-leevers and asparagus that we loaded by mistak', wi' a consequent saving o' money in the Steward's Department whuch Clifford & Castle is getting the benefeet o'. Also, through an owersight, and no being able to read Sponish, we got awa' wi' eight weeks' supply o' coal. Ah, weel!" he rolled his eyes resignedly, "I suppose, later on, the Repooblicans, or Purple Shirts, blamed it on the Syndicalists, or Gray Shirts; the Syndicalists blamed it on the Separatists, or Green Shirts, and the Sep . . ."

"Weel, great swith!" Mr. MacLean interrupted him. "Dom if you *Inchcliffe* lads aren't the lucky ones. But I onderstond that the *Bournecliffe,* whuch was in Shanghai, got awa' wi' half a shipload full o' odds and ends whuch they're still living on, the Jopanese army and the Chinese bondits catching the blame for it. And seeveral o' the other ships fared none too bodly, what wi' the wars, earthquakes and similar colomities whuch hae been sae popular throughoot the world o' late."

"Losh, losh, ye dinna say!" marvelled Mr. Glencannon. "Why, 'twud seem that the speerit o' diligence had peervaded the fleet lik' an epideemic o' scurvy! But after all, Davey, I'll bet that none o' ye've been pinching and toiling and driving half so conscientiously as the poor auld *Inchcliffe Castle!*"

"Weel, as to pinching, the most the *Northcliffe's* been able to snoffle to date was a few tons o' stuff off the dock i' Callao, during the Peruvian reevolution. But we've been toiling and driving lik' yersel's and lik' all the other ships—driving day and nicht! Why, this vurra afternoon, after Ball nosed us oot o' that pilot, the Auld Mon tuk the ship in by himsel', e'en wi'oot a tug, to save the expense. Dom if he wudna hae drove her clear through the lock gates if the dock pilot hadna come aboord and stopped him. But o' coorse the docking service is free, so Captain McCartney let reason prevail."

Mr. Glencannon sat back and drained his glass. "Weel, dearie me! Every officer and every mon in the whole dom fleet is vying wi' one another to save his skin and get that mystery ship!—What a speectacle!—What modness! Where will it all end, Davey, where will it all end?"

"Aloss!" sighed Mr. MacLean, with a shrug which rocked the table, "Aloss, who can say?" He coughed, glanced from the empty glasses to Mr. Glencannon, and back to the glasses again. Mr. Glencannon, catching the significance of the look, lurched impulsively to his feet. "Guid nicht, Davey!" he said. "Time's up, and I must hie me back to the ship. Effiffiff . . . er, efficienshish . . . weel onyway, it's Captain Ball's motto, and may the best mon win!"

v

Mrs. Alf Flynn, a year older, a trifle stouter, and a great deal warmer than she had been three hundred and sixty-five evenings previously, glanced up over the rim of her pot of 'arf and 'arf and perceived Mrs. O'Halloran ponderously settling herself in her portal across the way.

"Oh, 'ullo there, Missus O'Halloran, dear!" she screamed. "Well, 'ere we are in the fourth night of this 'ere 'orrible 'eat-wyve, and the pypers say there's no relief in sight. Orl day long, when I thought of yer slaving aw'y up there in the owners' orffices fer that fidgety little 'Azlitt, my 'eart went out to yer, Veronica dear."

"Oh yus?" screamed Mrs. O'Halloran, taking her nose out of her can of bitter. "Well, it was very kind of yer to think of me, I must say, fer a perishing busy day I 'ad of it. Sir John Castle, Mister 'Azlitt and the other gempmen 'ad their Hannual Meeting, and it larsted orl arfternoon."

"Oh, yer don't say!" said Mrs. Flynn, edging forward on the step. "Did anything himportant 'appen, dearie?"

Mrs. O'Halloran took a drag at the bitter and waited for her customary audience to assume their places. "Well, no," she said. "It was a pretty quiet and huninteresting meeting, from wot I could 'ear through the partition. Mister 'Azlitt said as 'ow 'e was 'appy to perdict that the Company would soon be declaring dividends agyne, but of course that wasn't no surprise in view of wot I told yer larst year. Then 'e went on to spill out a lot of bilge about 'ow throughout the year the orfficers and men on orl the ships 'ad mannerfested a wonderful spirit, and 'ad hincreased the hefficiency of the line no end, and so on. 'E said that this was hespecially remarkable because they'd bucked up and myde things jump without no urging from 'im, and brought the hexpenses down to next to nothing. Then 'e read a letter—'orrible slop it was —which 'e is sending with a gold watch to Captain Ball, of the *Inchcliffe*."

"Lawks!" chuckled Mrs. Jessup. "If 'e only knew wot the *Inchcliffe's* orfficers and men think about 'im, 'e wouldn't be 'arf so generous with 'is watches, 'e wouldn't!"

"Generous?" Mrs. O'Halloran sneered. "—'Oo, 'im? Haw, lydies, there's just the most comic joke of orl! That watch, as I 'appen to know, is a old second-'and one that 'Azlitt's been carrying fer years!"

"Oh, yer really don't mean it!"

"Second-'and? Why, the rotten skinflint!"

"Well, I never!"

"But wot about that fymous new ship 'e was talking about larst year—the one that was going to shyke the British Mercantile Marine and orl?—Did 'e mention it today, Missus O'Halloran?"

"Humph, yus. 'E said as 'ow Clifford & Castles ain't going in fer it arfter orl, that's 'ow much 'e mentioned it!"

"Wot?—Not going in fer it arfter orl?"

"No, dearie, and them was hexackly 'is own words. The little blighter 'as just simply welshed on the 'ole propersition!"

"—But 'ow's 'e think 'e's going to get them dividends if 'e 'asn't got the ship?"

Mrs. O'Halloran shrugged. "Arsk 'Azlitt!" she retorted, dismally.

From all around the Yard there came a murmur of disappointment.

"But wot kind of a ship was it, dearie? Was yer able to 'ear it's nyme today?"

"I was," said Mrs. O'Halloran. "Receivership, that was the nyme of it. But there ain't the faintest 'ope of our 'aving it now!"

Mrs. McCoy sniffed disgustedly. "Well, that shows yer 'ow much 'is word is worth!"

"Wot a ruddy old fraud 'e is!"

"Ain't 'e, just!"

"Not 'arf!"

Somewhere out in the Reach a steamer's siren bellowed, and in the distance, very faintly, Big Ben chimed nine strokes. Still clicking their tongues and shaking their heads at Mr. Hazlitt's astounding mendacity, the good ladies of Catsmeat Yard gathered their kimonos around them and went their pessimistic ways to bed.

BROILERS OF THE SEA

ONE morning in the summer of 1919 a British tramp ship called the *Paxton Merchant* was steaming down through the tepid waters and stifling airs in the mouth of Bab-el-Mandeb, when a great controversy arose between Mr. David MacCrummon, the Chief Engineer, and his senior assistant, a certain Mr. Colin Glencannon. In the course of their debate, which took place beneath the poop awning, the contenders waxed vehement, then sarcastic and finally so exceeding wroth that the stifling airs became sulphurous with acrimony, and the tepid waters turned torrid as volleys of blistering oaths ricochetted off the *Paxton Merchant's* decks and fell sizzling into her wake. So considerable was the uproar that snatches of it even reached the bridge, and at length Captain Birkhead sent Mr. Wart, his Second Mate, aft to ascertain its cause. Meanwhile, he gave attentive ear.

"Blosh!" he heard Mr. MacCrummon shouting. "Blosh and fuddlesticks, Glencannon, and I say it to yere ugly walrus face! Ye're no' only headstrong, ye're no' only vulgar, but ye're positively unsaniturra besides!"

Stepping out into the wing of the bridge, Captain Birkhead peered aft just in time to see Mr. Glencannon wrench his deck-chair asunder and hurl the fragments overboard in impotent fury. "MacCrummon," he cried, "oh, MacCrummon, ye pewling Dunvegan gowk, if ye had the inteeligence o' an idjiot ye'd ken that what I say is a motter o' undisputable scientific fact.—But ye dinna ken it, because ye're a dolt and a dimwit—aye, ye're nowt but a low untutored ignoramus, groping yere way through life with yere brains in yere breeks, thinking two and two mak's three, and spelling C with a K!"

Captain Birkhead watched Mr. MacCrummon's pipe sail over the taffrail to join the riven chair among the flotsam of the deep and also, peradventure, to poison a shark. The debaters called a

213

recess to collect breath and simultaneously Mr. Wart ascended the ladder to deliver his report.

"Sir," he explained, a faraway look in his eyes, "it's just them ruddy Scots altercating agyne.—Sitting back there in the shyde in their hunderdrawers, they are, going at it 'ammer and tongs."

"Oh, and are they?" snapped Captain Birkhead. "Well, what in the flaming blazes did you think I thought it was, Mister— meadowlarks? What I want to know is, what're they yaggling about?—What's the bone of contention between 'em this morning, hey?"

"Well," said Mr. Wart, squinting off to port into the mirage which danced and wavered above the sunblasted rocks of Araby the Blessed, "as near as I could sift it out from amongst their 'orrible language, Sir, it happears that Mr. MacCrummon main- tains that cats don't sweat, while Mr. Glencannon 'olds to the con- trary. Haccording to 'im, all felines prespire through the soles of their feet.—Copiously. Yus, Captain Birkhead, that was Mr. Glen- cannon's very word; —'copiously.' "

" 'Copiously'?" Captain Birkhead sniffed. "Ho, so 'copiously' is his word for it, hey? Well, Mr. Wart, you can take it from me, there's something more copious and a dam sight stronger than catsweat that's the matter with them two tinkers this morning, if anybody should happen to ask you!—Just which of 'em would you say was the drunkest, and whom of 'em's got the bottle?"

"Mm, well—" and again the Second Mate's gaze strayed off into the shimmering distances, "—well, as to which of 'em's the drunk- est, I'd call it a draw, I would. Neither of 'em's any drunker than usual, if you can imagine that; and as fer a bottle, why they 'aven't got no bottle at all.—No, Sir, they've got a ten-gallon swill bucket which they borrowed orff the cook, and they sucks out of it turn- and-turn-about through a glarss tube, the syme as wot they mykes their bleddy boiler gauges out of, Sir."

"Ah!" said Captain Birkhead icily, at the same time showing his eye-teeth. "A ten-gallon swill bucket they've got, is it? Well, at last I know what Mr. Glencannon stole those ninety pounds of dates off that Arab at Ismailia for, and why Mr. MacCrummon has been mucking about with steam in the donkey boiler and all them bottles and bits of copper pipe and things! Why, they've been brewing themselves a supply of *gok* or *bhing* or whatever's the native name for the filthy stuff, don't you see?—Making a distillery of my ship, yes, that's what they've been doing! Ah well, Mr. Wart, all I've got to say is, may the merciful heavens deliver me from engineers who are inventors!"

"Yus," said Mr. Wart, with an effort recalling himself from his intense preoccupation. "Yus, Mr. MacCrummon certainly is a genius when it comes to inventing gadgets and all such, I must say. But—but, well, I wonder if this time 'e 'asn't just slipped up a bit, so to speak?"

"Slipped up as how, Mr. Wart?"

"Slipped up in this 'ere controversy 'e's 'aving with Mr. Glencannon.—Arfter all, Captain, the cat is a mammal, the syme as you and I; it 'as 'air, and because it 'as 'air, it must 'ave pores for the 'air to grow out of, don't you follow me? And if it 'as pores— well, wot I says is, if you and I and all other mammals prespire through our pores, why don't a cat?"

Captain Birkhead's face clouded; he jerked his hands out of his jacket pockets and took a quick step toward the mate. "Look here, Mister, are you asking me questions?" he demanded, truculently. "—Isn't it enough that I've got to put up with them two Glasgow elocutors, without submitting to interrogations from you? Maybe cats have pores and maybe they haven't, but be dam if you or any other mate can call me a mammal on my own bridge, so just put that in your pipe and smoke it!" Snorting irefully he strode into the wheelhouse, glared at the steersman, then into the binnacle, and then back at the steersman. "And another thing," he shouted, leaning from the window, "I'm not so sure that Mr. MacCrummon's not right. Supposing a cat has got pores, hey?— Well, what then? Neither you or I or anybody else has ever seen a cat work up a lather, have you?"

"—No, Sorrh!" blurted the Quartermaster at the wheel, who from the outset had barely managed to restrain himself from taking part in the discussion. "Whoy, Oi moind one toime in Londonderry, Sorrh, whin a cot o' moy acquointance . . ."

"—Beggar you and the cats of your acquaintance, my man!" roared Captain Birkhead. "—Who in blazes asked you to stick your nasty mug into this marmalade, anyway? No! No!" he fumed, turning once more to Mr. Wart. "What I mean is, who are you to scoff at Mr. MacCrummon when he says that cats don't sweat, henh? Now me, I've petted 'em, I've fondled 'em, I've dandled 'em and I've strangled 'em in all kinds of weather and in every known climate, but be blowed if I ever remember one of 'em shedding a single drop through their pores."

Mr. Wart gulped once or twice. "But wot about Mr. Glencannon's theory?" he insisted. "Wot about felines prespiring through the soles of their feet? 'Aven't you never noticed their footprints, Sir?"

Captain Birkhead thrust out his chin. "Mister Mate," he said, "the habits of a cat is his own private business, bestowed upon him by nature. And besides that, I'll thank you not to bring such subjects up to your superior officers, or by George I'll have your ticket, Sir!"

Mr. Wart retreated in confusion to get the ladder in readiness for the Aden pilot.

"Mph!" grunted Captain Birkhead, stamping in to look at the chart. "Of course they don't sweat.—Through their pores or their feet or their ears or any other way!"

On the deck below, two grimy firemen were holding heated palaver. "—But a cat condenses, syme as the engines, don't 'e?" one of them was demanding. "Well, then, if 'e condenses, wot I says is, 'e's got to eject!"

"Eject, yer eye!" scoffed the other. "And 'ow can 'e eject through 'is ruddy feet when 'e's treading on 'em?"

By the forward winch, an engine room apprentice and the donkeyman were loud in a technical discussion involving cats, capillarity, osmosis and evaporation, while a sudden burst of oaths and outcries aft announced that the controversialists on the poop were under way again.

"Dam!" said Captain Birkhead.

Around the end of Ras Sanailah, Aden hove into view.

II

The *Paxton Merchant* had called at Aden to coal—a hot, noisy, dirty and altogether unpleasant process which frazzled men's nerves and raised hob with their tempers. Thus the universal discussion of feline hydraulics gave rise to much bad language, three fist fights, and considerable frenzied betting, in the course of which Messrs. MacCrummon and Glencannon waited upon Captain Birkhead bearing with them a quart bottle of whisky.

"We're osking ye to be our stake-holder, Captain," Mr. Mac-Crummon explained. "—As ye'll obsairve, it's a bottle o' Duggan's Dew o' Kirkintilloch, the excellence of whuch is the one thing in the world Glencannon and I can agree on. Due to the rigors o' the late War, the bottle noo in yere hands is pairhops the only one in existence East o' Suez, sae do ye guard it jealously, Captain, and dinna surrender it to either o' us till we come back together with the winner decided betwixt us."

"Unh!" said Captain Birkhead, locking the bottle in his cupboard. "But I say, I wish you buckos would hurry up and settle this thing. Not only is your constant bellowing and broiling a ruddy nuisance, not only is the question playing beer and skittles with the discipline of the ship, but I've got a three quid bet with Mr. Larkin on it myself."

"Whuch way are ye betting?" inquired Mr. MacCrummon.

"Why, 'no sweat,' of course! As I've said to Mr. Wart, as I've said to Mr. Larkin, as I've said to a dozen people, anybody that says a cat gives off is barmy."

"Haw, and is he?" demanded Mr. Glencannon, his voice vibrant. "Weel, Sir, speaking unofficially and withoot disrespect, if ye were no' the captain o' this rotten auld suet-kettle, I'd show ye richt here and noo who's barmy, and black both o' yere nosty squint eyes doing it! But as it is—weel, as it is, ye'll hae to wait till tomorrow, when yon puir deluded MacCrummon and I conduct cairtain conclusive experiments."

"Aye!" sneered Mr. MacCrummon. "—Conclusive in showing ye, Glencannon, that yere crack-pot theories is just so monny crack-pot theories, and that while ye're a mon o' vast knowledge, most o' it is wrong. Why, ye uncouth beet-nosed glaggy, the vurra idea o . . ."

"Get out! Get out of here, the both of you!" bawled Captain Birkhead, snatching up a Bechuana knobkerrie from the corner. "If you two miscreants think you can use my room for a ruddy bullring, you've got another think coming!" He shoved them out on deck, slammed the door after them, and stood scowling as the roars of rage grew faint in the distance. "Oh, Great Grimes, was there ever such a pair?" he muttered, feebly.

Next day as the *Paxton Merchant,* her decks gritty with coal dust, went snouting into the Gulf swell toward Zeila, in Somaliland Protectorate, Captain Birkhead repeated the mutter with lurid trimmings. For the *Merchant,* by nature the slowest and most sedate of tubs, was suddenly behaving like a horse that has swallowed a hornet. She surged ahead at an unprecedented pace, butting the blue seas and spattering them outwards in great sheets of spray which flashed with jewelled rainbows. From her funnel belched a black cloud that swept down low over her seething wake and then spread out in a pall upon the surface of the waters. Her decks throbbed and trembled like those of a destroyer running a speed trial, while from below came the ringing scrape of coal shovels, the thud of slice-bars and the general clank and rattle of a stokehold working with the devil in charge. From time to time firemen black as singed imps staggered out on deck and collapsed, to lie panting where they fell in broadening puddles of sweat.

Captain Birkhead strode to the Engine Room speaking tube and whistled down it. "See here!" he roared. "What the hell are you trying to do down there, anyway—shake the ruddy plates off her and burn up all the coal in the bunkers? We must be making 12 knots—yes, 13, by Moses!—and it's got to stop! Let me speak to the Chief! Let me speak to Mr. Glencannon!"

"Aye, Sir!" came the voice from the tube. " 'Arf a mo' while I calls 'em, Sir." The 'arf a mo' grew to a full one and the one to five; Captain Birkhead, waiting with his ear to the cup, was about to send for his knobkerrie and go below in person when "Bridge?" came the voice. "Sorry to keep you wyting, Sir, but the Chief and the Second was both busy. They're coming right up now to see you, Sir."

"Oh, they are, are they?" snarled Captain Birkhead, craning his neck over the dodger. "Well, I've a dam good mind to log the pair of 'em!" He had just become aware that the din from below had subsided and that the ship had resumed its accustomed plodding gait, when he saw the causes of his wrath emerge upon the deck. Mr. Glencannon was carrying a large roll of pale green blotting paper, while Mr. MacCrummon bore in his arms a japanned tin bread box. The pair of them walked to the rail, Mr. MacCrummon heaved his burden overboard, and then, with solemn faces, they proceeded up the ladder to the bridge. The Captain was waiting for them at the head of it.

"Well!" he began, "I want to ask you . . ."

Mr. MacCrummon stayed him with upraised hand. "'Twas a sorra failure—aye, a fiossco," he announced, shaking his head sadly. "The experiment came to nowt, and we're as far awa' from a settlement as we ever were. We tuk the cat and . . ."

"What cat?" demanded Captain Birkhead.

"Why, the cat we got in Aden last nicht;—we tuk the cat, whuch at the vurra ootset we'd imprisoned in the bread box, and lugged him doon into the stokehold, where 'twas guid and hot. Just to mak' the experiment more conclusive, we closed all the ventilators and stoked the auld tub up till we got a temperature o' 163 degrees Fahrenheit ten feet awa' from the boilers;—ah, whoosh, Captain, we could fair feel the marrow treekling within our bones! Weel, we tuk a shovel and pushed the box with the cat inside it richt close up against an open furnace door. I held the watch to check on the time, and Glencannon spread oot the blotting paper all ready to . . ."

"Yes, yes!" Captain Birkhead interrupted impatiently. "What happened, what happened?—Did he sweat or didn't he?"

"Aloss!" Mr. Glencannon took up the thread of the narrative, at the same time dabbing a tear from his eye with a handful of oily cotton waste, "whether he sweated or not, we dinna ken. At the end o' ten minutes we opened the box, and lo, nowt whatsoever was in it save a charred and shrivelled and shapeless corpus."

"No!" The Captain wilted back against the rail. "Well, I'll be damned!"

"Such is yere privilege, Sir," bowed Mr. Glencannon, politely. "And noo, ha'eing discharged our juties to science and consigned the puir broiled martyr's relics to the vasty deep, we've come to osk will ye kindly be guid enough to restore the bottle o' Duggan's which we recently left in yere custody."

"Aye," sighed Mr. MacCrummon. "All bets is off, so we've got to divide it equally. 'Tis e'en lik' the wise judgment o' Solomon, when he decreed that the Samaritan baby shud be chopped in twain."

"It is indeed," agreed Mr. Glencannon. "It's also summat lik' the time I saw a Dago cut a woman in half with a rip-saw in the auld Victoria Music Hall, in Cardiff, though I've often wondered since if there wasn't some sort o' flummery aboot it. And then, o' coorse, there was the time when an Uncle o' mine, the late Deacon Dugald Glencannon o' Ballachulish, came staggering hame with an axe, a cleaver and a butcher knife and . . . Ah, thonk ye, Captain!—Just gi' it here!"

"Ho, no ye don't!" shouted Mr. MacCrummon, snatching the bottle from him. "None o' that, ye grosping gowk, or I'll do ye in richt here and noo!"

"Ah, and will ye?" Mr. Glencannon's hand darted toward the knobkerrie in the corner, but Captain Birkhead beat him to it.

"Hold hard, you two," he rasped. "—Hold hard, I say, and take a look at this!"

The object to which he invited their attention was a .455 bull-dog revolver, and as he swung its muzzle back and forth across their wincing abdomens, they saw the dull gray gleam of lethal lead in all its several chambers.

"Now then, you Scotch scuts," he announced, "I've had a fair bellyful of your bickering and bellowing aboard my ship, and I'm going to put a stop to it once and for all. Sit down at that table, the pair of you, and write what I dictate. I'll write a third copy along with you, so's we'll all have one. Er, m'm:—

Whereinbefore and inasmuchas we, the undersigned, David Mac-Crummon and Colin Glencannon, do jointly and together own and possess a bottle bearing the label Duggan's Dew of Kirkin-tilloch, said bottle having been acquired by us in the course of scientific experiments in which we were jointly engaged, we hereby agree that the contents of said bottle does belong to each of us in equal shares, to wit, half of it to one and half to the other. We further agree that the division of said contents or of such proceeds as may result from its exchange, sale or other eventual use or disposal in any manner whatsoever, shall be made in a fair and equitable way, in order that no disputes shall arise between us either now or at future date regarding same. Er, er . . .'"

There was a knock at the door.

"Come in!" shouted Captain Birkhead, without lowering his pistol. "Ah, a wireless for me? H'm! . . ." He glanced through the message, and then, seeming not to comprehend it, went over it word by word. The engineers saw his face flush red and the red deepen to purple. His nostrils dilated. The gun thumped upon the table.

"Ah, what's amuss, Captain?" Mr. Glencannon inquired solicitously. "Has Mussis Birkhead finally eloped with that Swansea shipchandler, or has she finally decided not to?"

"Yes! No! Neither!" stammered Captain Birkhead, lurching to his feet and shaking his fists above his head in futile frenzy. "Oh, you web-footed sots, you! You hairy-eared Glasgow ghouls! Look, just look what you've done now! Here, read it, read it!"

The wireless message read:—

HAVE RELIABLE INFORMATION GRAY CAT ANSWERING TO NAME LADY DIANA MANNERS WAS STOLEN BY TWO OFFICERS YOUR SHIP STOP CAT CHERISHED PROPERTY MAJOR GENERAL SIR NEVILLE KEITH-ROSS GOVERNOR OF ADEN STOP UNLESS CAT IS DELIVERED GOOD CONDITION TO PORT AUTHORITIES AT ZEILA CULPRITS WILL BE RIGOROUSLY PROSECUTED FULL EXTENT OF LAW STOP ANSWER URGENT

"There!" moaned the Captain. "A fine mess you've got my ship into now! The only saving grace about the whole thing is that the pair of you'll go to jail, where you ought've been all along."

Mr. Glencannon wagged his head incredulously. "Weel, dearie me!" he mused. "So Lady Diana Manners was the little scolliwog's name, was it? I suppose the 'Lady Diana' part must hae been due to an owersight, and as for his manners, swith, they were fronkly onspeakable! All the same . . ."

"—But all the same, 'twas you who stole that cat, Glencannon!" thundered Mr. MacCrummon. "I warned ye ten times to leave it go and snare the black one which clawed ye in the alley! But oh no, ye stubborn headstrong lout, nothing would satisfy ye but . . ."

Mr. Glencannon leaned across the table and thrust a jaw like the ram of a battle cruiser to within a whisker's length of Mr. MacCrummon's, which rather resembled the bow of a Norwegian icebreaker. "Ye lie!" he hissed. "Ye lie in yere throat! 'Twas ye yersel' that stole the gray one, richt after the yellow one escaped fra' the bread box, and if ye'd no' been so befuddled ye'd vurra weel remember it!"

Captain Birkhead snatched up his revolver and intruded it brusquely between the bellicose chins, but just as he did so there came another knock at the door.

"It's fer you again, Captain," said the messenger. "—Sparks says as 'ow the Aden station is fair blistering the air on orl sides of its wyve-length, Sir!"

"Oh, how charming!" groaned the Captain, grinding his teeth. "—How perfectly delightful! Yes, and now, you ruddy guzzlers, just take a look at this!"

They looked and read:—

DEMAND NEWS OF CAT STOP MAJOR GENERAL SIR NEVILLE KEITH-ROSS COMPLETELY OUT OF CONTROL STOP APOPLEXY FEARED STOP HE THREATENS TO REQUEST CO-OPERATION OF NAVAL FORCES TO APPRE-HEND YOUR VESSEL UNLESS IMMEDIATE REPLY

"Foosh, Captain, I canna see aught so disturbing aboot that!" said Mr. Glencannon brightly. "After all, Sir, truth will prevail, and all ye hae to do is answer 'Cat not aboard ship.' "

"You leave the answer to me!" snapped Captain Birkhead. "Both of you sit down there where you were, and add on to that contract what I'm going to dictate, a-hem:—

We also certify by these presents that no person other than our-selves took part in or had knowledge of the experiments conducted by us, and that whatever the outcome, this partnership shall stand. It is further agreed that the responsibility for stealing a cat be-longing to the Governor of Aden rests solely upon us.

"There now!" Captain Birkhead took up the papers and checked them carefully. "I fancy that puts the responsibility for this whole mess right where it belongs! Sign all three of 'em, both of you, and then I'll sign as witness.—There, each of you take a copy—mine's going into the strong-box. Mr. MacCrummon, you're senior officer, so I'm handing over this bottle of whisky to you. Take it to your room, take your exact half share, and then turn the remainder over to Mr. Glencannon. But wait—there's another thing! I want you two to shake hands with each other, here in my presence. Come, come now—ah, fine, that's the spirit!"

"Let's let bygones be bygones, eh, Muster Mac?" said Mr. Glencannon, looking as sheepish as his resemblance to a walrus would permit.

"Aye, we'll let bygones be bygones," agreed Mr. MacCrummon. "We'll let the future tak' care o' itsel'!"

"Alright," said Captain Birkhead, "that's that! And now, scuttle to hell out of here, you pests, and pray to your ruddy Scotch gods that Major General Sir What-ever-his-silly-name-is pegs out with his apoplexy before we get to Zeila!"

It was time for Mr. Glencannon to stand his watch in the engine room, and as he descended the slippery iron ladders into the roaring, oven-like inferno—"May the hours fly swiftly!" he chuckled. "There'll be a pint o' braw Highland nectar awaiting me, and I'll just aboot hae time to doon it before supper." As the afternoon wore on, however, he found anticipation pleasant, and when his watch drew to an end, he almost wished that realization might be deferred. Thus, as he made his way aft toward his quarters and espied Mr. MacCrummon busy inventing something at the workbench on the after well-deck, he paused to pass the time of day with him.

"Weel, what is it this evening, Muster Mac?" he inquired genially. "What fair-haired child o' science are ye bringing forth the noo?"

Mr. MacCrummon, himself feeling mellow for reasons which the alcoholic content of the atmosphere surrounding him made obvious, looked up from the blow-torch in which he was heating a knob of brass, and blushed.

"Oh, 'tis nowt, nowt at all," he said modestly. " 'Tis just a vurra ingenious little device I hoppened to think up, that's all. It's a collapsible blackjack, d'ye see, convenient for carrying in the pocket. Pairhops its cleverest feature is this spiral spring in the handle, so adjusted that when ye hit a mon with it the feerst time, it bounces back o' its ain accord and clouts him again automatically."

"Neat, ho, vurra neat!" nodded Mr. Glencannon approvingly. "And noo—" he winked, "—and noo, Muster Mac, I think I'll just stup back to my room and discuss a drap o' that Duggan's, if that's where ye left it."

"Go richt ahead, Colin—ye'll find it on yere chest o' drawers, and may it comfort yere leathery gizzard as much as it has comforted mine!"

The bottle, sure enough, was on Mr. Glencannon's dresser, and as he held it up to the light and gauged its contents with a micrometric eye, he saw that the division had been accurate to the finest fraction of an inch and strictly according to contract.

He sighed luxuriously. He smacked his lips. "Weel, here goes!" he said, tilting back his head. There was rapturous silence, broken only by a slucking, guzzling sound, as when the tide recedes from a rocky cavern. But suddenly the guzzles gave way to gags, the slucking turned to sputters, and the erstwhile rapturous silence was shattered by a fearful oath.

"Oil!" gasped Mr. Glencannon, mopping off his tongue on the porthole curtain and retching somewhat. "Filthy roncid oil! Oh, by the black hoorns o' the deevil, this is the lost straw!" He seized the bottle by its neck and went sallying forth to the fray.

Then, as the saying has it, pandemonium reigned. Accounts differ as to just what transpired, although within a minute's time approximately two-thirds of the ship's company were involved. The pro-perspiration faction ranged themselves with Mr. Glencannon, while the bone-drys backed Mr. MacCrummon. When Captain Birkhead arrived upon the battlefield, knobkerrie in hand, he found the Chief Engineer *hors de combat,* covered with oil, surrounded by broken glass, and with a monumental lump upon his brow. Mr. Glencannon was sprawled beside him, wearing two lumps.

Now this extra excrescence upon Mr. Glencannon's cranium constituted a flattering testimonial to the efficiency of Mr. Mac-Crummon's new double-acting blackjack, and thus it might reasonably be assumed that the inventor was feasting his eyes upon it. But he wasn't. Instead he was staring fixedly at a little patch of flame which danced in the scupper, where the overturned blowtorch had ignited the mixture of coal dust and oil. "Swith!" he kept muttering. "Coal dust and oil! Coal dust and oil!" He was still repeating it like a wizard working a charm when he and Mr. Glencannon were put in irons and locked in their respective rooms, bandages and all.

During the night a wireless message from the *Paxton Merchant's* owners ordered Captain Birkhead to call at Djibouti, French Somaliland, instead of at Zeila; and there, with hymns and hallelujahs in his heart, he sent the pair ashore to the hospital.

Five hours later, short handed but once again habitable, the S.S. *Paxton Merchant* put back to sea.

III

On a morning in the summer of 1933, a British tramp ship called the *Inchcliffe Castle* lay berthed in Limehouse Commercial Docks, in the port of London, waiting for a cargo. Breakfast was over and now, there being nothing else to do, her officers lolled back in their chairs smoking, chatting, or picking their teeth, each according to his caprice, although it was to be remarked that one of them, who wore the stripes of a Chief Engineer, was doing all three at once. This gentleman was somewhat ruddier than of yore, his brow was more beetling and his mustache grown scragglier, but despite the changes wrought by the years, one would instantly have recognized him as Mr. Colin Glencannon.

"Aye," he was saying, at the same time giving an unexampled demonstration of versatility by inhaling a charge of snuff without disturbing his pipe or his toothpick. "Aye, Captain Ball, there's more than a modicum o' truth in yere obsairvations, Sir. I mysel' hae yet to meet a shipowner who was no' a scoundrel o' the deepest dye—treacherous, grosping, mean and . . ."

"Oh, ullo!" exclaimed the First Mate, looking up from his newspaper. "—MacCrummon—yus, David MacCrummon.—Why, ain't that the inventor cove wot used to be hengineer o' the *'Ardcliffe Castle?'*"

At the sound of the hated name, Mr. Glencannon tensed. "Aye, that's the swundler, richt enough, and before he was in the *Hardcliffe*, I sairved as his Second in the auld *Paxton Merchant*. What's the glod tidings o' him, Muster Montgomery—has he finally been hung?"

"No," said the Mate, " 'e 'asn't;—in fact it happears from this

'ere hinterview that 'e's well on the way to myking 'is ruddy fortune!"

Without ceremony Mr. Glencannon reached across the table
and snatched the paper to him. His face clouded and his breathing
quickened as he read:—

NEW SHIP READY FOR TEST
HIGH EFFICIENCY, LOW COST, INVENTOR'S
CLAIM FOR "COLLOIDAL" MIXTURE
"WILL REVOLUTIONIZE SHIPPING,"
SAYS MacCRUMMON

A new type of fuel for marine engines, it was learned today, has
been perfected by David MacCrummon, President of the Mac-
Crummon Patent Colloidal Fuel Company, Ltd., of 26 Leadenhall
Street. This fuel is a so-called "colloidal" mixture of coal dust and
oil, compounded after formulas developed and patented by Mr.
MacCrummon. Coal dust, generally considered a waste product,
costs practically nothing, and the oil in MacCrummon's specifications is of the lowest grade; thus the combustible colloid can be
produced with the utmost economy. "Any existing steam vessel
can be quickly and cheaply converted for the use of my fuel," said
Mr. MacCrummon, himself a marine engineer of wide experience.
"I confidently predict that in a few years time, 95% of the world's
shipping will be burning it. Our Company has chartered the S.S.
Samothrace, a 2800 ton cargo ship, for an actual test under strin-
gent deep-sea conditions. She will sail early next week." Shares in
the MacCrummon Patent Colloidal Fuel Co., Ltd., are now being
offered to the public. Mr. Coniston Gould, long active in Near
Eastern importing circles, is Chairman of the Board.

When he had finished the item, and as its full significance bore
in upon him, Mr. Glencannon's agitation became terrible to behold. "Infamous!" he whispered hoarsely. "Infamous! Why, the
dom thief is robbing me o' my richts!" Springing to his feet, he
hurled himself from the room.

Perhaps two hours later he ascended the stairs to the second
floor of No. 26 Leadenhall Street, and paused outside a door in-

scribed "The MacCrummon Patent Colloidal Fuel Company, Ltd. Walk In." Responding to the invitation, he entered and found himself in a handsome office furnished with a walnut desk and leather upholstered chairs. Upon the desk was a pair of feet in light tan shoes while behind it was the rest of Mr. MacCrummon, clad in a check suit. At the sound of the door, he glanced up from an illustrated feuilleton entitled "Parisian Nudities," and his involuntary start of recognition was followed by a look of extreme displeasure.

"Oh, so 'tis you, is it?" he observed sourly. "Weel, goodbye, Glencannon!"

Wholly unabashed, Mr. Glencannon came forward and settled himself in a chair, noticing as he did so that a frosted glass door on the left of the room was stencilled "Mr. Coniston Gould. Private."

"Weel, MacCrummon, I can tell ye're owerjoyed at seeing me," he beamed. "—Been inventing onything new lately?"

"Yes," said Mr. MacCrummon, producing a blackjack from the top drawer.—"This!" He held the weapon above the corner of the desk and twitched it slightly. So rapid was the ensuing vibration of the handle that the impacts of the head against the wood sounded like the roll of a drum.

"—Eight!" announced Mr. Glencannon, endeavoring to count the blows.

"No, ten," Mr. MacCrummon corrected him. "However, in octual proctice, ye'd only be conscious during the first two."

"Ah!" said Mr. Glencannon, "Ah!" He took out his pipe and went about filling it, at the same time surveying the office with a calculating eye. "Weel," he announced, striking a match on the arm of his chair, "I foncy there's room for it ower there next the window."

"—Room for what?" demanded Mr. MacCrummon.

"Room for my desk. Starting richt noo, you and I are co-presidents o' this company, so ye micht just as weel get used to it."

A peculiar sound emerged from Mr. MacCrummon's throat, and his hand moved toward the blackjack.

"Noo, noo, just a minute!" Mr. Glencannon restrained him. "Dinna turn ugly, MacCrummon—I warn ye it willna pay! If

ye'll regard this fist o' mine closely, ye'll obsairve that it's graced
with a set o' genuine imported American bross knuckles, and while
they only hit once, the once is enough. Oh, I expected richt alang
that ye'd no' voluntarily concede that my whocking ye ower the
head with that bottle o' oil, throwing the blow-torch at ye, and
setting fire to the coal dust mixture, was what gave ye the idea
o' yere dom patent fuel! Guid losh, come to think o' it, the whole
thing's really my invention!—But I'll no be greedy, MacCrummon—I'll let ye enjoy what's legally yours." From his wallet he
produced a greasy age-yellowed paper. "This document," he continued, "drawn up in legal form, signed by you and duly wut-
nessed, gi's me a full partner's share in this company, and ye canna
wurrm oot o' it!"

"Why, what in the heel are ye blethering aboot?" fumed Mr.
MacCrummon, shifting uneasily.

"I'm talking aboot this contract betwixt us, whuch ye signed in
Captain Birkhead's presence on the *Paxton Merchant* thirteen
years ago. Here, listen; I'll read ye some extracts—er . . . 'do
jointly and together own and possess a bottle bearing the label
Duggan's Dew of Kirkintilloch, said bottle hae'ing been acquired
by us in the course o' scientific experiments in whuch we were
jointly engaged' . . . er . . . 'the division of said contents or of
such proceeds as may come from its exchange, sale or other eventual use or disposal in any manner whatsoever (haw, get that, Mac-
Crummon!) shall be made in a fair and equitable way.' Aye, and
listen to this! . . . 'no person other than oursel's tuk part in or
had knowledge of the experiments . . . and that whate'er the
ootcome, this partnership shall stand.'—Guid losh, MacCrummon,
need I read ye more than that?"

"No!" retorted MacCrummon. "Ye can save yere breath! Ye
ken as weel as I do that all what ye've read had nowt to do wi'
my Colloidal Fuel, but only wi' that puir harmless little creature
whuch ye inveigled me into helping ye kidnop and broil in the
furnace at Aden, that time, barbarian that ye are! Get oot o' my
office, ye dom blackmailer! Get oot, get oot, I say!"

"Noo, dinna raise yere voice, and dinna attempt to get muscular
with me!" Mr. Glencannon shouted. "I'll hae my just and legal
richts, whuch means a full half share in this company! I'll gi' ye

twelve hours to think it ower, and if I hae no' heard fra ye by then—weel, I'll write an anonymous letter to a cairtain gentlemon in Scotland Yard!"

"Blosh!" scoffed Mr. MacCrummon. "What gentlemon do ye ken at Scotland Yard?"

Mr. Glencannon paused with his hand on the doorknob. "Why, do ye mean to say ye canna guess?" he asked incredulously. "Swith, MacCrummon, I've told ye before and I tell ye again, ye're ignorant enough to spell C with a K! Didn't ye ken that the newly-appointed Commissioner o' the Metropolitan Police is none other than Major General Sir Neville Keith-Ross, Retired, formerly Governor o' Aden?"

He slammed the door, and with the tinkle of its shattered glass panel still echoing pleasantly in his ears, descended the stairs to Leadenhall Street. He had proceeded scarcely more than halfway to Aldgate High Street when he heard hurried footfalls behind him and felt a nervous twitch at his sleeve. Turning, he confronted a stout, expensively-dressed gentleman with a very small black mustache and even smaller, blacker eyes.

"I beg your pardon," said this gentleman, bowing and going through the motions of a smile. "Believe me, Mr. Glencannon, I wouldn't have accosted you this way, except—er, except . . . But here, permit me to introduce myself!" He presented a card upon which was engraved

MR. CONISTON GOULD

IMPORTER

LONDON ISTANBUL SMYRNA

"Ah yes, Muster Gould, I've heard o' ye," said Mr. Glencannon. "And noo that I see ye, ye smell to me lik' a Levantine."

Mr. Coniston Gould rubbed his hands and laughed a laugh which suggested that his vocal chords were made of pork fat. "Well, I've heard of you too, Mr. Glencannon—or rather, I overheard what you were just discussing with Mr. MacCrummon. And speaking of, ah, smells—another spot of whisky wouldn't do you any harm, what say?"

"Muster Gould, ye've osked a question to whuch I hae only one onswer. Lead the way, Sir, lead the way!"

They turned into an establishment with a bar along one side
and booths along the other. "Here," Mr. Gould invited, ushering
Mr. Glencannon into one of the stalls "—here's a nice quiet spot
where we can have a little friendly business chat, eh?"

As he settled himself on the leather bench, Mr. Glencannon
made mental note that while Mr. MacCrummon spelled C with
a K, his elegant colleague pronounced S with a Z, and he wondered
if at some long-forgotten date Mr. Coniston Gould might not have
been called Constantine Gouldopolis, or Nestor Goulmoudjian,
or even plain Nick Goulikajian. But:—

"Yes," said Mr. Gould when the waiter had made his exit, "I
heard everything you said to Mr. MacCrummon—everything! I
judge that the pair of you are not, so to say, bosom friends, eh?"

"Yere judgment is correct, Sir," said Mr. Glencannon, sniffing
the contents of his glass. "And as lang as ye heard what I said to
him, I needna teel ye why. Suffice it to say that I loathe his vurra
entrails, and I'll hae my just share o' this invention if I hae to
tromple it oot o' him!"

"Ah, precisely!" nodded Mr. Gould, toying with one of the
emerald rings on his white and pudgy hand. "Speaking in strictest
confidence, Mr. MacCrummon has gotten a bit on my nerves, too.
The only thing is—ah—didn't I hear you mention something
about an anonymous letter to Scotland Yard?"

"Aye," said Mr. Glencannon, "ye cairtainly did."

Mr. Coniston Gould sat silent for a moment; then, "Mr. Glencannon," he said, "I'm a business man, and my reputation is of the
highest—oh yes, I assure you, the very, very highest! But nevertheless, to be perfectly frank, Scotland Yard is a name I don't care
to hear. Just at this time, to have them snooping about would be
exceedingly, ah, inconvenient, do you follow me?"

"I do," Mr. Glencannon nodded sympathetically.

"Precisely! I knew you'd get my point—even without having to
remind you that somebody else might write an anonymous letter
about your own part in a certain kidnapping and—ah—furnace-
murder, wasn't it?—A poor, harmless little creature, wrested from
its parents and . . . ugh! You see, my hearing's very acute, Mr.
Glencannon!"

Mr. Glencannon started violently and then wilted back against the cushion. He opened his mouth, but no sound emerged. Mr. Coniston Gould chuckled unctuously and rubbed his hands.

"Oh, there, there, please, I hope I haven't upset you!" he said. "It was only that I wanted to establish a common basis upon which you and I could talk business. I think that now we understand each other, don't you?"

"Aye!" whispered Mr. Glencannon, hoarsely. "What is it ye want of me, mon? Tell me, tell me!"

"I will," said Mr. Coniston Gould, his little black mustache twitching upward in a smile. "I'll start at the beginning. Now, in the first place, I own 51 percent of the stock of the MacCrummon Patent Colloidal Fuel Company, Ltd. I didn't pay a penny cash for it—ah, no, no, not I! Instead, I agreed to furnish the *Samothrace,* an old ship I happen to own, for experiments and tests. Well, MacCrummon's fuel is approved by Lloyd's and the French Bureau Veritas for vessels insured by them, but that's no proof it's any good. At best, it will be two or three years before it earns a penny. Meanwhile I need cash—yes I need cash, Mr. Glencannon—thousands and thousands of pounds of it! I need it desperately. Right away!"

"Ye hae my profoond sumpathy, Sir!" murmured Mr. Glencannon, rolling his eyes toward heaven.

"Thanks, but I'd rather have your help in getting the money!" Mr. Gould leaned across the table and laid a hand on Mr. Glencannon's arm. "The *Samothrace* sails next week," he whispered. "She's insured clear up to the masthead. Right now, we're mixing the coal dust and oil in my warehouse across from the Wellington Docks. What do you suppose would happen, Mr. Glencannon, if we were to put something besides coal dust into that oil—something which looks exactly like coal dust, but . . ."

"But what?"

Mr. Gould's lips scarcely moved. "Gunpowder!" he murmured. "Gunpowder! If you can arrange to buy it, pack it in coal dust sacks and deliver it, I'll sign over my 51 percent of the Company's shares to you the day the *Samothrace* sails.—Yes, and I'll advance you a hundred quid to cover your expenses right now!"

Mr. Glencannon scowled and gnawed the fringes of his mustache. "But, Muster Gould!" he protested. "While blowing up yere

ship wud cairtainly benefeet you, and wud e'en gi' me a guid
hearty laugh at MacCrummon, what wud it avail me to own the
stock if the fuel should thus apparently turn oot to be a failure?"

Mr. Gould shrugged and spread his hands. "If the fuel's actually
as good as MacCrummon claims, it would only be a temporary
set-back. In any case, you'll own the majority stock, and'll be able
to make him eat all the humble pie you choose to cram down his
neck."

"And if I don't agree to do as ye suggest?"

"Ah!" said Mr. Gould, softly "—Major General Sir Neville
Keith-Ross, of Scotland Yard, will receive an anonymous . . ."

"Sh-h-h!" and rather more violently than the circumstances
seemed to warrant, Mr. Glencannon's horny hand clamped over
the other's mouth. "Gi' me the money and the address o' yere
warehouse! I—I'm yere mon!"

                                    IV

Some weeks later, as the S.S. *Inchcliffe Castle* lay loading alongside the Quai Nord, at Algiers, Mr. Montgomery came into dinner
with a London paper only six days old. "Look 'ere!" he said.
"—'Ere's news for yer! It says 'ere that 'MacCrummon's Colloidal
Fuel Proves Huge Success. Shares Jump as *Samothrace* Returns
from Epic-Making Voyage.' Now wot in blyzes do yer think of
that?"

"Weel," a modest smile suffused Mr. Glencannon's countenance,
"inasmuch as I invented the fuel mysel', pairhops it wud be un-
becoming o' me to say. But I wonder what yon brute o' a Mac-
Crummon will say, when I march into his office and offer him the
alternative o' drinking a pint o' roncid oil or else buying my
majority stock at my ain figure?"

"Your majority stock!" exclaimed Captain Ball. "Why, do you
mean to say? . . ."

"Aye," Mr. Glencannon bowed, "exoctly!" A reminiscent light
kindled in his eye, and starting with the long ago day in the
Strait of Bab-el-Mandeb, he told them the story. It lost nothing
in the telling.

"But see 'ere!" protested Mr. Montgomery, as the saga drew to its stirring conclusion. "You still 'aven't explyned why the *Samo-thrace* didn't blow up, with all that ruddy gunpowder mixed in the fuel!"

"Weel," chuckled Mr. Glencannon, "when Muster Gould so shrewdly suggested that gunpowder looks exockly lik' coal dust, it at once occurred to me that coal dust looks exockly lik' gun-powder. And so . . ."

"Well, my word!" breathed Captain Ball. "So that's the way you did it! But now, see here, Mr. Glencannon; did you really intend to write that anonymous letter to Scotland Yard?"

Mr. Glencannon shook his head. "No," he said. "For to tell ye the truth, Sir, it wud hae availed me nowt. Unbeknowst to Mac-Crummon, who was sodly in his cups that nicht, I let the cat escape e'en before we got him back to the ship. I was worrit aboot losing the bet, don't ye see, so I feegured that half the bottle wud be better than none. No doot the little beastie got hame safe and sound shortly after the Aden station sent oot that second wireless."

"But the corpse!" insisted Mr. Montgomery. "Wot was the scorched and blackened hobject which yer chucked overboard in the bread box?"

"Why, bread, o' course!" replied Mr. Glencannon, spearing a slice with his fork. "—Please pass the margarine."

HAMS ACROSS THE SEA

THE short December day rolled on westward over the curve of the world, and the damp chill of evening flooded after it into the hollow of Marseilles. Here and there in the sky above the hills the mistral-streaked clouds glowed faintly yellow, but night, black night, smelling of the sea and of the docks and of a million garlic suppers, lay clammily upon the waterfront. From the windows of furtive bistros and slopshops crouched between the warehouses of the Quai de la Joliette, dim lights leaked out upon the sidewalk. Motor trucks like elephants with bulging luminous eyes went thundering over the cobbles, locomotives butted laden cars along the sidings, while above the roofs of the wharf-sheds loomed the funnels of great ships—some of them vaguely silhouetted against clouds as murky as themselves, and others jutting brightly out of billowing steam which rose from the winches as stevedores worked cargo in the glare of cluster-lights. Derricks clattered, men shouted, sirens hooted, tramcars clanged. Everywhere were tumult and confusion, as in one of those darkly-scrambled etchings customarily entitled either TOIL, THE TITANS, COMMERCE, or WATERFRONT NOCTURNE.

The artistic qualities of the scene were lost, however, upon the pedestrian who was shaping a somewhat zig-zag course along the sidewalk toward the Vieux Port. This gentleman was shivering with cold, but though his hands were shoved deep into his jacket pockets, the four gold stripes and purple insert of a Chief Engineer of the British Mercantile Marine were visible upon the cuffs. His skin was ruddy with recent tropic suns, his lip was adorned with a mustache of the type so popular among bull walruses of the more hirsute species, and his brow was furrowed with the wrinkles of an intense preoccupation.

"Nineteen fronks!" he muttered, his teeth chattering dismally. "Nineteen fronks, and nowt to show for it but a frozen marrow and a nosty taste! Braw, what a climate! But noo let's see—" he gnawed the fringe of his mustache, "there's H on the left and C on the right—that's the way it is i' British bathtubs. Aye, and according to International Law, the hot water is a'ways the West one and the cold the East, regardless o' race, creed or language. But though C stands for cold i' English, it stonds for hot i' French, and dommed if I can remember the wurrd for it. Noo, *caldo* sounds lik' cold but it means hot i' Eyetalian. And to mak' it a' the more cumpleecated, *frio*, which anybody'd think meant fire or summat to do wi' frying, octually means the revairse i' Spanish, and it starts wi' an F. And sae the vexing questions still pose themselves—what is the five-letter wurrd beginning wi' C that means hot i' French; and how the heel does a mon order a hot grog i' Marsails wi'oot it?"

He had reached the windswept bend of the quai behind Fort St. Jean and was shudderingly turning up his collar when an idea came to him. "O' coorse!" he chuckled, quickening his pace toward the lights of the Cafe de la Marine. "—The sign longuage! Losh, Glencannon, the money and the chills ye'd hae saved if ye'd thought o' it before!" Turning through the doorway, he presented himself at the deserted bar. The striped-jersied publican and most of his guests were gathered in a corner jabbering in undertones and glancing hostilely at a massive gentleman, moon-faced and middle-aged, slouched on the settee behind one of the tables along the opposite wall.

Mr. Glencannon cleared his throat, then snapped his fingers, impatiently, and finally, nothing happening, he dealt the bar a lusty kick.

"*A votre service, M'sieu!*" said the proprietor, hurrying forward apologetically.

Mr. Glencannon said not a word; instead, with his left hand, with vivid pantomimic suggestion, he opened the imaginary hot water tap of a bath tub. With his right, he went through the motions of raising a glass to his lips, blowing gustily as if to cool its steaming contents.

After a moment's hesitation a gleam of understanding lighted the publican's face. He slid a glass under a brass faucet, executed a rapid turn of his wrist, and bowingly presented a foam-collared scuttle of beer.

Mr. Glencannon considered the sudsy vessel with incredulity which turned into shuddering disgust. "Ah noo!" he said, "I fear ye're no vurra inteeligent, Muster Freenchmon! I osked ye plain as day for a drap o' something hot. Hot, don't ye ken? Hot— H-O-T—the left-hand tap wi' a C on it!—A drap o' Duggan's Dew o' Kirkintilloch, by preeference.—Nice and steaming, wi' maybe a loomp o' butter melted on the top, and a dosh or twa o' pepper! But hot—HOT!" And as before, he went through the motions of blowing into a glass.

The Frenchman nodded, and hastened to oblige. Disentangling a pink celluloid pocket comb from the side of his curly black hair, he scraped the dome of lather from the beer and replaced it with honest liquid out of the faucet.

"*V'la, m'sieu!*" he said, shoving it across the zinc. "*—V'la, plus d'ecume.*"

"Why hoorns o' the deevil!" shouted Mr. Glencannon, shoving it back again. "Ye're no' only a jock-oss, my mon, but ye're insolent i' the bargain! Coortesy has forced me to freeze my stomich wi' nine assorted brands o' French bilge a'ready i' other dram-shops where they misonderstood me, and it's cost me nineteen fronks. But dommed if ye'll cajole me into guzzling this bellywa . . ."

"—'Scuse me, Chief, but they don't serve hot drinks here."

The words thundered out like Big Ben chiming midnight in the fog, or even more, like The Lost Chord itself; for though there was no crimson twilight for them to flood, they filled the barroom like a deluge and fell upon the fevered spirits therein assembled like several tons of brick. For a fleeting instant Mr. Glencannon was inclined to believe that a battle-ship had blown up in the harbor; then he concluded that the drinking establishment was connected with a bowling alley; but finally he recognized the sound as a human voice, and turning, perceived that it belonged to the bulky moon-faced gentleman behind the wall table.

"Yair," the booming continued, "when I first come in here I hollered myself hoarse for a hot grog, but these good people just shook their heads and hollered back."

"A-weel," said Mr. Glencannon, noting that the voice, as well as the ponderous presence of its owner, seemed intensely distaste-

ful to the proprietor and the several clients, "what ye say, Sir, is
sod news to one just back fra' three months stewing i' the Indian
Ocean, a-sheevering and a-shoodering, the noo for want o' a guid
warm drappie to drive oot the raw December chill!"

"Say, and don't I know it!" the other sympathized. "Me, I'm
just in from Alexandria this morning, and I dam near froze all
day. Feelin' better now, though. Toomey's the name, Sir. Clement
Toomey—'Bass Drum' Toomey, as the boys say. I'm carpenter of
the *Arapahoe Chief,* of Baltimore, U.S.A.—one of the B. & B. Line
freighters, them which some folks calls the Bedbug Boats, and
they ain't so far wrong at that. Well, anyway, sit down, do, and
lemme pour you a drink, Mister—er . . ."

"Glencannon. O' the *Inchcliffe Castle.* Clifford & Castle, o' London. But, er, my dear Muster Toomey, though I've no deesposce-
tion to look a gift-horse i' the mouth, just what is this watery
concoction ye've poored so boontifully into my gloss?"

"Well," said Mr. Toomey, "when they first trotted it out, it was
a new one on me, too. *Marc,* the name of it is, and—but try it,
Mister Glencannon, try it!"

Somewhat skeptically Mr. Glencannon picked up the glass, introduced it beneath his mustache, and tilted back his head. Then,
after a few ruminative smacks of the lips, "Weel," he began, with
a disappointed shrug, "I feel constrained to infoorm ye, Muster
Toomey, that—er, ah, ag-GOPF!" His eyes stuck out and he
pressed both hands to his gizzard, like one who has swallowed a
scorpion with his salad.

"There!" roared Mr. Toomey, much gratified. "Ain't it a snug
little tipple, once it slips into the keyway?—Beats a hot toddy all
hollow, I do declare!"

"Aye," Mr. Glencannon managed to agree, and though his
voice emerged falsetto he was relieved at hearing it at all. "Er-haw!
Yes i'deed, Muster Toomey, huff, ye're absolutely right, Sir. It's
got a noble high theermal coefficient, beyant a doot; i' fact I shud
say it wud come in vurra hondy for welding steel. What did ye
say the name o' it is?"

"*Marc,*" said Mr. Toomey, referring to the label, "*Marc.*"

"Weel," chuckled Mr. Glencannon, now quite recovered and
raising his glass again, "I daresay it wudna tak' much o' it to mark

a mon for life, sae here goes!"

"That's the spirit!" applauded Mr. Toomey, joining him. "Once the first one's blasted out the channel, kinda, the rest of 'em slip down smooth as eels in jellyfish."

Mr. Glencannon proceeded to blast out the channel, at the same time taking stock of Mr. Toomey's somewhat peculiar lineaments. The red face seemed too round for the gray-thatched head, the head too big for the shoulders, the shoulders too massive for the body, and the body so enormously fat that Mr. Glencannon could only speculate as to the monumental proportions of the legs concealed beneath the table. In fact Mr. Toomey's vastness seemed to increase as he studied him feature by feature, the whole fittingly culminating in that bass-drum *grand finale* of a voice.

The Engineer put down his empty glass and sat back perspiring. "Muster Toomey," he said, "I congrotulate ye on discovering a cold drink fufty times hotter than the hottest o' hot ones. How i' the world did ye e'er hoppen to stoomble ower it?"

The other made a deprecating gesture, and the hand he made it with was the size of a catcher's mitt. "Why," he explained, "I was hankerin' for a nice hot jolt of Old War-Whoop, same as you was, so I come in here and asked for a *grog americain.*—That's the name I've always got 'em with in other French ports, but these-here brethren didn't seem to savvy. The louder I hollered *'grog americain'* the louder they hollered *'no, no, no americain!'* "

"It must hae soonded lik' Jutland!" mused Mr. Glencannon. "Didn't any of ye lose yere tempers?"

"Bless you, no!" bellowed Mr. Toomey jovially. "Oh, the French and us Americans is just one big happy family, Mister Glencannon—we don't lose our tempers and go to scrappin', like the rest of you Europelians! We believe in that good old doctrine about the lion laying down on the lamb.—'Course maybe once in a while we have a little tiff, like this here recent trouble about the debts, but I'm happy to see that even that's all settled now."

"Oh, aye?" inquired Mr. Glencannon, doubtfully. "I wish they'd pay me back my nineteen fronks, then! D'ye mean the American States is making them a present o' the money and pocketing the loss?"

"Hell, no! I mean that France is paying us every penny, like

the honest nation she is. Why, lookahere—" from the side pocket
of his coat he dragged an evening paper which he spread upon
the table. "There! Just get an eyeful o' that!"

Across the top of the page was a single black headline:—

PAS UN SOU A L'AMERIQUE

"—Oh, I knew they'd come through all right!" he continued,
wagging his two-gallon head. "The French is a fine honest people
and their word is as good as their bomb. Why, look how they paid
us that there now Lafayette Debt and discovered the Mississippi
River for us and all!—But whatsa matter, Mister Glencannon,
can't you read French?"

"Only small type," said the Engineer, knotting his brows and
staring at the headline.

"Well," Mr. Toomey explained, "it's hard to translate these
furrun tongues laterally, but this here certainly means that they'll
pay the installment that's due.—*PAS*, of course, means Pass; *UN*
means One; and *SOU* means Sow, a she-hog, same as in English;
—'Pass a Sow to America,' in other words."

"Ah yes," nodded Mr. Glencannon, judicially, "that's just aboot
the way I'd render it, too. But Muster Toomey, if ye'll pairdon
my obtuseness, what are they passing ye a sow for? The vurra idea
o' it sounds most insoolting to me!"

"'M, well," said Mr. Toomey, "I must admit that that part
ain't exactly so clear to me either. But knowin' French politeness
as I do, and seein' the lather they've worked up about this whole
thing, there's no question that their intentions is perfectly okay."

Mr. Glencannon took a drink and considered the headline
doubtfully. "Maybe it's their idiom—their slang," he suggested.
"But . . ."

"Idiom! Slang! Oh, sure, now you got it!" exclaimed Mr.
Toomey. "'Pass a Sow to Amereek'—'pay the whole debt,' 'go
the whole hog'!—Not just one installment, don't you see, but the
whole dang works! Sure, of course, that's what it means!"

"Ah, pairhops," Mr. Glencannon agreed. "—It's summat a case
o' 'hams across the sea,' as they say i' deeplomatic circles—though
I must confess I ne'er conseedered the anatomical implications o'
the phrase to be vurra complimentary. I'd noticed those same

wurrds chalked up on the walls ower town, but till this moment I'd no idea o' their purport."

"Well, Chief, you know now! And from their writin' it on the walls, you can see what a swell goodwill spirit the French public's got! By gosh, Mister Glencannon, as an American citizen I wanta say, I wanta say, I wanta s-s-s- —well, it sorta makes me glow all over!" He filled his glass and raised it.

Mr. Glencannon emptied his and lowered it. "Weel, as a Scot I can say the vurra same thing!" he declared fervently.

"Let's glow some more, then!" thundered the carpenter, reaching for the bottle. "This here's a night to celebrate! Hurray for America! Hurray for France! Hurray for Scotland! Hurray for America! Hurray for France! Hurray for . . ."

"Wait!" Mr. Glencannon restrained him, his tympanic membranes bruised and palpitating. "Ye've been once aroond, and there's no sense repeating. Let me repleenish yere gloss, Sir, and we'll drink a silent toast."

Mr. Toomey was about to reply when the proprietor appeared before them. "*Quel bruit!*" he complained, shielding his ears with his hands. "*C'est degoutant!*" Then, dropping into Marseilles-pidgin, "*Vous,*" he said, pointing at the crown-and-anchor on Mr. Glencannon's cap. "*Vous, Ingleesh, tres bon,* verree good, Jack! Yess! *Mais lui,*"—he jerked his head toward Mr. Toomey, "but him, Yankee, all *Americains,* are the *plus betes salauds du monde,* by dam!"

"There!" bawled Mr. Toomey, delightedly. "D'you hear that? He says you English is very good, but the American Yankees is the best sailors in the world, by dam!—Oh, pray don't be offended at his rankin' America first, Mister Glencannon—it's just French gratitude to America assertin' itself."

"Oh, I'm no' offended," the Engineer hastened to assure him, at the same time extending his glass. "I' fact, I'll e'en tak' a drink to it!"

The proprietor gazed toward the ceiling and shook his fists at it. "*Sacre nom! Payez et allez!*"

"Hear! Hear!" Mr. Toomey bass-drummed his approval. "He says 'Sacred signature! Pay our Allies!' Ah, what a spirit, Mister Glencannon, what a spirit!"

At this juncture, the sounds of a mighty commotion burst in upon them from the street. For the past five minutes these sounds had been growing steadily louder, but so had Mr. Toomey. Now, however, there was no drowning them, no mistaking the tumult of a marching mob. Clump, scrape, clump! went the hobnailed boots on the cobblestones, moving in time to a throaty barking chant:

> *"A bas le dette! A bas le dette!*
> *Pas un sou a l'Amerique!"*

As he heard the words, a tender smile lighted Mr. Toomey's face. Tears of happiness welled into his eyes. "Hark!" he said, "hark to the voice of France!

> *'Abate the debt! Abate the debt!*
> *Pass a sow to Amereek'"*

he translated, rapturously. "Why, they're makin' a regular rational restival—er, national nestival—wait, what I mean is, be dam if they ain't makin' a regular roliday out of this thing! Ah, gentlemen, gentlemen, this is all tust jouch juts troo touching!" His emotion got the better of him; he wept loud and unashamed.

The proprietor strode to the door, jerked it open and motioned toward the street. *"Marchez, marchez, bon Dieu!"* he ordered.

"I'd be honored, Sir, honored!" sobbed the carpenter, heaving himself erect. " He says 'March, march to God!' don't you get it?—Somethin' like 'Onward Christian Soldiers.' Why, he's invitin' me to march in the parade!" And booming "Viva for France! Abate the debt! Pass a sow to Amereek!" Bass Drum Toomey lurched out into the mob.

Mr. Glencannon, observing that the bottle of *marc* was still a good half full, lurched back to the table.

II

After the carpenter's departure a peaceful hush pervaded the Cafe de la Marine. The glasses on the shelves ceased to vibrate and the lamps to flicker. Though from somewhere along the Quai came a distance-dimmed bellowing about France, America, and sows, it merely served like the murmur of a faraway storm to accentuate the calm which prevailed within.

Mr. Glencannon, lolling back enjoying the *marc*, felt in some measure reconciled to the loss of his nineteen francs. He found it hard to believe that this was actually the same place he had entered less than an hour before, blue-lipped and shivering. He was warm, now, gratefully warm, and it occurred to him that perhaps the climate of Marseilles was changing. He wondered whether the Japan Current or the Gulf Stream might not have shifted its course, or the Equator have broken its moorings and drifted northward. He resolved to write the Royal Geographical Society about it first thing in the morning; meanwhile, he poured himself another drink, and unbuttoned his jacket. "Losh!" he panted, "if I'd e'er dreamed it wud turn oot lik' this, I'd hae left off a couple o' suits o' underwear!"

He sipped slowly, contentedly, from time to time saying "Whoosh!" and fanning himself with his cap. At length he arose, removed his coat, collar and tie, and with the cloth from the next table proceeded to dry himself thoroughly. "Great swith!" he breathed, "it's regular Red Sea weather!" He folded Mr. Toomey's newspaper into a Napoleon hat, set it crosswise upon his head, and adjusted it to shade his eyes against the glare of the kerosene lamps. "There noo, that's better!" he said. "I feared I was in for a nosty touch o' sun.—Weel, there's only one sure way to ward off sunstroke!" To make the assurance doubly sure, he took a good three-finger dose of *marc*, and battened it down with another.

Shortly, though, his temples commenced throbbing so he clapped his hands thrice at an elderly Frenchman engaged in working out chess problems at a neighboring table, and shouted, "Hut, ye lazy Chittagong *soor!* Tell the *punkah* coolies to get those fans going, and let's hae a bit o' air in here!" Then he removed his shirt and hung it over the back of a chair to dry.

"Ah, whoosh-a-ree!" he gasped. "Let pooets at hame sing praises o' the tropics, and o' the romance o' the flar-fung posts o' Empire, but just gi' one o' them a taste o' what it's like under a corrururu-gated iron roof on a corror-er, a coral beach lik' this, wi' the theermometer 110 i' the shade o' the old apple tree, where she promised my bride she wud be-e-e, and she looked so ni-hice that

I kissed her twi-i-I-CE—i' the shade o''. . . . o' . . . oh yes! Weel, as I was aboot to reemark when ye so rudely interroopted me aboot giving ye a taste, Sir—just bring one o' yon pooets oot here to the Nicobars, and he'll soon change his tune! Oh, any tune at a'! I can sing a lovely teenor to 'One-Eyed-Riley,' if ye hoppen to foncy it, and my barytune to 'The James Street Widow' is a vurritable gem. And so, Major MacIntyre, if the rest o' ye feel lik' singing, I'm sure I've no' the slichtest objection. But feerst, if ye'll pairdon me, I'll just peel off lik' the rest o' ye and mak' mysel' comfortable i' a loin-cloth."

He was well on the way toward realizing this project and was engaged in folding a tablecover into the proper triangular foundation, when he glanced out into the dancing heat-mirage and beheld a familiar face.

"Ho, Parkinson *Sahib!*" he shouted, dropping the loin-cloth and starting forward in spontaneous welcome. "Come in, come in oot o' the sun! Come in, Commissioner, and sit ye doon!" He pulled the chair from under the elderly chess-savant. "There, noo!" he said, bowing hospitably, "the whusky and soda are at yere eelbow, sae mak' yersel' at hame.—But, guid losh, Wutherspoon, ye lucky beggar, I thocht at this season ye'd be up cooling off i' the hills! How are the guid Mrs. MacBride and a' the little Feergusons?"

"Oh, shyme to yer!" said the newcomer, "behyving like this at your ayge, yer narsty nyked old beast!"

Something in the voice caused Mr. Glencannon to realize that his guest was not Colonel Connors-Fitz Maurice after all, but only a mendicant Arab. The Arab looked strangely familiar. Quick at penetrating disguises, Mr. Glencannon recognized him as young Mr. Levy, Wireless Operator of the S.S. *Inchcliffe Castle.* Despite the heat, Mr. Levy was wearing overcoat and muffler.

"Ah, Muster Levy, a vurra guid evening to ye!" he greeted. "How are ye, Muster Levy, and how are a' my worthy colleagues aboord the *Inchcliffe Castle?* Oh, they're a' vurra fit, thonk ye, and how are you?—Weel, I really canna complain, except for the heat. Ah, swith, lad, when ye've lived i' these lotitudes awhile, there's no telling what . . ."

"Put on yer socks!" ordered Mr. Levy, sternly. "—And if them 'orrid hobjects which I see dangling from the picture is your underwear, well, put 'em on, and let's get going!"

Mr. Glencannon dashed the perspiration from his chin, and shaded his eyes as he peered across the shimmering desert.

"Get going where?" he demanded.

"Get going out of 'ere, before the police nabs yer."

"Police!" scoffed Mr. Glencannon. "Police! Ah, dinna for one minute imogine that ye can threaten me wi' police, Sir! I've made a fool oot o' the Canadian Noorth-West Moonted! I've bilked the Royal South-Offrican Constobulary! I'm still laughing (haw haw!) at Scotland Yard! And as for the police o' France, why . . ."

Several large and formidable figures swam into his vision. They wore blue *kepis* and capes; automatic pistols were slung at their belts. The proprietor and guests were gathered around, pointing and jabbering.

"What's amuss?" demanded Mr. Glencannon, sizing up the situation. "Hae the tribes risen again?—Be quick, then, be quick, Muster Levy!—Sairve oot rifles and ammunition, and try to hold them off while I mak' a break for the coast!" He handed his watch to a waiter. "Goodbye, goodbye, old mon! Oh, dinna worrit aboot me—I'll . . . I'll win through somehow!"

"Now, wyte a minute, wyte a minute, and put yer pants on!" Mr. Levy restrained him at the door. "You ayn't going to myke a bryke for no plyce, you ayn't—not until yer've paid fer wot's been served yer orlready. The pub-keeper says you owe 'im sixty francs fer three bottles of this 'ere toilet water yer've been drinking, and if yer don't settle up 'e'll 'ave yer chucked into jyle."

"What?" barked Mr. Glencannon, the talk of jail and finance restoring him momentarily. "Three bottles! Why, the common swundler is a common swundler! I've had less than a bottle, and that as the guest of a vurra charming Noorth American gentlemon who'd paid for it a'ready!"

By way of answer, the proprietor pulled out the table and waved his hand toward two empty *marc* bottles on the floor beneath the bench lately occupied by Mr. Toomey.

"Well," shrugged Mr. Levy, "there yer are!—Tyke yer choice between paying and going to the jug."

"But sixty fronks!" moaned Mr. Glencannon. "I've been mulcted

oot o' nineteen fronks by the dom Freench bondits a'ready, and
noo it's sixty fronks more!"

"—Sixty-one francs, fifty centimes," corrected Mr. Levy, giving
heed to the publican's plaints. " 'E says 'e served yer a pint o'
beer besides. But 'e says if yer'll pay 'im now, 'e won't press the
charges of hindecent hexposure, dishorderly conduck, public
drunkenness and threats of hassault which 'e's got a dozen witnesses to."

Mr. Glencannon considered the policemen and his plight.
"Losh!" he fumed impotently, forking over the money, "I soobmit,
because I've no alteernative, and noo I'm oot seeventy-nine fronks
fufty! But once I locate my guid Yonkee friend Muster Toomey
and veerify my suspeecions aboot this being oot-and-oot skull-
duggery, I'll . . . I'll . . ."

"Oh, come on, do!" urged Mr. Levy, dragging him to the street.
"Let's get back aboard the ship before yer gets into trouble. And
tyke orff that silly pyper 'at and put yer cap on before yer catches
the pneumonyer!"

"Pneumoonia!" and Mr. Glencannon mopped the back of his
neck. "Pneumoonia, i' this climate!—Dengoo fever, ye mean!"

"Well, seeing it's you, per'aps I should've said deleery and
tremens. Now just 'old 'ard a bit, while we mykes our way through
this 'ere mob.—Lawks, they're in a 'orried narsty temper about
something!"

The debt-protest meeting was now in full swing. A dense crowd
packed the sidewalk and the roadway of the Quai de la Joliette—
a crowd which waved banners upon which were slogans decrying
the American debt-payment, and placards picturing Uncle Sam,
masked like a gangster and with pistols levelled, buried waist-
deep in money-bags. An orator was haranguing from the rear of a
motor truck; as he ranted of America's perfidious and cowardly
part in the World War, and of her present blood-sucking arro-
gance in suggesting that France repay at least some part of the
sums she had borrowed, the audience howled with indignation.
"Pas un sou!" three thousand hate-filled voices chanted. *"Pas un
sou a l'Amerique!"*

"Oh, ho!" said Mr. Glencannon, "hear their enthusiosm! I hae
no doot that I shall find the odmirable Toomey rejoicing wi'

them!" And despite Mr. Levy's attempts to restrain him, he set out upon a thorough search of the crowd, pushing and shoving his way, and pausing to peer into faces from under the edge of his paper hat.

It was while engaged in peering that he felt his right hand becoming heavy, then heavier, and glancing down, he saw several coins in the cap which he was holding by its visor. Even as he looked, these coins were joined by several coppers, a two franc piece and a pink five-franc note. Puzzled, he turned to call Mr. Levy's attention to the phenomenon, but Mr. Levy had disappeared. However, the man he chanced to be confronting said, *"Mais oui, mon vieux! Tout pour la cause!"* and dropped three francs twenty-five into the cap.

It was then Mr. Glencannon realized what was taking place. "Whoo!" he gasped in amazement, "they think I'm taking up a collection! As a matter o' fact, I do seem to be taking up a collection—I dinna ken for what, but I dom weel ken for whom!—Can it be that this whole mob is sunstruck?" There were a good three thousand people in the crowd; they were becoming more and more excited as the oratory reached new heights, and their liberality increased with their emotion. Thus Mr. Glencannon found himself garnering so rich a harvest that he was forced to transfer money from cap to pockets at short intervals; and soon his pockets were heavy and bulging.

"I'd ne'er hae believed it!" he marvelled. "—Freenchmen, Freenchmen octually giving their money away! Losh, I'd hae sooner believed it o' Glesga Scotsmen, or even o' . . ."

His musings were interrupted by a familiar booming voice from somewhere in the fringe of the crowd. "But I'm American!" it protested. "An American, I tellya! What the hell are you sluggin' at me for? Ouch! Ouch! Wait a minute, my friends, you don't understand me! I'm an American, savvy? *Viva for Amereek!"*

There were cries of *"Mort aux Americains"* and sounds of scuffling. "Now wait, wait!" Mr. Toomey was pleading.

But they didn't wait, and neither, finally, did Mr. Toomey. The last Mr. Glencannon saw of him, he was retreating ponderously into the black shadows of the quai, with fifty infuriated Frenchmen speeding in pursuit.

"Losh!" mused the Engineer, "if 'twas no so hot, I'd gae alang and see the finish o' it! 'Twull be a vurra, vurra trogic moment for those Freenchmen, once Muster Toomey lures them wi'in hailing distance o' the crew o' the *Arapahoe Chief!*" And then, grasping his jacket by the lapels and flapping it to cool himself, "Weel," he said, "by the weight o' this garment, I've collected aboot a' the money the congregation seems guid for—fufteen hoondred fronks by most consairvatif eestimate, or pairhops twa thousand. Sae noo I shall drap into the shade o' yon dram-shop and cool off wi' a nice cold gloss o' beer."

Behind the bar there was a mirror. Mr. Glencannon was surprised to discover that he was still wearing the paper hat, and that the big black headline, *PAS UN SOU A L'AMERIQUE!* extended like a band across the front of it.

"Weel," he said, removing it and putting on his cap, "Pairhops that explains it, and pairhops again it doesn't. But anyhow, though they passed the sow to America, Scotland got a vurra hondsome helping o' the gravy!" Beckoning knowingly to the barman, he raised his hand as though lifting a beer glass, and went through the motions of blowing off the foam.

The barman nodded, and served up a glass of steaming hot grog.

ONE GOOD TERN

THE second evening out of Port Elizabeth the S.S. *Inchcliffe Castle* thrust her bluff snout around the Dark Continent's darkest corner and girded her rusty loins for a long trek up the West African coast. All afternoon, below Good Hope, she had wallowed along through a sea patrolled by gray waterspouts which stalked across the surface like errant ghosts of gnarled apple trees; but now, as she nosed Northwestward, she was met by a gale that swept clear down from the Bight of Benin, bringing the hissing combers with it. She struggled past the lights of Cape Town and Stellenbosch, the seas smashing against her bows, rearing her backward and then sliding out from under, leaving her all a-smother forward and with her propeller racing futilely in the air. It was this latter circumstance, momentarily repeated, which aroused the indignation of Mr. Glencannon, the Chief Engineer. Giving over custody of the throttle to an assistant, he strode through the hot oily mists of the engine room and whistled into the speaking tube.

"Bridge, Sir," replied a distant piping voice like that of a ventriloquist's dummy talking in a trunk, "Quartermaster Birkett."

"Weel, jump off it and blost ye, Quartermoster Birkett!" bellowed Mr. Glencannon above the mighty whur-rum, whur-rum of the engines. "Tell the Mate I'll convairse wi' him, and be quick aboot it!"

After a due and dignified interval: "Chief Horfficer," shrilled a tinny tone which yet had in it the essence of pompous authority. "Wot the flyming 'ell's the matter down there now?"

"Matter?" repeated Mr. Glencannon. "Matter? Why nowt's the matter, ye swine, except that the whole dom coffee-mill is rising clear off the bed plates every time she pitches. No, nowt at a's the matter, except she's leaking steam at every pore, and the tail-shaft's due to snop at any minute. Oh, nowt's the matter beyant one or twa other little points such as hot bearings and sae forth, the whuch ye wudna onderstand e'en shud I expoond them fra' A to Izzard. The point is, will ye change the course and ease her off a bit before she tears her guts oot, or must I come up on the bridge i' pairson and tromple oot yere ain?"

There was a rattling in the tube as Mr. Montgomery cleared his throat. "Why, see 'ere, you ruddy Scotch walrus," he blustered, "I'm in charge hup 'ere, I am, and I warn yer to remember it. There's such a thing as discipline in the British Mercantile Marine, and the Board of Tryde will bear me hout! Now, let's just get this stryght; am I to hunderstand that you threaten me with physical wiolence hunless I halter the ship's course?"

"Aye!" screamed Mr. Glencannon, whacking on the mouthpiece of the tube with a spanner. "Boord o' Trade or no Boord o' Trade, if ye dinna slock her off i' the next twa minutes I'll come up there, snotch oot yere liver and wade i' yere gore, e'en at the cost o' a black mark on my Certeeficate and the price o' a pair o' new carpet slippers!—There, noo; if it's a threat ye want, tak' that one and mak' the most o' it!" Muttering to himself he resumed his place at the throttle, but soon the mutters gave way to chuckles. The motion of the vessel was changing, there could be no doubt about it. A slow roll was combined with the pitch. No longer was it necessary to shut her down each time the stern lifted, for now the screw remained safely under water.

"Haw, the glaggie!" gloated Mr. Glencannon. "I knew he'd ease her off if I got eeloquent wi' him. But noo, I've no doot he'll run straight to the Captain wi' a-muckle o' tittle-tattle aboot Communism, mutiny and my threats to do him in. Weel, let him, let him!" He thumbed a charge of snuff into his nostrils, carefully dusted back into the box those fugitive particles which clung to his mustache, and dismissed Mr. Montgomery from his mind.

Something less than an hour later he had fought his way forward along the gale-lashed deck, turned into the saloon, nodded to the company and was attacking his third bowl of mutton broth with a sound not unlike that of the last few inches of water escaping down the waste pipe of a bath tub, when the door swung open to reveal a horrid spectre. There, clutching at the door-frame, was Mr. Montgomery—nose bleeding copiously, both eyes rapidly becoming black, and head lolling about like that of a boxer still groggy from a knockout. At sight of Mr. Glencannon, however, he snapped up as though to a whiff of smelling salts.

"There 'e is!" he snarled, pointing an accusing finger. " 'E slugged me, 'e did, syme as 'e threatened! Yus, the ruddy coward— 'e lurked hout there on deck in the darkness and barshed me with a knuckle-duster without a hinkling of warning. Well, I'll show him!"

He lurched forward, the light of battle glinting in his puffy eyes. Mr. Glencannon, armed with a soup ladle, arose to meet him. Fortunately, however, Captain Ball and the other officers intervened and pushed Mr. Montgomery into his chair. He bunched up his napkin and buried his nose in it, muttering darkly.

Captain Ball, snorting like a grampus, resumed his place at the head of the board and surveyed the company sternly. "Oh damme, now see here, gentlemen," he said. "This thing is serious, mighty serious! Horseplay of this kind don't go on any ship of mine, and I'll have you know it!—Did you slug Mister Montgomery like he says, Mister Glencannon, or didn't you?"

"No Sir," declared the Engineer, "I didna hae the pleasure. As a motter o' fact, and ye yersel' can bear me wutness, I've been sitting here at the supper table for the past ten minutes."

"H'm," mused Captain Ball, "so you have, 'pon my word, so you have. Well, I fancy that vindicators you, all right. But if you didn't do it, who did? What I mean is, somebody must have done it. Oh, by gosh, gentlemen, this thing's a mystery, ker-huff, I mean to say it's a mystery!"

"Mystery my eye!" growled Mr. Montgomery. "The Chief threatened to do me in less'n an hour ago, 'e did, and if it wasn't hactually 'im wot barshed me, it was somebody 'oo 'e 'ired and put hup to it."

"Haw!" scoffed the Engineer. "Yere theories are as quaint as yere appearance, the whuch, I micht add, is no only quaint but revolting. And as for my hiring somebody to clout ye—weel, ye scut, there's monny a mon besides mysel' who'd pay guid money for the preevilege!"

"Yes, but who did it, that's what I'm trying to find out?" persisted Captain Ball. "There couldn't have been another soul out there on deck, so far as I can figure. But then, I mean to say, it couldn't be a ghost that done it, could it now?"

"Lawks, it ruddy well didn't feel like one," sniffed the Mate. Mr. Glencannon eyed him narrowly, and then gave vent to a chuckle. "Weel," he said, "if ye'll pairdon me for a bit, I think I can solve the mystery to the full satisfaction o' everybody." And tugging his flashlight from his hip pocket, he stepped out into the gale.

An uncomfortable silence fell around the table. "—Of course," Captain Ball explained ruminatively, "I really didn't mean I meant I thought it was a ghost, if you see what I mean. But I'm wondering now if maybe there ain't some sort of a mutiny brewing, what with all this Red improureganda the papers is full of nowadays. What I mean is, we'd . . ."

The door banged open and in strode Mr. Glencannon, bearing the limp form of a large gray-and-white sea bird. "There!" he announced, laying it tenderly upon the table. " 'Twas a storm-driven gull that hit ye, though at fairst, fra' the feathers that are still sticking to the front o' yere jocket, I was inclined to gi' the credit to an avenging angel."

"A gull!" cried Captain Ball delightedly. "A gull! Oh, Mister Montgomery—pardon my laughter, but if I was you, I'd jolly well be ashamed to . . ."

The bird stirred slightly, and emitted a feeble but derisive "Kw-e-e!" Mr. Montgomery dashed down his napkin, sprang to his feet and reached across the table. " 'Kw-e-e,' hey?" he rasped. "Well, I'll kwee yer, yer sneaky nose-bryking fish-chicken, yer! I'll wring yer bally neck, I will, and . . ."

"Hands off, ye hulking loomp, ye!" shouted the Engineer. "If ye so much as touch yon birdie, I'll fix yere mug so's ye can whustle Cockney folktunes into yere ain ear. Ho, shame, shame to ye, trying to vent yere nosty spleen upon a puir defeenseless doomb onimal!"

"Kw-e-e-e!" screamed the bird, pecking a V-shaped chunk out of Mr. Glencannon's forefinger. It struggled to its webbed feet and stood at the center of the table, ruffling its feathers and blinking its beady malevolent eyes.

Justly outraged by this display of ingratitude, Mr. Glencannon shook his fist in its face. "Noo, see here," he warned it. "Do ye be a bit more coorteous, ye oaf, or I'll hand ye ower to yon brute

Montgomery to do wi' as he wills." By way of answer the bird tore a half-inch patch of horny epidermis from Mr. Glencannon's knuckle and ate it with gusto.

"Haw, haw!" exulted Mr. Montgomery, who by this time had succeeded in getting his nose under control. "Well, I fancy that there'll learn yer to hinterfere between a bloke and 'is revenge! Oh, I 'ope 'e pecks yer silly heyes hout, that's wot I 'opes!"

"—Yus, and I 'ope 'e chokes before 'e scoffs up the rest of that bacon," said Mr. Levy, the Wireless Operator, as ruefully he watched rasher after rasher being gobbled by the uninvited guest. "Good lawks, 'e goes arfter it like it was hactually fit to eat!"

"Hem, ker-huff, well I must say he's got a ripping appetite," commented Captain Ball. "The only thing is, I—whup! There, you see? What I was about to say, Mister Glencannon—don't you think you'd better get him off the table?"

"Aye, I do i' vurra deed, Sir," agreed Mr. Glencannon. "The only question is"—he considered his bleeding hands—"The only question is, how to gae aboot it?"

Captain Ball waved his napkin and slapped it brusquely upon the tablecloth. "Scat!" he ordered. "F-s-s-s! Come, come now, my feathered friend, down on the linoleum you go!"

"Kw-e-e!" shrieked the bird, half spreading his wings and darting toward the Captain so savagely that the gallant mariner sought shelter beneath the table.

"M'ybe 'e'll fly hout by 'imself," volunteered Mr. Swales, the Second Officer, opening the door. "Lively, there, my bucko. Hup! Jump to it! Smartly now!" The bird, however, seemed to prefer his present surroundings, especially the bacon, and fiercely resented all attempts to dislodge him.

"A-weel, pairhops we'd better let him stay," opined Mr. Glencannon prudently. "Speaking for mysel', I conseeder his attochment to us deeply touching. Also, I feel so much indebted to him for what he did to Muster Montgomery that I hereby offeecially adopt him. But look, gentlemen, look ye there!—Whatever is that little metal bracelet he's wearing on his ankle?"

"Oh, why by George!" exclaimed Captain Ball. "Maybe he's a kind of a carrier pigeon of some sort, what? Take it off him, Mister Glencannon, take it off him."

Wrapping his hand in a napkin, Mr. Glencannon extended it cautiously toward the bird's right leg, upon which glistened an inch-wide nickel band. There was a "Kwe-e-e!", a lightning lunge of the beak, and a contented gobbling sound as a strip of napkin and a fragment of thumbnail went down to join the bacon.

"Whurra, drot ye!" fumed Mr. Glencannon, thrusting his thumb into his mouth. "Weel, it's plain to be seen that we canna subdue this voracious beastie by ordinurra meethods. Jessup!" he beckoned the Steward, "Jessup, do ye gae aft to my room and fetch the bottle o' Duggan's Dew ye'll find beneath the bunk. Remeember, I ken to a drap how much remains i' it, sae mind that ye dinna fa' prey to teemptation!"

The bottle having arrived, Mr. Glencannon held it up to the light to gauge its contents, poured out a tumblerful, drank all but an inch, and then nodded his head as though satisfied.

"Noo then, gentlemen," he announced, "ye're aboot to wutness a meethod o' anesthetizing birds whuch was oreeginated by my late father—a mon sae tenderhearted that he cudna bear to inflict pain on ony living creature. The guid mon owned a chicken farm, and by this little trick he no' only succeeded i' dulling the senses o' his birdies to the horrors o' the axe, but i' improving their flavor as weel. Here, lad—" he sopped a bread crust in the whisky and waved it at the gull "—Catch!"

There was a snake-like extension of the neck and a snap of the beak as the crust was caught in mid air.

"Bravvio!" Mr. Glencannon applauded. "Ye dooned it lik' a mon! Come on, chum, hae another. I'll join ye i' this one!"

The bird had another, a third and a fourth without visible effect. At the fifth, however, he seemed to feel a sudden elation. With a raucous "Kwe-e-e!" he scurried the length of the table on his clumsy webbed feet, took wing, and hurtled about the room in a series of dizzy circles, like a Panama hat in a cyclone. Consternation ran high, but at the peak of it, he decided to come in for a landing. Unfortunately—and perhaps because he mistook the table-top for a smooth pool of water—he neglected to put his feet down, and so executed a violent front somersault of the type known in aviation parlance as a ground loop. He lay on his back kwe-e-ing happily, and paddling his feet in the air.

"There, he thinks he's swimming!" declared Mr. Glencannon, emerging from behind a chair. "Losh, how weel do I mind the evening i' the middle o' Piccadilly Circus when I was tuk the same way! But noo, do ye pass me yon foork, Muster MacQuayle, and I'll pry open the birdie's bracelet."

By this time the patient was slumbering peacefully, and the metal band was removed without incident. All gathered around as the Engineer held it under the lamp. Upon it, in minute letters, was engraved:—

$25 REWARD, U.S. CURRENCY
will be paid to finder sending following information:—
Where found?
When found?
Condition of bird?
MENTION NUMBER 71
Address: Curator, Ornithological Survey
Webster Island, Mass., U.S.A.

"—Massachusetts, U.S.A."? repeated Captain Ball incredulously. "I mean to say, gentlemen, do you mean to say that there bird flew all the way from Massachusetts? Why, that's pretty near 8000 miles, almost, whichever way you figure it!"

"Aye!" agreed Mr. Glencannon, gleefully. "And twunty-five dollars is pretty near twunty-five dollars whucheever way I feegure it, too!" He dropped the band into his pocket, and gathered up his bottle and the bird.

"Come on, swift bearer o' glod tidings!" he addressed it. "I must frame an eepistol to yon Yonkee curator to post at Swakopmund, and you must get some sleep. Aloss, puir beastie, I dinna doot ye'll be feeling vurra sub-noormal i' the morning!"

II

As in the course of the ensuing weeks the *Inchcliffe Castle* called at Mossamedes, Libreville, Lagos, Bathurst and Dakar, Mr. Glencannon's pampered gray mascot became more or less a part of the hum-drum life aboardship, and more and more the bane of it. His favorite caprice was to roost on a davit or a ventilator cowl until he spied an enemy approaching on deck below; then, with a horrid scream of hate, he would fling himself downward and crash feet first into his prey—an experience, agreed those who underwent it, practically identical with encountering an Australian bushman's boomerang in full flight.

Although deeply attached to Mr. Glencannon and politely tolerant of Captain Ball, he held all the others in loathing and contempt. On several occasions his victims had succeeded in seizing him and throwing him over the side, but invariably, after a circle or two above the ship, he had returned aboard with a derisive Kweee! To Mr. Montgomery, he was especially antagonistic.

"Lawks, wot a narsty-tempered 'ellion!" the Mate complained to Mr. Levy, one day when the pair sat in the shade of the awning, watching the heat waves dance on the roofs of St. Louis de Senegal. "Larst night when I cyme orff watch, blarst me if I didn't catch 'im in my room eating hup a pile of temperance journals I subscribe to and which I treasure 'ighly. Drunk as a lord 'e was—yus, and ugly fighting drunk at that."

"Why didn't yer twist 'is perishing neck fer 'im?" inquired Mr. Levy.

"Hunh, m'ybe I didn't try—oh no, not arf! But just as I was habout to grarsp 'im, 'e leaps into the air like a ruddy fury, and first thing I knows, 'e's tore enough 'air out of my 'ead that you could stuff a mattress with it." He removed his cap and passed his hand tenderly over his lacerated scalp.

"Well, 'e done practically the syme thing to me," confessed Mr. Levy, "hup there in the Marconi room the hother night. Oh, now mind you, Mister Montgomery, I don't hobject to 'im 'opping habout on the tyble and walking orl hover my set, heven when I'm trying to send messages. But when 'e tykes to sneaking drinks hout of my jars of battery acid, well then, I s'y, 'e's going a bit too far!"

" 'E is indeed!" agreed the Mate. "But yer see, Mister Levy, the 'ole trouble is the w'y that blarsted Scotchman drinks with 'im. The bird 'as simply got a fighting jag on orl the time, or else 'e's in the 'eadaches and hagonies of 'ell's own 'angover. Either w'y, of course, 'is temper's rotten ragged, and orl of us suffers in consequence."

"Yus!" said Mr. Levy with deep passion, at the same time fingering a half-healed triangular wound on the lobe of his left ear.

"Yus, we suffers, we do, and orl the while that ruddy Scottish sot is looking forward to the twenty-five dollars that'll be w'yting fer 'im in London! Is that justice?—Now is it, I arsks you?"

Justice or not, the fact remained that two days after the ship tied up in Limehouse Commercial Docks, Mr. Glencannon found beside his place at table an envelope bearing the return address of the Department of Agriculture and the United States Government postal frank.

"Hoot!" he exclaimed, half to the company and half to the bird perched on his shoulder. "Here's my billyducks fra' the Yonkee fowl-fanciers! Haw, and look, look here, gentlemen—a twunty-dollar note and also a five, deescending on me lik' manna fra' the heavens! Oh, how pairfectly delichtfu'! But noo, what says the letter?"

As he scanned the comunication, his face was wreathed in smiles. "Weel, weel, weel," he addressed the bird, who had hopped to the table and then to the floor beside his chair. "It appears fra' this that ye're no' an ordinurra seagull after a', but a *Sterna hirundo*, or tern. And that, gentlemen"—he painstakingly arranged his face for the delivery of a jest —"And that, gentlemen, prompts me to the vurra droll reemark—'One good tern deesairves another.'—Tern. Haw, haw!—Tern, spelled t-e-r-n; oh losh, d'ye get it?"

With his right hand, he reached for the treasury notes to wave them triumphantly on high, but his fingers encountered only the vacant oilcloth. From his suddenly-palsied left, the letter fluttered down like a falling leaf. His jaw dropped. Slowly, he shifted his gaze from the table to the floor in time to see the last corner of the five-dollar bill disappearing into the tern's greedy gullet. All that remained of the twenty was the steel-engraved left eye of President Andrew Jackson, which stared at him disdainfully from the linoleum.

Terrible, then, was the wrath of Glencannon! With a hoarse cry, he seized the bird by the feet. Oblivious of thrashing wings and lunging beak, he struggled out on deck and hurled the mascot skywards clear beyond the rim of the *Inchcliffe Castle's* sooty funnel.

For a moment the tern hovered there, Kwe-e-ing insolently. Sud-

denly, from the distance, came an answering Kwe-e-e. Mr. Glencannon turned and saw a T & O liner sliding seaward down the
Reach, a lone gray bird dipping and wheeling across the suds of
its wake. Even as he looked, the gray bird was joined by another,
and then the pair of them faded away in the river mists.

III

Fifteen days had elapsed since the *Inchcliffe Castle* churned up
into the Port of London—fifteen days throughout which, with
much ado, profanity and perspiration, she had been groomed for
another four months' tramp around the seas. This time, however,
she was scheduled for a string of European ports—Baltic, Atlantic
and Mediterranean—and though even the meanest of these would
be paradise compared with the steaming miasmatic pestholes of
West Africa, Mr. Glencannon's spirits were low.

Thoughts of his betrayal, of his gobbled twenty-five dollars, still
rankled him bitterly. The unceasing jibes of his shipmates were
like stings of thistles to his soul. When hopefully he sought sur-
cease on shore he found that a monstrous governmental tyranny
had advanced the closing hour of the pubs and increased the tax
on whisky. For the first time in his career, he looked forward to
being at sea again.

Thus, as on the evening of the sixteenth day the tug cast off her
line and the *Inchcliffe Castle* slid out of the Estuary headed across
for Rotterdam, Mr. Glencannon sat down to his supper with something like an appetite. He sniffed the salty breeze that blew in
through the porthole, and found it good. But though avidly he
forked four slabs of boiled beef onto his plate and harpooned two
potatoes with a single masterly estocade of his knife, he was vaguely
aware that something, something was lacking. His right shoulder
felt light, uncomfortably light; it missed the friendly grip of web-
joined claws. With a sigh, he turned his head and contemplated
his right epaulette—vacant save for its quartet of gold stripes.

"Well, wot about it?" inquired Mr. Montgomery, who had been
watching him narrowly. "Wot price yer ruddy fish-chicken tod'y?
—Twenty-five dollars, per'aps?"

"Feesh-chicken?" repeated Mr. Glencannon, hastily concealing

his grief behind an air of vapid innocence. "Twunty-five dollars?
Oh, guid losh, Muster Montgomery—canna I sae much as con-
teemplate the dondruff on my shoulder-strop wi'oot ye rooshing
to mercenurra conclusions?"

"No!" declared Mr. Montgomery, with the assurance of one
who has his audience with him, "Gorblyme if you can! Oh, we've
got the larff on you this time, my giddy Scotch bucko! Pooh pooh
to you and yer ruddy nose-barshing bird and yer cheap tuppenny
puns habout one good tern deserving hanother! We've got the
larff on you, we 'ave, and now I'll tell yer 'ow!"

From his inside pocket he produced a letter and spread it flat
upon the table.

"This 'ere," he explained, "is the letter yer got from the Yonkee
bird people, and which yer dropped and fergot orl habout as soon
as yer pet scoffed hup yer money. Remember?"

"Aye," nodded Mr. Glencannon, leaning forward attentively. "I
remeember it only too weel!"

"Well, in this letter it says . . . 'the bird recovered by you,
Number 71, is the first of one 'undred similar Terns, consecutively
numbered and released, to be reported as found.' "

"Yes," said Mr. Glencannon, swallowing but not tasting half a
boiled potato. "Pray gae on."

"Well," Mr. Montgomery resumed, "with orl this hinformytion
to go by, wot d'yer suppose us fellow-sufferers done, hey? Why, I'll
tell yer wot we done! Me and Mister Swales and Mister MacQuayle
and Mister Levy, we heach of us wrote letters to this Yankee
curator cove, telling 'im 'ow we'd picked hup banded terns in the
different ports we're scheduled to call at on this voyage. Heach of
us gyve different numbers. We 'anded our letters to chaps on other
ships 'oo'll post 'em from the different ports before we get there.
And so lyter on, when we call at Bremerhaven, Mister Swales will
collect 'is twenty-five dollars, haddressed to *Poste Lagernd;* Mister
Levy and Mister MacQuayle will get theirs in Bordeaux and Marseilles, care of *Poste Restante;* and for myself, I've only to go to
the post horffice in Bilbao and arsk for a letter haddressed to
Chauncey Montgomery, care *Administracion de Correos,* and grab
my slice of good 'ard Yankee carsh. Ho, ho, ho! Oh, you think yer
a clever bloke, don't yer?—One good turn deserves another, don't

it? Well, 'ere's a good one yer've deserved for a long long time!"

A strange sound came from Mr. Glencannon's throat. His head sank forward on his breast. He rose to his feet and though with dignity he left the room, his step was like that of an aged and broken man. Here, it was apparent, walked a mortal whose burden was more than he could bear.

Once out upon the breeze-swept deck, however, he squared his shoulders and strode aft right briskly. Entering his room and bolting the door, he wrote four letters to the Postmasters of as many different foreign cities—letters which he signed, respectively, Chauncey Montgomery, B. Swales, Campbell MacQuayle, and A. Levy. The leters read:—

> "Kindly forward all mail for me to No. 33
> Kilmarnock Road, Milngavie, Scotland,
> care of Mr. Colin Glencannon."

GABRIEL'S TRUMPET

THE topsail schooner *Scorpena,* two hundred and seventy tons, belongs in shares to numerous members of the Costoli family of Via Reggio, an ancient port midway between Pisa's leaning tower and Carrara's marble mountains. One look at the trim little vessel as she scuds past at sea, chasing the tails of her plunging dolphin escort, is enough to tell you that she is a real sailors' ship, manned by sailors who are sons of sons of sailors clear back unto the shag-bearded, earringed ancestor whose Christian zeal in encouraging Admiral Andrea Doria's Moslem rowing slaves with a twelve-thonged scourge (one thong for each Apostle) gained for his galley the blue riband of the Genoese navy and for himself the foundation of the family fortune which the *Scorpena* represents today.

The *Scorpena* is commanded by Papa Costoli, whose potbelly is his sole badge of office. He smokes cigars gnarled and brittle as licorice root and patriarchally lords it over a crew of sons, nephews and assorted social errors with names like Tucci, Pucci and Mucci, all pronounced with an *ooch.* But if, as is likely, you see not a soul of them on deck and perceive that the wheel is lashed, it is because all hands are below, eating polenta, drinking wine, playing the accordion and trusting in St. Gabriel.

You will surely see St. Gabriel. He is the *Scorpena's* figurehead—a votive image of olive wood, right arm extended with the golden trump of doom, plundered in times remote from some cathedral in Calabria or Sicily. Such is the Costolis' faith in his usefulness, so often have they transferred him from old ships to new, that he has outgrown the status of family heirloom and become a sort of doyen of their house. It is St. Gabriel who brings good health, good weather and good cargoes—in sum, *la buona fortuna.* With him at the prow, what need of mortal lookout to warn of rocks, shoals or the low-lurking derelict? Never in the centuries since he took over his job has a Costoli ship piled up, but if ever one does—why, then the archangel's trumpet will sound a blast, the gates of paradise will swing wide, and in will troop the Costolis, caps and rosaries in hand. Each twenty-fourth of March, which is St. Gabriel's own day, they give him a fresh coat of paint, doing his robe crimson, his wings pale blue and his flowing beard the black of night. His halo and trumpet they gild most splendidly.

Thus secured against the manifold hazards of the deep, it is the Costolis' wont to put to sea with light hearts, rollicking song and a certain amount of accordion music, as in fact they quitted their home port one bright warm morning last May. Their ship was laden with bulrushes of the sort the infant Moses was found among, but which in our more practical times are used for making saxophone reeds and caning the seats of chairs in the lesser restaurants. These bulrushes were consigned to Bagnoles, in the French Department of Var, where the *Scorpena* would exchange them for a cargo of bauxite and scrap metal for La Spezia and home. It was a chore she had done so often that had her course lain across dry land, instead of the Ligurian Sea, she could have followed her own well-worn pathway like a milch cow between barn and pasture.

Now, May is a month of light airs below the Gulf of Genoa, and sundown of the second day found the vessel with all sails set, lazing along somewhere southwest of Cape Mele in a faint breeze stirring off the land. As the long chaplet of coastal beacons flickered to life as one, Papa Costoli buttoned the top of his trousers and came ponderously on deck for the evening rite of taking the ship's position. Ignoring the lighthouses (he could never remember their intervals of flash and doubted their accuracy anyway), he subjected the blood-red sky and sea and purple mountains to a scowling scrutiny, as though daring them to start something. Next, puckering his cheeks and expanding his equator to a prodigious dimension, he spat into the air and gauged the wind velocity by the descending curve of the gobbet. Finally, tilting back his head until the fat on his neck rolled into a series of distinct bulges, like the spare tires on the back of a motorbus, he took a succession of deep sniffs.

"Ha! Petroleum!" he announced to the barefoot sons, nephews and informal fry gathered in reverence to witness the mystery.

"Petroleum—fm-m-miff! Smell it? Well, you stupid apes, that means we are off Imperia, where the oil refineries are. May San Gaby guide us clear of their cursed tank ships in the night!" Turning to Bucci (or it may have been Lucci), who was dozing at the helm, "Hold her as she bears as long as you smell petroleum," he ordered. "Then ease her off a couple of spokes until you can see the flashes of the electric trains in the Bordighera yards, being careful not to turn your head sideways. Wait until you can no longer hear the locomotives whistle at the Ventimiglia tunnel on the French frontier, then lash her and come right in for supper. It's my turn to cook again, damn and damn and damn it all!"

Easing his paunch through the galley doorway, he observed that the clouds, become unstuck from the mountain peaks, were drifting lazily seaward down the slopes, perhaps to settle as fog. "Zucci," he demanded, "did you remember to put oil in the lights?"

"Oil?" mumbled Zucci, waking up and scratching his back against the mainmast. "Oh, did you finally remember to buy the oil, Papa?"

"M-m, well, that is, er . . . Nucci, did you remind me to buy the oil?"

"What was the use, when you forgot to buy the wicks?"

"Why should I buy wicks when there wasn't any oil?" Papa Costoli forced his midriff past the jamb and slammed the door testily. Grumbling to himself, he lit the candle, gulped a tincupful of the purple wine of Montecatini to take the moss off his teeth, unmuzzled the garlic and set about preparing the pasta. He made a good, substantial job of it. Afterward, they all sat around and sang to an obbligato of pancreatic gurgles and Stucci's pearl-inlayed accordion.

It was a snug, family evening. The air in the low-ceilinged cabin became thicker and thicker with the fumes of cigars, cigarettes, cooking and Costolis. It was almost as dense as the fog into which the vigilant St. Gabriel, alone in the bows, was thrusting his golden trumpet.

II

Mr. Colin Glencannon, Chief Engineer of the British tramp ship *Inchcliffe Castle*, lay sound asleep in his bunk, the sound emanating from the region due south of his adenoids and resembling the whimper of wind through the ribs of a gibbeted skeleton. From time to time, heightening the realism, he gave off strangled cackles as of ravens gorging a cadaveric feast and a sudden menacing "whoosh!" as though to frighten the ravens away.

Early that evening, in a laudable effort to keep the supper table conversation from flagging, Mr. Glencannon had remarked that Mr. Montgomery, the Mate, was incompetent, cowardly, untruthful and unsanitary. Mr. Montgomery, who chanced to be present, resented these allegations with spirit and offered to bet one million pounds Sterling that Mr. Glencannon, himself, was a ruddy, thumping liar. Snorting his disdain for such niggardly stakes, the Engineer proclaimed his readiness to hazard fifty million pounds against ten million pounds in support of his original claims. Swayed by the generous odds, the Mate accepted the wager; then, not agreeing on just how to settle it, the pair embarked upon a fresh controversy, in which Mr. Glencannon's superior elocutionary gifts enabled him to smite his adversary hip and thigh.

In retrospect, he had found the debate most satisfying; besides, the night had fallen clear and calm, and the gentle dew which moistened him after his bedside orisons was the justly esteemed distillation of Messrs. Mackenzie Duggan & Co., Ltd., of Kirkintilloch; thus, Mr. Glencannon dozed off free from care and aglow with well-being certified by the makers to test one-hundred-proof. But presently, seeping into his slumbers, came an uncomfortable awareness that the ship was proceeding through fog. Mr. Glencannon knew this, not by virtue of clairvoyance, but because the engines were turning at half speed. He had nursed and cursed the *Inchcliffe's* decrepit old teapots for such a weary tale of years that, waking, sleeping, or even sober, he was more sensitive to their pulse beats than to his own. And now, suddenly, they thrashed full astern!

Wide awake and terror-frozen, Mr. Glencannon jerked upright. Simultaneously, the whistle blasted a panic of hoots which seemed to kick him in the pit of the stomach. He heard shouts, the scurry of feet and the steering engine gnashing its teeth as the wheel was jammed hard over. Something crashed against the vessel's starboard side, scraped rendingly along full half its length and after an agonizing age slid clear. In a flash, the supper table controversy came back to him. "Foosh!" he gasped. "Montgomery! The dom lout's done it this time!"

Not pausing to don even the suit of droop-tail underwear which served him as pajamas in the harsher climates, he snatched up a lifebelt and the bottle of Duggan's, dashed out on deck and flung himself into a lifeboat, where he cowered, trembling, under a thwart. "Och, horrors!" he croaked. "Little did I dream, when I told him what I thocht o' his seamanship, that his stupidity wud soon be the death o' us all! . . . Ye're aboot to tenant a watery grave, Glencannon, so proof yersel', lad, proof yersel'!"

He had proofed himself to midway down the well-known Duggan label before he realized that Captain Ball was on the bridge and that the *Inchcliffe Castle,* instead of sinking, was proceeding on her course beneath a sky now clear and starlit.

"Not a blarsted light was showing on 'er, sir—no, rot me if there was!" he heard Mr. Montgomery explaining shrilly. "First thing I knew, there we was right on top of 'er in the fog. We barshed 'er ruddy bowsprit orff and she yanked down a lot of 'er own top 'amper by 'er forestays, but I 'ad time to see she wasn't really damaged no more than wot we are, sir!"

"Humph, ker-huff, well I mean to say, that makes it all the worse!" stormed Captain Ball a trifle thickly, he having in the first excitement installed his false teeth backward and bitten himself in the palate. "If you'd only hit her amidships and sunk her with all hands, everything would've been settled neat and tidy then and there. As it is, maybe she got our name and will report the collision and then we'll have a lot of forms and things to fill out. Shocking nuisance, ker-hem! But I can't understand why you didn't hear her. Even these ruddy French coasters, which you ought to know the waters around here is always thicker'n mutton stew with, usually blow bells and ring fish horns in a fog, ker-hem, which is incidentally more than you was doing, Mister Mate, to say nothing of they are also usually beating on dishpans!"

"B-but blyme, sir, she wasn't making a sound, not a sound! . . . You can arsk the steersman and the lookout if she was!"

"Oh, I can, can I? Well, I ain't asking you to go asking me to start asking anybody anything, and I'll ask you please to remember it!" bellowed Captain Ball. "The steersman's here to steer, the lookout's there to look, but you're the officer responsible here to hear and see that this ship ain't climbed aboard of by every ruddy Frenchy that happens to be out at night! Oh, it looks to me as if you was asleep on your job, Mister Montgomery; it does indeed! Well, a-hem, ker-huff, we'll discuff this ker-busineff further‚ in the morning!" He ejected his false teeth into his palm, gathered up the skirts of his nightshirt and descended the ladder to his room, scolding gummily.

"Haw!" chuckled Mr. Glencannon, swinging himself over the gunwale to the deck and draping his lifebelt around him kilt-fashion. "It all bears oot what I told yon odious Cockney to his face!" He strolled forward and gazed at the litter of splintered wood, ripped canvas and tangled cordage caught in the starboard stays. "Losh, thanks to him, it micht just as weel have been a frichtful tragedy which— But, oh ho, what's that?" He hurried down to the welldeck, picked up the object which had caught his eye and examined it perplexedly. A canny smile wreathed his countenance; he turned and mounted to the bridge.

"A-weel, Muster Montgomery," he greeted the scowling Mate, "I see that the grave charges I lodged against ye last evening are being abundantly confeermed already."

"Wot the 'ell d'yer mean?" snapped the other. "And wot the 'ell are yer doing up 'ere with nothing on but that there lifebelt, yer shameless Scotch walrus?"

"Why, as to my costume, I o' course knew that ye yersel' wud be panic-stricken in the recent emergency, so I turned oot in all haste to set an example o' coolness and courage to the men. As to the meaning o' my statement—weel, ye'll recall that I publicly accused ye no' only o' gross incompetence, but o' being a liar besides. The collision was proof o' the one—and here's proof o' the other!" From behind his back he produced a long gilded trumpet, something like a coach horn, and shook it triumphantly under the Mate's nose.

"Here's the vurra foghorn ye swore to Captain Ball that they weren't blawing! Aloss, the puir frogeater who was sounding it in their bows, and who hurled it at ye in a last despairing effort to wake ye up, is dootless droonded dead! His bluid is on yere hands, so who's the walrus noo?"

"Now, wait, wait, wait a minute!" blustered Mr. Montgomery, albeit paling somewhat. "Supposing that there really is their fog'orn, why, that's still no proof they was blowing it, any more than they was showing lights! I saw no lights, I 'eard no 'orn, and—"

"Aye, ye saw no lichts, ye heard no horn—and for why? Weèl, I'll show ye for why!" He brushed past the Mate into the wing of the bridge and from the deck snatched up a freshly charged pipe, three burnt matches and an open matchbox. "There!" he shouted, "there's for why! Instead o' attending to yere job, ye were ducking doon under yon weather cloth trying to licht yere pipe! E'en if ye glanced ahead between tries, which I doot, yere eyes were blinded by the match flames—just as yere ears were deefened and useless from stooping ower in the lee and then standing up in the wind again. Ye were deleeberately violating the rules o' common prudence and the Thirty-one Articles. In the midst o' yere criminal neegligence, the dread emergency arose—and ye were no' equal to it!"

Mr. Montgomery's mouth fell ajar and his knees trembled. He grasped a stanchion for support. "Now, see 'ere, Mister Glencannon!" he managed to stammer. "I—I'm only 'uman, ain't I? I like a bit of a smoke on watch, same as anybody else. Orl of us make our little mistakes sometimes. . . . Come, now, don't we?"

"Aye, but we dinna all lie aboot them!" thundered the Engineer. "Lying, Muster Montgomery, is a vurra expensive luxury!"

"Hexpensive? Why, wot d'yer mean?"

"I mean that either ye'll pay me the ten mullion poonds ye lost to me in a fair and sporting wager, or I'll blaw this horn, wake up the Captain and expose yere shame to him and the whole dom ship!"

The Mate smiled half-hopefully and then laughed aloud. "Lawks, I thought for a minute yer were serious!" he said, mopping his brow. "Ten million quid? Ho, ho, that's a good one, that is! I ain't got much over ten quid to me name, let alone ten million!"

"Then," said Mr. Glencannon, solemnly, "ye'd better stir yersel' aroond in Nice in the morning and raise the rest o' it. Who knows? Perhaps this thing will be the making o' ye! But I do know that a foormal bet is a binding contract, and that ye owe me the full and stipulated sum. I'll thank ye the noo to hand ower a numminal doon payment o' two quid."

The smile withered on Mr. Montgomery's face. "Oh, so ye're really serious, then!" he sneered. "Well, yer vampire, if yer think I'm going to pay yer a single brarss farthing on a crazy bet that was made in fun, ye're— Stop! Sh-h-h! Don't blow it! Please!"

Mr. Glencannon lowered the trumpet and shrugged. "The doon payment has gone up to three quid," he announced, evenly. "In another ten seeconds, it will be . . ."

Mr. Montgomery glanced fearfully over his shoulder toward the bridge ladder. "Orl right, orl right. 'Ere, take it!" he whispered hoarsely, shoving the money into the Engineer's hand.

"Thank ye," said Mr. Glencannon. "The balance o' yere debt is noo rejewced to a mere nine mullion, nine hoonderd and ninety-nine thoosand, nine hoonderd and ninety-seven poonds. Kindly remit same at yere airliest convenience and oblige."

He tucked the trumpet under his arm and departed down the ladder, the cork slabs of the lifebelt drumming hollowly against his knees. In the privacy of his room, he locked the money away in the dresser and then set about examining the curious gilded instrument. "How vurra unique!" he mused. "I ne'er saw anything exoctly lik' it! And there's paint all ower it a quarter-inch thick, except on this one place aroond the middle." He pressed the mouthpiece against his lips and essayed a breath into it. The breath was of a nature to penetrate solid concrete but it failed to pass through the trumpet. "Clogged up—useless! Weel, that explains why the Frenchies were throwing it awa'—and o' course is the real reason why yon jockoss Montgomery didna hear it. But —haw, haw, haw!—'twill be a lang, lang time before he hears the last o' it!"

III

Outside the entrance of Bagnoles harbor, a little fleet of Italian schooners and *tartanas* were idling at anchor while three or four more of them, including the *Scorpena*, lay tied up in the shelter of the gray stone mole behind the cathedral. This untoward congestion of shipping was due to a shortage of bauxite, or aluminium ore; for although a red and dusty mountain range of the stuff was piled upon the Quai du Mistral, it had all been bought up by cable for shipment to England. The first of the British carriers, the *Inchcliffe Castle,* of London, had arrived and started loading that morning; now, as the Italian vessels continued to wait for additional ore trains from the mines, the crews of most of them were whiling away the time in slumber, song and the noisy game of *mora.*

The master and men of the *Scorpena,* however, were prey to a gnawing malaise. Slouching elbows-on-rail, they talked in hushed voices or in silence spat moodily into the waters of Bagnoles harbor. For the direst of all calamities had befallen them. They had lost their luck.

Nine days had passed since their midnight misadventure, four of which they had slaved at sea and five spent wearily waiting for bauxite. Papa Costoli, knowing that the collision had occurred in French waters, fearing that the vessel he had rammed was one of the Nice-Ajaccio mailboats, and quaking in his carpet slippers whenever he thought of the seven kinds of hell he would catch if responsibility for the accident were fastened upon him, had prudently contrived by carpentry and camouflage to efface all signs of it before putting into port.

All signs, that is, save one; St. Gabriel was without his trumpet. His splintered fingers patched with putty and touched up with paint, he presented the anomalous spectacle of an archangel shaking his fist at the world—a gesture scarcely calculated to bring good luck to the ship, cargo and crew in his charge. And the luck, the proverbial Costoli luck, had vanished with the trumpet. St. Gabriel had saved the ship, but without his horn, the horn that he had carried for so many centuries—well, he was no longer St. Gabriel! Immediately upon the *Scorpena's* arrival in Bagnoles, the *douaniers* had come aboard and confiscated eight thousand lira's worth of Gorgonzola cheeses and choice Parma hams which Papa Costoli was attempting to smuggle into France in observance of a privily recognized custom established by Italian skippers back in Garibaldi's time. The confiscation was bad enough luck, but on top of it the headstrong Zucci had berated the *douaniers* and kicked one of them in the shins at cost of a drubbing for himself and a five hundred franc fine for the ship. And now there was this waiting, this irksome, expensive waiting which, Papa Costoli was convinced, would end at any minute with his arrest, imprisonment and disrating for running in fog without lights and ramming a government mail vessel. He shuddered, spat down at a big gray mullet that was swimming just under the surface and returned his gaze to the sun-baked town.

A uniformed figure came striding purposefully along the quay! Was he an insurance inspector from the Bureau Veritas? An official of the *Administration Maritime?* A policeman with a warrant? Like a sea turtle, Papa Costoli retracted his head into the fat of his neck; his nostrils dilated and his paunch turned cold. He nudged Bucci, Bucci nudged Tucci, Tucci nudged Lucci, and so the alarm sped down the rail. They saw the uniformed one come straight for their vessel. They held their breaths as they watched him eying it. They heaved a great sigh of relief as they distinguished on his cuffs the four gold stripes and purple inset of a Chief Engineer of the British Mercantile Marine.

"He is not a Frenchman!" announced Papa Costoli. *"San Gabriele, vi ringrazio!"*

"San Gabriele, vi ringrazio!" came the fervent echo.

The Engineer, now that he had paused, seemed much less steady on his feet than he had been while under way. Also, he seemed less interested in the *Scorpena* than in the several tons of scrap metal which lay ready for loading on the quay alongside her. Hands in jacket pockets and swaying back on his heels, "Losh!" he exclaimed rapturously, "a truly mognificent pile o' junk! Weel, noo I shall spend a delichtful hour browsing amongst it!" He peeled off his jacket, hung it on the jutting leg of a crippled iron bedstead and set about his browsing with the eagerness of a bibliomaniac at large in the Bodleian Library.

For a considerable time, then, the Italians watched in perplexity as he clambered, tripped and sprawled upon the junk pile, hoisting out cracked tram wheels, wrestling with a twisted motorcar chassis and gloatingly clicking his tongue over a set of manhole covers, the inscriptions upon which left no doubt of their authenticity as a limited edition. At length, however, he seemed to feel an embarrassment of riches; reluctantly, he laid aside the greater part of his incunabula and concentrated his attention upon the rarer and more readily portable gems. These consisted of a worn locomotive brakeshoe, the fittings from a horse collar, a Louis XV chandelier, and a hollow copper ball of the sort used to stay the rushing waters which symbolize our civilization.

He had gathered up his prizes and was heading for the *Inchcliffe Castle* when Papa Costoli, welcoming the chance to bolster his sagging morale with a little bullying and at the same time air his English to his tribe, sounded off with a challenging hail.

"Hey, looka you!" he shouted. "Whata for to hell you are take-a da junk, hey?"

The Engineer halted guiltly in his tracks and stood blushing. "Eh? Beg pardon?" he simpered sheepishly. "Oh! Weel, to tell ye the truth, sir, I'm just indulging an innocent little whimsy. Ye see, I—I'm a great one to fuddle and tinker aboot, making things in my spare time. Aye, making things!" His hand swept upward in a spacious fluid gesture. "Little, pairfict, artistic things! Bross knuckles! Skeleton keys! All manner o' dainty trifles. . . ." He glanced at his collected treasures and his eyes kindled with a fond light. "Perhaps I'm owersensitive to beauty, but the cockroach trap which I made for mysel' in Nice the other day really does seem more lovely than any pooem I hope to see climb up a tree, or howe'er that song goes, although I play it vurra sweetly on the bagpipe. . . . Anyway, whene'er my guid foortune guides me to a truly monumental pile o' junk such as yon, I always avail mysel' o' the oppor—"

"Putta back!" ordered Papa Costoli, sternly. "Putta back dam queeck! I proheebitta you steal-a my junk!"

"Oh, but, my vurra dear sir!" Mr. Glencannon protested, crestfallen. "Surely ye dinna mean to say that these few puir frogments o' this-and-that are o' any value to ye! Pray what wud ye do with them if ye had them?"

"Whata we do?" screamed Papa Costoli, pounding on the rail. "Whata we do? We make-a da bomb, we make-a da cannon, we make-a da shell! Blow uppa all dam Inglese sheep. BOOP!"

"Weel, blaw them up and see if I care!" said Mr. Glencannon, airily. "The best mutton comes from Scotland anyway, so BOOP yersel'! But noo, I hope ye'll forgive me if I remark that yere accent is faulty, yere manners uncouth and yere odor stifling. In a word, my vurra dear sir, ye're nowt but a filthy bum."

Papa Costoli turned purple; his paunch vibrated like a stratosphere balloon about to burst. He sputtered impotently.

"And moreover," the Engineer continued, drowning him out, "ye're no' e'en a feerst-class genuine bum! Ye're merely a renegade and a Communist, as yon figurehead plainly reveals! Foosh, fie and for shame! Whoe'er heard o' a loyal Eyetolian Foshist putting a statue o' whuskery auld Karl Marx in a red nichtshirt on the bow o' a ship! Look! His fist is e'en clenched in the Communist salute!"

"No! No! No *Communista!*" bawled Papa Costoli, attempting to beat his breast but in his fury punching Bucci in the eye.

"Blosh! I'll report ye to Ben Mussolini, that's what I'll do!" declared Mr. Glencannon, righteously. "I'll mak' a meemorandum o' this whole international incident, and ye'll see what happens to ye when ye get back to Italy with yere dom Moscow pig barge!"

Notebook and pencil in hand he strode along the quay and scowled up at the vessel's transom. " '*Scorpena* o' Via Reggio,' " he read aloud, ominously. "Vurra weel, ye dom red radical reevolutionaries! Just wait till the guid Muster Mussolini hears how ye behave when ye're oot o' his country, and he'll rub yere noses in it till ye dom weel wish ye'd all been shot in Abyssinia!"

As he snapped the rubber band around his notebook, his fiery glance fell upon a square brass plate screwed to the *Scorpena's* after-deckhouse. Upon the plate was engraved "*San Gabriele, Fateci la Grazia di Salvarci.*" "San Gabriele?" he muttered. "San Gabriele? . . . That must mean Saint Gabriel, the Archangel who'll blaw the trumpet on Doomsday. But—but—trumpet? Aye, guid losh, why, o' course!" Ignoring the chorus of invective howled at him by the entire Costoli family, he stalked off toward the *Inchcliffe Castle,* covertly observing, as he passed the *Scorpena's* figurehead, that its freshly painted fist was indeed posed exactly to accommodate the mysterious golden trumpet.

IV

Once aboard the *Inchcliffe Castle,* Mr. Glencannon hurried to his room and thence, with the recently scoured and brightly polished trumpet wrapped in a newspaper, he went in search of Mr. Montgomery. He found him lying in his bunk, reading a temperance journal and looking glum.

"Well, wot the 'ell is it now?" the Mate demanded as his visitor very carefully closed the door behind him. Then, spying the trumpet, "Oh, more blackmail, is it?" he groaned. "Well, blarst yer soul, ain't yer ever going to let up on a chap? As far as I can see, Captain Ball 'as forgot orl about the haccident, but now, if yer should just blow that thing—why, it might cost me my job and even my ticket!"

"Aye, I ken it vurra weel," said Mr. Glencannon. "But I must insist that ye withdraw yere insinuations aboot me being a black-mailer. If ye're referring to those trifling installments ye've paid me on our wager, why—"

"Trifling hinstallments?" echoed Mr. Montgomery. "Trifling, yer've got the cheek to call 'em? Three pounds at sea, two pounds when we was in Nice, three more at sea yestiddy, and now—"

"And noo," said Mr. Glencannon, sudden good will throbbing in his voice and illumining his face, "and noo, dear lad, yere worries are aboot to be ended once and for all! Surely, ye didna think the money interested me—foosh to money! No, Muster Montgomery, I was merely teaching ye a valuable lesson ne'er to sleep on yere job—I was trying in all altruism to mak' a better mon o' ye!"

"Oh, see 'ere, cut out the bilge!" growled the Mate. "Stop bleat-ing around the bush and explain wot's yere gyme! I told yer at the start I only 'ad ten quid and now yer've bled me down to two."

"Two?" repeated Mr. Glencannon, smiling brightly. "Weel, weel, weel, I must say that's handsome o' ye! One poond was the price I planned to sell ye this foghorn for, but as lang as ye insist upon paying two, why—"

"Yer—yer really mean yer'll sell it to me?" gasped the Mate. "Yer mean yer'll sell it and keep yer mouth shut about—about . . . 'Ere—'ere's two pounds—take it!"

"Aye, I'll ne'er mention it, e'en in my cups," the other promised, tucking away the money and handing over the trumpet. "As to our little bet—weel, as lang as ye've no money left, I dinna mind telling ye it was only a joke all alang, haw, haw, haw!"

"Joke, eh? Bleddy fine joke!" snapped Mr. Montgomery. He rose from his bunk, rapped out a savage oath and was just about to shove the trumpet through the open porthole when Mr. Glencannon grasped his arm.

"Foosh, mon, foosh—dinna be reckless!" he counseled. "Dinna ye realize that yon horn is worth money?"

"Worth money to 'oo?"

Mr. Glencannon shrugged. "Worth money to yersel'. Fronkly, if I was as broke as ye are, I'd go aroond aboot the port and try to sell it for whate'er I cud get to a French ship—aye, or e'en to yon Dago schooner astern o' us. All Mediterranean windjammers use foghorns o' that same pattern."

"Oh, do they? Well, then, maybe that's an idea!" assented Mr. Montgomery. "Even a ruddy 'arf-crown would look as big as the moon to me right now! Yus, I'll just go back there and try it on them Dagos."

Mr. Glencannon accompanied him on deck and then stood watching him as he headed along the quay toward the *Scorpena*.

"Haw, losh, what a spectacle!" he gloated. "I shudder to think what yon Dagos will do to the gowk, and my only regret is that I canna be there to see it! Thanks to my recent gentle efforts, they're no doot feeling slichtly anti-British. And as soon as they recognize their ain horn being offered for sale to them by an English officer off a ship they'll instantly realize must be the vurra one that dom near sunk them, they'll, they'll—oh, dearie me, haw, haw, haw!"

For twenty minutes he stood there, shaken by spasms of laughter and craning his neck *Scorpena*-ward to see the carnage begin. But strangely enough, it didn't begin. Instead, to his consternation, he saw the fat Italian captain escort Mr. Montgomery to the ladder, embrace him warmly and wring his hand.

Mr. Glencannon grew tense. "Weel, what happened? Did ye sell it?" he demanded, as the Mate, beaming, came up the *Inchcliffe Castle's* side.

"Sell it? Yus, I sold it!" Mr. Montgomery appeared to be in a pleasant sort of daze. "Lawks, I—I can't quite figure it out! When I first went aboard, they was orl very narsty and 'ostilelike, but as soon as I unwrapped the fog'orn, they seemed scared to death of me. The skipper actually wanted to know if I'd come to arrest 'im! I told 'im 'eavens no—orl I wanted was to sell the ruddy 'orn. Then 'e arsked me, very suspicious, where I'd got it, and it was my turn to be scared, you bet! But as soon's I told 'im I'd stole it orff a drunken French sailor in Nice, 'e gave me this 'ere money and then—now don't larff—they orl gathered around and kissed me! Look!"

Mr. Glencannon looked, and saw two banknotes, from each of which scowled an engraved likeness of Il Duce. Mr. Glencannon returned the scowl. "Two thoosand liras!" he read. "Two—thoosand—liras! Why, it's ower twenty English poonds!" He trembled as though stricken with palsy. He steadied himself against the rail. "Laugh!" he repeated dully. "Laugh, did ye say? No, Muster Montgomery, I willna laugh. Oh, I assure ye, Muster Montgomery, I've no slichtest intention o' laughing! As a matter o' fact—as a m-matter o' f-act, I—I . . ."

His emotion overcame him. Fumbling in his pocket for a cork-screw, he turned and lurched toward his room. From somewhere not far off came voices raised in song to the rollicking lilt of an accordion.

CAPTAIN SNOOTY-OFF-THE-YACHT

IT WAS a balmy January morning. Between the Mediterranean Sea and a cerulean, or travel folder, sky, the sugar-white city of Monte Carlo reared in terraces up the sides of nougat mountains crested with clouds of crème Chantilly. The fashionable half-world's motorcars with half the world's license plates zoomed through steep streets and flashed between exotic gardens. Outside the Café de Paris expensive people sat sipping expensive drinks to whip up expensive appetites, while out of the Casino just opposite came pensive people with expensive whippings and no appetites at all. Down in the harbor between Monte and the Rock, yachts brave with brass and gala bunting basked in ranks along the moles, completing the scene as it has been made so familiar by E. Phillips Oppenheim and the horn-rimmed young gentlemen in airshaft offices who write advertisements for cruises to far lands. Completing the scene as it actually exists were the gasworks.

The gasworks are over on the Monaco side of the port, at the foot of the cliffs beneath Fort Antoine. Though with their coal piles, rusty tanks and sooty smokestacks they look neither better nor worse than the gasworks of Liverpool, Brooklyn or Odessa, to encounter them in this pastry principality is like finding a Saturday night cigar butt in the center of a Sunday dinner angel cake. On this particular morning their aesthetic value was by no means increased by a British tramp ship which lay unloading alongside them at the Quai du Commerce. Her name was *Inchcliffe Castle* and, like the gasworks, she was frankly disreputable. The black of her snub-nosed hull was streaked with filth and pocked with red lead where half-hearted efforts had been made to check corrosion's ravage; her superstructure, once white, was now a mottled gray and fast becoming grayer as swirling clouds of dust arose from the coal which great steel scoops were dredging out of her holds.

This coal-dust blizzard had been in progress since early morn-

275

ing and showed no signs of abating. The Mates, as in duty bound, were out on deck in the gritty, grimy thick of it; Captain Ball had escaped ashore, while Mr. Glencannon, the Chief Engineer, had taken refuge in the ship's saloon, where he was deep in an experiment destined ultimately to result in the harnessing of a mighty natural force.

Now, as in so many of mankind's epoch-making explorations of the obscure, of which by way of illustration we need only cite Newton's with the apple, Galileo's with the lamp and Franklin's with his kite and key, Mr. Glencannon's experimental apparatus was the simplest imaginable, and his manner of devising it is therefore doubly worthy of note. The previous evening he had gone ashore with a system, mathematically flawless, for breaking the Monte Carlo bank; but after losing seventy-one francs in two spins, he loudly impugned the integrity of the roulette wheel, threw a croupier through a glass door and kicked the shins out of a lifesize oil portrait of His Late Majesty, Leopold II, King of the Belgians. Returning shipward smarting from his losses and several abrasions caused by the Casino steps, he limped into an English bar in La Condamine and ordered a stimulant known as the Dew of Kirkintilloch, distilled by Messrs. Mackenzie Duggan & Co., Ltd., in Scotland.

"Duggan's?" said the barman, producing the bottle and, in response to the patient's nod, dispensing a double dollop of it. "Right-o and 'ere you are, sir! Oh, and by the way—'ere's a bit of a new novelty that the Duggan firm 'ave just got out. It's an advertisement, don'tcher see, and I 'opes yer'll accept it with the compliments of the 'ouse." With a snap of his thumb and forefinger he spun a little green top across the bar.

As the top waltzed and teetered on the mahogany, Mr. Glencannon considered it sourly over the rim of his glass.

"Weel, I must confess I canna return the compliment," he growled. "Ah, foosh, but ye'd think a great firm lik' the Duggan people wud have more commercial sense than try to odvertise with nursery toys! Why, e'en a fool shud know that there's dom few children can afford to drink whusky at twelve sheelings a bottle, in these hard times!"

"Oh, but this ain't for the kiddies," explained the barman,

eagerly following the top's gyrations. "Wait, now wait! Just you watch it!"

It skittered against an ash tray, bounced off a glass, executed three dizzy swoops and then, after a final frenzied fluttering like that of a singed June bug, flopped down and lay still.

"There, look! It says 'Put Two,' " announced the barman. "If we was playing for money, now, that would cost me two francs!"

"Ye mean it's a gombling game?" inquired Mr. Glencannon, with a pious shudder. "Oh, my dear mon!" Examining the top, nevertheless, he saw that it was a six-sided affair of celluloid, the respective facets marked "Take One," "Put Two," "Take All," "Put One," "Take Two" and "All Put." Around the upper part of it, in gold letters, was stamped "But All Take Duggan's, the Tip-Top Tipple!"

"A-weel," he said, "I soobscribe to the sentiment, at least. Duggan's Dew is monkind's solace—indeed, 'tis a vuritable boon to the race. Therefore I deeply deplore seeing its name coupled with a curse lik' gombling."

He took the top by its stem and spun it experimentally. It stopped with "Take Two" showing.

"There, you'd've won the pot!" said the barman.

Mr. Glencannon spun once more. The top showed "Take All."

"Crickey!" gasped the barman. "Well, did you ever? Why, I mean to say, I never seen such luck!"

"Ah, noo, noo!" protested Mr. Glencannon, at the same time digging for his purse. "As one o' the stonchest pillars o' the Presbyterian Kirk, I'm opposed to gombling on pruuciple and in all its foorms. But still, barmon—weel, as lang as ye insist, I'll yield to yere blondishments and spin ye for a fronc or so."

Two hours later, his limp complicated by a stagger, he boarded the *Inchcliffe Castle* minus one hundred and thirty-seven francs, which, with the sum already dropped in the Casino, made him two hundred and eight francs loser for the day. The little green top was in his pocket but red was the rage in his soul.

Far into the night he lay tossing and turning, thinking of spinning roulette wheels, spinning tops and spinning francs until he felt that his brain was spinning within his skull. And it was this which gave him inspiration.

"Centrifugal foorce!" he exclaimed, sitting up in his bunk with a slight list to starboard to take the weight off the bruises on his keel. "Centrifugal foorce, aye, there's the onswer! . . . Weel, I'll get richt to work in the morning and we'll soon see what hoppens when this swundling town o' Monte Carlo tries to diddle with the austere science o' physics!"

As we have already discovered him in the ship's saloon, he had sawed through the top horizontally and was carving a spiral tunnel, rather like a worm-hole, in the lower half. This tunnel was minutely gauged to accommodate a small steel ball bearing. Later, the ball imprisoned within, he would cement the halves together so that only a microscope could detect the seam. A spin to the right, or clockwise, as a person naturally spins a top, would not be affected by the weight of the ball, which would rest at the central axis. But a spin to the left—and a snap of the fingers is quicker than the eye!—would cause the ball to fly out into the spiral and lodge at the end of it. There, its weight would cause the top to fall with the opposite, or "Take All," side upward, to the cost and confusion of sport-loving spinners untutored in the infallible laws of dynamics.

It was delicate work requiring deep concentration, but as he sat happily filing, fitting, humming, muttering and champing on the overhang of his walrus mustache, Mr. Glencannon became aware of an angry bellowing in the distance. This was annoying. The bellowing increased in amplitude and he stayed his hand, frowning petulantly. Footfalls pounded along the deck outside. As he snatched up the pieces of the top and dropped them into his pocket, the saloon door was flung open and in burst two hundred and twenty pounds of purple rage clad in yachting costume.

As the stranger towered snorting in the doorway, Mr. Glencannon sized him up as an elderly yacht captain who had served his time as mate of a windjammer, bruising Swedes. If there was one class of mariners more repugnant to the Engineer than yacht people, it was sail people—and here, beyond a doubt, was a very nasty combination of both. He raised his eyebrows in inquiry, at the same time feeling for his brass knuckles.

"It's got to stop!" declared the irate one, finding voice and to spare. "It's got to stop! Unh!" He leaned across the table and beat upon it with a five-pound fist.

"Aye, stop it must," agreed Mr. Glencannon, retrieving his tools from the floor. "If it doesn't stop at once, ye uncouth boor, ye'll collide with something solid.—Come, control yersel', Captain Snooty-off-the-Yacht! Explain what ye mean by running amuck aboot my ship and intruding here in my private study!"

The yachtsman puffed out his purple cheeks and endeavored to swallow his apoplexy. "Your damned coal dust!" he blustered. "Look!" With a Corona-size forefinger he pointed through the porthole at an opulent Thornycroft sea cruiser berthed at the adjacent mole. Carried by a freshening breeze, the coal dust was swishing along her bone-white decks, eddying in drifts in nooks and crannies and wafting down her ventilators to sully parquetry and furniture. "Coal dust, coal dust, can't you see it? You're ruining the yacht!"

"Aye, coal dust, coal dust, indeed," nodded Mr. Glencannon. "Pairhops I shud explain it's because we're unloading coal, whuch rarely gives off dondruff. If we'd only a cargo o' hacksaws, noo, I foncy we'd be stifled by the sawdust or pairhops have hacking coughs, whuch is a pun, haw, haw! Ostriches, on the other hond, wud no doot yield us feather dusters. The point is, ye odious auld blunty, what in the heel d'ye come snirtling to me aboot it for?"

"Because it's got to stop and you've got to stop it!" bawled the yachtsman, snatching off his cap and indicating a smudge across the white top of it. "There, look at that!"

Mr. Glencannon hesitated, shuddered, took the elegant headgear between thumb and forefinger and examined it as though it were a leper's bandage. "A-weel," he said doubtfully, "if ye mean this dark spot here, 'tis nowt but a bit o' a blemish. Losh, my guid mon, I've a mole, a birthmark and nine seeparate bruises on my nether anotomy that—"

"Blast you and your nether anatomy! My new cap's ruined! Unh! Ruined!"

With a shrug of resignation Mr. Glencannon tossed it through the porthole into the harbor. "Weel, in that case ye'll no more be wanting it. But noo, Captain"—his right fist, formidably garnished, appeared from his jacket pocket—"I obsairve another streak o' soot on the point o' yere chin, so I'll just proceed to dust it off with this custom-tailored knuckle duster, whuch ye'll note has four steel spikes cunningly mounted in the bross foondation. Or wud ye rather have me kick ye owerboard so ye can wash yere chin for yersel'?"

He took a quick step forward, his fist at half-cock. The intruder hesitated for an instant, then turned and fled. From his chest came a rasping rumble as of empty barrels being dragged across a wharf. Mr. Glencannon pursued him to the gangway, at the head of which he halted while the other scrambled ashore.

"All right!" bawled the purple yachtsman, stamping on the quay and shaking both fists at once. "All right, you vandal, you ruffian, you thug! You haven't heard the last of this yet, by gad, and—"

"Captain, I salute ye!" chortled Mr. Glencannon, thumbing his nose and waggling his brass-knuckled fingers most insolently. With a truculent swagger he returned to the saloon and his labors in the realm of science.

II

Fussy old Mr. Virgil Hazlitt, Managing Director of Clifford, Castle & Co., Ltd., the London shipowners, clipped a pince-nez on the knifelike bridge of a beak already occupied by spectacles and refocused his horrified squint at the letter which lay before him. "Phew!" he gasped. "Oh, Lord!" He pressed his thin fingers against his blue-veined temples and swayed back and forth in his swivel chair. "It's—it's just—phew!" Snatching up the letter he hurried across the room and pushed open a door marked "Sir John Castle." There was a resounding crash from the far side as a bag of golf clubs toppled to the floor.

"Fore, Hazlitt!" cried Sir John, glancing up from a pale pink journal with pictures of jockeys, of boxers and of wrestlers writhing in Gordian knots. "Have a chair, Hazlitt, and—but, oh, I say! What's the matter?"

"This!" Mr. Hazlitt extended the letter in a palsied hand. "Look —look at it, Sir John!"

"H'm," said the baronet, complying. " 'On Board *M.Y. Velella*, Harbor of Monte Carlo.' . . . *Velella?* Why, the *Velella's* Major

Duggan's boat! Hurray! So he's finally giving us that business, eh, Hazlitt?"

Mr. Hazlitt, incapable of speech, merely waved toward the letter. It read:

Messrs. Clifford, Castle & Co., Ltd.,
St. Mary Axe, London, E.C.

Sirs:

After the failure of your persistent and, I may say, impudent efforts to secure the shipping business of the several enterprises which I control, I am not surprised to have one of your officers insult me in a most scurrilous manner and then threaten me with a lethal weapon.

I am not a man to take half measures with a firm employing thugs and *bravi*, and I need not remind you that my wide industrial and financial connections place me in a position to make things most unpleasant for you.

Pending receipt of your acknowledgment of this letter, I shall be taking legal advice and planning the additional measures which this outrage so clearly warrants.

(Signed) Mackenzie Duggan.

"Insults? Weapons? W-why, what in the world is he talking about?" demanded Sir John, blankly.

"I haven't the faintest idea, but whatever it is, it's—awful."

"Awful's no name for it, Hazlitt! Here we've worked on this thing for months and months and now—phut! Who d' you s'pose did it—whatever it was?"

"Somebody from the *Inchcliffe*. Must've been. She's been in Monte Carlo since Monday. We'd better wire Captain Ball at once for full information and order him to use his own judgment until further instructions." He buzzed for a stenographer and dictated the telegram.

"Hell!" groaned Sir John. "Duggan's charters on those six Royal Victoria Maritime ships expire on the fifteenth and I'd have sworn we stood a good chance to snaffle the business!"

"We did," sighed Mr. Hazlitt, "but—we don't. And we mustn't overlook Duggan's threat about what else he can do to us, either!"

"Don't tell me!" said Sir John grimly. "Oh, this chap Duggan's a frightful old savage, once he gets his back up! He's shrewd, Hazlitt, shrewd, and utterly ruthless. And—vengeful!"

"Oh, dear!" said Mr. Hazlitt, miserably. "What a horrible, horrible mess! We make a standing offer of bonus and commissions
to our ships' officers for getting business, and the best they can do
is drive prospective customers away. . . . And get us sued. . . .
And get us ruined!" A trembling rage swept over him and he unleashed his most fearful oath.

"Drat!" said Mr. Virgil Hazlitt.

III

Captain John Ball, Master of the S.S. *Inchcliffe Castle,* settled
his bulk in his chair at the head of the table and harpooned a
slab of mutton from the platter in the center. "Well, gentlemen,"
he announced, "I've just spent a most interesting and instructive
morning in the Monaco Oceanographic Musee, which is French
for museum, up there on that hill up there. Ker-hem! Their word
for 'oceanographic' is the same as ours, except that they compli-
cate it with a *q* and also some other letters, but that's neither here
nor there. The point I'm trying to get across is, they've got the most
extraordinary collection of fish I ever came across. It's all arranged
very scientific and educational, with the correct as well as the Latin
names on each and every specimen. To a real fish lover like me
—well, gentlemen, to watch 'em swimming about in their beautiful rocky caverns, with hidden lights shining on their gorgeous
flaming colors, it fairly made me drool for a good solid gutful of
fried fish cooked as only Missus B. knows how! First she takes a
good hot stove, a gob of butter, a sprig of pursley, a—Er, I say,
you know, this here mutton don't smell so pristine to me. . . .
Jessup! Steward! Now see here, my man, what in the— Oh, a telegram for me?"

"Yus, sir," said Jessup. "It just came aboard with a boy."

"H'm," grumbled Captain Ball, tearing it open. "I'll bet it's
from—yes, it's from Hazlitt, and will you just take a look at the
length of it! Why, the sniveling old gimlet, he spends a fortune
wiring us a lot of blather and then makes up for it by supplying
us with motten rutton, rutton motten—er, with stinking viands,
to phrase it more genteelly. Why, bless me, what in the world's
he talking about? Listen:

'Owner yacht *Velella* complains of insults and threats from officer your ship. Plans drastic legal and other action. Send full details. Whoever did this has jeopardized our chances for important charters and will be sacked on return to London. If possible go aboard *Velella* asking to see Major Mackenzie Duggan in person and doing all you possibly can to . . .' "

"Duggan?" barked Mr. Glencannon, springing to his feet and clenching his fists. "Mackenzie Duggan, the distiller? Ho, so that's who he was! Weel, Captain"—his voice dropped to a rasping croak and the glint in his eye was baleful—"Hazlitt canna sack me because I've just resigned. And because I've resigned ye canna prevent me from going aboord yon *Velella* richt the noo and speaking my mind to the blackest-hearted, most ungrateful scoondrel that e'er was spawned in Scotland!"

IV

Like the king in his counting house, Major Mackenzie Duggan sat in the leather-lined smoking room of the motor yacht *Velella*, counting up his winnings from the Casinos of Menton, Monte, Nice and Cannes. Following his annual custom, he had gone through these scarcely philanthropic institutions like a hurricane hooked up to a vacuum cleaner, but as he jotted down the grand total of his loot he felt no slightest elation. Rather, he was half scornful, half bored and wholly unsatisfied. He had won so much so often so easily that there was no longer any kick in it. "Unh!" said Major Duggan.

A self-made man of moderate intelligence, vast diligence and phenomenal luck, he had begun by making the world's best whisky by mistake and then patenting the mistake. From then on, all he touched turned to gold. The newspaper caption writers had long since promoted him from Wealthy Distiller to Well-known Industrialist and expected soon to be styling him The Prominent Scottish Baronet. But none of it mattered to Major Duggan. His heart and soul were in his business enterprises. There was, of course, his distillery in Kirkintilloch. There were the great Port Glasgow Refineries and the foundry at Ardrossan. Then there was the Clydeside Paper Mill, Ltd., a thundering big concern. But though he was personally active in the direction of all of them, the distillery was his first love and ever remained the apple of his eye. And he remained the distillery's star salesman.

His yearly cruises to the Mediterranean were really busman's holidays. With sample case, order book and well-sharpened pencil, he made his daily rounds of the Riviera resorts, singing the praises of the Dew of Kirkintilloch to hotel owners, wheedling purchasing agents, high-powering barmen, bribing waiters and—selling the merchandise! Not until evening would he reluctantly relax at roulette or baccarat, growling, unh, that it was more fun unloading a single case of Dew on a back street bar with doubtful credit than shaking down the *Société des Bains de Mer* for the price of a complete new distillery, by gad. This, of course, was hardly the orthodox sporting attitude, and often, after closing time, the pasty-faced gentlemen with lizard eyes and little black mustaches who had shoved across his winnings all evening, sat over their *cafés crèmes* and wondered how this big fat blusterer of a *milor' Écossais* would behave if he ever, ever were to lose. But—and they shrugged their narrow shoulders—he never, never did. . . .

"No, never!" Major Duggan mused aloud, crumpling up the sheet of figures and chucking it into the waste basket. "It's all a howling bore, by gad! . . . Unh! Now what do you want, Mackintosh?"

"Pairdon, sir," said the steward, "but there's a gentlemon come aboord wud lik' to see the owner, and vurra irate he do seem, sir."

"Gentlemen? Irate? Unh, he is, is he? What's his name?"

"His name I dinna ker., sir. When I osked him, he—"

"Kick him off the yacht, kick him off, I say!" and Major Duggan rapidly assumed his familiar tint of purple. "Why, blast it, Mackintosh, how often must I tell you that when people won't give their names, you—"

"Pairdon, sir, but he says he's a customer," interrupted Mackintosh, placidly.

"A customer? Unh? A customer?" Automatically an unctuous smile wreathed the Major's countenance, to remain for but an instant. "An—an angry customer, you say? Great heavens, Mackintosh, bring him here at once! Must straighten him out myself!

Personal touch! Got to mollify him immediately!" He rose and paced back and forth. "A customer—angry! Well, it must be that damned distributor's fault! Plain as day! Here I call on every account in this territory, do a bang-up good-will and selling job, and then it's all spoiled by a—a—UNH!"

Rooted in his tracks, he stood glowering at the figure across the room. "Mackintosh!" he bawled. "Ferguson! Campbell!"

"The name's Glencannon," the Engineer corrected him, bolting the door, moving to the sideboard and pouring himself a slug of Dew. "Noo dinna raise an uproar, Muster Distiller, for 'twull avail ye nowt beyant the shattered yowp whuch ye so richly desairve." He gulped his drink and with a lordly gesture tossed a sixpence on the table. "There," he said scornfully, "tak' it, ye grubby mosh boiler! 'Tis the last bawbee ye'll e'er get oot o' the best, most steadfast customer ye e'er had!"

Major Duggan opened his mouth and let it hang ajar. His ample face was a battleground for his conflicting emotions. Rage thumped like a war drum in his soul but in time with its rhythm a still, small voice was chanting, "The customer is always right! . . . The customer is always right! . . ."

"But you scoundr—unh—my good man!" he stammered, his supersalesman's smile colliding midway with his Jovian scowl, his right hand spread for a friendly back slap and the left all set to crack a jaw. "Blast—unh—bless your soul, won't you please explain what's troubling you? If it's that little matter of the coal dust the other day, why, surely you must realize that I—"

"That ye didn't know I was the goose that laid yere golden egg —that I was yere mainstay, yere ooltimote consumer! Weel!"—and from his pocket Mr. Glencannon dragged the little green top, dashed it to the floor and spurned it with his foot—"now ye've got me sacked oot o' a job I've held for years, and from a quart-a-day friend ye've made a no-quarter enemy! I give ye my word that in every last barroom in the world's four corners I'll spread the news o' what an ungrate ye are. I'll tell them in Pandanus Charlie's in Kalong Betok. I'll cry yere shame in the Dingo at Marseels. When I speak my piece in Claude's in Leeverpool yere ears will sizzle lik' frying liver, and when I step up to the bar in The Captain's in Shonghai and sing oot, 'Give me a drink o' anything but Duggan's Dirty Dogwash,' and then explain why, weel, pairhops ye'll—"

"Please! Please!" Major Duggan interrupted, *vox angelica*. "Oh, my dear Mister Glencannon, you can't mean what you're saying! Why, Claude's in Liverpool is one of our best accounts, and The Captain's in Shanghai buys over a thousand cases annually! Surely, you wouldn't have us lose all this business, all this good will—in addition, of course, to your own! I—unh—I was hasty, that was all. I'll see that you get your job back, Mister Glencannon, don't you worry about that. I'll wire your owners in London tonight and if they don't reinstate you, I'll put 'em out of business, by gad! Come," he urged, extending his hand, "let bygones be bygones! Sit down, do, and we'll have a friendly drop together!"

Mr. Glencannon hesitated, licking his lips. Then his mustache twitched slightly and he smiled a sheepish smile. "A-weel," he said, diffidently accepting the proffered hand, "as lang as ye're willing to do the richt thing, sir, I—I, weel, Major Duggan, pairhops I was a wee bit hasty mysel'!"

"There, that's the spirit!" boomed the Major, exuding perspiration and personal magnetism in approximately equal quantities. " 'We are advertised by our friends' is what I always say, and we can't afford to lose a good one like you. Here, pour for yourself, Mister Glencannon—and please, old man, ha, ha—please take back that sixpence!"

Mr. Glencannon reached toward the coin and then glanced floorward at the little green top. He flickered his eyelid in a playful wink. "Haw! I'll just spin ye for it—what d'ye say?"

"Right-o, sportsman!" laughed Major Duggan, retrieving the top. "Accepting your sixpence as payment would be one thing, but winning it will be another!"

"A-weel," murmured Mr. Glencannon, "ye've no' exoctly won it yet!"

v

When late that afternoon brought no signs of Mr. Glencannon, Captain Ball donned his Sunday uniform, installed his shore-going teeth and in some trepidation presented himself aboard the

M.Y. *Velella.* After a considerable delay he was ushered below to the smoking room, which was so filled with the fumes of Havana leaf and Nigger Wool Shag that at first he could scarcely see across it.

"Unh! Well, come in!" invited a snarl from somewhere in the murk. Stumbling over an empty bottle and a bucket of ice, the visitor groped his way to a table at one end of which sat a large, purple gentleman whom he assumed to be Major Duggan. Across from him sat Mr. Glencannon. Both were disheveled, red-eyed and stripped to their undershirts. Evidently the situation was critical.

"Good afternoon, sir," said Captain Ball, hastening with oil for the troubled waters. "I've taken the liberty of—"

"Sit down and be quiet!" barked Major Duggan. "Can't you see we're busy?"

"Aye, if ye'll be patient just a minute, Captain . . ." said Mr. Glencannon, casily. "There's ower foorty poonds in this pot, d'ye see, but as soon as I've won it—"

"Well, you won't win it!" roared the Major, "You won't win again! You can't, you can't, you can't, I tell you! Here, it's my spin."

With a savage snap of the fingers he sent the little green top teetering across the table and then leaned over as though preparing to bite it. The veins of his forehead stood out like bunches of prime hothouse grapes. Mr. Glencannon sat back calmly, sorting out English and French banknotes from the great stack at his elbow and arranging them in neat piles.

Captain Ball shifted uneasily. "Pleasant day," he observed. "Er, I've taken the lib—"

"Unh! Put Two! Damn!" rasped Major Duggan, shoving out two pounds to the mound in the center. "Why, blast me if I ever saw such putrid luck! Still, though"—and he looked eagerly from one to the other of them as if seeking encouragement—"I didn't actually lose the pot now, did I? It was only Put Two, which'll make it all the jollier win for me when I spin next time. Oh, my luck's not out yet, gentlemen!" He took a drink and at once re-filled his glass. "No, no, no, my luck's not out and don't you ever think it is! I'm Lucky Duggan, I am! Ask them at Menton! Ask

them at Cannes! Ask 'em here at Monte! Ask 'em—unh—ask them
at Camenton, er, Camonte, unh, ask 'em here at Carlo! 'Lucky
Duggan,' that's who they'll tell you I am! So come on, Glencannon, you blasted good old customer you—spin out a Put to swell
the pot and then watch good old Lucky Duggan rake it in!"

Mr. Glencannon, having arranged his winnings to his liking
and taken his nose out of his glass, picked up the top and spun it
nonchalantly and with right good will. The spin, however, was to
the left. As was inevitable, its centrifugal and gyroscopic resultants
checked exactly with the already well-demonstrated Glencannon
theory, to say nothing of those of Einstein, Sperry, Brennan, *et al.*
The reading was "Take All."

As Mr. Glencannon did so with both hands, Major Duggan
lurched out of his chair with such violence that he took the arms
of it with him.

"Hell's fury!" he bellowed. "I've lost again!"

"Ah, er, ker-hem!" said Captain Ball, "I've taken the liberty of
coming aboard here, sir, becau—"

"That makes the seventy-third consecutive pot I've lost this
afternoon! It's not the money that bothers me—no, no, beggar
the money! But"—the Major paused, pressed a trembling hand to
his brow; when he resumed, his voice was but a whisper— "but
I—I wonder if it means my luck has gone! My business luck as
well! Ah, heavens, just think what that would mean!"

"Ah, heavens, just think!" Captain Ball nodded solemnly.
"However, I have taken the lib—"

"Shut up, you!" snapped Major Duggan. "Now see here, Glencannon, you've collared all the ready cash on the yacht, but we
can't let this thing stop at that! I've got to play with you again—
I've got to play and play and play you until I win, even if it's
only a farthing. It's my luck I've got to win back. See what I mean?
Come aboard first thing tomorrow and—"

Mr. Glencannon shook his head, meanwhile bundling up his
winnings in his jacket. "The *Inchcliffe Castle* sails at midnicht for
London," he announced, "and e'en the noo I must go see aboot
getting up steam. Aloss, sir, I fear we've had our farewell game
together."

"B-but that can't be, I tell you! You don't know, you can't

realize, what this means to me! But wait!" He grasped the other's forearm eagerly. "When will you be in Glasgow?"

"Glesga? Probably never," said Mr. Glencannon. "We've no business oot o' Glesga at all—in fact, the owners have ne'er been able to secure any. If we'd only a charter there—weel, then, o' coorse—"

"Ha! A charter, you say? Why, bless your soul, there's the very solution! I'm using six of those rotten Royal Victoria ships for my Clydeside Paper Mills—Glasgow to North African ports for esparto grass. The charter parties expire on the fifteenth. Well, I'll just turn over the whole business to Clifford & Castle!"

"Copital!" Mr. Glencannon applauded. "In that way we can get together and test yere luck at least once each month." He picked up the top and very carefully stowed it away in his pocket. "And noo, sir, may I osk that ye word that teelegrom, whuch ye promised to send to the owners, in such a way that ye infoorm them o' yere decision and leave no doot aboot me desairving full credit for it? Ye see, there'll be a bit o' a commission and a bonus for me."

"Oh, depend on it!" beamed Major Duggan. "I'm a star sales-man myself—yes, I always was and always will be—unh—well, that is, I've always been successful in the past—" His self-confidence wilted again and his words trailed off uncertainly.

"Ker-hem!" said Captain Ball, somewhat dazed. "Well, now, Major Duggan, if I may take the liber—"

"Haw, losh, Captain, ye've spoken the vurra words oot o' my mouth!" chuckled Mr. Glencannon. "I was just aboot to suggest to the Major that if he has any spare cases o' auld whusky kicking aroond loose and cluttering up his yacht we'd be pairfickly willing to debarrass him o' it and tak' it richt alang with us the noo."

THE MONTE CARLO MASSACRE

THE city of Nice has been described by flamboyant tourist litera-
ture as Europe's sunniest resort and by flimflammed tourists as
the resort of Europe's shadiest characters. Whatever the truth, the
native Niçois, most of whom are waiters, prudently preserve their
neutrality by keeping out of the sun, avoiding the tourists until
presenting the check, squeezing hush money from the shady characters, and watching their step at all times, but especially after
dark in the Albert Premier Gardens.

On this March night a baleful moon shone down on the park
from a melodramatic sky; silhouettes of wind-swept palms sprawled
and writhed across the graveled pathways like tortured tarantulas,
while on the inky surface of the lake swans drifted mistily as ghosts.
Eerie, sinister was the scene, and drear as the mood of Mr. Colin
Glencannon as he stalked through it on his way from the Casino
des Sports to the motor-bus terminal. From time to time the stalk
was varied by a stagger which was aggravated by a stumble, until
at length Mr. Glencannon was astonished to find himself proceeding backward across the center of a flower bed.

"Whoosh!" he breathed, the breath turning to steam in the
chill night air and the steam condensing into practically pure
alcohol which descended upon the flowers in globules of dew.
(The Dew of Kirkintilloch; Messrs. Mackenzie Duggan & Co.,
Ltd., Distillers. *Adv.*) "Ah, whoosh, and even foosh! Pairhops I'd
better pause and rumminate a bit, lest my spirits sag so low that
I trip and fall ower them!"

Heading for a bench drawn into the shadow of the municipal
bandstand, he was about to effect an emergency landing upon it
when he perceived that it was already occupied. The occupant, a
bulky gentleman, was standing precariously on the wooden slats,
fumbling with a length of rope and emitting horrid moans. As
there seemed but little doubt that he was about to hang himself

from the bandstand railing, Mr. Glencannon subsided into the upper rim of a wire refuse basket and prepared to view the proceedings in stability and comfort.

Although the bulky gentleman continued his fumbling and reinforced his moaning with sniffles, sighs, and sobs, he managed to return the scrutiny with something of calculation and appraisal. What he saw seemed to give him confidence, as indeed it should have done, for Mr. Glencannon was wearing the uniform of a chief engineer of the British mercantile marine.

"Say, friend," he said sepulchrally, "do you happen to know any English?"

"Aye, hoonderds o' them," replied Mr. Glencannon—"though I'm o' the orthodox Scottish persuasion, mysel'."

"Um," said the bulky one, "um, yair, sure. Still, though, that ain't exactly what I was driving at. What I was gonna say was, 'a man may be down, but he's never out,' see, and I was wunnering whether you'd unnerstand me. Then I was gonna say something about extenning the good old helping hand to a poor guy who's way, way down in his luck."

"Ah, and were ye really?" said Mr. Glencannon, brightening. "Weel, that's jolly decent o' ye! Noo that ye've mentioned it, auld mon, if ye cud see yere way clear to letting me have—"

"As I was saying," the bulky one interrupted hastily and loudly —"as I was saying, I'm a poor unfortunate guy that's in turrible need. I'm right up against it, see? I'm—desperate! Well, what's it to be, friend? Will you help me, or—" He held up the rope and dangled it dismally.

"Oh, dearie me, noo I understond ye!" cried Mr. Glencannon, with sudden comprehension and ready sympathy. "O' course, I'll help ye, puir lad—o' course, I'll help ye!" He disengaged himself from the refuse basket and snatched the lethal hemp. "There, noo! Just let me tak' charge o' everything," he invited soothingly. "Ye'll find that I've a vurra skillful hond when it comes to tying knots."

The bulky one pondered this at length, but with little enthusiasm. His sole audible conclusion was a grunt. Then he scratched his head and climbed down from the bench. "Um," he repeated gloomily, producing some American cigarettes.

"Yes, thonks, I will," murmured Mr. Glencannon, reaching out

and helping himself to three of them, two of which he crumbled
into the bowl of his pipe and the other he placed in reserve over
his right ear. "And noo, if ye'll just oblige me with a licht off that
match— Ah, ye're really vurra polite! Heigh, ho!" Deftly he bent
a hangman's knot in the rope and slipped open the noose. "Weel,
ye'll soon be rid o' the fulthy and expensive tobacco habit; we've
always got that to console us," he observed, rolling his eyes toward
the firmament.

The bulky one stared at him incredulously. "Aw, hey, now, hell,
friend! You don't really mean that you'll—you'll just stand there
and watch me go through with this awful business, do you?"

Mr. Glencannon shrugged, then sank down on the bench. "If
'twill sweeten yere last moments, I'll humor ye and sit," he said
magnanimously.

"Hell!" The bulky one dashed his cigarette to the ground and
stamped his heel upon it. "You think I'm kidding, do you? You
think I ain't game to hang myself, hey? Okay, buddy, okay! I'll
show you whether I'm game—and then maybe you'll be sorry!"

He mounted the bench, adjusted the noose around his neck
and secured the free end to a cast-iron curlicue in the bandstand's
ornamental railing. Then, fixing Mr. Glencannon with an accusing eye, he stepped off into space.

The engineer leaned back, cocked his head to one side and considered the dangling form critically.

"A-weel, it looks just aboot the way I'd always pictured it," he
mused. "Indeed, it tak's me back through the ages to ancient
Babylon's Honging Gardens, though it also reminds me summat
o' McKipling's ceelebrated jingle aboot Danny Deever, beginning—er—

" '*What mak's ye look so white, so white?*' *said Files-on-parade*. . . .
'*A touch o' sun, a touch o' sun,*' *the Colored Sergeant said,*

"Though be domned if I cud ever see why the bard thocht a
touch o' sun wud turn a neeger white. . . . But come, come!" he
addressed the hanging man impatiently. "Stop holding yere chin
doon and get on with yere job! Those strongling noises ye're
making are extremely unmeelodious!"

The other ceased his struggles and his gurgles, put his chin down even farther and scowled at Mr. Glencannon as he swayed. Without relaxing the bulging muscles of his bullneck, "Now, see here, you!" he said hollowly. "Ain't you gonna do nothing? Ain't you gonna cut me down?"

"Cut ye doon?" scoffed Mr. Glencannon. "Cut ye doon, blosh! Ye're no' half hung, and I've no knife anyway, so dinna talk nonsense! Be proctical, lad, be proctical!"

"Well, ain't I trying to be?" croaked the other plaintively. "Oh, please, have a heart, friend! Say! Exactly how long do you think I can stay up here, hanging like this, anyway? An hour? All night? All week?"

"Ho!" cried Mr. Glencannon indignantly, springing to his feet. "Oh, ho! So that's yere little game, is it? Trying to pin me doon and trop me into making a bet, are ye? Weel, ye cheap swundler, let me warn ye I've been swundled once too often in this domned swundling town and I willna fall for any sure-thing bet at this time o' the clock! I'm in a black mood, a mood to see a genuween honging, and a genuween honging I'll see! If ye dinna lift up yere chin, relox yere neck and let nature tak' its course, I'll grab ye by the legs and—"

Hastily, the bulky one reached over his head and grasped the rope.

With an ease that was astonishing in one of his weight, he pulled himself up on it until the noose fell slack upon his chest.

"Oh, so you're a real Scotch tough guy in a real tough mood, hunh?" he grunted, his feet groping for the bench. "Well, Scotch tough guy, I'll just come down outta here and show you who's a— No! Please! Leggo! Ar-r-r-rgh!"

With a flying tackle, Mr. Glencannon had caught him by the ankles. He clung there, swinging, swaying and bearing down hard.

II

In view of our several references to Mr. Glencannon's melancholy mood and because of this mood's importance in our story, we must briefly touch upon the circumstances which induced it before proceeding with the hanging in the Albert Premier Gardens.

For some months past, the S.S. *Inchcliffe Castle,* of which Mr. Glencannon was chief engineer, had been ferrying coal cargoes from the Welsh ports to the Riviera cities of Cannes, Antibes, Nice, Monte Carlo and Mentone. In each of these cities, which lie within a twenty-franc bus fare, was at least one gambling casino, and in each of the casinos Mr. Glencannon had lost at least one shirt. At length, fearing for the very hair on his chest, already streaked with gray from anxiety and chagrin, he very sensibly decided to abandon haphazard play at roulette in favor of a tested scientific system. The first system to engage his attention was one called *La Pous-sette*—"the little push." This consisted in so arranging his chips in the outer margin of the green baize that the merest flick of the forefinger would shoot them across the line into the so-called "even chances"—*Rouge, Noir, Pair, Impair,* and so on. If, at the instant the little ivory ball dropped into a compartment of the wheel, Mr. Glencannon saw that the chance opposite which he was sitting had won, he would flick a chip into the square, collect his gains, politely stifle a yawn and saunter off to another table.

Although the even chances pay only double, he played this system against the Monte Carlo bank so effectively that he won eight hundred francs in fifty-five minutes. At the fifty-sixth minute, however, just as he was counting his loot behind a potted palm, he was surrounded by four dress-suited officials, hustled into an ante-room, despoiled of his money, beaten with rubber bludgeons of the sort commonly used for interpellating reticent guests in police stations, and thrown down the back steps. He could not help but recall that on the occasion of a visit to the Monte Carlo Casino three years previously, he had been thrown down the front steps, and he felt the present indignity keenly.

Persuaded that there were flaws in the *Poussette,* mathematical or otherwise, Mr. Glencannon resolved to devise a less-fallible system of his own. He had observed that all confirmed system play-ers carried little morocco notebooks which they frequently con-sulted and in which they jotted calculations. He purchased such a book and proceeded to work out the new Glencannon System within it. First he glued the back cover and all but the first half dozen pages together, thus converting them into a solid block. Next, he cut out the center of this block, transforming it into a box, the sides of which were the gilt edges of the glued pages and the bottom the morocco-leather back. With a razor blade, then, he slit an inverted V in the leather, its point about an inch and a half from the top of the book. In shape, position and purpose, this slit resembled the mouth of a shark. Its lower edges—as it were, the under jaw of it—he reinforced inside with flat steel springs. Seen either closed or with any number up to five of its six loose pages open, the book showed no external signs of tampering. Closed and held in the hand, however, a gentle squeeze caused the V-shaped slit in the back of it to open, the lower jaw projecting slightly. When pressure was relaxed, the slit sprang shut.

Having tested the system in private until convinced of its theoretical soundness, Mr. Glencannon decided to prove it in actual play in the Casino des Sports de la Méditerranée, newest and most lavishly chromium-plated deadfall in the city of Nice. He edged his way through the crowd around the first table in the *salle,* took out his notebook and frowningly checked half a dozen spins against certain cryptic combinations of figures written on the opening, or unglued, pages. Apparently satisfied with the tendency of the wheel, and observing that a stout lady opposite him had staked a handful of hundred-franc chips on Number 22, *en plein,* he endeavored to toss a ten-franc chip on Number 23. It fell short. He reached over and with the upper edge of the closed notebook pushed his chip into the proper square. As he did so, he squeezed gently. The slot opened and scooped up two hundred francs from the stout lady's pile, momentarily concealed beneath.

Number 7 won. The stout lady shrugged, watched the croupier gather in her stake and turned her attention elsewhere. Mr. Glencannon shrugged, watched the croupier gather in his stake, slipped his notebook into his pocket and shook the stout lady's chips out. He had risked ten francs and won one hundred and ninety! The great Glencannon Shark Jaw System had proved itself. The key to riches was his. As he moved on to another table he felt as if he were walking on air.

Two hours later found him still playing—playing as one possessed. A conservative estimate of his possessions would put them somewhere between four and five thousand francs. True, there were occasional protests from winning players who accused the bank of withholding portions of their just gains, but whenever such dissensions occurred, Mr. Glencannon would frown petulantly upon the disturbing parties, murmur something about the putrid sportsmanship of the lower classes, and transfer his activities to the opposite end of the *salle,* visiting the bar on the way.

Along toward midnight the disputes increased in frequency. Mr. Glencannon realized that in common prudence he should call a halt. But the gambling fever was in his blood. His face was flushed, one eye was glazed, the other was bloodshot, and the overhang of his walrus mustache glistened with great beads of whisky.

"One more! Just one more!" he kept promising himself. He repeated the promise at bar and gaming tables alike, dizzied, dazzled, intoxicated by visions of wealth beside which that of Croesus dwindled to a beggarly handful of counterfeit Albanian pennies.

"One more! Positively the last! Aye, and I'll drink this one to the great Glencannon System!" He had actually raised the glass to his lips before he realized that it was his notebook and that people were staring and even pointing at him. This served to remind him that he had left the bar some moments previously and was now standing at a crowded roulette table.

"Haw!" he chuckled. "Weel, if any mon thinks that playing a system is no' a frichtful mental strain, it's because he thinks that playing a system is no' a frichtful mental strain! H'm"—he consulted his formulas and then scanned the layout—"let see, noo; let's see!"

What he saw was a sprawling mound of five-hundred-franc chips on Number 30. He flipped a ten-franc chip toward Number 29 and missed it by a comfortable margin. Reaching over the mound on Number 30, he shoved his own chip into the proper square with his notebook. As nearly as he could judge, the scoop gulped down fifteen hundred francs. To his astonishment and dismay, however, the book resisted his efforts to withdraw it from the table. He tweaked it gently. He tugged it hard. He jerked it—alas, to no avail! He realized with horror, then, that the point of the scoop had pierced the green baize and that its steel-spring shark jaws were gripping the padded cloth as though locked with tetanus.

He felt the eyes of the croupiers, of the players, of all the world upon him. "Monsieur," the *chef de parti* addressed him coldly, "please to have the goodness to retire your book from the table."

"Moonseer," said Mr. Glencannon, drawing himself up to his full height, which he felt at the moment to be something less than six inches, "yon book, as ye see, refuses to budge. It's a strange thing, it's a domned suspicious thing, but ye know the reason better than I! . . . Ladies and gentlemen!" he harangued the players. "Fellow victims! As most of ye have noticed, there's been crooked work going on in this room all evening. Weel, here's the climox o' it! This wheel is fixed—aye, they've got electro-magnets concealed in the table, and if ye dinna believe me, just try to pick up yon book! Why, o' all the fulthy swundles—"

At this point he felt himself moving rapidly elsewhere. As at Monte Carlo, his first stop was an anteroom. Here in Nice, however, there were six dress-suited officials instead of four, and the steps of the service entrance down which they kicked him were even higher, steeper and harder than the back steps at Monte.

All of which serves to explain Mr. Glencannon's mood as we left him helping with the hanging in the Albert Premier Gardens.

III

The longer Mr. Glencannon clung to the hanging man's ankles the longer the latter's neck became, until it seemed in imminent danger of stretching from a bullneck into one quite suitable for a racing whippet. Fortunately, before this transformation could take place, the iron curlicue to which the rope was attached snapped under the strain and the pair pitched to the ground.

Mr. Glencannon, his head somewhat cleared by the exercise, scrambled to his feet and seized the loose end of the rope. "Come!" he chided. "Do ye stop yere gulping and get up!"

"I can't get up!" wheezed the bulky one.

"But dinna ye want me to hong ye some more?"

The other groaned and shook his head, but through a rather restricted arc. "Unh-uh!" he said. "Not me! I'd hung myself three times tonight before you showed up, but now"—he rubbed his throat gingerly—"now, I guess I'll quit and call it a day!"

"Eh? Ye'd hung yersel' three times? Ah, foosh! Explain yersel'!"

The sufferer lay silent for a moment; then he grinned wryly, dragged himself to the bench and slumped down upon it. "Yair, I'll explain," he said. "Why not? After all, I s'pose I'd orter seen that you—you wasn't one of the—suckers!" He swallowed experimentally. "Um. Well, I'm a perfessional hanger, as you might say. I just wait here in this park till I spot English or American tourists coming along, and then I put on my act for 'em. Mostly they slip me a hunnerd francs as soon as I show 'em the rope. But if they don't—well, I simply hang myself."

"But what hoppens then?"

"Why, then they cut me down and fork out double!"

"Weel, great swith, ye astoond me!" cried Mr. Glencannon. "O' course, I knew, from the way ye held yere chin, that ye were an impostor o' some sort. But all the same, there must be a cairtain amoont o' wear and tear on the gullet!"

"Unh-uh, not on mine!" said the other, with a note of pride. "It's a stunt I practiced in the gym as part of my regular training." He expanded his mighty neck muscles. "There, just looka that for a development! By rights, you see, I'm a perfessional wrestler."

"Aye, I'd suspected something o' the sort from yere architecture. But do ye mean to say ye can mak' more money oot o' honging than oot o' wrestling?"

"Well, no, though wrestling ain't no bed of roses either. Particularly all-in wrestling, the kind I do."

"Oh, aye, I've seen it in the London Blackfriars' Ring," chuckled Mr. Glencannon. "They bit, kicked, gouged, choked and ruined one another throughout a lang winter's evening. Losh, it looked lik' a noble sport, but I heard whuspers that it was faked."

"Sure it's faked, but that didn't make my specialty any easier. Me, I was the guy that gets jumped on, see? Why, some of them bruisers that jumped on me weighed over three hunnerd pounds!"

"But why didn't ye break the monotony by jumping on some o' them, when opportunity presented?"

"Because there was a clause in my contrack against it, that's why," sighed the wrestler. "You see, when René Desfourneaux, this French permoter, come over to the States to sign up a stable of us for a Europeen tour, he seen me get jumped on five times in one match and was very enthusiastic about my style. He said he could see I had a real gift for getting jumped on, sort of, and he would build me up into the biggest drawing card on the Continent."

"But he bruck his wurrd?"

"No, I broke three ribs," said the other ruefully. "That is, a big palooka by the name of Earthquake Garfunkel broke 'em for me by jumping before I give him the high sign. That happened right here in Nice, a month ago."

"Earthquake Garfunkel—braugh, it's a vurra muscular name!" said the engineer. "By the way, I am Muster Colin Glencannon, Esquire. Who micht you be?"

"My name's Lilly," said the other. "Peter Alastair Lissington Lilly. But my perfessional name is The Brooklyn Behemoth, and I shouldn't be surprised if it's probably familiar to you."

"I canna say that it is," confessed Mr. Glencannon. "However, I'm faiily fameellar with the Brooklyn Bridge and intimately so with the Sand Street police station, if that's any sop to yere vanity. However, my dear Muster Lilly, pray continue with yere vurra interesting dissertation."

"Well, with my slats busted I couldn't stand getting jumped on, so Desfourneaux gimme the sack. Yair, the skunk, he even talked about suing me for breach of contrack, but that's really because he wants to get out of the wrestling game and tie in with some new syndicate that's trying to build up a heavyweight boxing champeen. Well"—the Behemoth spread his ample hands—"I seen it was either starve or set up in business for myself, so I bought that hunk of rope and here I am!"

"Extraordinurra!" murmured Mr. Glencannon. "Why, the whole thing's pairfictly astoonding! To think that for ower a month ye've made a living sumply by honging yersel' on this bondstond!"

"Three or four hunnerd francs a night!" the wrestler assured him complacently.

"And ye've had no trouble with the police?"

"Unh-uh! Nobody's ever reported me, because I only work English and American tourists. Anyway, here in France there's no law against committing suicide, as long as you don't lay on the railroad track and slow up the trains. Once you've shelled out a

hunnerd and eighty francs for your identity card, you can hang
yourself as often as you feel like, see?"

"Aye, I do see," said Mr. Glencannon pontifically. "I do see indeed! I see that ye've been peddling yere God-given talent for a
piddling pittance, when ye ocht to be rich, rich, rich! Ho, ye puir,
sumple gowk, yere vurra brains are muscle-boond! Dinna ye realize
there's a foortune to be made oot o' honging yerself', if ye'll only
hong where the honging's guid?"

"Good? Friend, I guess I haven't done so bad, hanging around
right here in this park!"

"Three or four hoonderd froncs a nicht? Phut!" scoffed Mr.
Glencannon. "What ye need is a business monager! Noo, I'll be
sailing for England a week from tonicht, but I guarontee that we
cud airn thoosands and thoosands if ye'd just let me hondle things
in the meanwhile!"

"Um!" answered The Brooklyn Behemoth cautiously. "Well,
I dunno. Of course, thousands and thousands is plenty of jack,
even if it's only francs. But I got a very nice little trade built up
here, and I been gypped by managers so often that I'm getting
pretty leery. Just what was you figuring as your cut?"

"A trifling fifty per cent," said Mr. Glencannon, not even bother-
ing to snap his fingers.

"Well, I'd hafta have it in black and white in a real hidebound
contrack. And even at that, maybe I wouldn't like your proposition."

"Oh, ye'll lik' my proposition, dinna fear! As for the contract
being hideboond—weel, my dear Muster Behemoth, I'll write it
with my ain fair hond, and I promise it'll tak' a cannier wrestler
than yersel' to wriggle oot o' it."

IV

Monsieur Louis Vidal, principal owner of the Casino des Sports
de la Méditerranée and all-around big shot in Continental sporting circles, bowed to the visitor who had just been ushered into
his private office. For all his Parisian suavity, his London tailoring
and his three ruby rings, M. Vidal looked very like a rat, though
not a rat in which anyone would repose a sacred trust.

"Good morning," he greeted. "You are the British gentleman who teleph—er—oh! Why, you damned crook! You're the fellow who was thrown out of here the other night!"

"No' thrun oot; kicked oot. Ye'll find there's an expensive difference!" chuckled Mr. Glencannon, settling into a chair.

"Bah! *Fichez le camp* or you'll get kicked out again! If it wasn't for the scandal, I'd have you arrested!"

"Scondal? Oh, aye, to be sure!" Mr. Glencannon nodded comprehendingly. "Noo that ye mention it, I realize that scondal micht be a vurra costly business to a gombling casino. Especially to a new one lik' this, that's having a lean time getting started."

M. Vidal winced slightly and then reached toward the push button on his desk. "Don't you worry about my casino! You just clear out of it! Understand?"

"Bless ye, puir fellow, o' course I understond! It's yersel' who's doing the worriting—and ye'll be doing a domn sicht more o' it if ye shud chonce to push yon buzzer!"

As a professional gambler, M. Vidal did not believe in taking chances; thus, he stayed his hand and scrutinized his visitor with eyes which had seen through some of the slickest scoundrels in Europe. But now, strangely enough, the old principle of diamond-cut-diamond didn't seem to work. M. Vidal was puzzled at its failure—puzzled and vaguely uneasy. "Er—who are you, anyway?" he asked.

"A-weel, my name doesna matter," said Mr. Glencannon, "though were I to whusper it in yere ear, I promise it wud flabbergast ye. The important thing is, I hoppen to be secretary and treasurer o' The Riviera Social and Suicide Club."

"The—what? Oh, *blague!* Do you take me for an idiot?"

"On the contrary, moonseer, I know ye to be almost as shrewd as other people think ye. That is why I have called upon ye, with unimpeachable credentials, to announce that the club's inaugural suicide festival and picnic was conducted last nicht. The officiating member, who had recently been mulcted o' a foortune here in yere nice, new, shiny casino, hung himsel' just ootside it."

M. Vidal paled, then recovered himself. "Ridiculous!" he sneered. "If anything—anything like that had happened, don't you suppose I'd have heard of it?"

"If we'd left the cadaver oot there, I suppose ye cairtainly wud," conceded Mr. Glencannon. "However, richt in the midst o' a lovely and most impressive ceremony, a weel-meaning non-member came blundering alang and cut doon the candidate prematurely. Foortunately, I had already taken the souvenir photograph."

"The—photograph?"

"Aye! It's a vurritable gem! Here, look at it!" He tossed the print upon the desk, but prudently withheld the negative.

M. Vidal snatched up the picture and studied it in horror. The horror was due partly to the bulky form dangling from a tree, but mostly to the background against which it was silhouetted. For there—no mistaking them—were the white-marble façade and brilliant neon signs of the Casino des Sports de la Méditerranée.

"Nom du diable!" His voice was tense. "Have you shown this to —anyone else?"

"Not yet," Mr. Glencannon assured him. "Ye see, when I obsairved how pairfictly all the details o' yere building had turned oot, it occurred to me that pairhops ye'd lik' to use the picture in yere odvertising. And so, instead o' taking it aroond to the newspapers, I—"

"How much do you want for it? Speak up!"

Mr. Glencannon picked thoughtfully at his front teeth with a corner of the negative. "A-weel, photographs o' hongings are priced on a sliding scale," he said, flicking a fiber of the S.S. *Inchcliffe Castle's* breakfast ham from the celluloid. "If I'd no' been ejected oot o' here the other nicht, I'd noo have at least five thoosand froncs, and there wudn't have been any honging. Therefore, there wudn't have been any photograph, and so it wud have cost ye nothing. If, on the other hond, ye'd merely thrun me oot, I'd noo be asking only seven thoosand for the picture. But as lang as ye kicked me oot, its price is ten thoosand froncs, net. Ah, losh!" He held the negative up to the light. "Just look at the lovely pattern o' the shadows, and the amusing abstract design formed by the writhing arms and legs as the subject strongles to death in the full glare o' yere electric signs! Why, 'tis enough to give yere customers nichtmares and ruin yere trade for years!"

"Don't I know it?" snapped M. Vidal. "Still, ten thousand francs is—"

"Is exockly the price o' the picture," finished Mr. Glencannon. "How in the world did ye guess it?"

M. Vidal grimaced, unlocked a drawer, produced a packet of broad *mille* notes and peeled off ten of them. "Here!" he said. "Now give me that print and the *pellicule!* Ah!" He snapped a flame on his lighter, touched it to paper and film, and watched them crinkle to cinders in the ash tray. Then he mopped his forehead and studied Mr. Glencannon with a mixture of curiosity, aversion and respect.

"Well, blast you, I wish I knew just how it was that you worked this game," he growled. "More than that, I wish you'd worked it on somebody else. Why didn't you, eh? On some casino that's already well established. On a casino that can really afford to—pay!" He paused. "Monte Carlo, for instance."

"Monte Carlo? Ah, exockly!" agreed Mr. Glencannon. "I've a bit o' a grudge against Monte Carlo too. But, fronkly, I understond that the laws o' Monaco, unlik' those o' Fronce, are vurra severe with anyone who attempts to diddle the weel-known casino."

"They are, worse luck!" said M. Vidal grimly. "That's one more reason why Monte has such an unfair advantage over the rest of us! Monte—well, I don't mind confessing that the Monte Carlo Casino is my biggest competition." He leaned back and blinked his rat eyes at Mr. Glencannon. "I wonder," he continued slowly —"yes, I wonder if you couldn't conduct your next—er—little soiree in the casino gardens at Monte Carlo?"

"Vurra easily," said Mr. Glencannon. "But as I wudna dare try to interest them in a photograph, how wud the club mak' oot on its expenses?"

"Oh, I'd take care of that part!" M. Vidal assured him, warming to his subject. "There'd be no trouble about the photograph, because nobody would be asked to buy it. As a matter of fact, I'd give it away, and the Monte crowd wouldn't even know about it till they saw it in the English and American newspapers."

"Ah, losh, noo I'm beginning to understond ye!" Mr. Glencannon chuckled admiringly. "Ye mean ye'd lik' to strongle their competition with a little advairse publicity! Haw, haw, haw, it's a most intriguing idea!"

"You like it? So! Then let's get down to business. What do you say to another ten thousand for a hanging at Monte, to be done tonight?"

"Weel, I canna think o' any nicht likely to be more propitious," said Mr. Glencannon. "However, the Suicide Club's customarra terms are half in advonce; remainder, cash on cadaver, or its photograph."

M. Vidal reopened the drawer, fished out another packet of notes and snipped them through the middle with scissors. "Half in advance, you said? Here you are! You'll get the other half as soon as you've hung your man and I've got the picture. Now, listen! At midnight, sharp, I'll be in my car at the foot of the gardens across from the Casino entrance. My photographer will be with me, and so will—certain other people. Ha! Yes, yes, I warn you, my friend! Don't try any more funny business with me!"

v

Rows of cars flanked the floodlit flower gardens which slope down from the Boulevard du Moulin to the Monte Carlo Casino. Their chauffeurs, like all chauffeurs after eleven P.M., were drowsing in their seats or discussing in vehement undertones the parsimony, perversity and general pusillanimity of their employers. Mr. Glencannon, pacing nervously back and forth across the short stretch of sidewalk at the foot of the gardens, cast alternate glances at his watch and at the curb-side traffic sign which faced the entrance of the casino opposite. This sign, he had decided, would make an ideal gallows. But though the rope, neatly coiled, was ready beneath his jacket, and the photographer, his camera set, was waiting in Vidal's car at the head of the line, Mr. Peter Alastair Lissington Lilly, professionally known as The Brooklyn Behemoth, was nowhere to be seen.

From the tower of the Prince's palace, cresting the moon-bathed Rock beyond the harbor, came twelve solemn strokes. "Ah, swith!" muttered Mr. Glencannon. "After all my careful plonning, is he going to let me doon? Where, oh where, can the domn lout be?"

The minute hand of his watch had dragged on to fifteen past midnight when he felt a tap on his shoulder. He wheeled to find himself confronted by four strangers in caps. These gentlemen loomed even more bulkily than the absent Mr. Lilly himself, and they shared among them a notable collection of beetle brows, lantern jaws and cauliflower ears.

" 'Ere, you," said the spokesman in a whisper which he delivered from the corner of his mouth. "We're Vidal's men. Are you the bloke from the Suicide Club?"

"I am, indeed, none other than he," replied Mr. Glencannon, with dignity. "Ye can infoorm yere master, with my cumpliments, that all is in readiness for the hoppy event. Look!" Cautiously he opened his jacket and exposed the rope. "Unfoortunately, there seems to have been a slicht delay, but—"

"Nuts to your buts!" the other interrupted him. "It's a quarter arfter midnight, guv'nor, and you're bleddy well due to swing! . . . C'mon, chums; string him up!"

Mr. Glencannon felt the rope snatched from under his jacket. He felt the noose jerked tight around his neck. He felt himself hauled clear of the ground. He tried to scream. He managed only to gurgle. His neck was stretching. His lungs were bursting.

He saw bright flashes before his eyes, and heard, as from across vast distances, the shouts and thuds of conflict. With a final agonized whinny, he swooned.

When Mr. Glencannon opened his eyes, he found himself in a speeding automobile. When he tried to open his lips, he found that they were already open and encircling the neck of a bottle.

"*Ça y est!*" he heard M. Vidal's voice. "He's coming out of it!"

"Sure, he's okay now," agreed The Brooklyn Behemoth. "He'd orter held his chin down, that's all."

Feeling that the bottle was empty and his strength in some measure regained, Mr. Glencannon sat up. "Foosh!" he snorted. "What in the heel do ye mean, having me lynched by a gang o' thugs and—"

"There, there! Everything's all right!" M. Vidal was exuberant. "Here is the rest of your money. You see, when it got so late and there hadn't been a hanging, my men became a bit—er—restive. And so—"

"And so ye let them hong me! Weel, ye unscruppulous rat, dinna ye s'pose I noticed it?"

"I dare say you did! But, my dear fellow, please be reasonable! I was going to have them cut you down as soon as we'd got the pictures."

"Who did cut me doon?"

"Why, your athletic friend here. Ha, how well you'd arranged it! He came rushing upon the scene, knocked out all four of my men with as many blows of his fist, and then jumped—yes, actually jumped upon them! With you hanging there strangling and the others laid out cold in the foreground, the photos will look like a wholesale massacre! A massacre at Monte Carlo!"

Mr. Glencannon counted the halves of the *mille* notes and shoved them into his pocket. Then he turned upon the wrestler. "Weel, what are ye smirking at, ye stupid lump? If ye think I'll pay ye a plugged bross farthing for this nicht's bungling work, ye're domn weel mistaken!"

"Aw, hey, now!" sulked The Brooklyn Behemoth. "How'd I know I was gonna miss that bus? Lucky for you that I—"

"Oh, you needn't worry," M. Vidal assured him. "I don't know who you are, but I do know that you knocked out the four best heavyweight prospects that my scout, Desfourneaux, has been able to locate in Europe. I head the syndicate that's out to build up a new world's champion and I'll put you under contract in the morning."

"Ye'll do nothing o' the sort!" growled Glencannon. "He's already under a hideboond contract with me."

"I'll buy the contract."

"A-weel," said Mr. Glencannon, "in that case, pairhops we can arrange it. But feerst, how much am I bid for the eleeven additional photos I tuck the other nicht, when yere new heavyweight chompion was honging by his neck ootside yere nosty, swundling casino?"

THE HUNTING OF THE HAGGIS

CAPTAIN BALL smiled paternally as he watched his officers take their places at the supper table, but the smile was a trifle tremulous at the edges. In his throat—he ker-huffed, unresultfully—he could feel the same lump that was always there when he came down the lane to Kozey Kottage after a long voyage and saw Missus B. standing in the doorway beneath the mail-order trumpet vine, which they loved just as much as though it hadn't turned out to be a peculiarly repulsive sort of warty climbing squash. *Ten years,* Captain Ball was thinking. *Yes, tomorrow'll make the tenth Christmas this very same crowd of us has been together in the* Inchcliffe Castle. *M'm—well, all of us is older now than we was then, but particularly me. Yes, most damned particularly me.* He reminded himself that this was only because he'd had a head start of years on the rest of them, but there was scant consolation in the thought.

The steward brought in a covered dish and placed it on the table before him. "Ker-hem!" Captain Ball recalled himself brusquely. "Good evening, gentlemen, good evening!" He shook the crumbs and fragments of the noontime curry from his napkin. "Well, I s'pose we might as well learn the worst!" With the air of a coroner lifting a coffin lid at an overdue exhumation, he uncovered the dish and peered within. "Bwah!" he recolled. "Curry! Again!" He sat back shuddering, and from the depths of his considerable paunch came murmurs and complaints, like the voices of a rebellious mob heard dimly in the distance. For some seconds he and the company hearkened to this ventriloquial *tour de force;* then, when the tumult and the shouting died, "Well, there you are, and I won't say 'pardon me'!" Captain Ball spread his hands. "You heard it, gentleman, you heard my innermost sentiments, and I'm not ashamed to state I stand behind my stomach exactly one hundred per cent!"

"Bravvio!" applauded Mr. Glencannon, the chief engineer. "Yere spirit o' solidarity does ye proud, sir—e'en though I suspect ye're feeling as hollow as the rest o' us." He dragged the dish toward him, spooned out a heaping portion of curried rice and codfish, and fell to stowing it away in the hatchlike orifice beneath his walrus mustache.

"Hollow?" repeated Captain Ball. "Indeed, Mr. Glencannon, my stomach's as hollow as a cargo of bass drums! But my heart— ah, my heart is full to overflowing, both with joy and with sadness!" He paused lamely and smiled that same tremulous smile. "Maybe you'll say I'm a sentimental old fool, gentlemen, but, you see, I was just now figuring that this is the eve of our tenth Christmas together. Well, here we ought to be gloating over the bang-up dinner we ought to be having tomorrow and singing carols about good cheer and yew logs and what not and et cetera and so on—instead of which—ker-huff—where are we? Well,"— he turned to the mate—"literally, of course, I s'pose such sticklers for accuracy as you, Mr. Montgomery, would say we was right here in Aden harbor, anchored in five fathoms and a little over, and the chart would back you up. But what I really mean to say is— er—er—well, here it is the tenth anniversary of our happy family, as it were, but instead of looking forward to a fine old feed to celebrate it, our very constitutions is roaring riot and rebellion!"

"Yus!" agreed Mr. Montgomery, sourly. "And orl on account of the curry. Curry, curry, curry, day in, day out, and the narsty stuff is only a sort of lowgrade dandruff they comb out of 'orses anyway! Welp, I wish a very curry Christmas to the rest of yer! Myself, I'll eat my dinner ashore tomorrer or my name's not Chauncey Montgomery!"

"Eh? Ah, now, see here! You don't really mean that, do you?" demanded Captain Ball in dismay. "Oh, come, come, Mr. Montgomery; surely you wouldn't, you couldn't, break up our regular Christmas family party on our tenth anniversary, will you? Maybe I'm silly, maybe I'm superstitious, but it—it's so unusual for the same old crowd to stick together so long in one ship and always get along so free from friction!"

"Per'aps," grunted Mr. Montgomery. "Orl I know is that I've got barnacles on my stomach from the fodder, and blisters on my soul from the friction." He glanced sidewise at Mr. Glencannon, who, from the shelter of his napkin, thumbed his nose in return. "No, captain, I've choked down all the curry and the hinsults I can stand! I'm going ashore tonight, I'm going to arsk Shapiro, the ship chandler, for the name of the least worst 'otel in Aden, and then I'm going to order a dinner for myself for tomorrow. I know I won't get turkey, I 'ope I won't get potomaine poisoning, but damned if I'll get curry!"

"No, no, of course you won't!" sighed Captain Ball. "I s'pose it was really pretty selfish of me to try to dissuade you. But—ha-ha!—there's no fool like an old fool, eh? H'm'm. Ten years!" He essayed a forkful of the curry, but either it or the lump in his throat choked him, so he gave it up. "Well, let's change the subject and talk about something pleasant! Turkey, you said?" The sounds from within him soared to the wild crescendo of hunger marchers chanting the "International," then died on a gurgle of utter despair. "Ah, turkey! All roasted to a nice, rich tobacco-juice brown, with its abdomen stuffed with chestnuts and sausages and thyme and bread crumbs, like Missus B. always stuffs hers at home—though damme if I can ever remember whether the accent is on the 'ab' or the 'do.' She also makes a lovely, thick gravy out of the giblets."

"Lawks, 'ow delicious! The thought of it fair makes my teeth water!" declared Mr. Montgomery. "If we could only 'ave turkey with giblet gravy tomorrer, even watching Mr. Glencannon eat it couldn't spoil my happetite! But look,"—he pointed through the open doorway toward the black rock mountains which reared above the lights on Steamer Point—"look! Why, blyme, yer'd find gold coins in the streets o' Glasgow before yer'd find a turkey in Aden!"

"A-weel," said Mr. Glencannon, "oot o' respect for the captain's vurra evident distress at yere decision, I'll owerlook for the moment the crude pairsonal slurs ye've just noo cast at me. And noturally, I willna attempt to dispute the fact that the turkey is a vurra noble and palatable bird. But all the talk o' stoomachs has reminded me that for great ceremoonial occasions—birthdays, bonquets, brawls and e'en such sacred, sentimental gatherings as Captain Ball was plonning for tomorrow—there's another dish

fully as deleecious as the turkey. I refair, o' coorse, to the haggis.
Noo, look ye, Muster Montgomery; I'll give ye a chonce to be
decent for once in yere life, e'en though it sprains ye! If I guarontee
to cook up a nice, ploomp haggis for our little party, will ye no'
accede to the captain's cherished wishes and eat yere Christmas
meal with him and the rest o' us?"

"M'm, well, that depends," said Mr. Montgomery, loftily. "Just
wot the 'ell's a 'aggis?"

Mr. Glencannon gazed at him in astonishment mingled with
pity. "The haggis," he explained with a spacious gesture, "the
haggis, Muster Mate, is the fruit o' a romonce o' lang, lang ago,
involving the humble pudding and the lordly sossage. It is the
culinary triumph o' Scotland, which is to say, o' the entire world!
Oh, surely, my puir fellow, e'en in all yere pewling ignorance, ye
dinna mean to say ye've ne'er thrilled to the deathless lines o'
Robert Burns in his Address to a Haggis? Er—

> "Great chieftain o' the pudding race,
>   Aboon them a' ye tak your place!
>   His knife see rustic Labour dight
>   And cut ye up wi' ready sleight,
>   Trenching your gushing entrails bright
>   Lik' any ditch.
>   And then, oh what a glorious sight,
>   Warm-reekin', rich!"

"H'mph, it sounds ruddy nausyeating to me," said Mr. Montgomery. "Besides, leaving out the silly tuppenny poetry, you've
only 'arf answered the question I arsked yer in the first place—to
wit, wot the 'ell's a 'aggis?"

"Yes, yes, tell him!" urged Captain Ball, eagerly. "Explain him
the full modus operanda of how you prepare this—er—delicious
Highland titbit, Mr. Glencannon!"

Mr. Glencannon squinted a fishy eye at the gnats which swarmed
around the polished brass lamp above the table. "Weel, making
the haggis is rideeculously sumple," he declared. "Ye merely need
a certain amoont o' oatmeal, some onions, and a five-gallon bucket.
Er"—he turned to the second engineer—"what else wud ye say
was needed for a haggis, Muster MacQuayle?"

"Pepper," said Mr. MacQuale. "Ye must have plenty of pepper.

Losh, I can see my auld Aunty Meg in Killiecrankie making a haggis the noo!"

"Oatmeal, onions and pepper—is that orl there is to it?" sneered Mr. Montgomery.

"Weel, proctically," said Mr. Glencannon, placidly filling his pipe, "though in enumerating the ingredients, ye left oot the five-gallon bucket. But once ye've got those four succulent essentials ready at hond, yere haggis is as guid as made. All that remains to do, then, is slaughter an ox, cut his hoofs off, skin him, rip his insides oot and—"

"Not an ox—a sheep!" Mr. MacQuayle objected. "Ye commence by chopping his head off. My Aunty Meg in Killiecrankie always did the job with an auld claymore whuch belanged to my great-grandfather, Piper Jaimie McTooth, o' Stronachlachar. He went oot to India with the Argyll and Dumbartons in 1857 and won a bronze medal for getting shot in half at Lucknow. Aunty Meg cud fetch a sheep's head off with that auld claymore in one lick—squirp!—till the rheumatism cromped her style. After that, she'd sneak up on him through the heather and bosh him ower the head with a rock. While the sheep would be laying there groggy, she'd sit hersel' astroddle o' him with a cross-cut saw and—"

Mr. Glencannon frowned and raised a hand for silence. "Pairdon me, Muster MacQuale," he said, "ox! Ye hong up yere ox and ye let his bluid drain into the five-gallon bucket. His stoomach, his liver, his heart and all his heavier machinery ye put carefully to one side where the collies canna snotch them. His other, or auxiliary, mechanism is vurra useful to mak' glue oot of, so ye mustna throw any o' it awa'. Ah, losh, gentlemen"—Mr. Glencannon smacked his lips—"as ye can readily judge for yersels, the haggis is a vurritable feast for the gods!"

Mr. Montgomery shook his fists toward heaven. "But now, see 'ere!" he fumed. 'Never mind the collies and the glue—it's the 'aggis, the 'aggis I want to know about!"

"Haw, listen to him, captain!" chuckled Mr. Glencannon. "His eagerness betrays his oppetite, and I dinna blame him! Oh, he'll be here with us tomorrow with a fork in each hond, mark my wurrds!" He struck a match, applied it to his pipe and puffed thoughtfully before continuing. "Ye tak' the heart o' yere ox—"

"Sheep," said Mr. MacQuale.

"Ox! Great swith, Muster MacQuale, if—"

"Oh, my eye!" snapped Mr. Montgomery. "Get a'ead with it, can't yer?"

"Aye, glodly, if ye'll only stop interrupting! Ye tak' all the parts ye dinna plon to use for glue except the stoomach. Ye hash them up. Ye mix them with yere oatmeal, yere onions and yere pepper. Then ye throw the whole business into the five-gallon bucket, soshing it aroond with a broom hondle or a guid, stoot walking stick until it gives off a scupping sound, lik' when ye wade through the ooze in the bottom o' a dry dock. At this point, if ye care to, ye can add a sprig o' pursely and a few leaves o' rosemary, gently crushed betwixt the finger and the thumb, although discriminating haggis eaters o' the auld school maintain that this detrocts from the soobtile and deelicate flavor o' the whole."

"Ugh! Me, I'd add some disinfectant an 'eave the 'ole mess overboard!" declared Mr. Montgomery. "Yus, gorblyme, and I'd 'eave the bucket arfter it!"

Mr. Glencannon raised his eyebrows. "Muster Montgomery," he said, "pairmit me to obsairve that I think ye're vurra uncouth."

"Yes, shush, shush—softly, Mister Mate," Captain Ball admonished, pacifically. "So far, the haggis is raw, don't you see? . . . But—ker-hem—I mean to say, how do you cook it, Mr. Glencannon?"

"Ye cook it to a turn, sir," said the engineer. "For that, incidentally, ye must use a fire. But feerst ye pick up the ox's stoomach in yere left hond, grosping it firmly aroond the waistline, as in the auld-fashioned Viennese waltz. Then, with yere richt, ye stoof it full o' the stoof ye fish oot o' the five gallon bucket. . . . Do ye check wi' me, Muster MacQuale?"

"Dom, no, by no means!" blurted Mr. MacQuale. "Ye dinna stoof the stoofing into an ox's stoomach at all; ye stoof it into a sheep's liver! My auld Aunty Meg in Killiecrankie—"

"Foosh to yere auld Aunty Meg in Killiecrankie!" Mr. Glencannon banged on the table and stamped on Mr. Montgomery's foot. "Come, mon, come; dinna let us bicker and quibble ower details! Instead, let us combine our talents in making a haggis for the captain's Christmas party and a treat for Muster Montgomery whuch I doot he'll have the guid taste to appreciate!"

"Now, never you mind about my taste!" said Mr. Montgomery, tartly. "I don't think either of you two Scotch cannibals 'ave got the foggiest notion of 'ow to make yer 'orrid 'aggis, and I wouldn't eat it anyway. Besides that, where'll you get the ox, the sheep or wotever else you need to make it with? The only animals I've seen in Aden is camels, and I could 'ardly see them for the ticks."

"Ticks dinna matter, but camels willna sairve," said Mr. Mac-Quayle, sullenly. "To mak' a proper haggis, ye must have a shee—"

"Oh, blosh and fuddlesticks!" shouted Mr. Glencannon, springing to his feet. "I'm at the end o' my patience! . . . Captain Ball, sir!" He turned to the shipmaster. "Here and noo I give ye my soleinn promise to provide a Christmas dinner worthy o' our tenth anni ersurra under your commond, and in spicht o' heel, I'll do it!" With a farewell snort at Mr. Montgomery, he stalked from the room, went over the side to the dinghy and rowed away into the night.

When the sound of the oars had died away in the distance, "Welp!" the mate leered sardonically. "That settles that—wotever it was! Now I'll just nip back to my room, put on a fresh suit o' whites, 'ail a bumboat and go ashore myself. . . . Sure you wouldn't like to 'ave a proper 'otel meal with me tomorrer, Captain Ball and the rest o' yer? Er"—he squirmed—"I mean, I don't suppose it could cost you more than about five bob apiece."

For a moment there was silence; then Captain Ball spoke for the crowd in a voice that quavered more than a little. "Why, no," he said, "no, thank you! I fancy we'd all rather eat together, here on the ship, like we've done for the past nine years, and—and as I was hoping you would, too, Mr. Montgomery! Tradition, sentiment, superstition—see what I mean? Damned silly of me, what? But—uh—well, anyway, m'boy, I really do hope you'll enjoy your Christmas dinner."

II

As Mr. Montgomery had remarked, Aden and its environs are anything but pastoral; lowing herds, bleating flocks and all else bucolic and edible are there as scarce as in the more arid purlieus of Hades. Instead of heading for this sterile shore, Mr. Glencannon rowed down the inner harbor toward the oil-bunkering berths, where, near the terminal buoy of the pipe line, a great gray vessel lay pale in the moonlight. She was the refrigerator ship *Northern Princess,* on her regular run from Majunga, Madagascar, to Marseilles with frozen meat. The still air around her throbbed to the muffled, monotonous pulsation of pumps, some of them handling the fuel oil, others driving through her complex metal arteries the chemicals which proofed her cargo against even such withering heat as there was that night in Aden.

"Losh!" murmured Mr. Glencannon, resting on his oars and measuring her bulk. "She's carrying enough dead oxen to mak' a haggis the size o' the Rock o' Gibraltar! Noo, if only Wee Wully Anstruther is still her engineer—"

From somewhere aft came thuds, shouted oaths and peals of ribald laughter. A bottle whizzed through the moonlight and plunged into the water like a three-inch shell.

"Haw!" chuckled Mr. Glencannon, "'Wee Wully Anstruther's still in her, beyant the shadow o' a doot! I only hope he's not in one o' his tontrums, because I forgot to bring my bross knuckles."

He made fast the dinghy to the platform of the ladder, ascended to the deck and strode aft toward the sounds of disturbance. In the open doorway of the engineer's saloon he halted, amazed at the strange rite in progress within. Around the table at the center of the smoke-filled room stood a number of lumpy, ruddy-faced gentlemen, as well as a number of others slightly less lumpy and ruddy, but obviously equally tough. Mr. Glencannon identified the former as butchers and refrigeration engineers and the rest as the engine-room staff of the *Northern Princess.* All were shouting advice and encouragement to a diminutive four-striped officer who, blindfolded and with his hands bound behind him, was kneeling on the table apparently endeavoring to drown himself in a dish of consommé.

"He looks lik' Wee Wully," muttered Mr. Glencannon. "He is Wee Wully. But what in the world is he doing?"

Moving closer, he perceived that the diminutive one was lapping up the consommé with the thirst of the worn hart that panteth after the water brooks. At length, strangling but triumphant, he straightened up, a silver coin between his teeth.

"Four minutes, thirteen seconds!" announced somebody.

Amidst hoarse cheers, bonds and blindfold were stripped from the hero and he was assisted to the floor. Swaying slightly, he acknowledged the plaudits of the multitude and wrung out his sodden necktie.

"Anstruther!" exclaimed Mr. Glencannon. hurrying forward and shaking his hand. "How are ye, Wee Wulliam, how are ye?"

The little man blinked up at him uncertainly; then, "Colin Colcollin!" he proclaimed, raspingly. "Merry Chrishmash, Crolin, Mrerry Chrishmash! . . . Come, fill up the plate again, ladsh, and let my auld friend Grencrarron have a gro at it!"

"Oh, thonk ye, Wully; ye're really too kind!" Mr. Glencannon demurred. "I'd dearly love to tak' part in yere innocent little game, espeecially as I obsairve that the prize is a half crown. But to tell ye the honest truth, Wully, I simply canna drink clear soup."

"Who osked ye to drink clear soup?" demanded Mr. Anstruther, truculently. "Who osked ye to drink thick soup? Who osked ye to drink green-turtle soup, pink-turtle soup, purtle-turtle soup or mocking-turtle soup? Thash no' soup in yon plate, ye gowk; it's whushky!"

"Eh?" Mr. Glencannon vaulted to the table, knelt before the dish and sniffed a magical aroma. "Why, it's Duggan's Dew o' Kirkintilloch!" he cried. "Come, blindfold me, gentlemen! Tie my honds! . . . There, noo! Ready, timekeeper? Go!"

He found the pastime distinctly to his taste, especially as his walrus mustache, acting like a sponge, augmented his natural prowess. So rapidly did he lower the level of the plate's contents that Mr. Anstruther, fearing for his own record, approached on tiptoe and restored it from a fresh bottle. Sensing despite his blindfold that he was the victim of sharp practice, Mr. Glencannon redoubled his efforts, emptied the plate and retrieved the half crown in the phenomenal time of four minutes flat.

The plaudits which acclaimed his exploit were perfunctory, and in them he sensed a vaguely hostile note. Moreover, his teeth were so firmly embedded in the half crown that he suspected it was lead.

"Dom!" rasped Mr. Anstruther, making a wry face. "Why, ye've qualified for the finals with yere vurra feerst try! But then, Glencannon, ye auld snake, ye always were a dangerous mon at parlor games and parties!"

"True," admitted Mr. Grencannon, disengaging the coin from his lower incisors and tossing it through the porthole. "As a matter o' fact," he raised his voice to make himself heard above the considerable din—"as a matter o' fact, Wully, it's precisely because o' a party that I've come aboord to consult ye. Ye see, I've promised to mak' a Christmas haggis."

"A haggis?" repeated Mr. Anstruther. "Ye mean a guid, auld, steaming, peppery, juicy, Heeland haggis? Weel, weel, weel, let's drink a drink to it! The only trooble is, where are ye going to get the billy goat's blodder?"

"A-weel," said Mr. Glencannon, "if I hoppened to want a billy goat's blodder, one o' the feerst places I'd look for it wud be in the neighborhood o' a billy goat. But why shud I want it?"

"Because, dom it, ye canna mix it, stoof it, cook it, have it or eat it withoot it!" asserted Mr. Anstruther. "I can't, eh? Who says I can't?" He arose, bit a crescent-shaped fragment out of the visor of his cap and sat down again. "Yes, yes, precisely! I've followed ye to a *T*, so noo ye can follow me to a whusky."

"Glodly!" said Mr. Glencannon. "However, Wully, I fear we dinna quite understond each other. I cudna use a billy goat's blodder, because I dinna want to mak' a futball, a bagpipe or a hot-water bottle. What I told ye I wanted to mak' was a haggis."

"A haggis?" Mr. Anstruther repeated again. "Ye mean a guid, auld, steaming, peppery, juicy, Heeland haggis? Weel, weel, weel, let's drink a drink to it! The only trooble is—er—er— Trooble? Ho! If it's trooble ye're looking for, ye ugly brute, ye've only to—"

"Noo, wait, Wee Wulliam!" Mr. Glencannon restrained him. "You and I are auld friends and ye're *Bura Misteri Sahib* o' the *Northern Princess*, the whuch is a vurritable Noah's Ark full o' frozen cattle. Weel, I was thinking that if ye cud see yere way clear to lending me the loan o' a nice, tender dead ox oot o' yere cargo, I—"

Mr. Anstruther yawned, removed his trousers, pulled them over his head as though they were a nightshirt, thrust his arms through the legs and buttoned the fly snugly around his neck. Then he stared down at his bare, gnarled knees. "Why, look!" he bawled. "Look! There's somebody aroond here, there's some skulking thief aroond here, that has stole the vurra troosies off my breech!" He lurched forward and leveled an accusing finger at Mr. Glen-cannon. "There he is, lads!" he shouted. "Let's heave the scoondrel owerboord!"

With a menacing growl they made for him. Mr. Glencannon snatched up a full whisky bottle from the sideboard and, wielding it clubwise, fought his way to the door. He fled along the deck toward the ladder, the pack at his heels, but so hotly were they pressing him when he reached it that he dared not attempt to descend to his dinghy. Through alleyways, up and down companions, round and about the ship they sped, the decks drumming to their footfalls and the night made hideous with the sounds of hue and cry.

Turning a corner and momentarily out of sight of his pursuers, Mr. Glencannon slid halfway down a steep iron ladder and fell the remainder of the distance. Thanks to his presence of mind in clutching the bottle to his breast, there were only personal casualties. He found himself in a narrow, dimly lit passage at one end of which was a door marked KEEP OUT; THIS MEANS YOU! "Aye, but it doesna mean me!" he gasped, turning the knob. It was not, as he had surmised, a collision door, for despite its considerable thickness it was surprisingly light in weight. He stepped over the high sill, slammed the portal after him, and was in Stygian darkness. Instantly, miraculously, the sounds of pursuit were stilled; in fact, as he stood there straining his eyes and ears, he felt that the blackness was palpable, that it was packed in around him under pressure and that it shut him off from all the world. Here, at last, was sanctuary!

He lit his pocket flash. Its beam licked an ebonite panel upon which were various switches and instruments and a brass plate, engraved HANDLING CHAMBER, NO. 3 HOLD. " 'Let there be licht!' " he quoted, closing several switches at once. Suddenly dazzled, he saw that he was in a spacious, white-enameled room. There were banks of pipes on the bulkheads, and from the deckhead above, chain hoists hung on curving steel tracks. The tracks ran from doors in the port and starboard sides of the vessel, converging amidships at the entrance to the hold.

"H'm, weel, it's all vurra tronquil and commendably saniturra," he remarked. "I'll mak' mysel' comfortable till yon murderers get tired o' sairching for me, and then I'll sneak oot. Whoosheroo, it's a job to mak' a haggis!" He sat with his back against the pipes and broached his bottle. The silence was broken by a liquid, gurgling sound. This was natural enough in the circumstances, but when he had recorked the bottle, the gurgling continued.

"Strange!" he mused. "Uncanny! Weel, they're peculiar craft, these great floating ice chests! Noo, evidently this so-called Hondling Chamber is insulated, so that frozen meat can be unloaded through it withoot opening the hatches and raising the temperature in the hold proper. They sumply open yon door amidships, hook their oxen on the chain hoists and drog them ower to the door on whichever side they hoppen to be discharging from. I wonder—noo, I wonder—if a mon cud steal an ox oot o' here singlehonded? O' coorse, if Wee Wully Anstruther and his butchers and his bondits shud catch him at it—brhh!"

The very thought made his blood run cold, so he fortified himself with a few thermal units from the bottle. Feeling no reaction, he consumed a few more. As he did so, the neck of the bottle rattled dismally against his teeth, and vice versa. "Why, guid losh, mon, yere hond is treembling lik' a leaf! Ye're—ye're treembling all ower! Can it be ye're in for a bout o' fever?" He felt a dull ache across his shoulder blades and another farther down. "Spinal meningitus!" he gasped, endeavoring to rise. "But, heavens! I canna stond up! Paralysis! Help!" he bawled. "Anstruther! Somebody! Help!"

He realized with a surge of horror that no voice, no human sound, could penetrate those insulated walls.

"Aloss!" he moaned. "They'll unload my puir cadaver at Marseels with the rest o' the meat! Christmas Eve—ah, what a nicht to die!"

Resignedly, he bowed his head and buried his face in his hands. Soon he was conscious of a painful constriction in his armpits and across the chest. His first diagnosis was pleurisy; then he discovered that he was leaning forward into the slack of his jacket like a papoose in a blanket, and that the back and shoulders, crusted with hoarfrost, were firmly frozen to the pipes.

"Ah, come!" he growled, his breath turning to steam in the icy air. "What silly horseplay is this?" He undid the buttons and squirmed out of the garment, which hung rigid as a knightly panoply on the wall. "Ho, I see it all, noo! Anstruther has turned on the freezing system—that explains the gurgling! He intends to freeze me to death alive!" With difficulty he unstuck his jacket from the brine pipes, stamped upon it until it regained some measure of flexibility, and donned it. Skidding across the frosty floor, he made for the instrument panel. A dial, marked FAHRENHEIT TEMPERATURE, HANDLING CHAMBER, registered 26 degrees. Even as he scanned it, the needle dropped to 24, then to 22, and so continued downward. "Och, horrors!" croaked Mr. Glencannon, holding his bottle to the light, gauging its contents and taking a mammoth sowp of them. "If I'm no rescued soon, I'll have to put mysel' on half rations! Where are the Soviet ice-breakers? Where are the Yonkee planes? Where are the Alaskan dog teams, the Canadian Quintriplets and the doughty Odmiral Byrd? Am I to be abondoned here to freeze?"

Very cautiously he unlatched the door by which he had entered and pressed his ear to the crack. "Noo, two o' ye wait richt here," he heard Mr. Anstruther's rasping voice. "If he comes down this way, clout him ower the head and—"

Mr. Glencannon let the latch click back into place. He crossed to the door of the hold and swung it open. From the shadowy spaces beyond came a gust like the polar breath of Antarctica.

"Ah, foosh!" he cringed, fumblingly uncorking the bottle. "Grim death confronts me where'er I turn! I'd better drink up this whusky before it freezes solid, for my teeth are chottering so I cudna hope to chew it!"

He was about to close the door when he discerned within the hold a level expanse of beef carcasses so vast that its limits were lost in the gloom. It was the top layer of the cargo; the legs of the beasts, hewn off to stumps in precise conformity to market specifications, jutted up in ranks as orderly and rigid as the Grenadier Guards on parade. Here, dead, frozen and far from their lush native pastures, was a whole Malagasy herd! Here was meat to feed a multitude! Here, to a quester after haggis, was El Dorado!

For a moment, Mr. Glencannon stood gnawing at the frozen fringe of his mustache and expelling the brittle fragments. Then he dragged the fall of one of the chain hoists into the hold, fixed the hook in the nearest carcass and hoisted it clear. Pulling, hauling and butting it with his shoulders, he slid it along the overhead conveyor rail to the starboard side. He swung open the insulating panel which covered the loading door in the hull and unscrewed the dozen iron dogs which secured the clamps.

"Noo, then!" he panted. "All I've got to do is open it, let my ox doon into the water and climb doon the chain mysel'. It'll be a short swim forward to the dinghy; I'll row it back, tak' my ox in tow and return in triumph to the *Inchcliffe Castle*. But I'd best turn oot the lichts, lest Anstruther and his thugs shud spot me."

One by one he flipped the switches; the lights went out and simultaneously the liquid gurgling ceased. "Shish-shish!" he simpered, blushing in the darkness. "Weel, wud ye believe it? It must have been I, mysel', that turned on all the winter weather in the feerst place!"

Slowly, soundlessly, he swung back the hull door and stood gratefully in the flood of tropic air which wafted through the opening. But though the heat was as a benison to his body, it had a strange effect upon his brain.

"Whoa!" He swayed dizzily. "Hold hard, Glencannon, hold hard! Ye've had only a little ower a bottle and a half o' whusky, but anybody'd think ye'd had a drap too much!"

Not without difficulty he slung the carcass clear of the side and lowered it until the slack in the chain indicated that it was afloat. It lay on its back with its stump legs in the air. He clambered down the chain and, still grasping it, stood on the buoyant beef while he took stock of the situation. He could see his dinghy bobbing at the ladder foot with Wee Willy Anstruther drowsing in the stern of it. Due to the manner in which he was wearing his trousers, Mr. Anstruther had a sinister, hunchbacked look about him. Even more sinister, however, was the twelve-inch Stillson wrench which lay ready to his hand on the thwart.

"Ho, dearie me!" groaned Mr. Glencannon. "What's to be done the noo?" He moved a trifle aft along the beef and sat down to lower its metacenter and increase its stability. This brought its neck out of water like a clipper's bow, but caused the after portion to float almost awash. To avoid wetting his feet, Mr. Glencannon stepped down into the vent in the belly as though it were a cockpit and seated himself in the stern sheets. "Haw, vurra snoog," he murmured, conning the little craft with an appreciative eye. "Vurra tidy and vurra shipshape. If only it had a bit more sheer and another strake o' freeboard, it wud be the most seaworthy ox in all the Gulf o' Aden. What more cud an auld sailor osk?" He squinted across the harbor and distinguished the lights of the *Inchcliffe Castle.* "Foosh to the dinghy, they'll bring it back when they've sobered up. I'll novigate hame in my ain' haggis!" He unhooked the chain hoist and, paddling with his hands, made off into the night.

"Ah, but it's grond to be at sea again." He sniffed the breezes gratefully. "Although come to think o' it, I havena been ashore since we left Mombasa." He raised his voice in a rollicking bluewater chantey. He was putting his whole soul into the chorus of "yo heave ho's!" when he realized that his lingual mechanism was actually giving off the words and music of a sentimental ballad that he recalled as Sweet Mary of Argyll.

Weel, weel, let it have its ain way; he thought, tolerantly. *After all, Sweet Mary is a beautiful auld song. Listen.* But he listened vainly, for now, despite himself, he was reciting Burns' "Address to a Haggis."

"Ah, swith!" he growled, when the poem ended. " 'Tis all vurra oggrovating! I suspect there must have been a certain amoont o' alcohol in Wee Wully's whusky!"

Whether or not the suspicion was justified, he found it increasingly difficult to hold to his course or even to remember where the course lay. From time to time he paused in his splashing to take a star sight, but the stars were swooping and dipping in the celestial vault, playing tag with the lights on shore and generally behaving in a scandalous manner.

"Peerplexing!" he said, lifting his hands out of the water and raising them smartly on high in the Toss Oars position prescribed in the Royal Navy. "I almost wish I had Montgomery aboord to novigate this craft for me. But, no, on second thocht, no! Though

I'm forced to associate with him on the *Inchcliffe Castle,* domned if I'd tolerate him on my ain private yacht! But where, oh, where is the *Inchcliffe Castle?"* He strained his eyes into the night and descried Djebel Ishan and its brood of lesser peaks looming black against the sky. His view of them was somewhat obstructed by a row of tree trunks rising out of the water in the near foreground. "Tut, tut!" he objected. "There's no forest in the middle o' Aden harbor, and therefore I doot if I see one. There's some sort of a swundle, here, or pairhops it's a mirage. But"—he reached out and touched the nearest trunk—"but no; it's solid!"

There was a soft swish, a gleam of phosphorescence on the starboard beam. Something struck his frail craft amidships, causing it to tremble from brisket to rump. The sea gushed onto his lap through a gaping puncture just below the water line.

"Torpedoed!" he cried. "We're holed in the tenderloin! All honds abandon ship!"

He scrambled to his feet. The beef rolled gunwales-under. To prevent it capsizing, Mr. Glencannon threw his arms around the tree trunk. There was a second shock, a ripping, rending sound and lo, the carcass was dragged from under him by an eight-foot shark! Clinging to the tree with everything but his eyelashes, he saw the great fish tearing at the meat, saw it joined by another and another, and watched in horror as they churned the water to foam a scant yard beneath his wincing coattails.

"Quick!" he urged himself. "Get higher, mon, get higher! Pull yersel' up onto a limb!"

He groped overhead and grasped a heavy, square-hewn timber. He realized, then, that he was not on a tree at all, but on one of the supporting piles of a wharf. He hoisted himself to the moon-bathed planking and sank down in a state of collapse.

"Whurra!" he panted. " 'Tis a sorra, thonkless tosk to mak' a haggis! Why, noo that I come to think o' it, e'en yon ox had all o' his machinery removed and so was useless anyway! If it wasna for my promise to guid auld Captain Ball and my loathing for that snipe o' a Montgomery, I'd say foosh to the whole domned party! But noo, let's see, let's see!"

III

Messrs. Raoul and Cyril Shapiro (Shapiro Brothers, Ltd., Shipping Suppliers to H.M. Navy, Contractors to Leading Mail, Passenger and Freight S.S. Lines, General Chandlers, Furnishers and Direct Importers of Fresh Provisions. Shapiros' Prices Please and Shapiros' Service Satisfies) were just about to close up the office in their premises on the Aden Crescent when they were visited by Mr. Montgomery.

"Good evening, gempmen," said the mate. "I'm orff the *Inchcliffe Castle*, that C. & C. ship that's laying out there by the Fairway buoy. You'll remember us, of course; our steward got drunk and bought a 'undredweight of curry powder off yer on the voyage out. That's why I've just stopped in to arsk yer if yer could direct me to a 'arfway decent 'otel in this 'ere town where a chap could eat 'is Christmas dinner tomorrer without choking on it."

"Well," said Mr. Raoul Shapiro, "if I may express myself candidly, sir—although, for obvious reasons, I must beg of you not to quote me—the hotels of Aden are uniformly of a distinctly inferior order."

"They are, indeed, lousy," agreed Mr. Cyril Shapiro. "But, why, sir, if I may venture to ask, are you thinking of eating your Christmas repast in Aden when such a magnificent meal will be served aboard your own ship?"

"Eh?" said Mr. Montgomery. "Magnificent meal? On the ruddy *Inchcliffe Castle*? 'Ere, now, don't make me weep!"

"Yes, yes, on the *Inchcliffe Castle*," affirmed the other, referring to a ledger on the table. "The gentleman, our valued client, said he was giving a party for his colleagues and insisted on everything being of the very best. Er—two tinned Gold Seal Royal Banquet Roasting Turkeys, three tinned The Chef of Windsor Castle's Own Recipe Plum Puddings, five tins of Extra Selected Imported French Asparagus, four boxes of The London Jockey Club's Private Brand Havana Cigars, three cases of—er—yes, pepper, four cases of Duggan's Dew of Kirkintilloch Whisky—"

"Duggan's Dew? Four cases? Lawks!" gasped Mr. Montgomery. "Why, it must 'ave been the chief hengineer! And you say he bought all that stuff for—for the party 'e's giving tomorrer? Think of it! Well, I always did say 'e was a decent sort, bless 'is dear old soul!"

"Yes, quite," said Mr. Shapiro. "He came in here a trifle—er—under the weather, if I may say so, sir. Gave us to understand that he was looking for an ox's—er—stomach. But when he saw the vast assortment of fancy high-grade delicacies on our shelves, he favored us with his most valued order."

"Tùrkey! Sparrowgrass! Plum pudding!" Mr. Montgomery was rolling his eyes. "Of course I know 'e can afford it, but orl the same, I must say it's right down jolly noble of 'im! Wot a meal! Wot a Christmas! And—yus, wot a pal!"

When he had gone, "Phooey!" said Mr. Raoul Shapiro. "Am I glad to hear what he said about that Scotchman being able to afford it? After all, you know, he only signed a personal chit for it, so I was worrying maybe we was stuck. What was his name again?"

Mr. Cyril Shapiro consulted the sprawling signature in the chit book. "Chauncey Montgomery," he read.

MONKEY BUSINESS AT GIBRALTAR

A STREAKY PALL of smoke hung low over the bay. Most of it was
coming from the funnels of the anchored convoy that filled the
roadstead from the inner moles to well beyond Europa Point,
while the rest—it formed the lighter streaks—had drifted across
the strait from brush fires burning on the African mountainsides.
Rising above it against the dazzling noonday blue, the Rock of
Gibraltar loomed like a gigantic lion basking in the sun.

Mr. Glencannon stood straddled in the cockpit of a shore-
bound water taxi, balancing himself against the slap and surge
and gazing up at the great limestone bulk as it dwarfed the
arsenals, the dockyards, and the clustering town. In the course of
a long and distinguished career as an engineer of ocean tramps,
he had beheld Gibraltar times without number, and always with
profound emotion. Others might call it the hub of the world, a
symbol of modern might, and, in particularly obnoxious cases,
even liken it to a gigantic lion basking in the sun; but Mr.
Glencannon had never subscribed to any such grandiloquent
tosh. To him, Gibraltar's significance was personal, practical,
real. "Hail! Hail to thee, prood rock. Lang may ye wave!" he
addressed it with simple reverence. "Within thy noble shadow,
whusky sells for six bob less per bottle than anywhere else in the
British Empire!"

At the North Mole landing stage, the native boatman was
reluctant to accept a Japanese five-yen note in payment of the
fare; this led to a brief exchange of views, at the conclusion of
which Mr. Glencannon removed his brass knuckles and strolled
leisurely up through the public market place. Placards in the
windows of the several pubs fronting upon the square announced
that by order of the Provost Marshal, the establishments would
remain closed until Evening Gunfire at 17:00, but to a sophisti-

cated traveller with a sensitive nose, this intelligence was of interest only in exemplifying man's inhumanity to man. Turning into a dank alley somewhere beyond the Casemate Barracks, he halted at a doorway which bore carved upon its lintel the two-thumbed hand of Mohammed's daughter Fatma, reminder of the long ago day when British Gibraltar was Moorish Djebel-Tarik.

"Noo, here," he said, "if my memory sairves, is a vurra snug little shebeen in whuch to improve a shining hour." He rapped upon the nail-studded door in a special manner. After due interval it was opened by an old lady with one tooth and three warts, who greeted him effusively in Spanish.

"Cheerio, senior, and a vurra bonus tart to usted!" he responded, dropping effortlessly into the pure Castilian. *"I have como to get uno drinko o' whusky, or pairhops duo, three-o or four-o. —Right-o?"*

"Si y bien lo sabe usted," she assured him, flashing her tooth in a coquettish smile. He bowed his way past her into a narrow, pitch black passage and waited until she had opened a door at the far end of it. Framed in the oblong of light, he saw a little two-wheeled cart, painted in camouflage and marked with the stencilled broad arrow which identifies His Majesty's ordnance property. Instead of the machine-gun ammunition which it had been designed to carry, the cart was loaded with bananas, cumquats, turnips, and other vegetables.

"Ah, foosho!" cried Mr. Glencannon in dismay. *"Have usted turned this place into a dom green grocerio, senior? I didna como acqui to swillo el tomato juice! I . . ."*

He was interrupted by a low, rumbling mutter which came through the doorway from somewhere beyond the vegetable cart —a sound like that of an impending earthquake or of summer thunder on the heights of Gibraltar. It was a human voice—but what a voice! "Ah, whurra—there's something rodically wrong!" it was saying petulantly. "Noo, two-and-six for cumquats plus five-and-eight for banonas mak's eight-and-two, plus five-and-four for turnips mak's theerteen-and-six, plus six-and-a-penny for carrots mak's nineteen-and-seeven—weel, call it an even poond and buy another drink—plus, er no, no, wait! Ah, great swith—I've left oot the six-and-four for the cobbages! Tsk, tsk, tsk! Weel, I bocht the cobbages before I bocht the turnips, and I bocht the turnips before I bocht the carrots, so noo I'll have to go clear back to the cumquats and figure it oot all ower again! *Dom!*"

Something dark shot out from behind the edge of the door and struck the cart with a resounding crash. For an instant Mr. Glencannon mistook the object for a valise, then recognized it as a hobnailed infantry boot of mammoth proportions. The ankle above it wore a khaki gaiter like the cover of a ham, while the leg—a veritable Pillar of Hercules—was sheathed in a green woolen stocking topped with the red-and-heather tartan of the Argyll and Dumbarton Highlanders. Mr. Glencannon knew that there could be but two such legs in Gibraltar, if not in the entire world. "Why, Cousin Dooglas!" he cried, hurrying into the room. "Foncy meeting you!"

"Cousin Colin!" boomed the giant, rising to greet him but having a good six inches to go when his head thumped the ceiling. "Weel, weel, weel! Weel, weel, weel! Weel, weel, w . . ."

"Yes, I know," said Mr. Glencannon. "But—guid heavens, Cousin Dooglas, yere lips are all blue! Have ye got the dengoo fever, lad?"

"M'm?" The Highlander wiped his mouth with his hand, considered the indigo smear on the palm and then wiped the palm on the seat of his kilt. "No," he growled, his sweat-beaded brow clouding. "No. 'Tis only the undullable pencil whuch I've been wurrking oot some vurra cumplex prublems in mothemometry with." He gestured helplessly toward a chewed pencil stump and a litter of printed government forms on the table. "Cousin Colin, ye've come at an opportune moment! Pray sit ye doon, dear lad, and figure oot this bluidy mess for me, won't we?"

"All in guid time, all in guid time! Dinna be so impatient!" said Mr. Glencannon, settling into a chair. *"Ho, senior!"* he addressed the proprietress. *"Duo o' Duggan's Dewo! Si, and while usted are about it, ye micht as weel fetcho el bottle and leave it acqui.* And noo, Cousin Dooglas ye can go ahead and tell me the news. Why, may I osk, have they sent ye back here from the front in Italy?"

"Um, oh—weel, ye see, every time I started digging mysel' a fox hole, I'd strike bed rock before it was deep enough to fit me. At feerst they thocht they'd sumply retire me for auld age, but when they realized what a scondal it wud be to lose the benefit o' my twunty-eight years' experience in the sairvice, they put me in commond back here."

"In commond? Why Cousin Dooglas! Ye're only a sergeant!"

"What's so only aboot it?" demanded the giant, tartly. "Haven't ye heard that What's-his-name, er, that nosty little Hun —oh, you know the twirp I mean!—anyway, he was only a corporal, wasn't he?"

"Aye, Dooglas, but dinna be evasive. What I meant was, what are ye in commond of?"

"A-weel . . ." Cousin Dooglas reddened with embarrassment and beneath the table his feet shuffled with a sound like cases of machinery being dragged across a wharf. "Er . . ." He gulped his drink as though to bolster his courage for a confession. "I'm in commond o' the apes, that's who I'm in commond of!" he blurted, glowering defiantly.

"The, er, Apes?" Mr. Glencannon raised his eyebrows. "D'ye mean lik' the Wrens—an auxiliary corps o' lady Highlanders, or summat such?"

"No, I mean apes," said Cousin Douglas, still scowling. "Barbary apes. —The kind that are pink and purple in the south. Surely, ye must have heard o' the wurrld-famous apes o' Gibraltar, Colin!"

Mr. Glencannon groomed his walrus mustache with his lower lip. "Aye, noo that ye speak o' it, I foncy I have. Noturally, I always dismussed it as a mere auld wives' tale, cooked up to swundle the tourists in peace time. D'ye mean to say it's really true?"

"O' course it's true!" cried Cousin Douglas, beginning to regain his confidence. "Why, the apes o' Gibraltar are among the most cherished traditions o' the Empire! There's even an auld provairb whuch says, quoot, 'When the apes leave the Rock, the British will go with them.' "

Mr. Glencannon sniffed skeptically. "Go where?" he asked.

"What for?"

"How shud I know?" said Cousin Douglas. "Dom it all, Cousin Colin, I didna invent the provairb! I'm only telling ye what Auld Stickychin told me, and he ocht to know!"

"Auld Stickychin? Weel, it's a fitting name for an ape who'd go aroond drooling silly provairbs to the ignorant soldiery!"

Cousin Douglas pushed back his Glengarry and dashed the sweat of exasperation from his brow. "But Auld Stickychin isn't an ape! He's Major the Richt Reeverend Stickley Chenwith, Senior Choplain o' the Fortress o' Gibraltar! The War Office sent him doon here to write a book aboot the history and traditions o' the Rock."

"H'mph! Worse and worse!" scoffed Mr. Glencannon. "Things have come to a pretty pass for us tox payers when the Army sends a Major Choplain to Gibraltar to scribble books aboot ossinine traditions, and a seeven-foot Sergeant to be chambermaid to a pack o' apes!"

"But—but dom it, Cousin Colin—these apes here on Gib are the only apes on the entire continent o' Europe! They're uniquee! Some think the Moors brocht them from Africa and some think they came ower through a tunnel under the Strait— in any case, they've been here since time immoral. The great prublem noo, the thing whuch worrits the government so much, is that they dinna fructify. Consequently, they're getting fewer and fewer and are in danger o' becoming extink."

"Indeed?" Mr. Glencannon stifled a yawn with his glass. "Exockly how fewer and fewer o' them are there, Dooglas?"

The Highlander produced a notebook from his sporran and frowned at it importantly. "A-hem! As o' yesterday, they mustered a strength o' exockly theerty-seeven—er, no, wait! —Um, . . ." He counted on his fingers. "Theerty-four and one mak' theerty-five and one more mak's theerty-six, doesn't it? —Aye, and that reminds me, Cousin Colin—won't ye please help me figure oot these dom ration forms? I've sumply got to get yon vegetables up to the Rock!"

Mr. Glencannon sighed, drew one of the documents to him and scanned it listlessly. It was headed:

SUPPLEMENTARY RATION RETURN
(FORM NO. 902 AMENDED TO FORM NO. 902-A)
To be used in connection with purchases (cash) of comestibles
(leguminous, green, but not including fruits, citrus) as authorized
under Par. 41, S.O. 461, H.Q.H.M.C., for troops (dismounted), in
garrisons other than in (a) Mauritius (b) the Indian Northwest
Frontier Command and (c) the Andaman Islands. To be executed
in quadruplicate and filed under R (2) 42-184.

Below, a smeared and almost illegible scrawl, were Cousin
Douglas's calculations.

Mr. Glencannon ran his eye down the column of figures, then
turned and scanned the contents of the vegetable cart apprais-
ingly. "Why, Dooglas," he said, his interest visibly aroused, "am
I to understond that they give ye cauld, hard cash in hond to buy
all yon ape fodder with?"

"Aye, and that's only the feerst o' my respunsibilities! After
I've bocht the stuff in the market, I have to drog it two miles
through the broiling heat to Number Six Ammunition Hoist,
where the artillera lads give me a lift up to the South-East Bas-
tion. From there I have to scromble alang the sheer face o' the
Rock to way beyant O'Hara's Tower, where the apes hong oot.
Then, I . . ."

"How much cash do they give ye?"

"One poond cash per ape per month. Ye see . . ."

"Foosh! Ye're dom richt I see!" Mr. Glencannon's fist crashed
down upon the table. "—I see sitting before me the stuppidest
gowk that ere disgraced the blessed name o' Glencannon! Ye've
been contenting yersel' with robbing the apes o' a few pitiful
pennies while letting the vurritable wealth o' Crocus slip
through yere clumsy fingers! Shame, shame upon ye, ye hulking
lump!"

"Um?" Cousin Douglas shrank back against the wall and considered his fingers blankly. His lower lip trembled. Two tears,
each a brimming teaspoonful, rolled down his beefy cheeks and
spattered, plop! plop!, upon the floor. "Ah, please!" he begged.
"Dinna scold me, dinna be cross with me! —Please, please,
Cousin Colin!"

"Vurra weel!" said Mr. Glencannon, sternly. "Drink some

more whusky and brace up, and try to answer my questions."

"Whuch questions?" asked Cousin Douglas, drying his tears on his kilt and reaching for the bottle.

Mr. Glencannon sat back frowning and blowing smoke toward the ceiling. "Weel, in the feerst place, ye're drawing doon theerty-six quid each month for feeding theerty-six apes. If there were more apes, ye'd draw more money. Is that richt?"

"Aye, but . . ."

"Wait! I want ye to think vurra hard and tell me exockly what these theerty-six apes look lik."

Cousin Douglas thought. "They look almost exockly lik' theerty-six apes," he said. "One end o' them ye already know aboot and the rest is hairy and even uglier."

"How big are they?"

"They're roughly aboot as big as a dog."

"Roughly aboot as big as a dog aboot how big do ye mean?"

"Aboot as big as a dog aboot up to yere knee."

"Ah, precisely! And noo," Mr. Glencannon leaned across the table impressively and shook his pipe stem in his cousin's face, "and noo, aboot how big wud ye say the baby ones are?"

"I cudna say because I've never seen one," said Cousin Douglas, blinking a gob of pipe gravy from his eye. "I dinna ken anybody who has. There's none been born for years and years."

"Copital! Copitol! But noo, just supposing ye shud see one when ye go up there this afternoon, what wud ye do aboot it?"

"Oh, my orders in such an event are vurra clear. Feerst I'd have to lug the wee bairn doon from the Rock and get it examined by Veterinary Sergeant Joe Pyle. If Joe was sober enough, whuch he sometimes is, he and I wud tak' it ower and show it to Auld Stickychin. Auld Stickychin wud register its birth in his history o' Gibraltar and have it entered on the ration roll so's I cud draw one quid cash per month for it."

"Ha! And if ye brocht doon another wee ape a week from noo and still another one ten days after that, and so on at reasonable intervals—ye'd draw a quid more per month for each and evey one o' them?"

"Aye, the more the merrier! As I told ye before, the government is worriting aboot them becoming extink, so . . ."

"So noo its worrits are ower! Haw!" His face wreathed in smiles, Mr. Glencannon reached up and slapped his cousin resoundingly upon the shoulder. He filled the glasses to the brim, raised them politely, and drained them one after the other. "Dooglas, you and I are aboot to render a great and patriotic sairvice to the Empire! I want ye to listen vurra, vurra closely to the plon I'm aboot to unfold . . ."

*   *   *   *

Shortly after five o'clock that afternoon, Mr. Glencannon again entered the nail-studded portal beneath the two-thumbed hand of Fatma and waited in the passage until the single-toothed lady with the three warts had opened the door at the far end of it. This time there was revealed no vegetable cart, no infantry boot the size of a valise, but a pair of thin and very bowed legs encased in cavalry breeches and puttees. "Cousin Dooglas!" he cried, hurrying into the room as before. "I'm sorra I'm late but, er—Oh, I beg yere pairdon, sir!"

"It's quite orl right, quite orl right!" said the owner of the legs, a horsey looking gentleman of a certain age whose uniform identified him as a Veterinary Sergeant of the 117th Lancers. "If it's Duggie Glencannon yer looking for, 'h should be 'ere any minute, sir. —'Appens I've got a dyte with 'im meself. 'Ere, 'ave a chair, wontcher?"

"Why yes, thonks, I will," said Mr. Glencannon, with a diffident but charming bow. "I am Muster Colin Glencannon, Esquire, Sergeant Dooglas Glencannon's cousin; I'm chief engineer o' the *Inchcliffe Castle,* one o' the mognificent ships oot there in yonder convoy. While we're waiting for Dooglas, I wonder wud ye care to join me in a modest sowp o' whusky, sir?"

"Coo, not 'arf I wouldn't!" said the other, with enthusiasm. "This 'ere bleedy beer mykes me belly slosh abaht like a ruddy foundered 'orse's! —There, just listen to it! I'm Veterinary Sergeant Joseph Pyle, Mr. Glencannon—Honest Doc Pyle I was, in civil life, and I wish to 'ell I was back there now! If yer 'appened to be down at the Grand National per'aps yer'll remember my nyme in connection with the big 'orse-doping scandal of that year."

"Aye, why o' course, o' course!" cried Mr. Glencannon, who had passed the whole of 1921 in the South China coastal trade. "Weel, weel, weel, it's a small wurrld, isn't it? What are ye doing here at Gibraltar, Sergeant Pyle?"

"H'mph! Cooling me ruddy 'eels and going to seed, that's wot I'm doing! I ain't 'ad me 'ands on a decent case o' glanders, spavin, epizootic, or blind staggers since they mechanized the cavalry and tinned orl the 'orses fer bullybeef. The only veterinary practice I get nowadays is on the bleddy apes."

"The, er, apes?" Mr. Glencannon raised his eyebrows. "D'ye mean lik' the Wrens—an auxiliary corps o' lady horse doctors, or summat such?"

"No, I mean apes—Barbary apes," said Sergeant Pyle, sourly, "—the narsty, 'airy beggars that the gov'ment 'as got mucking aralind 'ere on Gibraltar Rock, though gorbly-me if I knows wot for. Yer Cousin Duggie can tell yer orl abaht 'em, if yer intristid which I most definitely ain't. —As a matter of fack, Duggie telephoned down from O'Hara's Tower a while ago that a new ape's just been born, and that's wot I'm wyting 'ere to see 'im abaht."

"Congrotulations to one and all o' us!" said Mr. Glencannon, filling the glasses again. "I haven't seen Dooglas since the feerst year o' the war, but I sent a message ashore to him this morning on the odd chance he cud meet me here. How is the dear lad, Sergeant Pyle?"

"Welp, Duggie ain't no brighter than usual and even a bleddy sight less, to be perfickly candied with yer, Mr. Glencannon. If yer should 'appen to arsk my opinion as a medical man, I'd say 'e'd outgrown 'is brains in boy'ood and they've never caught up with 'im since."

Mr. Glencannon pursed his lips and nodded sagely. "A vurra shrewd and peenetrating diagnosis, sir," he said. "But also, if ye'll pairdon a layman's opinion, we shudna owerlook the matter o' his spituitary glonds. Fronkly, my puir cousin Dooglas has always been a pronoonced hyberbolic. At the age o' nine, when he was only a wee lout less than six feet high, his glonds were already the size o' rump steaks. His late lamented father, Hamish Glencannon, a munstrosity who was affectionately known throughoot the region as the Dumb Ox o' Ecclefechan, endeavored to discourage the lad's growth by making him carry an onvil aroond on his head. Unfoortunately, however, the . . ."

There was a knocking at the outer door that shook the house to its foundations, followed by a sound as of a squadron of tanks playing hockey in the hall. Puffing and sweating, Cousin Douglas burst into the room. He was carrying a khaki duffel bag which he deposited upon the table. "Joey!" he boomed. "The apes! They've fructified! They've—they've—er—eh? Oh, why hello there, Cousin Colin—they just noo delivered me yere message, and ye've come at a hoppy and historic moment! —Pairdon me half a jiffick, dear lad, till I show Sergeant Pyle what the angels have brocht!" He loosened the strings of the bag and stood back dramatically. Out of it leaped a little gray beast with the face of a very old and very evil Irishman. Pausing only to sink its teeth in Cousin Douglas's thumb, it sprang to the lamp bracket, swung by its tail for a moment, and then dropped down upon Mr. Glencannon's shoulder. It perched there chattering volubly and searching his scalp for fleas.

"Weel, weel, weel—what an itsy-bitsy-witsy 'ittle darling!" he exclaimed, twisting his head and beaming at it. "Kitchy-witchy-wee!" he tickled it in the ribs. "—No, haw, haw, please, sweetie —uncle's mustosh is oot o' bounds!"

"Um, mum—playful little beggar, isn't he?" mumbled Cousin Douglas, sucking his thumb. "Weel, Joey, ye can plainly see he's a pairfict physical speecimen, so what d'ye say we have a drink or two and then lug him ower to Auld Stickychin's? I foncy I ocht to restore him to his parents as soon as possible."

"Oh, do yer?" Veterinary Sergeant Pyle's horsey front teeth were bared in a derisive grin. "Well, ain't that just too lovely of yer! The only trouble is, I'm afryde yer'll find it's a bleddy long swim to Brazil!"

"Brazil?" said Cousin Douglas, vacantly. "What kind of a Brazil?"

"The kind of a Brazil where that there full-grown, long-tyled Brazilian monkey came from, that's wot kind of a Brazil!" said Sergeant Pyle. With a disdainful snort, he turned his back upon the Highlander and confronted Mr. Glencannon. "Now look 'ere, chum—I don't know much abaht apes, but I do know they 'aven't got no tyles. I don't know much abaht you, neither—but I've been around touts, 'orse tryders, and dog thieves orl me life, and I can spot a crook as far as I can see one. Yer might as well come clean and tell me wot yer gyme is!"

"My, er, game?" Mr. Glencannon's mien was severe and his tone as cold as ice. "I dinna comprehend yere meaning, sir, but I am forced to point oot that yere monner is distinctly offensive."

"Oh, come, climb down off yer 'igh 'orse!" said Sergeant Pyle, winking and poking him in the ribs most insolently. "I suspected there was sumping fishy cooking when Duggie phoned me from the Rock! Do yer really think I can't see through this little swindle—you and yer cousin and yer precious monkey? Why, yer've simply brought Jocko ashore from yer ship so's Duggie can palm 'im off as a baby ape whenever 'e feels like it and draw down an extra quid a month each time! Maybe Old Stickychin won't know the difference, but me—welp, I wasn't born yestiddy, old cock!"

Mr. Glencannon stiffened. His brows beetled with righteous indignation and his Adam's apple bobbed up and down like a glass ball in a shooting gallery. "Noo, see here, my guid mon," he said, severely. "I feel it my duty to warn ye that yere thinly veiled insinuations, in-so-far as they impugn my ain pairsonal integrity, are o' a nature to entail the gravest consequences to yersel'. And while, o' course, I canna obsolutely vouch for Sergeant Dooglas Glencannon —for, after all, no mon is his brother's keeper, much less his cousin's, and Dooglas, unfoortunately, has for many years been exposed to the demoralizing influences o' the brutal and licentious soldiery o' whuch you, whole dom business for me! It's—it's just too sod!" He buried his face in his hands.

"Aye, but look ye here!" rumbled Cousin Douglas, in sudden panic. "What am I going to tell Auld Stickychin? I phoned him I was fetching doon a baby ape and noo he's in a frichtful dither to see it."

"Right, me bucko, and see it 'e will!" Sergeant Pyel promised him, confidently. "Now that I'm in on this thing, we can myke it the coziest sure-thing propersition since the time at Ascot I fed Golden Chieftain the bushel of celluloid oats!"

"Um? What d'ye mean, noo that ye're in on it?" demanded Cousin Douglas, truculently. "Even as it was, I was to get only five shillings in the poond, and if . . ."

"Shut up, Dooglas! Mind yere monners and let the gentlemon talk!" said Mr. Glencannon, sharply. "Aye, Sergeant Pyle—I readily concede that having a veterinary specialist o' yere talents associated with us gives the project a new and much more favorable ospect. As a basis for discussion, what do ye say we split the proceeds fifty-fifty and mak' suitable arrangements with Cousin Dooglas at a subsequent date? —Is that satisfactorra?"

"Wot could be fairer? Let's drink to it! —Cheers, dears!" Sergeant Pyle drank and then cleared his throat professionally. "Now, first, as to regarding this 'ere monkey, 'ere . . . As I said before, Old Stickychin probably couldn't tell 'im from a baby ape, but yet agyne, 'e might. —Come 'ere, Jocko, lemme look yer over. H'm! Welp, 'is color is a bit too gray, but I can fix that some other time with a pot of strong tea—jest fer tonight, it don't matter. Nope, nope—it's this 're long tyle that's our real problem."

"Weel, just as a suggestion—cudn't ye explain to the worthy choplain that apes, lik' todpoles, are born with tails whuch drap off when they attain puberty?"

"I could explyne it, yus, but would 'e believe it? —Also, Mr. Glencannon, yer mustn't forget that a lot of the orfficers arahnd 'ere 'ave served in India, Africa and orl o' them monkey countries, and they know wot's wot."

"Um, er, but look," said Cousin Douglas. "As lang as everybody but me is splitting up the profits o' this thing, why dinna ye sumply declare Auld Stickychin in on the deal and offer him his cut?"

Mr. Glencannon looked up at him with something approaching admiration. "Indeed," he nodded thoughtfully, "there's almost a modicum o' sense in yere suggestion, Dooglas. Unfoortunately, however, the choplain micht misconstrue the offer as a bribe and snitch to the higher authorities. —Some clergymen are not entirely honest, lad.''

"Yus, yus, I fancy the only way we can get arahnd this 'ere monkey's tyle is to cut it off," said Sergeant Pyle, pinching the root of it exploringly. "It's only a minor operytion, of course, and I can perform it in a jiffy right 'ere and now."

A gasp of horror burst from Cousin Douglas. "Ah, no! No!" he protested. "Ye canna do it, Joey! Ye mustna, shallna do it, lad! Ye—ye havena got the chlorofurrm! Ye havena got the instruments!"

"No, and I don't need 'em," said Sergeant Pyle, with obvious professional pride. "Fer simple caudal amputytions, I've got a special technique of me own. The way I do it is to simply slam 'em in a door. —Swish! Bang! and it's off. Why, when I was in private practice, back 'ome in Kidderminster, I bet I processed a thousand ordinary alley cats in my barthroom door and turned 'em into valuable pedigreed Manxs as quick as I could slam it. Ah, yus, gempmen!" He closed his eyes and smiled nostalgically, "I was doing right 'andsome in the 'igh-clarss Manx tryde till the bleddy war come along and crabbed it orl!"

"B-But how aboot the stump?" insisted Cousin Douglas, his face deathly pale. "Auld Stickychin expects to see the baby ape this vurra evening, but surely we canna show him the puir little beastie with his stump all sore!"

"No, by crikey, we can't—I'd forgot abaht the stump," Sergeant Pyle agreed. "M'm I say, though! —'Ow would it be if we simply let Jocko sit on Duggie's shoulder and shoved 'is tyle down out of sight inside the neck of his tunic?"

"Eek! Ecky! It wud tickle!" the giant squirmed and shuddered. "—No, I canna stond the thoucht o' it! A better idea wud be to put diapers on him and hide his tail underneath. —After all, he' supposed to be a new born baby, isn't he?"

"Dooglas, dinna be vulgar!" Mr. Glencannon admonished him. "Kindly remember ye're in the presence o' gentlemen and that the digniturra we're shortly going to visit is a clerk in holy orders."

"Yus, and 'e's a ruddy Major, which is worse!" said Sergeant Pyle, grimly. "Think 'ow it would look fer a couple of noncoms to barge into a Major's quarters with a monkey dressed in dipers! For 'eaven's sykes, Duggie, use yer 'ead!"

Cousin Douglas grunted sullenly. "Oh, vurra weel—if that's the way ye feel aboot it, I won't say another wurrd! I won't even suggest what I was aboot to suggest aboot togging him oot in a little pair o' breeks."

"Breeks? Why, o' course!" cried Mr. Glencannon. "Breeches— troosies—ponts—they're the vurra thing! Losh, what a hoppy inspiration! Oh, I knew I'd hit upon something, if I thocht aboot it lang enough!"

"And sure enough, gorbly-me, so yer 'ave!" said Sergeant Pyle, admiringly. "Call in the old 'ag, Mr. Glencannon, and start 'er sewing a pair at once. Tell 'er to myke 'em good and droopy in the seat, like them silly plus-fours the Algerian camel jockeys wear. —Better tell 'er to fetch another bottle, too, while yer abaht it."

Cousin Douglas consulted the Messerschmitt dash clock that served him as a wrist watch. "Um! Tell her to fetch two bottles," he mumbled. "Joey and I have got to be at Auld Stickychin's in a little less than an hour."

"Oh, dinna worrit—I'll see that ye get there on time!" Mr. Glencannon assured him. "I have implicit confidence in yere honesty, gentlemen, and I intend to prove it by coming richt alang with ye!"

*   *   *   *

Beyond the Rock, the moon rose dripping from the sea. Britannia's lion, which had basked so grandly in the noonday sun, was now an even grander silhouette as it crouched alert to the unseen menaces that lurk and prowl in nights of war. Its shadow, cast upon the town, made the narrow streets perhaps the blackest on all the blacked-out continent of Europe.

It was partly due to this almost palpable darkness that our trio of conspirators were having difficulty in reaching the chaplain's house. "I canna see my hond before my face," complained Cousin

Douglas, who was groping his way on all fours. "I literally canna tell front from back nor up from doon."

"Weel, at least ye can pull doon the back o' yere kilt, ye shameless booby!" Mr. Glencannon rebuked him sharply. "What kind o' an exomple are ye setting for this little monkey here?— No, here—I thocht he was on my other shoulder."

"Lawks, poor Jocko!" chuckled Sergeant Pyle. "Look—'e can't even balance 'imself, with 'is tyle inside 'is nice red breeches! If I didn't know I didn't know 'e didn't drink, I'd say 'e'd been drinking. 'E reminds me of the time little Artie Stevens was riding a three-year-old nymed—no, wyte a minute, it wasn't little Artie Stevens, it was a 'orse nymed Sir Lancelot. A fine big jumper, this 'orse was—sixty-seven 'ands 'igh and a sort of a light bay color. —Macaroni, 'is owner called 'im, in honor of the dago that discovered the first radio, but I dyed 'im chestnut in no time with a tub of good, strong tea. Welp, this 'ere jockey, Reynolds or O'Laughlin or some such nyme like that, was riding 'im in the Doncaster 'Andicap on a 'orse by the nyme of Cuckoo Clock, little Artie Stevens up. Welp, gempmen, I 'ope I may rot in me tracks if unbelievable as it may seem, but that's exackly wot 'appened! It was August Bank 'Oliday and twenty-three thousand people was there to see it with me own eyes. I never larffed so 'ard in orl me bleddy life!"

"Um!" said Cousin Douglas, "That's the trouble with horses. But if Cousin Colin still insists on coming in with us when we report to Auld Stickychin, who are we going to tell him he is?"

"Ah, Dooglas, Dooglas—will ye never lairn that honesty is always the best policy?" Mr. Glencannon chided him, warily. "If necessurra, I'll sumply tell him the plain, varnished truth."

"Saddle soap would be orl right, too," said Sergeant Pyle. "It works best if yer spit on the sponge. Anyway, get ready, because 'ere we are." He lead the way along a brick-paved walk between flower beds, raised the polished brass door knocker and banged it once. "Now, brace up military, Duggie—get yer bally backbone into it!" he whispered. *"Hup!"* The pair came to attention and stood rigid as ramrods.

The door swung open and a little pink-cheeked old gentleman

stood blinking and beaming out at them. Under his uniform tunic he wore a clerical vest and collar; but even had he been dressed in spangled tights, there would have been no mistaking him for anything but an English clergyman. "Ah! Well, well—come in, men, come in!" he invited, an excited throb in his voice. "So it's happened at last, eh, Sergeant Glencannon? —Eh, Sergeant Pyle? Er, where is—I mean to say—ah, yes, yes, to be sure this other gentleman has it! Well, well! My, my, my! What a little beauty, and all dressed up in red silk breeches! Bring it in, please—yes, come in, all of you. —The Commanding Officer and his staff are waiting."

"Um!" said Cousin Douglas dismally. He and Sergeant Pyle marched behind Major Chenwith and Mr. Glencannon into a sombre oak-panelled study. The room was lit only by candelabra and filled with old, dark furniture and red-tabbed officers.

"A-hem!" the chaplain tapped a glass on the table. "General Ennersleigh and gentlemen! It is a privilege—indeed, I may say, er, a most distinguished honor—to introduce to you a new and welcome arrival upon the Rock." He paused, smiled, and then raised his glass. "Sir and gentlemen, let us drink the health of this diminutive living symbol of Britain's secure and enduring tenancy of the Fortress and Crown Colony of Gibraltar!"

"Hear! Hear!" said a dozen voices. Some one switched on the phonograph. The record was *Land Of Hope And Glory*. At the first solemn note, the monkey leaped down from Mr. Glencannon's shoulder and turned three somersaults on the rug; then it snatched an ash tray from the table and pirouetted around the room, taking up a collection.

"Hem, aw . . ." Lieutenant-General Sir Clive Ennersleigh dropped the monocle from his right eye and put on a pair of horn-rimmed spectacles. The monkey clambered up his leg, hung from his breast pocket while it inspected his decorations, and then mounted to his shoulder. "Er, ka-humph!" said General Ennersleigh.

There was a sudden gasp—an expression of sheer, cold horror that was echoed and repeated throughout the shadowy room. For there, slowly crawling and writhing about on General Ennersleigh's chest was—a snake!

"Sir!" said a voice, tense and sibilant. "Sir! As you value your life, don't stir a muscle!"

"No, don't move—anybody!" said another. "It's a cobra sir. It's climbing up you, just below the ape's right foot."

General Ennersleigh's port wine complexion faded to one of gray. He was a brave man but he had served in India and knew his snakes. He stood immovable, the awful, ominous, aching silence broken only by his stertorous breathing.

"Now, quiet, everybody—here's what we've got to do," whispered his aide. "That chap nearest the door—yes, you!" he nodded at Mr. Glencannon. "You just ease down the hall to the kitchen and fetch a saucer of milk. On your way back, pick up a walking stick from the hall stand. Spill the milk on the floor over there in the corner and when the snake comes down to get it—whack him!"

"Aye!" murmured Mr. Glencannon. With admirable presence of mind he tiptoed out into the hall. Just as he crossed the threshold, the monkey threw its arms around the general's neck. "Skeek!" it said in a high falsetto, biting him in the nose. It sprang to the table, out to the hall, and then through the front door into the night.

"*Allez-oop,* Jocko—hold on tight!" cried Mr. Glencannon, catching it on his shoulder and dashing headlong across the shadowy flower beds. "From here to the waterfront, ye're going to see some speed! But losh, puir little laddie! How vurra uncomfortable ye must be, with yere tail hanging oot o' yere troosie leg and the end o' it all wrapped aroond the general's wallet and his gold cigarette case!"

"Skeek!" said the monkey as it bit off a fragment of Mr. Glencannon's left ear.